THE ORB
SCIENCE FICT
YEARBOOK
THREE

Also edited by David S. Garnett and
available from Orbit:

ZENITH
ZENITH 2
THE ORBIT SCIENCE FICTION YEARBOOK ONE
THE ORBIT SCIENCE FICTION YEARBOOK TWO

THE ORBIT
SCIENCE FICTION
YEARBOOK
THREE

Edited by
David S. Garnett

An Orbit Book

First published in Great Britain in 1990
by Futura Publications, a Division of
Macdonald & Co (Publishers) Ltd
London & Sydney

ISBN 0 7088 8337 0

Typeset by Leaper & Gard Ltd, Bristol
Printed and bound in Great Britain by
BPCC Hazell Books
Aylesbury, Bucks, England
Member of BPCC Ltd.

Futura Publications
A Division of
Macdonald & Co (Publishers) Ltd
Orbit House
1 New Fetter Lane
London EC4A 1AR
A member of Maxwell Macmillan Pergamon Publishing Corporation plc

ACKNOWLEDGEMENTS

'Introduction' by Iain M. Banks. Copyright © 1990 by Iain M. Banks. Published by arrangement with the author.

'At the Rialto' by Connie Willis. Copyright © 1989 by Byron Preiss Visual Publications, Inc. First published in *The Microverse*. Reprinted by permission of the author.

'The Gates of Babel' by J.R. Dunn. Copyright © 1989 by Omni Publications International, Ltd. First published in *Omni* May 1989. Reprinted by permission of the author.

'Dori Bangs' by Bruce Sterling. Copyright © 1989 by Davis Publications, Inc. First published in *Isaac Asimov's Science Fiction Magazine* September 1989. Reprinted by permission of the author.

'Surrender' by Lucius Shepard. Copyright © 1989 by Davis Publications, Inc. First published in *Isaac Asimov's Science Fiction Magazine* August 1989. Reprinted by permission of the author.

'Chimera' by Jayge Carr. Copyright © 1989 by Marj Krueger. First published in *Synergy 4*. Reprinted by permission of the author.

'Out of Copyright' by Charles Sheffield. Copyright © 1989 by Mercury Press, Inc. First published in *The Magazine of Fantasy and Science Fiction* May 1989. Reprinted by permission of the author.

'Abe Lincoln in McDonald's' by James Morrow. Copyright © 1989 by Mercury Press, Inc. First published in *The Magazine of Fantasy and Science Fiction* May 1989. Reprinted by permission of the author.

'Dogwalker' by Orson Scott Card. Copyright © 1989 by Davis Publications, Inc. First published in *Isaac Asimov's Science Fiction Magazine* November 1989. Reprinted by permission of the author.

'Lunar Triptych: Embracing the Night' by Richard Paul Russo. Copyright © 1989 by Davis Publications, Inc. First published in *Isaac Asimov's Science Fiction Magazine* Mid-December 1989. Reprinted by permission of the author.

'Privacy' by David Brin. Copyright © 1989 by Mercury Press, Inc. First published in *The Magazine of Fantasy and Science Fiction* September 1989. Reprinted by permission of the author.

'The Asenion Solution' by Robert Silverberg. Copyright © 1989 by Agberg, Ltd. First published in *Foundation's Friends*. Reprinted by permission of the author.

'In Blue' by John Crowley. Copyright © 1989 by John Crowley. First published in *Novelty*. Reprinted by permission of the author.

'Why Didn't the Crowd Boo?' by Brian Aldiss. Copyright © 1990 by Brian Aldiss. Published by arrangement with the author.

'Science Fiction Novels of the Year' by John Clute. Copyright © 1990 by John Clute. Published by arrangement with the author.

The introductions and afterwords to each story have been specially written for this anthology and are copyright © 1990 by the authors.

All other material in this volume is copyright © 1990 by David S. Garnett — whose thanks go to John Jarrold of Orbit Books, and to all those people who made material available for the collection or helped in various ways.

CONTENTS

CONTENTS

INTRODUCTION:

Hot damn; Mandela released, Havel scooting around the Prague presidential palace, bits of the Berlin Wall, wood-mounted, adorning desks inside the Lloyds building, and — whether such conditions really are part of the Effect or not — a succession of near hurricanes convincing lots of welly-wearing brits carrying torches, candles and huge mortgages that Oh-oh; the geezers in the white coats woz rite!

Strange days indeed, Mr Cornelius.

Meanwhile, the implication is that it's actually getting harder to write Science Fiction as the future lowers and events cram closer. Certainly near-future SF — always the hardest to get right, and the first to go out of date, from Flash Gordon's riveted space-ships, through the magazine cover featuring a grim-faced engineer climbing a space ship (with many more sleek shapes in the back-ground), a slide rule clenched in his perfectly formed teeth, to Luke's wimpily ineffective aiming computer (or: 'plot-device') and beyond — is going to have to be even more careful about leaving the political ambience rather vague (cf *Neuromancer* and cousins for object lessons) or not be afraid to spell things out. (Jeez ma, and we thought we only had to worry about getting the *technical* stuff right. Now these dumb politicos are treating our reality like they're in a Shakespeare play. Sheech.) Still, it could be worse, think of all those poor Red Menace thriller writers, sitting in their tax havens gritting their dentures, whistling the Horst Wessel song under their breath and sweatily praying that somebody wastes Gorby and *fast.*

But, to focus; another year another *Year's Best.* The SF short story is alive and well and living in hope, much like the rest of us. I recall, as a something between a nipper and a callow youth — category nomenclature suggestions on a post-card, please — being slightly surprised that there were short stories that weren't Science Fiction. (Shows you the scope and depth of *my* literary background, eh?) What — I thought — could people possibly find to write about in the short form that could be said with anything like the impact that even a merely competent SF short story was able to summon up? The answer, I found — for me at the time at least — was not all that much, aktcherly. Where were the ideas, dammit? (Psychological subtlety counted as a pretty low suit for me at the time, and is still all too easily trumped; lightly weighted, gameplayers.)

Well — grudging admission follows after the dash — I might have been looking for the wrong things, but there is a sense of force, of impact and dislocation in the best SF (and, horror) short stories that it is almost impossible to duplicate in more conventional short fiction. The reason is simple; in either of the former you can be plunged instantly — from the first few words — into a world as outrageously different from your own as the writer has the wit to devise, skill to write and courage to stick with. The story set in what we laughably term the real world is by implication only just shaving off from the mundane plane at the shallowest of angles; seconds or less. Over the course of a novel, cranking up the flight path of this fancy so that it at least gives the impression of being exponential in nature, the enterprising scribbler can end up with something devoutly weird. But over the course of five thousand words or whatever, it's not just difficult, it's the sort of exercise you end up feeling distinctly peeved about if nobody uses the words 'masterpiece' or 'tour de force' or something of a similar writerly-heart-warming description when they review it. Easier conceived than executed, in short.

Auden said that a poem was never finished, it was abandoned; I've always hoped and — 'umbly, onist — suspected that he was wrong, or at least attempting to add an overly-modest (or over-insured) caveat to the critical matrix of his own work; that there must be a point, in some — perhaps many poems, where there is nothing more that can be profitably added, deleted or otherwise altered; where whatever feeling or image the poet had in his or her mind has been translated as fully and exactly into language as possible given the limitations of writer and language (and, in a few cases, perhaps only given the limitations of the language). Scale alone tends to make such controlled precision inapplicable where the novel is concerned, and Auden's prescription might, optimistically, be more relevant to that form, where process is the point (even if you're called Robbe-Grillet; ha!). The short story, however — I'd like to suggest — can approach this level of perfection; it can be held in the mind — transmitting or receiving as a complete entity, and so pretend to the ideal of un-improvable wholeness; irreproachability. (To be banal, apart from anything else, you can get more stabs at it writing short stuff rather than long.)

Enough; let me pause only to doff a metaphorical hat to Mr Clute, providing the latest in a series of invaluable annual overviews of the SF novel as she is wrote, and a metaphysical one to Mr Aldiss, who seems to be able to be himself despairingly more illuminatingly than the rest of us — their contributions damn well near worth the price of the tome along — and pass you over to

Connie Willis has had short fiction published in *F&SF*, *Asimov's*, *Omni*, *Twilight Zone* and *Galileo*, and in 1982 she won two Nebula Awards: for her novelette 'Fire Watch' and for her short story 'A Letter from the Clearys'. The former also won the 1983 Hugo as best novelette. Her novella 'The Last of the Winnebagos' won the 1988 Nebula and the 1989 Hugo.

She has written two novels with Cynthia Felice, *Water Witch* and *Light Raid*. Her first novel was *Lincoln's Dreams*, which won the 1988 John W. Campbell Memorial Award. Her second novel will be *Doomsday Book*, which has the same background as 'Fire Watch'.

Willis lives in Greeley, Colorado, and the following story was a finalist for the Nebula and Hugo.

AT THE RIALTO
by
CONNIE WILLIS

Seriousness of mind was a prerequisite for understanding Newtonian physics. I am not convinced it is not a handicap in understanding quantum theory. — Excerpt from Dr. Gedanken's keynote address to the 1989 International Congress of Quantum Physicists Annual Meeting, Hollywood

I got to Hollywood around one-thirty and started trying to check into the Rialto.

'Sorry, we don't have any rooms,' the girl behind the desk said. 'We're all booked up with some science thing.'

'I'm with the science thing,' I said. 'Dr. Ruth Baringer I reserved a double.'

'There are a bunch of Republicans here, too, and a tour group from Finland. They told me when I started work here that they got all these movie people, but the only one I've seen so far was that guy who played the friend of that other guy in that one movie. You're not a movie person, are you?'

'No,' I said. 'I'm with the science thing. Dr. Ruth Baringer.'

'My name's Tiffany,' she said. 'I'm not actually a hotel clerk at all. I'm just working here to pay for my transcendental posture lessons. I'm really a model-slash-actress.'

'I'm a quantum physicist,' I said, trying to get things back on track. 'The name is Ruth Baringer.'

She messed with the computer for a minute. 'I don't show a reservation for you.'

'Maybe it's in Dr. Mendoza's name. I'm sharing a room with her.'

She messed with the computer some more. 'I don't show a reservation for her either. Are you sure you don't want the Disneyland Hotel? A lot of people get the two confused.'

'I want the Rialto,' I said, rummaging through my bag for my notebook. 'I have a confirmation number. W37420.'

She typed it in. 'Are you Dr. Gedanken?' she asked.

'Excuse me,' an elderly man said.

'I'll be right with you.' Tiffany told him. 'How long do you plan to stay with us, Dr. Gedanken?' she asked me.

'Excuse me,' the man said, sounding desperate. He had bushy white hair and a dazed expression, as if he had just been through a horrific experience or had been trying to check in to the Rialto.

He wasn't wearing any socks. I wondered if *he* was Dr. Gedanken. Dr. Gedanken was the main reason I'd decided to come to the meeting. I had missed his lecture on wave/particle duality last year, but I had read the text of it in the *ICQP Journal*, and it had actually seemed to make sense, which is more than you can say for most of quantum theory. He was giving the keynote address this year, and I was determined to hear it.

It wasn't Dr. Gedanken. 'My name is Dr. Whedbee,' the elderly man said. 'You gave me the wrong room.'

'All our rooms are pretty much the same,' Tiffany said. 'Except for how many beds they have in them and stuff.'

'My room has a *person* in it!' he said. 'Dr. Sleeth. From the University of Texas at Austin. She was changing her clothes.' His hair seemed to get wilder as he spoke. 'She thought I was a serial killer.'

'And you said your name is Dr. Whedbee?' Tiffany asked, fooling with the computer once again. 'I don't show a reservation for you.'

Dr. Whedbee began to cry.

Tiffany got out a paper towel, wiped off the counter, and turned back to me. 'May I help you?' she said.

Thursday, 7:30–9 P.M. *Opening Ceremonies*. Dr. Halvard Onofrio, University of Maryland at College Park, will speak on 'Doubts Surrounding the Heisenberg Uncertainty Principle.' Ballroom.

I finally got my room at five after Tiffany went off duty. Till then I sat around the lobby with Dr. Whedbee, listening to Abey Fields complain about Hollywwod.

'What's wrong with Racine?' he said. 'Why do we always have to go to these exotic places, like Hollywood? And St. Louis last year wasn't much better. The institut Henri Poincaré people kept going off to see the arch and Busch Stadium.'

'Speaking of St. Louis.' Dr. Takumi said, 'have you seen David yet?'

'No,' I said.

'Oh, really?' she said. 'Last year at the annual meeting you two were practically inseparable. Moonlight riverboat rides and all.'

'What's on the programming tonight?' I said to Abey.

'David was just here,' Dr. Takumi said. 'He said to tell you he was going out to look at the stars in the sidewalk.'

'That's exactly what I'm talking about.' Abey said. 'Riverboat rides and movie stars. What do those things have to do with quantum theory? Racine would have been an appropriate setting for a group of physicists. Not like this . . . this . . . do you realize we're practically across the street from Grauman's Chinese Theatre? And Hollywood Boulevard's where all those gangs hang out. If they catch you wearing red or blue, they'll —'

He stopped. 'Is that Dr. Gedanken?' he asked, staring at the front desk.

I turned and looked. A short, roundish man with a mustache was trying to check in. 'No,' I said. 'That's Dr. Onofrio.'

'Oh, yes,' Abey said, consulting his program book. 'He's speaking tonight at the opening ceremonies. On the Heisenberg uncertainty principle. Are you going?'

'I'm not sure,' I said, which was supposed to be a joke, but Abey didn't laugh.

'I must meet Dr. Gedanken. He's just gotten funding for a new project.'

I wondered what Dr. Gedanken's new project was — I would have loved to work with him.

'I'm hoping he'll come to my workshop on the wonderful world of quantum physics,' Abey said, still watching the desk. Amazingly enough, Dr. Onofrio seemed to have gotten a key and was heading for the elevators. 'I think his project has something to do with understanding quantum theory.'

Well, that let me out. I didn't understand quantum theory at all. I sometimes had a sneaking suspicion nobody else did either, including Abey Fields, and that they just weren't willing to admit it.

I mean, an electron is a particle except it acts like a wave. In fact, a neutron acts like two waves and interferes with itself (or each other), and you can't really measure any of this stuff properly because of the Heisenberg uncertainty principle, and that isn't the worst of it. When you set up a Josephson junction to figure out what rules the electrons obey, they sneak past the barrier to the other side, and they don't seem to care much about the limits of the speed of light either, and Schrödinger's cat is neither alive nor dead till you open the box, and it all makes about as much sense as Tiffany's calling me Dr. Gedanken.

Which reminded me, I had promised to call Darlene and give her our room number. I didn't have a room number, but if I waited much longer, she'd have left. She was flying to Denver to speak at CU and then coming on to Hollywood sometime tomorrow morning. I interrupted Abey in the middle of his telling me how beautiful Racine was in the winter and went to call her.

'I don't have a room yet,' I said when she answered. 'Should I leave a message on your machine, or do you want to give me your number in Denver?'

'Never mind all that,' Darlene said. 'Have you seen David yet?'

To illustrate the problems of the concept of wave function, Dr. Schrödinger imagines a cat being put into a box with a piece of uranium, a bottle of poison gas, and a Geiger counter. If a uranium nucleus disintegrates while the cat is in the box, it will release radiation which will set off the Geiger counter and break the bottle of poison gas. Since it is impossible in quantum theory to predict whether a uranium nucleus will disintegrate while the cat is in the box, and only possible to calculate uranium's probable half-life, the cat is neither alive nor dead until we open the box. — From 'The Wonderful World of Quantum

Physics', a seminar presented at the ICQP Annual
Meeting by A. Fields. Ph.D., University of Nebraska
at Wahoo

I completely forgot to warn Darlene about Tiffany, the model-
slash-actress.

'What do you mean you're trying to avoid David?' she had
asked me at least three times. 'Why would you do a stupid thing
like that?'

Because in St. Louis I ended up on a riverboat in the
moonlight and didn't make it back until the conference was
over.

'Because I want to attend the programming,' I said the third
time around, 'not a wax museum. I am a middle-aged woman.'

'And David is a middle-aged man who, I might add, is
absolutely charming. In fact, he may be the last charming man
left in the universe.'

'Charm is for quarks,' I said and hung up, feeling smug until
I remembered I hadn't told her about Tiffany. I went back to
the front desk, thinking maybe Dr. Onofrio's success signaled a
change. Tiffany asked, 'May I help you?' and left me standing
there.

After a while I gave up and went back to the red and gold
sofas.

'David was here again,' Dr. Takumi said. 'He said to tell you
he was going to the wax museum.'

'There *are* no wax museums in Racine,' Abey said.

'What's the programming for tonight?' I said, taking Abey's
program from him.

'There's a mixer at six-thirty and the opening ceremonies in
the ballroom and then some seminars.'

I read the descriptions of the seminars. There was one on the
Josephson junction. Electrons were able to somehow tunnel
through an insulated barrier even though they didn't have the
required energy. Maybe I could somehow get a room without
checking in.

'If we were in Racine,' Abey said, looking at his watch,
'we'd already be checked in and on our way to dinner.'

Dr. Onofrio emerged from the elevator, still carrying his

bags. He came over and sank down on the sofa next to Abey.

'Did they give you a room with a semi-naked woman in it?' Dr. Whedbee asked.

'I don't know,' Dr. Onofrio said. 'I couldn't find it.' He looked sadly at the key. 'They gave me 1282, but the room numbers only go up to 75.'

'I think I'll attend the seminar on chaos,' I said.

> *The most serious difficulty quantum theory faces today is not the inherent limitation of measurement capability or the EPR paradox. It is the lack of a paradigm. Quantum theory has no working model, no metaphor that properly defines it.* — Excerpt from Dr. Gedanken's keynote address

I got to my room at six, after a brief skirmish with the bellboy-slash-actor who couldn't remember where he's stored my suitcase, and unpacked.

My clothes, which had been permanent-press all the way from MIT, underwent a complete wave-function collapse the moment that I opened my suitcase, and came out looking like Schrödinger's almost-dead cat.

By the time I had called housekeeping for an iron, taken a bath, given up on the iron, and steamed a dress in the shower, I had missed the 'Mixer with Munchies' and was half an hour late for Dr. Onofiro's opening remarks.

I opened the door to the ballroom as quietly as I could and slid inside. I had hoped they would be late getting started, but a man I didn't recognize was already introducing the speaker: '— and an inspiration to all of us in the field.'

I dived for the nearest chair and sat down.

'Hi,' David said. 'I've been looking all over for you. Where were you?'

'Not at the wax museum,' I whispered.

'You should have been,' he whispered back. 'It was great. They had John Wayne, Elvis, and Tiffany the model-slash-actress with the brain of the pea-slash-amoeba.'

'Shh,' I said.

'— the person we've all been waiting to hear, Dr. Ringgit Dinari.'

'What happened to Dr. Onofrio?' I asked.

'Shhh,' David said.

Dr. Dinari looked a lot like Dr. Onofrio. She was short, roundish, and mustached and was wearing a rainbow-striped caftan. 'I will be your guide this evening into a strange new world,' she said, 'a world where all that you thought you knew, all common sense, all accepted wisdom, must be discarded. A world where all the rules have changed and it sometimes seems there are no rules at all.'

She sounded just like Dr. Onofrio, too. He had given this same speech two years ago in Cincinnati. I wondered if he had undergone some strange transformation during his search for room 1282 and was now a woman.

'Before I go on,' Dr. Dinari said, 'how many of you have already channeled?'

> *Newtonian physics had as its model the machine. The metaphor of the machine, with its interrelated parts, its gears and wheels, its causes and effects, was what made it possible to* think *about Newtonian physics* — Excerpt from Dr. Gedanken's keynote address

'You knew we were in the wrong place.' I hissed at David when we made it out to the lobby.

When we stood up to leave. Dr. Dinari had extended her pudgy hand in its rainbow-striped sleeve and called out in a voice a lot like Charlton Heston's, 'O unbelievers! Leave not, for here only is reality!'

'Actually, channeling would explain a lot,' David said, grinning.

'If the opening remarks aren't in the ballroom, where are they?'

'Beats me,' he said. 'Want to go see the Capitol Records Building? It's shaped like a stack of records.'

'I want to go to the opening remarks.'

'The beacon on top blinks out *Hollywood* in Morse code.'

I went over to the front desk.

21

'Can I help you?' the clerk behind the desk said. 'My name is Natalie, and I'm an actress —'

'Where is the ICQP meeting this evening?' I said.

'They're in the ballroom.'

'I'll bet you didn't have any dinner.' David said. 'I'll buy you an ice cream cone. There's this great place that has the ice cream cone Ryan O'Neal bought for Tatum in *Paper Moon.*'

'A channeler's in the ballroom,' I told Natalie. 'I'm looking for the ICQP.'

She fiddled with the computer. 'I'm sorry, I don't show a reservation for them.'

'How about Grauman's Chinese?' David said. 'You want reality? You want Charlton Heston? You want to see quantum theory in action?'

He grabbed my hands. 'Come with me,' he said seriously

In St. Louis I had suffered a wave-function collapse a lot like what had happened to my clothes when I opened the suitcase. I had ended up on a riverboat halfway to New Orleans that time. It happened again, and the next thing I knew I was walking around the courtyard of Sid Grauman's Chinese Theatre, eating an ice cream cone and trying to fit my feet in Myrna Loy's footprints.

She must have been a midget or had her feet bound as a child. So, apparently had Debbie Reynolds, Dorothy Lamour, and Wallace Beery.

The only footprints I came close to fitting were Donald Duck's.

'I see this as a map of the microcosm,' David said, sweeping his hand over the slightly irregular pavement of printed and signed cement squares.

'See, there are all these tracks. We know something's been here, and the prints are pretty much the same, only every once in a while you've got this' — he knelt down and pointed to the print of John Wayne's clenched fist — 'and over here' — he walked toward the box office and pointed to the print of Betty Grable's leg — 'and we can figure out the signatures, but what is this reference to 'Sid on all these squares? And what does this mean?' He pointed at Red Skelton's square. It said, THANKS SID WE DOOD IT

'You keep thinking you've found a pattern.' David said, crossing over to the other side, 'but Van Johnson's square is kind of sandwiched in here at an angle between Esther Williams and Cantinflas, and who the hell is May Robson? And why are all these squares empty?'

He had managed to maneuver me over behind the display of Academy Award winners. It was an accordionlike wrought-iron screen. I was in the fold between 1944 and 1945.

'And as if that isn't enough, you suddenly realize you're standing in the courtyard. You're not even in the theater.'

'And that's what you think is happening in quantum theory?' I said weakly. I was backed up into Bing Crosby, who had won for Best Actor in *Going My Way*. 'You think we're not in the theater yet?'

'I think we know as much about quantum theory as we can figure out about May Robson from her footprints,' he said putting his hand up to Ingrid Bergman's cheek (Best Actress, *Gaslight*) and blocking my escape. 'I don't think we understand anything *about* quantum theory, not tunneling, not complementarity.' He leaned toward me. 'Not passion.'

The Best Movie of 1945 was *The Lost Weekend*. 'Dr. Gedanken understands it.' I said, disentangling myself from the Academy Award winners and David. 'Did you know he's putting together a new research team for a big project on understanding quantum theory?'

'Yes,' David said. 'Want to see a movie?'

'There's a seminar on chaos at nine,' I said, stepping over the Marx Brothers. 'I have to get back.'

'If it's chaos you want, you should stay right here,' he said, stopping to look at Irene Dunne's handprints. 'We could see the movie and then go have dinner. There's this place near Hollywood and Vine that has the mashed potatoes Richard Dreyfuss made into Devils Tower in *Close Encounters*.'

'I want to meet Dr. Gedanken,' I said, making it safely to the sidewalk. I looked back at David.

He had gone back to the other side of the courtyard and was looking at Roy Rogers's signature.

'Are you kidding? He doesn't understand it any better than we do.'

'Well, at least he's trying.'

'So am I. The problem is, how can one neutron possibly interfere with itself, and why are there only two of Trigger's hoofprints here?'

'It's eight fifty-five.' I said. 'I am going to the chaos seminar.'

'If you can find it,' he said getting down on one knee to look at the signature.

'I'll find it,' I said grimly.

He stood up and grinned at me, his hands in his pockets. 'It's a great movie,' he said.

It was happening again. I turned and practically ran across the street.

'*Benji IX* is showing,' he shouted after me. 'He accidentally exchanges bodies with a Siamese cat."

> Thursday, 9–10 P.M. 'The Science of Chaos.' I. Durcheinander, Leipzig. A seminar on the structure of chaos. Principles of chaos will be discussed, including the butterfly effect, fractals, and insolid billowing. Clara Bow Room.

I couldn't find the chaos seminar. The Clara Bow Room, where it was supposed to be, was empty. A meeting of vegetarians was next door in the Fatty Arbuckle Room, and all the other conference rooms were locked. The channeler was still in the ballroom. 'Come!' she commanded when I opened the door. 'Understanding awaits!'

I went upstairs to bed.

I had forgotten to call Darlene. She would have left for Denver already, but I called her answering machine and told it the room number in case she picked up her messages. In the morning I would have to tell the front desk to give her a key. I went to bed.

I didn't sleep well. The air conditioner went off during the night, which meant I didn't have to steam my suit when I got up the next morning, I got dressed and went downstairs.

The programming started at nine o'clock with Abey Fields's 'Wonderful World' workshop in the Mary Pickford Room, a breakfast buffet in the ballroom, and a side presentation on 'Delayed Choice Experiments' in Cecil B. DeMille A on the mezzanine level.

The breakfast buffet sounded wonderful, even though it always turns out to be urn coffee and donuts. I hadn't had anything but an ice cream cone since noon the day before, but if David were around, he would be somewhere close to the food, and I wanted to steer clear of him. Last night it had been Grauman's Chinese. Today I was likely to end up at Knott's Berry Farm. I wasn't going to let that happen even if he *was* charming.

It was pitch-dark inside Cecil B. DeMille A. Even the slide on the screen up front appeared to be black. 'As you can see,' Dr. Lvov said, 'the laser pulse is already in motion before the experimenter sets up the wave or particle detector.'

He clicked to the next slide, which was dark gray. 'We used a Mach-Zehnder interferometer with two mirrors and a particle detector. For the first series of tries we allowed the experimenter to decide which apparatus he would use by whatever method he wished. For the second series, we used that most primitive of randomizers —'

He clicked again, to a white slide with black polka dots that gave off enough light for me to be able to spot an empty chair on the aisle ten rows up. I hurried to get to it before the slide changed, and sat down.

'— a pair of dice. Alley's experiments had shown us that when the particle detector was in place, the light was detected as a particle, and when the wave detector was in place, the light showed wavelike behavior, no matter when the choice of apparatus was made.'

'Hi,' David said. 'You've missed five black slides, two gray ones, and a white with black polka dots.'

'Shh,' I said.

'In our two series, we hoped to ascertain whether the consciousness of the decision affected the outcome,' Dr. Lvov clicked to another black slide. 'As you can see, the graph shows no effective difference between the tries in which the experimenter chose the detection apparatus and those in which the apparatus was randomly chosen.'

'You want to go get some breakfast?' David whispered.

'I already ate,' I whispered back, and waited for my stomach to growl and give me away. It did.

'There's a great place down near Hollywood and Vine that has the waffles Katharine Hepburn made for Spencer Tracy in *Woman of the Year*.'

'Shh,' I said.

'And after breakfast, we could go to Frederick's of Hollywood and see the bra museum.'

'Will you please be quiet? I can't hear.'

'Or see,' he said, but he subsided more or less for the remaining ninety-two black, gray, and polka-dotted slides.

Dr. Lvov turned on the lights and blinked smilingly at the audience. 'Consciousness had no discernible effect on the results of the experiment. As one of my lab assistants put it, "The little devil knows what you're going to do before you know it yourself."'

This was apparently supposed to be a joke, but I didn't think it was very funny. I opened my program and tried to find something to go to that David wouldn't be caught dead at.

'Are you two going to breakfast?' Dr. Thibodeaux asked.

'Yes,' David said.

'No,' I said.

'Dr. Hotard and I wished to eat somewhere that is *vraiment* Hollywood.'

'David knows just the place,' I said. 'He's been telling me about this great place where they have the grapefruit James Cagney shoved in Mae Clarke's face in *Public Enemy*.'

Dr. Hotard hurried up, carrying a camera and four guide-books. 'And then perhaps you would show us Grauman's Chinese Theatre?' he asked David.

'Of course he will,' I said. 'I'm sorry I can't go with you, but I promised Dr. Verikovsky I'd be at his lecture on Boolean logic. And after Grauman's Chinese, David can take you to the bra museum at Frederick's of Hollywood.'

'And the Brown Derby?' Thibodeaux asked. 'I have heard it is shaped like a chapeau.' They dragged him off. I watched till they were safely out of the lobby and then ducked upstairs and into Dr. Whedbee's lecture on information theory. Dr. Whedbee wasn't there.

'He went to find an overhead projector.' Dr. Takumi said. She had half a donut on a plate in one hand and a Styrofoam cup in the other.

'Did you get that at the breakfast buffet?' I asked.

'Yes. It was the last one. And they ran out of coffee right after I got there. You weren't at Abey Field's thing, were you?' She set the coffee cup down and took a bite of the donut.

'No,' I said, wondering if I should try to take her by surprise or just wrestle the donut away from her.

'You didn't miss anything. He raved the whole time about how we should have had the meeting in Racine.' She popped the last piece of donut in her mouth. 'Have you seen David yet?'

> Friday, 9–10 P.M. 'The Eureka Experiment: A Slide
> Presentation.' J. Lvov, Eureka College, Descriptions,
> results, and conclusions of Lvov's delayed conscious/
> randomized choice experiments. Cecil B. DeMille A.

Dr. Whedbee eventually came in carrying an overhead projector, the cord trailing behind him. He plugged it in. The light didn't go on.

'Here,' Dr. Takumi said, handing me her plate and cup. 'I have one of these at Caltech. It needs its fractal basin boundaries adjusted.'

She whacked the side of the projector.

There weren't even any crumbs left of the donut. There was about a millimeter of coffee in the bottom of the cup. I was about to stoop to new depths when she hit the projector again. The light came on 'I learned that in the chaos seminar last night.' She said, grabbing the cup away from me and draining it. 'You should have been there. The Clara Bow Room was packed.'

'I believe I'm ready to begin.' Dr. Whedbee said. Dr. Takumi and I sat down 'Information is the transmission of meaning.' Dr. Whedbee said. He wrote MEANING or possibly INFORMATION on the screen with a green Magic Marker.

'When information is randomized, meaning cannot be

transmitted, and we have a state of entropy.' He wrote it under MEANING with a red Magic Marker. His handwriting appeared to be completely illegible.

'States of entropy vary from low entropy, such as the mild static on your car radio, to high entropy, a state of complete disorder, of randomness and confusion, in which no information at all is being communicated.'

Oh, my God. I thought *I forgot to tell the hotel about Darlene.*

The next time Dr. Whedbee bent over to inscribe hieroglyphics on the screen, I sneaked out and went down to the desk, hoping Tiffany hadn't come on duty yet. She had.

'May I help you?' she asked.

'I'm in room 663.' I said. 'I'm sharing a room with Dr. Darlene Mendoza. She's coming in this morning, and she'll be needing a key.'

'For what?' Tiffany said.

'To get into the room. I may be in one of the lectures when she gets here.'

'Why doesn't she have a key?'

'Because she isn't here yet.'

'I thought you said she was sharing a room with you.'

'She *will* be sharing a room with me. Her name is Darlene Mendoza.'

'And your name?' she asked, hands poised over the computer.

'Ruth Baringer.'

'We don't show a reservation for you.'

> We have made impressive advances in quantum physics in the ninety years since Planck's constant, but they have by and large been advances in technology, not theory. We can only make advances in theory when we have a model we can visualize. — Excerpt from Dr. Gedanken's keynote address

I high-entrophied with Tiffany for a while on the subjects of my not having a reservation and the air-conditioning and then switched back suddenly to the problem of Darlene's key, in the hope of catching her off guard. It worked about as well as

Alley's delayed-choice experiments.

In the middle of my attempting to explain that Darlene was not the air-conditioning repairman, Abey Fields came up.

'Have you seen Dr. Gedanken?'

I shook my head.

'I was sure he'd come to my "Wonderful World" workshop, but he didn't, and the hotel says they can't find his reservation,' he said, scanning the lobby. 'I found out what his new project is, incidentally, and I'd be perfect for it. He's going to find a paradigm for quantum theory, is that him?' he said, pointing at an elderly man getting in the elevator.

'I think that's Dr. Whedbee,' I said, but he had already sprinted across the lobby to the elevator.

He nearly made it. The elevator slid to a close just as he go there.

He pushed the elevator button several times to make the door open again, and when that didn't work, tried to readjust its fractal basin boundaries. I turned back to the desk.

'May I help you?' Tiffany said.

'You may,' I said. 'My roommate, Darlene Mendoza, will be arriving sometime this morning. She's a producer. She's here to cast the female lead in a new movie starring Robert Redford and Harrison Ford. When she gets here, give her her key. And fix the air-conditioning.'

'Yes, ma'am,' she said.

> *The Josephson junction is designed so that electrons must obtain additional energy to surmount the energy barrier. It has been found, however, that some electrons simply tunnel, as Heinz Pagels put it, 'right through the wall.'* —
> From 'The Wonderful World of Quantum Physics,' A. Fields, UNW

Abey had stopped banging on the elevator button and was trying to pry the elevator doors apart.

I went out the side door and up to Hollywood Boulevard. David's restaurant was near Hollywood and Vine. I turned the other direction, toward Grauman's Chinese Theatre, and ducked into the first restaurant I saw.

'I'm Stephanie,' the waitress said. 'How many are there in your party?'

There was no one remotely in my vicinity. 'Are you an actress-slash-model?' I asked her.

'Yes. I'm working here part-time to pay for my holistic hairstyling lessons.'

'There's one of me,' I said, holding up my forefinger to make it perfectly clear. 'I want a table away from the window.'

She led me to a table in front of the window, handed me a menu the size of the macrocosm, and put another one down across from me.

'Our breakfast specials today are papaya stuffed with salmonberries and nasturtium/radicchio salad with a balsamic vinaigrette. I'll take your order when your other party arrives.'

I stood the extra menu up so it hid me from the window, opened the other one, and read the breakfast entrées. They all seemed to have *cilantro* or *lemongrass* in their names.

I wondered if *radicchio* could possibly be Californian for *donut*.

'Hi,' David said, grabbing the standing-up menu and sitting down. 'The sea urchin pâté looks good.'

I was actually glad to see him. 'How did you get here?' I asked.

'Tunneling,' he said. 'What exactly is extra-virgin olive oil?'

'I wanted a donut,' I said pitifully.

He took my menu away from me, laid it on the table, and stood up. 'There's a great place next door that's got the donut Clark Gable taught Claudette Colbert how to dunk in *It Happened One Night*.'

The great place was probably out in Long Beach someplace, but I was too weak with hunger to resist him. I stood up. Stephanie hurried over.

'Will there be anything else?' she asked.

'We're leaving,' David said.

'Okay, then,' she said, tearing a check off her pad and slapping it on the table. 'I hope you enjoyed your breakfast.'

Finding such a paradigm is difficult, if not impossible.
Due to Planck's constant the world we see is largely

AT THE RIALTO

dominated by Newtonian mechanics. Particles are particles, waves are waves, and objects do not suddenly vanish through walls and reappear on the other side. It is only on the subatomic level that quantum effects dominate.
— Excerpt from Dr. Gedanken's keynote address

The restaurant was next door to Grauman's Chinese, which made me a little nervous, but it had eggs and bacon and toast and orange juice and coffee. And donuts. 'I thought you were having breakfast with Dr. Thibodeaux and Dr. Hotard,' I said, dunking one in my coffee. 'What happened to them?'

'They went to Forest Lawn. Dr. Hotard wanted to see the church where Ronald Reagan got married.'

'He got married at Forest Lawn?'

He took a bite of my donut. 'In the Wee Kirk of the Heather. Did you know Forest Lawn's got the World's Largest Oil Painting Incorporating a Religious Theme?'

'So why didn't you go with them?'

'And miss the movie?' He grabbed both my hands across the table. 'There's a matinee at two o'clock. Come with me.'

I could feel things starting to collapse 'I have to get back,' I said, trying to disentangle my hands. 'There's a panel on the EPR paradox at two o'clock.'

'There's another showing at five. And one at eight.'

'Dr. Gedanken's giving the keynote address at eight.

'You know what the problem is?' he said, still holding on to my hands. 'It isn't really Grauman's Chinese Theatre; it's Mann's, so Sid isn't even around to ask. Like, why do some pairs like Joanne Woodward and Paul Newman share the same square and other pairs don't? Like Ginger Rogers and Fred Astaire?'

'You know what the problem is?' I said, wrenching my hands free. 'The problem is you don't take anything seriously. This is a conference, but you don't care anything about the programming or hearing Dr. Gedanken speak or trying to understand quantum theory!' I fumbled in my purse for some money for the check.

'I thought that was what we were talking about,' David said, sounding surprised. 'The problem is, where do those lion

31

statues that guard the door fit in? And what about all those empty spaces?'

Friday, 2–3 P.M. *Panel Discussion on the EPR Paradox.* I. Takumi, moderator, R. Iverson, L. S. Ping. A discussion of the latest research in single-state correlations, including nonlocal influences, the Calcutta proposal, and passion. Keystone Kops Room.

I went up to my room as soon as I got back to the Rialto to see if Darlene was there yet. She wasn't, and when I tried to call the desk, the phone wouldn't work. I went back down to the registration desk. There was no one there. I waited fifteen minutes and then went into the panel on the EPR paradox.

'The Einstein–Podolsky–Rosen paradox cannot be reconciled with quantum theory,' Dr. Takumi was saying. 'I don't care what the experiments seem to indicate. Two electrons at opposite ends of the universe can't affect each other simultaneously without destroying the entire theory of the space–time continuum.

She was right. Even if it were possible to find a model of quantum theory, what about the EPR paradox? If an experimenter measured one of a pair of electrons that had originally collided, it changed the cross-correlation of the other instantaneously, even if the electrons were light-years apart.

It was as if they were eternally linked by that one collision, sharing the same square forever, even if they were on opposite sides of the universe.

'If the electrons *communicated* instantaneously, I'd agree with you,' Dr. Iverson said, 'but they don't; they simply influence each other. Dr. Shimony defined his influence in his paper on passion, and my experiment clearly —'

I thought of David leaning over me between the Best Pictures of 1944 and 1945, saying, 'I think we know as much about quantum theory as we do about May Robson from her footprints.'

'You can't explain it away by inventing new terms,' Dr. Takumi said.

'I completely disagree,' Dr. Ping said. 'Passion at a distance

is not just an invented term. It's a demonstrated phenomenon.'
It certainly is, I thought, thinking about David taking the macrocosmic menu out of the window and saying, 'The sea urchin pâté looks good.'

It didn't matter where the electron went after the collision. Even if it went in the opposite direction from Hollywood and Vine, even if it stood a menu in the window to hide it, the other electron would still come and rescue it from the radicchio and buy it a donut.

'A demonstrated phenomenon!' Dr. Takumi said. 'Ha!' She banged her moderator's gavel for emphasis.

'Are you saying passion doesn't exist?' Dr. Ping said, getting very red in the face.

'I'm saying one measly experiment is hardly a demonstrated phenomenon.'

'One measly experiment! I spent five years on this project!' Dr. Iverson said, shaking his fist at her. 'I'll show you passion at a distance!'

'Try it, and I'll adjust your fractal basin boundaries!' Dr. Takumi said, and hit him over the head with the gavel.

Yet finding a paradigm is not impossible. Newtonian physics is not a machine. It simply shares some of the attributes of a machine. We must find a model somewhere in the visible world that shares the often bizarre attributes of quantum physics. Such a model, unlikely as it sounds, surely exists somewhere, and it is up to us to find it. —
Excerpt from Dr. Gedanken's keynote address

I went up to my room before the police came. Darlene still wasn't there, and the phone and air-conditioning still weren't working. I was really beginning to get worried. I walked up to Grauman's Chinese to look for David, but he wasn't there. Dr. Whedbee and Dr. Sleeth were behind the Academy Award winners folding screen.

'You haven't seen David, have you?' I asked them.

Dr. Whedbee removed his hand from Norma Shearer's cheek.

'He left,' Dr. Sleeth said, disentangling herself from the Best Movie of 1929–30.

'He said he was going out to Forest Lawn,' Dr. Whedbee said, trying to smooth down his bushy white hair.

'Have you seen Dr. Mendoza? She was supposed to get in this morning.'

They hadn't seen her, and neither had Drs. Hotard and Thibodeaux, who stopped me in the lobby and showed me a postcard of Aimee Semple McPherson's tomb. Tiffany had gone off duty. Natalie couldn't find my reservation. I went back up to the room to wait, thinking Darlene might call.

The air-conditioning still wasn't fixed. I fanned myself with a Hollywood brochure and then opened it up and read it. There was a map of the courtyard of Grauman's Chinese on the back cover. Deborah Kerr and Yul Brynner didn't have a square together either, and Katharine Hepburn and Spencer Tracy weren't even on the map. She had made him waffles in *Woman of the Year*, and they hadn't even given them a square.

I wondered if Tiffany the model-slash-actress had been in charge of assigning the cement. I could see her looking blankly at Spencer Tracy and saying. 'I don't show a reservation for you.'

What exactly was a model-slash-actress? Did it mean she was a model *or* an actress or a model *and* an actress? She certainly wasn't a hotel clerk.

Maybe electrons were actually the Tiffanys of the microcosm, and that explained their wave-slash-particle duality. Maybe they weren't really electrons at all. Maybe they were just working part-time at being electrons to pay for their single-state lessons.

Darlene still hadn't called by seven o'clock. I stopped fanning myself and tried to open a window. It wouldn't budge. The problem was, nobody knew anything about quantum theory. All we had to go on were a few colliding electrons that nobody could see and that couldn't be measured properly because of the Heisenberg uncertainty principle. And there was chaos to consider, and entropy, and all those empty spaces. We didn't even know who May Robson was.

At seven-thirty the phone rang. It was Darlene. 'What

happened?' I said. 'Where are you?'

'At the Beverly Wilshire.'

'In Beverly Hills?'

'Yes. It's a long story. When I got to the Rialto, the hotel clerk — think her name was Tiffany — told me you weren't there. She said they were booked solid with some science thing and had had to send the overflow to other hotels. She said you were at the Beverly Wilshire in Room 1027. How's David?'

'Impossible,' I said. 'He's spent the whole conference looking at Deanna Durbin's footprints at Grauman's Chinese Theatre and trying to talk me into going to the movies.'

'And are you going?'

'I can't. Dr. Gedanken's giving the keynote address in half an hour.'

'He is?' Darlene said, sounding surprised. 'Just a minute.' There was a silence, and then she came back on and said, 'I think you should go to the movies. David's one of the last two charming men in the universe.'

'But he doesn't take quantum theory seriously. Dr. Gedanken is hiring a research team to design a paradigm, and David keeps talking about the beacon on top of the Capitol Records Building.'

'You know, he may be on to something there. I mean, seriousness was all right for Newtonian physics, but maybe quantum theory needs a different approach. Sid says —'

'Sid?'

'This guy who's taking me to the movies tonight. It's a long story. Tiffany gave me the wrong room number, and I walked in on this guy in his underwear. He's a quantum physicist. He was supposed to be staying at the Rialto, but Tiffany couldn't find his reservation.'

The major implication of wave/particle duality is that an electron has no precise location. It exists in a superposition of probable locations. Only when the experimenter observes the electron does it 'collapse' into a location.

The Wonderful World of Quantum Physics,' A Fields, UNW

Forest Lawn closed at five o'clock. I looked it up in the Hollywood brochure after Darlene hung up.

There was no telling where he might have gone: the Brown Derby or the La Brea Tar Pits or some great place near Hollywood and Vine that had the alfalfa sprouts John Hurt ate right before his chest exploded in *Alien.*

At least I knew where Dr. Gedanken was. I changed my clothes and got in the elevator, thinking about wave/particle duality and fractals and high-entropy states and delayed-choice experiments. The problem was, where could you find a paradigm that would make it possible to visualize quantum theory when you had to include Josephson junctions and passion and all those empty spaces? It wasn't possible. You had to have more to work with than a few footprints and the impression of Betty Grable's leg.

The elevator door opened, and Abey Fields pounced on me.

'I've been looking all over for you,' he said. 'You haven't seen Dr. Gedanken, have you?'

'Isn't he in the ballroom?'

'No,' he said. 'He's already fifteen minutes late, and nobody's seen him. You have to sign this,' he said, shoving a clipboard at me.

'What is it?'

'It's a petition.' He grabbed it back from me. '"We the undersigned demand that annual meetings of the International Congress of Quantum Physicists henceforth be held in appropriate locations." Like Racine,' he added, shoving the clipboard at me again. '*Unlike* Hollywood.'

Hollywood.

Are you aware it took the average ICQP delegate two hours and thirty-six minutes to check in? They even sent some of the delegates to a hotel in Glendale.'

'And Beverly Hills,' I said absently. Hollywood. Bra museums and the Marx Brothers and gangs that would kill you if you wore red or blue and Tiffany/Stephanie and the World's Largest Oil Painting Incorporating a Religious Theme.

'Beverly Hills,' Abey muttered, pulling an automatic pencil out of his pocket protector and writing a note to himself. 'I'm presenting the petition during Dr. Gedanken's speech. Well, go on, sign it,' he said, handing me the pencil. 'Unless you want the annual meeting to be here at the Rialto next year.'

I handed the clipboard back to him. 'I think from now on the annual meeting might be here every year,' I said, and took off running for Grauman's Chinese.

> *When we have that paradigm, one that embraces both the logical and the nonsensical aspects of quantum theory, we will be able to look past the colliding electrons and the mathematics and see the microcosm in all its astonishing beauty.* — Excerpt from Dr. Gedanken's keynote address

'I want a ticket to *Benji IX*,' I told the girl at the box office. Her name tag said, WELCOME TO HOLLYWOOD. MY NAME IS KIMBERLEY

'Which theater?' she said.

'Grauman's Chinese.' I said, thinking, *This is no time for a high-entropy state.*

'Which theater?'

I looked up at the marquee. *Benji IX* was showing in all three theaters, the huge main theater and the two smaller ones on either side.

'They're doing audience reaction surveys.' Kimberly said. 'Each theater has a different ending.'

'Which one's in the main theatre?'

'I don't know. I just work here part-time to pay for my organic breathing lessons.'

'Do you have any dice?' I asked, and then realized I was going about this all wrong. This was quantum theory, not Newtonian. It didn't matter which theater I chose or which seat I sat down in. This was a delayed-choice experiment and David was already in flight.

'The one with the happy ending.' I said

'Center theater,' she said.

I walked past the stone lions and into the lobby. Rhonda Fleming and some Chinese wax figures were sitting inside a glass case next to the door to the rest rooms. There was a huge painted screen behind the concession stand.

I bought a box of Raisinets, a tub of popcorn, and a box of jujubes and went inside the theater.

It was bigger than I had imagined. Rows and rows of empty red chairs curved between the huge pillars and up to the red curtains where the screen must be. The walls were covered with intricate drawings. I stood there, holding my jujubes and Raisinets and popcorn, staring at the chandelier overhead. It was an elaborate gold sunburst surrounded by silver dragons. I had never imagined it was anything like this.

The lights went down, and the red curtains opened, revealing an inner curtain like a veil across the screen.

I went down the dark aisle and sat in one of the seats. 'Hi,' I said, and handed the Raisinets to David.

'Where have you been?' he said. 'The movie's about to start.'

'I know,' I said. I leaned across him and handed Darlene her popcorn and Dr. Gedanken his jujubes. 'I was working on the paradigm for quantum theory.'

'And?' Dr. Gedanken said, opening his jujubes.

'And you're both wrong.' I said. 'It isn't Grauman's Chinese. It isn't movies either. Dr. Gedanken.'

'Sid,' Dr. Gedanken said. 'If we're all going to be on the same research team. I think we should use first names.'

'If it isn't Grauman's Chinese or the movies, what is it?' Darlene asked, eating popcorn.

'It's Hollywood.'

'Hollywood,' Dr. Gedanken said thoughtfully.

'Hollywood,' I said. 'Stars in the sidewalk and buildings that look like stacks of records and hats, and radicchio and audience surveys and bra museums. And the movies. And Grauman's Chinese.'

'And the Rialto,' David said.

'Especially the Rialto.'

'And the ICQP,' Dr. Gedanken said.

I thought about Dr. Lvov's black and gray slides and the disappearing chaos seminar and Dr. Whedbee writing MEANING or possibly INFORMATION on the overhead projector. 'And the ICQP,' I said.

'Did Dr. Takumi really hit Dr. Iverson over the head with a gavel?' Darlene asked.

'Shh.' David said. 'I think the movie's starting.' He took hold of my hand. Darlene settled back with her popcorn, and Dr. Gendanken put his feet up on the chair in front of him. The inner curtain opened, and the screen lit up.

After a reasonably successful career in business, J.R. Dunn began writing as a political journalist before turning in despair to sf. His work has appeared in *Writers of the Future, Amazing* and *Omni*. He has also written a number of critical articles on the genre for such general circulation magazines as *The World and I, Reason,* and *Liberty*. His current projects include a novel entitled *This Side of Judgement*. He lives in New Jersey, through no fault of his own.

He has written an afterword to his story for the *Yearbook*.

THE GATES OF BABEL
by
J.R. DUNN

The thing appeared a few minutes after they left the highway for the coast road: a huge, gray-white blockhouse peering over the hills outside of Lompoc, distorted by distance and the afternoon heat. McCune stared at it for a few seconds before turning to Parkinson. 'That's it? That's Vandenberg?'

'That's it,' Parkinson said, shifting in the seat. 'It won't be too far now.'

McCune studied him before turning back to the road, wondering for the dozenth time what was on his mind. He looked normal enough, considering his story. He was well dressed, in an academic sort of way — tweed jacket, corduroys, loafers — but that didn't mean much. They didn't have to wear medallions or flowing robes. McCune had seen them all since he had started at the *Journal*: Atlanteans, witches, flat-earthers. California bred 'em like oranges and the first place they headed was a newspaper. He'd had his fill early and had hoped he'd see the end of them somewhere along the line, but no such luck. The nuts are always with us.

He had to admit that Parkinson was different. It wasn't the usual line, and a surprising amount of his information had checked out. There had been someone named Vandenberg, an Air Force general back in the Forties, and a base had been named after him on the coast north of Santa Barbara. It was a test center of some sort, though there was no mention of it being abandoned as Parkinson had said. And there was that other item, too, the booklet marked SECRET, TRANSPOLAR SHUTTLE PROBLEMS, or something.

'What was the name of that handbook you gave me again?'

Parkinson rubbed his forehead and sighed. '*STS Polar Launch Parameters.*' He put his hand out the window and began to tap the side of the car. 'Did you read it?'

McCune shook his head. 'I tried, but I couldn't follow any of it. I meant to bring it along so that I could ask you about a few things, but like I said, I lost it.'

'You didn't lose it.'

He glared at Parkinson for a moment, then turned his eyes back to the road. 'You know, you'd do a lot more for your case if you thought twice about remarks like that. Your story is wild enough as it is without implying that I threw your evidence away, much less trying to tell me what I wrote three years ago.'

'You didn't bother to check your files?'

'Why the hell should I? You think I wouldn't remember?'

'How about a three-part series on cost overruns at Slick-6?'

McCune answered with a snort of disgust. Parkinson, for his part, smiled sourly before turning his head back to the road. He sat up suddenly and pointed. 'There you go,' he said. 'Gantries.'

They had topped the last hill overlooking the coastal plain. Scattered across it was a collection of large metal structures, openwork towers painted orange and white. They were big, over a hundred feet high, and McCune had never seen anything like them.

'And what are they?'

'Missile launching platforms.'

McCune shrugged. 'Right.'

As they drove down the hill, he inspected the rest of the base. There was little that he recognized: no runway, no control tower, no aircraft of any kind, just roads, a few buildings, the huge concrete blockhouse surrounded by smaller structures of the same type, and the enigmatic towers running up the coast against the blue of the Pacific. A long paved track meandered from the big blockhouse south to the hills near the shore, and for a moment he thought that might be a runway, but no, it wasn't wide enough and it made a number of hairpin turns, avoiding the hummocks and gullies of the plain for level ground.

The road went past a chain-link fence topped with barbed wire before leading to a gate. It was wide open; the guardhouse next to it was wrecked, with only small shards of glass in the windows. Despite this, McCune stopped the car. He sat clutching the steering wheel for a moment before turning to Parkinson. 'Maybe we should check in with somebody.'

'Nobody to check in with,' Parkinson said. 'We passed administration five minutes ago, past Lompoc. You saw it was empty.'

McCune thought back. It hadn't struck him at the time, but the last stretch of buildings they had passed had seemed deserted, with no one in sight and no cars on the streets. He looked out again at the guardhouse. There had been a sign beneath the front window, but all that remained now were twisted bolts and discolored brick. 'How could they leave a military base open like this?'

'They didn't, the first few months. They kept up a guard for a while, but that petered out just like everything else.'

'But this damage . . .'

'Kids,' Parkinson said, nearly spitting the word. 'They ride their minibikes on the tow route. You can't keep 'em out.'

Nodding, McCune put the care in gear and drove through the gate. The road took them past other buildings, most of them brick but a few made of prefab metal. None were in any better shape than the guardhouse, and a few were much worse: doors kicked down, smoke stains showing around the windows, with desks and wrecked office equipment scattered across the parched lawns.

After a few blocks Parkinson told him to take the next left, and they drove out into the base itself, toward the towers that rose above the sand.

For about a mile they paralleled the curved path he had noticed from the top of the hill, heading for the blockhouse at the center of the base. He was unable to take his eyes off it as they drew nearer and it began to dominate the landscape. He didn't hear Parkinson telling him to turn until they were well past the spur, and he had to back up fifty yards to get to the right road.

A few minutes later they pulled up in front of a building that was in much better shape than those they had passed near the gate. The windows were intact, the door undamaged, and though the chaparral was making a valiant effort to reclaim the small hill it stood on, the area in front had been kept clear. A four-wheel-drive Blazer was parked next to it, and as they pulled up, a man not much smaller than the truck stepped out to meet them.

'Running a little late,' he bellowed cheerfully as Parkinson got out. He was dressed casually in slacks, a *guayabera* shirt that flapped over his ample belly, and a baseball cap with an odd acronym in front: NASA with the bars of the A's removed so that they looked like arrowheads. Like McCune he was bearded, but in proportion to the rest of his frame; it took up most of his face and spilled down to meet his shirt, giving him the air of a prospector or robber baron.

'Sorry about that,' said Parkinson. 'He kept me sitting in the waiting room all morning.' He took a step toward the building, then looked questioningly at the big man. 'Where's everybody else?'

'Sherry saw one of those spheres floating around the assembly building about noon,' the big man said, waving an arm to the south. 'I sent everybody home after she told me.'

McCune was halfway out of the car, arm draped over the open door. Spheres, floating spheres — that brought back something. Hadn't there been some kind of flying ghosts people were seeing a few years back? Ofos or something? He was trying to catch the thought when the big man stepped around the front of the car. He closed the door and held out his hand. 'Robert McCune, *LA Journal*.'

'Ben Everly, avionics engineer,' the big man boomed back. 'Welcome to North Vandenberg.' He released McCune's hand and glanced at Parkinson with a crooked smile. Parkinson scowled and turned away.

McCune eyed them for a moment, then looked at the blockhouse, grown overwhelming at this distance. From where he stood he could see an American flag painted on the side. Everly followed his gaze. 'Impressive in a miserable sort of way. Makes you wonder what Baikonur looks like these days.' He saw McCune frown and said, 'Baikonur, the Russian . . . well, forget it, it's not important.'

Tearing his eyes away, McCune turned back to him. 'These spheres you just mentioned. What are they like? Glowing? Making noises?'

Crossing his arms. Everly leaned back against the car, which settled alarmingly under his weight. 'No, sir, nothing like that

Black. Blacker than anything you've ever heard of. No lights, no sound, no emissions at all, as far as we can tell. There's supposed to be a shimmer directly underneath from close up, but I've never seen it. They show up once a month, sometimes more often. We think they're unmanned.' He smiled through his beard. 'Or whatever.'

'Who's we?'

'Bunch of people trying to salvage what they can. People who remember.'

McCune was about to ask him what it was they remembered when Parkinson spoke. 'Look, we haven't got much daylight left, and there's a lot to look at. We ought to get started.'

Everly nodded and pushed himself away from the truck. 'Don's right. There's too much to see here in one day and we haven't even got that.' He hitched up his pants and walked over to Parkinson. 'Well, what do you think? Where do we hit first?'

Parkinson pointed to the concrete structure, 'Slick-6.'

The big man ran his fingers through his beard. 'That's a hell of a lot to take in at once. let's build up to it, show him the Titan first.'

'Fine by me,' said Parkinson. 'Just as long as he gets a look at the orbiter.'

'Oh, he will,' Everly said. He walked with bulky grace toward the Blazer. 'I'll take the truck and you follow me.'

They drove about five miles north, through the shadow of the blockhouse that stretched for hundreds of yards across the sands. Again McCune was unable to tear his eyes away and kept staring at the thing as they drove past. The size of the towers, now that he was down among them, was bad enough, but this, this thing was something else. He could not imagine what it was for. The other side of it was hollow, and a tower similar to the others but much larger stood a short distance away, attached to it by a sort of track. Inside he caught a glimpse of a white shape before the glare of the sun forced him to turn his eyes back to the road. Ahead was one of the towers, standing near the low hills that ringed the base. Even from this distance he could see that it differed from the others. A long, low object lay behind it, bending upward so that one end rested on the platform below the tower. He looked away, taking in the rest of the base, nearly shivering as he did so. Incomprehensible as most of it was, the place had an air of bleakness, of total desolation that he could barely stand. He glanced at Parkinson, wondering if he felt the same. 'What's this Titan he was talking about?'

Parkinson nodded at the tower ahead 'Titan 34D7. Standard military lifter.'

McCune turned back to the road. 'Uh-huh. Standard military lifter. I should have known.' Parkinson stared blankly out the windshield, resting his chin on his hand. 'You'll see.'

Neither of them spoke again before reaching the tower. Everly had pulled up near the metal object behind it and was surveying the thing, his hands on his hips. He turned as they approached. 'Well, here we are. A Titan, or most of one, anyway.' He and Parkinson walked up to it, McCune following reluctantly.

It was in three parts, sheet-metal tubes about ten feet in diameter and ninety feet long, each attached on one side to another. The ends of the two on the outside were rounded off to blunt cones, while the one in the middle was flat and open. They had broken a little more than halfway down, and the other ends, hidden from McCune, leaned against the platform and jutted toward the sky. The tubes were badly damaged, with sheets of metal cracked, torn, and curling from the sides. McCune could see that it had fallen from the platform, where it had rested with the cones pointing upward. Looking at the tower he could see where it, too, had suffered, with struts and beams bent and left hanging by the fall of the thing.

Everly had stopped at the side of it and was patting the metal affectionately when McCune reached him. There was writing on the metal: numbers, symbols, and strange words. 'What is it?'

'It's a rocket,' said Everly, taking a few steps back. 'Two-stage, two solid boosters, nearly three million pounds thrust at liftoff.' He pushed back the baseball cap. 'Came down in that big storm spring of last year. We thought it was secure enough, but we were wrong.' There was a windblown piece of chaparral stuck in a curled sheet of metal, and Everly kicked it away.

'Wasn't fueled, of course, except for the boosters. If it had been, people would have noticed. I was here in '86 when that one blew at Slick-4. That was something to write home about.'

McCune looked back at the pointed ends. 'They look like fuel tanks to me.'

Parkinson, who had been watching him intently, snickered and turned away. 'Fuel tanks, my God . . .'

'Wait a second, Don,' said Everly. 'He's not wrong. They are fuel tanks, except for the engines.' He began to walk the length of the tubes toward the tower. 'We may as well take a look at those now.'

Parkinson glared at McCune and followed, muttering. After a few seconds McCune set out after them, keeping well away from the side of the tubes.

They had already climbed the metal stairs to the platform when he reached the base of — what had Parkinson called it? — the gantry. He hesitated, staring up at them before mounting the steps himself. When he reached the top, a brisk wind was coming in off the Pacific, bringing with it the salt smell of the sea. He had left his jacket in the car, and he shivered in the cool breeze. The two of them stood near the center of the platform, gesturing at the tubes twenty feet overhead. McCune looked up and studied them. Like the center tube at the far end, they were flat but set with flaring nozzles that gaped at the sky. The middle nozzle was relatively small, only a few feet in diameter, but the outlying two were enormous: He could have walked into them without bending over. He shivered again and looked down at the two men standing underneath them. Everly had noticed him standing at the railing and he led Parkinson over. 'Well,' he said as they drew nearer, 'I guess they're not fuel tanks.'

'Yep,' Everly said as he rested his bulk against the railing. 'It's true they are not.'

'They look like jet engines.'

'Close,' said Everly, 'real close. They operate roughly the same as jets.' He gestured at the tubes, buckled and torn by the edge of the platform. 'Fuel and oxidizer flow from the tanks into a chamber just behind the nozzles and they ignite and the exhaust pushes this sucker' — he thrust his palm into the air — 'straight up.'

McCune bit his lip, looking again at the nozzles, then back at Everly. 'Okay, granted. Obviously a lot of hard work went into these things and that may be what they're for. But why would anybody want to do such a thing?'

'You took a course in physics in college, am I right?' McCune nodded, wondering how he knew. 'Well, remember your Newton. You push an object hard enough and fast enough, it doesn't come down. It goes into a circular path around the planet, an orbit.'

McCune thought for a minute before speaking. 'But . . . that'd be fifteen or twenty thousand miles an hour.'

'Sure,' Everly said. He pointed at the nozzles above them. 'You think those couldn't do it?'

He looked up and tried to picture flames shooting out of the tubes but felt a shiver of unease and dropped his eyes. 'But what good would that do? Something floating around out there?'

It seemed Parkinson had been awaiting his moment. He leaned forward eagerly. 'Satellites. From orbit you can see anything. Reconnaissance, meteorology, communications, astronomy . . .' His voice fell. 'Space stations . . .' He took a step back, his mouth twisted. 'This doesn't mean a damn thing to you, does it? Just words.' He looked desperately at Everly. 'We're not getting through to him.' Everly remained silent, and Parkinson, shaking his head, pushed past him to the stairs. McCune leaned over the railing and watched Parkinson descend. 'What the hell is his problem?'

The big man leaned back on the railing with his arms crossed and his lips pursed. A few seconds passed before he answered. 'Don,' he said slowly, 'is going through something the rest of us have left far behind. He's an astrophysicist from back East with no direct connection to the program, although he was working on a project for the space telescope — but that's Greek to you anyway. He's only been out here for two months and still has to get his feet on the ground.'

'All well and good; I did him a favor coming out here.'

'I know.' Everly said, stepping away from the railing. 'I

appreciate it. Believe me, most people wouldn't have gotten this far.' He turned and looked out over the base. 'This beginning to mean anything to you?' he asked, sweeping an arm across the vista.

'I can't really say. I don't know if it means anything concrete, but I'm getting a weird feeling from it all.'

Everly nodded. 'As if you've forgotten a word, and it seems ready to pop out of your mind, but you can't quite grasp it.'

'Right. But a lot stranger than that.'

'How so?'

McCune looked the big man in the eyes. 'I'm scared,' he said. 'Really scared.'

He pointed at the tubes looming up against the sky. 'I tried to picture that thing working, and I couldn't make myself do it. And the rest of the place.' He gripped the top of a railing. 'The towers, that block over there.' He shivered in a gust of wind. 'It frightens me, and I don't know why.'

Everly nodded and walked to the top of the stairs. 'I think I understand.' After a moment McCune let go of the railing and followed. The two of them silently descended the metal steps and walked over to the cars. Parkinson was leaning on the front of the truck, looking out to sea, ignoring their approach. When they were a few years away, McCune stopped and Everly turned to him, his eyebrows raised. 'Those satellites he was talking about, those are real?'

'Sure. There's one of them not five minutes from here.'

'Here? Now?'

Everly laughed. 'Yeah. Want to see it?'

'Well . . .' McCune thought for a minute. 'Why not?'

'Okay. It's in a hangar a couple miles down the road.'

Parkinson didn't ride with him this time, instead getting into the truck with Everly. The wind had grown colder, and McCune put his jacket on before starting the engine. Out to sea, the sun nearly touched the horizon as he followed the truck down the long, bare road to the white hangar near the shore.

Everly stopped in front of it but stayed inside talking to Parkinson while McCune waited. This close to the water the smell of the sea was overwhelming, the salt odor overlaid with the iodine of rotting kelp and the smell of dead things.

The gulls wheeled across the sky, calling to each other, silhouetted by the setting sun. Finally Everly emerged from the Blazer, flashlight in hand, followed by Parkinson. 'We'll need this,' he said, waving the flash, a big utility model, at McCune. 'They cut the damn power off and it'll be dark in there.' They walked to the sliding door of the hangar, which had been left open a few feet.

Everly flicked on the flashlight as they entered, pointing it at an object resting on a wheeled pallet at the center of the concrete floor. It was the same diameter as the tubes — the rocket — that they had just seen but was much shorter, about forty feet overall. The shape was different as well, lacking the smooth aerodynamic simplicity of the Titan. The bulk of it was an irregular polygon, set with circular hatches flush against the surface. From the rear end protruded a rectangle with a number of metal plates, antennas, and boxes poking from it. The other end was covered, umbrellalike, by a folded panel of shiny metal. There was nothing startling or extraordinary about it — it looked like any machine — but McCune felt the same sense of discomfort, of foreboding, that had touched him back at the gantry.

'KH-14,' said Everly. '*KH* stands for *Keyhole*. It's a long-duration recon satellite, a modification of the KH-12 that went up on the shuttle. Never was a 13. We figured we'd had enough bad luck.' He walked toward the machine, the circle of the flashlight beam shrinking against the side of it. 'It was supposed to go up on that bird we just saw, on the twentieth.' He paused for a moment, staring at the thing, 'Mice and men.'

Oppressed by the place's darkness, McCune whispered, 'What does it do?'

Apparently this was Parkinson's forte. He walked to the machine and began rattling off a string of terms that made no sense: *pixels, multispectral scanners, digital filters.* Everly must have seen him shaking his head. 'Cameras,' he said quietly. 'Fancy cameras.' McCune made no response. His gaze was drawn to the shadows dancing around the hangar as the flashlight beam followed Parkinson. He kept seeing that block of concrete and steel in the growing darkness outside, the tomb of a devil or a god. The smell of the sea had penetrated the hangar, underlining the sense of bleakness while the cries of the gulls mocked it all. After a few minutes he said, 'I've heard enough,' and walked stiffly outside. Behind him he heard Parkinson's voice raised in anger but could make out no words.

The sun had vanished, leaving the western sky awash with red and yellow that faded as he watched. He sat down on the hood of the car, breathing deeply, trying to understand what he felt. The wind from the sea was much colder than it had any right to be. Everly and Parkinson walked out of the hangar, the big man shutting off the flashlight as he neared the car. He sat down next to McCune. 'A little too much, eh?'

McCune nodded. He looked out at the dark shapes of the base, beginning to fall into night. A glow from the eastern hills backlit the gantries strangely. He shook his head. 'I don't know,' he said. 'This place must have cost millions . . .'

'Billions,' said Everly.

'Billions, then, and nobody knows about it. It's abandoned.' He looked back at the Titan pad. 'That thing, that rocket, you'd see it fifty miles off when it went up, but nobody ever has.' He turned to Everly. 'How many of them have been . . .'

'Launched? Hundreds, worldwide.'

McCune stared at the sand in front of the car. 'I guess you'd better tell me how this happened.'

Parkinson held his hands out, as if speaking to a child. 'On August eighteenth, two years ago . . .' he began, but Everly cut him off. 'Hold on, Don, one thing at a time.' He got up and brushed off his pants. 'We'll drive over to Lompoc, get a drink maybe, something to eat. It's too dark . . .'

'No, sir. He sees the orbiter.'

'Don . . .'

'God damn it, Ben, that's why I brought him out here in the first place. He sees the STS. If that doesn't shake him up, nothing will.'

'He's already shook up quite a bit, Don.' Nonetheless, he looked questioningly at McCune, who rose from the hood of the car and said, 'Okay, I'll look at your orbiter, whatever the hell that is. But first, I want you to tell me everything.'

Everly shrugged. 'No problem. I can do it on the way over, if you don't mind riding with me.'

'Not at all,' McCune said. He turned to Parkinson. 'I suppose that I can trust you to drive?'

'I've driven a car,' Parkinson said, and walked around to the door.

McCune got into the Blazer and sat back looking at the glow in the eastern sky. 'By the way, where is this thing?'

Everly started the truck, then pointed to the blockhouse that brooded in darkness two miles away. 'Slick-6.'

'Well,' McCune said after they had driven a few hundred yards from the hangar. Everly didn't answer and sat steering the truck with one hand, a thoughtful look on his face. 'I'd like you to clear this up before we get over there,' he went on. 'And one other thing: I'll look at this orbiter from outside, but I'm not going in that building.'

'You won't have to.'

McCune relaxed and sank back into the seat. 'All right, but tell me the rest of it. I'd sooner believe you than what's-his-name there.' He gestured toward the lights of the car ahead of them.

'Yeah, you would at that,' Everly said. 'We got along pretty well last time we met, even though you were here to give me a hard time.'

McCune turned and stared. 'What?'

Without a word, Everly leaned over and opened the glove compartment. He took out a small cassette recorder and handed it to McCune. 'Listen to it,' he said.

McCune took the recorder and turned it on. Everly's voice boomed out. '. . . have it, Bob. You can't make polar launches from the Cape, not with Miami and the Caribbean islands in the way. Here you've got a clear shot down the Pacific, straight to the South Pole.'

There was a short pause, then another voice continued. 'But isn't it true that a lot of congressmen have been criticizing the shuttle complex here since the *Challenger* disaster?'

He gasped, and his grip on the recorder tightened convulsively. He fumbled with it, punching several buttons until it shut off.

It was his voice.

He hit the eject button and the tape popped out, nearly falling to the floor of the truck. He held it close to his face to see what was written on the label, but the trembling of his hand made it impossible. He took a deep breath and looked again. *Bob McCune — Journal* and a date three years ago. He dropped it all, recorder and tape, into his lap and was shaking uncontrollably when he felt the big man's hand on his shoulder. 'Easy, son.'

Still shaking, McCune looked up at him. 'What is this?'

The truck was stopped, sitting in the middle of the road. Ahead the lights of his car disappeared in the direction of the blockhouse. Everly bent forward, his eyebrows resting on the dash, his arms enveloping the steering wheel. He stared out of the windshield a moment before speaking. 'You came here to do a hatchet job three years back. Your target was Slick-6. As I recall, you supported the space program but didn't like military launches. You wanted to see a working engineer, so PR sent you to me. We toured the base, same as we did today. I recorded the interview, just as I always . . . did, to avoid, ah . . . honest errors.'

He looked at McCune and smiled. 'You were pretty amused.'

'I don't remember any of it.'

The big man's eyes dulled, and he looked back at the road. 'Nobody does. Two years ago, on August seventeenth, they remembered it all. *Sputnik*, Apollo, the shuttle. Glenn, Gagarin, Armstrong. They went to bed that night — at least in this country — and when they got up the next day, it was gone.' He sat back, and his arms dropped to his sides. He looked very old. 'I came here that morning — Christ, I'll remember it on my deathbed — it was like a dead city. Weber was in hysterics. Couldn't reach the base commander, couldn't reach the Pentagon. There were about twenty of us here that knew. Some of the others had shown up for work but were just wandering around, not knowing what they were here for.' He closed his eyes as if in pain. 'Some of the best men I've ever known, lobotomized. Their whole lives taken from them.' He shook his head. 'It took us days to get a handle on it, weeks to believe it. Some of us never have.'

He sat silently for a moment before continuing. 'After a couple of months we set up a network, and started getting data from the observatories — the ones that were still operating, anyway. Strange things going on in the rest of the system. Gravitational waves of incredible magnitude, point sources of laser and ionizing radiation, disturbances in the atmosphere of Jupiter . . . then, after a while, you could see them.' He looked out the side window at the eastern hills, then turned back, his mouth a thin line. 'We don't know where they came from, what they look like, what they're doing.

'We don't know how they did it either, a tailored virus, a field, something we can't even understand, but they wiped the idea of space travel from the mind of the race.'

He put the truck in gear and started the engine. 'Not all of us, of course, or I wouldn't be here. Some remember. One, two percent, tops. A hundred million worldwide, maybe. We're trying to keep it alive. Fargas at Transorbit remembers, thank God. He's got money and a launch site in Peru we can use to put up essential stuff, communications, weather. Otherwise when whatever is in orbit now runs down, the whole planet goes down the tubes.' He raised a hand and waved it out the window at the base. 'And we stay here. Me, Don, a few others, salvaging what we can. Scavenging. Don thought that bringing you up here would waken the dormant memories, that you'd write something about it, start an investigation. The rest of us know better.' He put the truck in gear and started it rolling. 'Well, how do you like that story?'

McCune realized that he was gaping at the man and turned to the windshield. His thoughts would not come together. There were images floating through his mind: something like the rocket he had seen back there leaping into the sky on a pillar of smoke and flame; a group of smiling men dressed in outlandish silvery suits holding glass-visored helmets; another suited man, wearing the helmet now, saluting the flag in a dark, barren landscape. Something that Everly had said — Apollo? — he kept seeing the moon. He searched the sky for it, but it was nowhere in sight. Of course not. It was — a new moon.

Was there such a thing? 'No,' he said finally. 'No, that's insane. There isn't anything like that. People would know. The government. There'd be more evidence . . .' He was beginning to babble, and he cut himself off.

Not taking his eyes off the road, Everly nodded. 'Oh, there is. You can check unemployment figures for science professors, aerospace — sorry, aeronautics — engineers, and research scientists. Look at the companies, hundreds of them, that have gone out of business in the last few years, particularly down your way, and check what they were involved with. And some of it is worse. The Indian Ocean weather satellite broke down a year back, just before the monsoon. A typhoon hit Bangladesh the week after and killed two million people. Their UN ambassador, Basra, was one of us. He couldn't take it. He shot himself.'

'I heard about that,' McCune said. 'He had a breakdown. He made a crazy speech in the Assembly. They were going to send him home.'

'Yeah,' said Everly, smiling bitterly. 'A crazy speech. All about weather satellites and what had happened to his country.'

McCune shook his head. 'I don't care, it's still insane. There aren't any things up there. If you think . . .'

Chuckling, Everly raised his hand. 'Okay, okay, I've heard it before.' They were now driving through the mass of smaller buildings that surrounded the blockhouse. Turning the last corner, he saw his car a few hundred yards away with Parkinson standing next to it. He took a step toward the truck as they pulled up, but Everly shook his head, and he turned away abruptly. McCune opened the door before they stopped moving and was getting out when the cassette clattered to the floor. He picked it up and was about to hand it to Everly when the big man spoke. 'As long as you're here why not take a look? I'll light it up for you.' McCune gazed up at the blockhouse and the white shape inside, barely visible with the glow of the sky behind it. He wanted to get away from there as soon as possible, but he turned back to Everly. 'All right, but then I'm leaving.'

Everly nodded. 'Sure. No hard feelings.' He shut the door and drove toward the blockhouse. McCune took a step in the direction of his car, but Parkinson was standing there, and he turned away, in the direction of the sea.

They were both nuts. They couldn't possibly believe that story. God alone knew what they were actually doing here. He'd thought Everly was normal, but no, he was just as bad. How had Parkinson ever talked him into this, anyway? Wouldn't he ever learn to say no?

He looked past the dunes at the gray ocean. The wind seemed to have increased and grown colder, and the odor it brought made him want to gag. He knew he would never again come upon the smell of the sea without feeling an echo of the fear that he felt now. He wished he had never left Los Angeles. He clasped his jacket closed and shivered. The cassette was still in his hand, so he shoved it in the jacket pocket. Then Parkinson spoke, he turned to look, and he knew.

It stood in sharp relief, lit by the spotlight on Everly's truck. It was gigantic, gleaming while in the harsh glare, the stubby wings, the wide body, the single fin rising from the tail. A picture rose in his mind of this thing roaring into the night in a burst of fire that lit up the sky, a vision of power and glory, fearsome beyond dreams. Moaning, he drove the image away and stumbled toward the car. Parkinson stood in front of it, blocking his way McCune stopped and stared at him. 'It's an airplane,' he said through clenched teeth. Parkinson frowned.

'It's an airplane,' McCune shouted. 'You brought me here to see an airplane!' He tried to push past, but Parkinson grabbed his arm and held him there, smiling fixedly. 'So it's an airplane. What about the rest?'

'Do you think I'm crazy?' He flung an arm toward the sky. 'Something coming down from those lights up there?'

Parkinson yanked McCune closer, nearly pulling him of his feet. 'Those lights up there.'

Chin trembling, McCune looked away. 'The stars,' he said, his voice a croak.

'Right,' said Parkinson, shaking him. 'But what are they?'

McCune looked up at them, the cold dots in the sky, nearly washed out by the glare from behind the blockhouse. His eyes returned to Parkinson's grinning face. 'They're lights up there.'

Parkinson gave a wordless cry of disgust and pulled him to the car, shoving him inside and across the passenger seat. He sat behind the wheel and started the engine. The gears screamed in protest as he swung around and drove off to the shore. McCune huddled against the door, staring at him. In a moment they were out of the shadow of the buildings, into the full glare of the light from the east. Parkinson drove to the top of a small hill, stopped the car, and got out. McCune nearly fell to the ground when the door was yanked open but was caught and dragged out past the front of the car. Parkinson let him go and pointed to the eastern sky. 'What about that?' he shouted. 'Is that just a light up there?'

McCune had no words for what was rising above the horizon. It was two handspans wide and half that high, and bright enough to make him squint. It seemed shapeless at first glance, with bright wings of shining matter reaching out in all directions, but there were hints of an inner structure impossible to make out past the sharp, actinic flashes that came every few seconds from its center. The white edges changed as he watched, turning to deep crimson and then to purple that spread out and faded into darkness. Around it points of light moved in elaborate patterns, sometimes disappearing into the thing itself while others emerged to join in the dance. 'It's been growing out there for a year and a half,' Parkinson bellowed. 'The asteroids are gone, along with most of Jupiter. It doesn't rotate, doesn't revolve, doesn't move at all. I've seen Mars rise in front of it and it's just a spot, a particle. Do you know what that means?'

McCune whimpered, shook his head, and turned back to the car. He struck out blindly when Parkinson tried to stop him hitting him in the face. The door was open when he reached it, and he collapsed inside. He shut it and pushed down the lock, then realized the window was open and fumbled with the switch, but nothing happened. He sat back in the seat shaking, then looked up to see Parkinson approaching the front of the car, his face wet, his teeth clenched in fury. He nearly screamed when a bright light touched Parkinson's face before he became aware of the truck pulling up next to him.

It stopped a few feet away, and the big man leaned out the inside window. 'Now you know, Donny,' he said in a quiet voice. 'You can't get through to them. Sometimes it's panic, sometimes contempt, sometimes confusion, but it always ends the same way. They've lost it, and they can't get it back.'

He looked over at McCune and seemed about to go on but instead just dropped his eyes and looked away.

McCune waited no longer. He reached for the keys and tried to start the car, but the engine died, and for a moment he was convinced that they had done something to it to keep him there. He thought of running, anything to get away from that place, and was about to bolt out the door when the engine caught and the car shot forward, nearly hitting Parkinson. He did not look back.

Breathing heavily, Parkinson watched the taillights recede. He looked up at the eastern sky, his expression unreadable, then turned to Everly. 'It's over,' he said.

The big man shook his head. 'No, it's not over, not yet anyway.' He fell silent, looking out over the dark sea as if there were something out there that he wanted but did not quite know how to obtain. 'There's still us, few as we are. It'll be a hard road, no question, but I promise you this: Someday we'll go out there and ask them who the hell they think they are.'

Parkinson rubbed his face, nodded, then walked head down back to the truck. 'I guess I've made a fool of myself,' he said as he got in.

'No, you didn't,' the big man replied. 'It's something we all go through.' He looked back at the base, the towers and buildings nearly lost against the black of the sea. 'Rite of passage,' he said softly, then swung around and started the truck toward the gate.

As they went up the ramp to 101 they passed McCune parked at the side of the road. He was looking at a cassette he had found in his pocket, wondering how it had gotten there, and he failed to see them. But it didn't matter. They had nothing more to say to him, and after all, he didn't know them anymore.

This is a Challenger *story; it was written in the fall of 1986; a few months after the disaster.*

One of the things that struck me at the time was how soon people forgot. Part of the explanation of this is the natural tendency to dismiss unpleasant events from memory — no one, to mention a similar case, remembers the names of the U.S. Army mail pilots who died in droves during the 1930s — but a larger part, I think, is due to the indifference that the conquest of space has met with in the public mind. ('Conquest of space' — sounds corny these days, doesn't it?)

Whatever the source of that indifference — faulty public relations, cynicism over government programs, a general loss of will — such an attitude is a matter of choice. If it wasn't, if it was imposed from outside, would its tragic nature become clearer? I thought it would.

J.R. Dunn

Bruce Sterling's short stories have been published in *The Magazine of Fantasy and Science Fiction, Interzone, Isaac Asimov's Science Fiction Magazine, Hayakawa's Science Fiction Magazine* and numerous 'best' anthologies. Many of these are in his first collection *Crystal Express*, and he also edited *Mirrorshades: The Cyberpunk Anthology*.

He is the author of the novels *Involution Ocean, The Artificial Kid, Schismatrix* and *Islands in the Net*. His most recent novel, *The Difference Engine*, is a collaboration with William Gibson.

Sterling once produced his own journal, the legendary *Cheap Truth*, and now writes a regular column for *Interzone*.

The following story was a Nebula and Hugo finalist, and the author comments: 'This story was, of course, inspired by the lives of Lester Bangs and Dori Seda, but it was truly catalysed by the work of their friends: Greil Marcus, a rock critic, and Krystine Kryttre, a graphic artist. With generous devotion, they kept the memory of their colleagues alive. Thank you, Greil; thank you, Krystine.'

DORI BANGS

by
BRUCE STERLING

True facts, mostly: Lester Bangs was born in California in 1948. He published his first article in 1969. It came in over the transom at *Rolling Stone*. It was a frenzied review of the MC5's 'Kick Out the Jams.'

Without much meaning to, Lester Bangs slowly changed from a Romilar-guzzling college kid into a 'professional rock critic.' There wasn't much precedent for this job in 1969, so Lester kinda had to make it up as he went along. Kind of *smell* his way into the role, as it were. But Lester had a fine set of cultural antennae. For instance, Lester invented the tag 'punk rock.' This is posterity's primary debt to the Bangs oeuvre.

Lester's not as famous now as he used to be, because he's been dead for some time, but in the '70s Lester wrote a million record reviews, for *Creem* and the *Village Voice* and *NME* and *Who Put The Bomp*. He liked to crouch over his old manual typewriter, and slam out wild Beat-influenced copy, while the Velvet Underground or Stooges were on the box. This made life a hideous trial for the neighborhood, but in Lester's opinion the neighborhood pretty much had it coming. *Epater les bourgeois,* man!

Lester was a party animal. It was a professional obligation, actually. Lester was great fun to hang with, because he usually had a jagged speed-edge, which made him smart and bold and rude and crazy. Lester was a one-man band, until he got drunk. Nutmeg, Romilar, belladonna, crank, those substances Lester could handle. But booze seemed to crack him open, and an unexpected black dreck of rage and pain would come dripping out, like oil from a broken crankcase.

Toward the end — but Lester had no notion that the end was nigh. He'd given up the booze, more or less. Even a single beer often triggered frenzies of self-contempt. Lester was thirty-three and sick of being groovy; he was restless, and the stuff he'd been writing lately no longer meshed with the surroundings that had made him what he was. Lester told his friends that he was gonna leave New York and go to Mexico and work on a deep, serious novel, about deep serious issues, man. The real thing, this time. He was really gonna pin it down, get into the guts of Western Culture, what it really was, how it really felt.

But then, in April '82, Lester happened to catch the flu. Lester was living alone at the time, his mom, the Jehovah's Witness, having died recently. He had no one to make him chicken soup, and the flu really took him down. Tricky stuff, flu; it has a way of getting on top of you.

Lester ate some Darvon, but instead of giving him the buzzed-out float it usually did, the pills made him feel foggy and dull and desperate. He was too sick to leave his room, or hassle with doctors or ambulances, so instead he just did more Darvon. And his heart stopped.

There was nobody there to do anything about it, so he lay there until a friend showed up and found him.

More true fax, pretty much: Dori Seda was born in 1951. She was a cartoonist, of the 'underground' variety. Dori wasn't ever famous, certainly not in Lester's league, but then she didn't beat her chest and bend every ear in the effort to make herself a Living Legend, either. She had a lot of friends in San Francisco, anyway.

Dori did a 'comic book' once, called *Lonely Nights*. An unusual 'comic book' for those who haven't followed the 'funnies' trade lately, as *Lonely Nights* was not particularly 'funny,' unless you really get a hoot from deeply revealing tales of frustrated personal relationships. Dori also did a lot of work for *WEIRDO* magazine, which emanated from the artistic circles of R. Crumb, he of 'Keep On Truckin'' and 'Fritz the Cat' fame.

R. Crumb once said: 'Comics are words and pictures. You can do anything with words and pictures!' As a manifesto, it was a typically American declaration, and it was a truth that Dori held to be self-evident.

Dori wanted to be a True Artist in her own real-gone little '80s-esque medium. Comix, or 'graphic narrative' if you want a snazzier cognomen for it, was a breaking thing, and she had to feel her way into it. You can see the struggle in her 'comics' — always relentlessly autobiographical — Dori hanging around in the 'Café La Boheme' trying to trade foodstamps for cigs; Dori living in drafty warehouses in the Shabby Hippie Section of San Francisco, sketching under the skylight and squabbling with her roommate's boyfriend; Dori trying to scrape up money to have her dog treated for mange.

Dori's comics are littered with dead cig-butts and toppled wine-bottles. She was, in a classic nutshell, Wild, Zany, and Self-Destructive. In 1988 Dori was in a car-wreck which cracked her pelvis and collarbone. She was laid up, bored, and in pain. To kill time, she drank and smoked and took pain-killers.

She caught the flu. She had friends who loved her, but nobody realized how badly off she was; probably she didn't know it herself. She just went down hard, and couldn't get up alone. On February 26 her heart stopped. She was thirty-six.

So enough 'true facts.' Now for some comforting lies.

As it happens, even while a malignant cloud of flu virus was lying in wait for the warm hospitable lungs of Lester Bangs, the Fate, Atropos, she who weaves the things that are to be, accidentally dropped a stitch. Knit one? Purl two? What the hell does it matter, anyway? It's just human lives, right?

So Lester, instead of inhaling a cloud of invisible contagion from the exhalations of a passing junkie, is almost hit by a Yellow Cab. This mishap on his way back from the deli shocks Lester out of his dogmatic slumbers. High time, Lester concludes, to get out of this burg and down to sunny old Mexico. He's gonna tackle his great American novel: *All My Friends are Hermits.*

So true. None of Lester's groovy friends go out much any more. Always ahead of their time, Lester's Bohemian cadre are no longer rock and roll animals. They still wear black leather jackets, they still stay up all night, they still hate Ronald Reagan with fantastic virulence; but they never leave home. They pursue an unnamed lifestyle that sociologist Faith Popcorn — (and how can you doubt anyone with a name like

Faith Popcorn) — will describe years later as 'cocooning.'

Lester has eight zillion rock, blues, and jazz albums, crammed into his grubby NYC apartment. Books are piled feet deep on every available surface: Wm. Burroughs, Hunter Thompson, Celine, Kerouac, Huysmans, Foucault, and dozens of unsold copies of *Blondie*, Lester's book-length band-bio.

More albums and singles come in the mail every day. People used to send Lester records in the forlorn hope he would review them. But now it's simply a tradition. Lester has transformed himself into a counter-cultural info-sump. People send him vinyl just because he's *Lester Bangs*, man!

Still jittery from his thrilling brush with death, Lester looks over his lifetime of loot with a surge of Sartrean nausea. He resists the urge to raid the fridge for his last desperate can of Blatz Beer. Instead, Lester snorts some speed, and calls an airline to plan his Mexican wanderjahr. After screaming in confusion at the hopeless stupid bitch of a receptionist, he gets a ticket to San Francisco, best he can do on short notice. He packs in a frenzy and splits.

Next morning finds Lester exhausted and wired and on the wrong side of the continent. He's brought nothing with him but an Army duffel-bag with his Olympia portable, some typing paper, shirts, assorted vials of dope, and a paperback copy of *Moby Dick*, which he's always meant to get around to re-reading.

Lester takes a cab out of the airport. He tells the cabbie to drive nowhere, feeling a vague compulsive urge to soak up the local vibe. San Francisco reminds him of his *Rolling Stone* days, back before Wenner fired him for being nasty to rock-stars. Fuck Wenner, he thinks. Fuck this city that was almost Avalon for a few months in '67 and has been on greased skids to Hell ever since.

The hilly half-familiar streets creep and wriggle with memories, avatars, talismans. Decadence, man, a no-kidding *death of affect*. It all ties in for Lester, in a bilious mental stew: snuff movies, discos, the cold-blooded whine of synthesizers, Pet Rocks, S&M, mindfuck self-improvement cults, Winning Through Intimidation, every aspect of the invisible war slowly eating the soul of the world.

After an hour or so he stops the cab at random. He needs coffee, white sugar, human beings, maybe a cheese Danish. Lester glimpses himself in the cab's window as he turns to pay: a chunky jobless thirty-three-year-old in a biker jacket, speed-pale dissipated New York face, Fu Manchu mustache looking pasted on. Running to fat, running for shelter . . . no excuses, Bangs! Lester hands the driver a big tip. Chew on that, pal — you just drove the next Oswald Spengler.

Lester staggers into the cafe. It's crowded and stinks of patchouli and clove. He sees two chainsmoking punkettes hanging out at a formica table. CBGB's types, but with California suntans. The kind of women, Lester thinks, who sit crosslegged on the floor and won't fuck you but are perfectly willing to describe in detail their highly complex postexistential *weltanschauung*. Tall and skinny and crazy-looking and bad news. Exactly his type, really. Lester sits down at their table and gives them his big rubber grin.

'Been having fun?' Lester says.

They look at him like he's crazy, which he is, but he wangles their names out: 'Dori' and 'Krystine.' Dori's wearing fishnet stockings, cowboy boots, and strapless second-hand bodice-hugger covered with peeling pink feathers. Her long brown hair's streaked blonde. Krystine's got a black knit tank-top and a leather skirt and a skull-tattoo on her stomach.

Dori and Krystine have never heard of 'Lester Bangs.' They don't read much. They're *artists*. They do cartoons. Under-ground comix. Lester's mildly interested. Manifestations of the trash aesthetic always strongly appeal to him. It seems so American, the *good* America that is: the righteous wild America of rootless European refuse picking up discarded pop-junk and making it shine like the Koh-i-noor. To make 'comic books' into *Art* — what a hopeless fucking effort, worse than rock and roll and you don't even get heavy bread for it. Lester says as much, to see what they'll do.

Krystine wanders off for a refill. Dori, who is mildly weirded-out by this tubby red-eyed stranger with his loud come-on, gives Lester her double-barreled brush-off. Which consists of opening up this Windex-clear vision into the Vent of Hell that is her daily life. Dori lights another Camel from the butt of the last, smiles at Lester with her big gappy front teeth and says brightly:

'You like *dogs*, Lester? I have this dog, and he has eczema and disgusting open sores all over his body, and he smells *really* bad . . . I can't get friends to come over because he likes to shove his nose right into their, you know, *crotch* . . . and go *Snort! Snort!*'

'"I want to scream with wild dog joy in the smoking pit of a charnel house,"' Lester says.

Dori stares at him. 'Did you make that up?'

'Yeah,' Lester says. 'Where were you when Elvis died?'

'You taking a survey on it?' Dori says.

'No, I just wondered,' Lester says. 'There was talk of having Elvis's corpse dug up, and the stomach analyzed. For dope, y'know. Can you *imagine* that? I mean, the *thrill* of sticking your hand and forearm into Elvis's rotted guts and slopping around in the stomach lining and liver and kidneys and coming up out of dead Elvis's innards triumphantly clenching some crumbs off a few Percodans and Desoxyns and 'ludes . . . and then this is the *real* kick, Dori: you pop these crumbled-up bits of pills in your *own mouth* and bolt 'em down and get high on drugs that not only has Elvis Presley, the *King*, gotten high on, not the same brand mind you but the same *pills*, all slimy with little bits of his innards, so you've actually gotten to *eat* the King of Rock and Roll!'

' *Who* did you say you were?' Dori says. 'A rock journalist? I thought you were putting me on. 'Lester Bangs,' that's a fucking weird name!'

Dori and Krystine have been up all night, dancing to the heroin headbanger vibes of Darby Crash and the Germs. Lester watches through hooded eyes: this Dori is a woman over thirty, but she's got this wacky airhead routine down smooth, the Big Shiny Fun of the American Pop Bohemia. 'Fuck you for believing I'm this shallow.' Beneath the skin of her Attitude he can sense a bracing skeleton of pure desperation. There is hollow fear and sadness in the marrow of her bones. He's been writing about a topic just like this lately.

They talk a while, about the city mostly, about their variant scenes. Sparring, but he's interested. Dori yawns with pretended disinterest and gets up to leave. Lester notes that Dori is taller than he is. It doesn't bother him. He gets her phone number.

Lester crashes in a Holiday Inn. Next day he leaves town. He spends a week in a flophouse in Tijuana with his Great American Novel, which sucks. Despondent and terrified, he writes himself little cheering notes: 'Burroughs was almost fifty when he wrote *Nova Express!*" Hey boy, you only thirty-three! Burnt-out! Washed-up! Finished! A bit of flotsam! And in that flotsam your salvation! In that one grain of wood. In that one bit of that irrelevance. If you can bring yourself to describe it . . .'

It's no good. He's fucked. He knows he is, too, he's been reading over his scrapbooks lately, those clippings of yellow newsprint, thinking: it was all a box, man! *El Cajon!* You'd think: wow, a groovy youth-rebel Rock Writer, he can talk about *anything*, can't he? Sex, dope, violence, Mazola parties with teenage Indonesian groupies, Nancy Reagan publicly fucked by a herd of clapped-out bull walruses . . . but when you actually READ a bunch of Lester Bangs Rock Reviews in a row, the whole shebang has a delicate hermetic whiff, like so many eighteenth-century sonnets. It is to dance in chains; it is to see the whole world through a little chromed window of Silva-Thin 'shades . . .

Lester Bangs is nothing if not a consummate romantic. He is, after all, a man who *really no kidding believes* that Rock and Roll Could Change the World, and when he writes something which isn't an impromptu free lesson on what's wrong with Western Culture and how it can't survive without grabbing itself by the backbrain and turning itself inside-out, he feels like he's wasted a day. Now Lester, fretfully abandoning his typewriter to stalk and kill flophouse roaches, comes to realize that HE will have to turn himself inside out. Grow, or die. Grow into something but he has no idea what. He feels beaten.

So Lester gets drunk. Starts with Tecate, works his way up to tequila. He wakes up with a savage hangover. Life seems hideous and utterly meaningless. He abandons himself to senseless impulse. Or, in alternate terms, Lester allows himself to follow the numinous artistic promptings of his holy intuition.

He returns to San Fransisco and calls Dori Seda.

Dori, in the meantime, has learned from friends that there is indeed a rock journalist named 'Lester Bangs' who's actually kind of *famous*. He once appeared on stage with the J. Geils Band 'playing' his typewriter. He's kind of a big deal, which probably accounts for his being kind of an asshole. On a dare, Dori calls Lester Bangs in New York, gets his answering machine, and recognizes the voice. It was him, all right. Through some cosmic freak, she met Lester Bangs and he tried to pick her up! No dice, though. More Lonely Nights, Dori!

Then Lester calls. He's back in town again. Dori's so flustered she ends up being nicer to him on the phone than she means to be.

She goes out with him. To rock clubs. Lester never has to pay; he just mutters at people, and they let him in and find him a table. Strangers rush up to gladhand Lester and jostle round the table and pay court. Lester finds the music mostly boring, and it's no pretense; he actually *is* bored, he's heard it all. He sits there sipping club sodas and handing out these little chips of witty guru insight to these sleaze-ass Hollywood guys and bighaired coke-whores in black Spandex. Like it was his *job*.

Dori can't believe he's going to all this trouble just to jump her bones. It's not like he can't get women, or like their own relationship is all that tremendously scintillating. Lester's whole set-up is alien. But it *is* kind of interesting, and doesn't demand much. All Dori has to do is dress in her sluttiest Goodwill get-up, and be This Chick With Lester. Dori likes being invisible, and watching people when they don't know she's looking. She can see in their eyes that Lester's people wonder Who The Hell Is She? Dori finds this really funny, and makes sketches of his creepiest acquaintances on cocktail napkins. At night she puts them in her sketch books and writes dialogue balloons. It's all really good material.

Lester's also very funny, in a way. He's smart, not just hustler-clever but scary-crazy smart, like he's sometimes profound without knowing it or even *wanting* it. But when he thinks he's being most amusing, is when he's actually the most incredibly depressing. It bothers her that he doesn't drink around her; it's a bad sign. He knows almost nothing about art or drawing, he dresses like a jerk, he dances like a trained bear. And she's fallen in love with him and she knows he's going to break her goddamn heart.

Lester has put his novel aside for the moment. Nothing new there; he's been working on it, in hopeless spasms, for ten years. But now juggling this affair takes all he's got.

Lester is terrified that this amazing woman is going to go to pieces on him. He's seen enough of her work now to recognize that she's possessed of some kind of genuine demented genius. He can smell it; the vibe pours off her like Everglades swamp-reek. Even in her frowsy houserobe and bunny slippers, hair a mess, no makeup, half-asleep, he can see something there like Dresden china, something fragile and precious. And the world seems like a maelstrom of jungle hate, sinking into entrophy or gearing up for Armageddon, and what the hell can anybody do? How can he be happy with her and not be punished for it? How long can they break the rules before the Nova Police show?

But nothing horrible happens to them. They just go on living.

Then Lester blunders into a virulent cloud of Hollywood money. He's written a stupid and utterly commercial screenplay about the laff-a-minute fictional antics of a heavy-metal band, and without warning he gets eighty thousand dollars for it.

He's never had so much money in one piece before. He has, he realizes with dawning horror, sold out.

To mark the occasion Lester buys some freebase, six grams of crystal meth, and rents a big white Cadillac. He fast-talks Dori into joining him for a supernaturally cool Kerouac adventure into the Savage Heart of America, and they get in the car laughing like hyenas and take off for parts unknown.

Four days later they're in Kansas City. Lester's lying in the back seat in a jittery Hank Williams half-doze and Dori is driving. They have nothing left to say, as they've been arguing viciously ever since Albuquerque.

Dori, white-knuckled, sinuses scorched with crank, loses it behind the wheel. Lester's slammed from the back seat and wakes up to find Dori knocked out and drizzling blood from a scalp wound. The Caddy's wrapped messily in the buckled ruins of a sidewalk mailbox.

Lester holds the resultant nightmare together for about two hours, which is long enough to flag down help and get Dori into a Kansas City trauma room.

He sits there, watching over her, convinced he's lost it, blown it; it's over, she'll hate him forever now. My God, she could have died! As soon as she comes to, he'll have to face her. The thought of this makes something buckle inside him. He flees the hospital in headlong panic.

He ends up in a sleazy little rock dive downtown where he jumps onto a table and picks a fight with the bouncer. After he's knocked down for the third time, he gets up screaming for the manager, how he's going to *ruin that motherfucker!* and the club's owner shows up, tired and red-faced and sweating. The owner, whose own tragedy must go mostly unexpressed here, is a fat white-haired cigar-chewing third-rater who attempted, and failed, to model his life on Elvis' Colonel Parker. He hates kids, he hates rock and roll, he hates the aggravation of smart-ass doped-up hippies screaming threats and pimping off the hard work of businessmen just trying to make a living.

He has Lester hauled to his office backstage and tells him all this. Toward the end, the owner's confused, almost plaintive, because he's never seen anyone as utterly, obviously, and desperately fucked-up as Lester Bangs, but who can still be coherent about it and use phrases like 'rendered to the factor of machinehood' while mopping blood from his punched nose.

And Lester, trembling and red-eyed, tells him: fuck you Jack, I could run this jerkoff place, I could do everything you do blind drunk, and make this place a fucking *legend in American culture,* you booshwah sonofabitch.

Yeah punk if you had the money, the owner says.

I've *got* the money! Let's see your papers, you evil cracker bastard! In a few minutes Lester is the owner-to-be on a hand-shake and an earnest-check.

Next day he brings Dori roses from the hospital shop down-stairs. He sits next to the bed; they compare bruises, and Lester explains to her that he has just blown his fortune. They are now tied down and beaten in the corn-shucking heart of America. There is only one possible action left to complete this situation.

Three days later they are married in Kansas City by a justice of the peace.

Needless to say marriage does not solve any of their problems. It's a minor big deal for a while, gets mentioned in rock-mag gossip columns; they get some telegrams from friends, and Dori's mom seems pretty glad about it. They even get a nice note from Julie Burchill, the Marxist Amazon from *New Musical Express* who has quit the game to write for fashion mags, and her husband Tony Parsons the proverbial 'hip young gunslinger' who now writes weird potboiler novels about racetrack gangsters. Tony & Julie seem to be making some kind of go of it. Kinda inspirational.

For a while Dori calls herself Dori Seda-Bangs, like her good friend Aline Kominsky-Crumb, but after a while she figures what's the use? and just calls herself Dori Bangs which sounds plenty weird enough on its own.

Lester can't say he's really *happy* or anything, but he's sure *busy*. He re-names the club 'Waxy's Travel Lounge,' for some reason known only to himself. The club loses money quickly and consistently. After the first month Lester stops playing Lou Reed's *Metal Machine Music* before sets, and that helps attendance some, but Waxy's is still a club which books a lot of tiny weird college-circuit acts that Albert Average just doesn't get yet. Pretty soon they're broke again and living on Lester's reviews.

They'd be even worse off, except Dori does a series of promo posters for Waxy's that are so amazing that they draw people in, even after they've been burned again and again on weird-ass bands only Lester can listen to.

After a couple of years they're still together, only they have shrieking crockery-throwing fights and once, when he's been drinking, Lester wrenches her arm badly Dori's truly afraid it's broken. It isn't, luckily, but it's sure no great kick being Mrs. Lester Bangs. Dori was always afraid of this: that what he does is *work* and what she does is *cute*. How many Great Women Artists are there anyway, and what happened to 'em? They went into patching the wounded ego and picking up the dropped socks of Mr. Wonderful, that's what. No big mystery about it.

And besides, she's thirty-six and still barely scraping a living. She pedals her beat-up bike through the awful Kansas weather and sees these yuppies cruise by with these smarmy grins: hey we don't *have* to invent our lives, our lives are *invented for us* and boy does that ever save a lot of soul-searching.

But still somehow they blunder along; they have the occasional good break. Like when Lester turns over the club on Wednesdays to some black kids for (ecch!) 'disco nite' and it turns out to be the beginning of a little Kansas City rap-scratch scene, which actually makes the club some money. And 'Polyrock,' a band Lester hates at first but later champions to global megastardom, cuts a live album in Waxy's.

And Dori gets a contract to do one of those twenty-second animated logos for MTV, and really gets into it. It's fun, so she starts doing video animation work for (fairly) big bucks and even gets a Macintosh II from a video-hack admirer in Silicon Valley. Dori had always loathed feared and despised *computers* but this thing is *different.* This is a kind of art that *nobody's ever done before* and has to be invented from leftovers, sweat, and thin air! It's wide open and way rad!

Lester's novel doesn't get anywhere, but he does write a book called *A Reasonable Guide to Horrible Noise* which becomes a hip coffeetable cult item with an admiring introduction by a trendy French semiotician. Among other things, this book introduces the term 'chipster' which describes the kind of person who, well, didn't really *exist* before Lester described them but once he'd pointed 'em out it was *obvious to everybody.*

But they're still not *happy.* They both have a hard time taking the 'marital fidelity' notion with anything like seriousness. They have a vicious fight once, over who gave who herpes, and Dori splits for six months and goes back to California. Where she looks up her old girlfriends and finds the survivors married with kids, and her old boyfriends are even seedier and more pathetic than Lester. What the hell, it's not happiness but it's something. She goes back to Lester. He's gratifyingly humble and appreciative for almost six weeks.

Waxy's does in fact become a cultural legend of sorts, but they don't pay you for that; and anyway it's hell to own a bar while attending sessions of Alcoholics Anonymous. So Lester gives in, and sells the club. He and Dori buy a house, which turns out to be far more hassle than it's worth, and then they go to Paris for a while, where they argue bitterly and squander all their remaining money.

When they come back Lester gets, of all the awful things, an academic gig. For a Kansas state college. Lester teaches Rock and Popular Culture. In the '70s there'd have been no room for such a hopeless skidrow weirdo in a, like, Serious Academic Environment, but it's the late '90s by now, and Lester has outlived the era of outlawhood. Because who are we kidding? Rock and Roll is a satellite-driven worldwide information industry which is worth billions and *billions*, and if they don't study *major industries* then what the hell are the taxpayers funding colleges for?

Self-destruction is awfully tiring. After a while, they just give it up. They've lost the energy to flame-out, and it hurts too much; besides it's less trouble just to live. They eat balanced meals, go to bed early, and attend faculty parties where Lester argues violently about the parking privileges.

Just after the turn of the century, Lester finally gets his novel published, but it seems quaint and dated now, and gets panned and quickly remaindered. It would be nice to say that Lester's book was rediscovered years later as a Klassic of Litratchur but the truth is that Lester's no novelist; what he is, is a cultural mutant, and what he has in the way of insight and energy has been eaten up. Subsumed by the Beast, man. What he thought and said made some kind of difference, but nowhere near as big a difference as he'd dreamed.

In the year 2015, Lester dies of a heart attack while shoveling snow off his lawn. Dori has him cremated, in one of those plasma flash-cremators that are all the mode in the 21st-cent. undertaking business. There's a nice respectful retrospective on Lester in the *New York Times Review of Books* but the truth is Lester's pretty much a forgotten man; a colorful footnote for cultural historians who can see the twentieth century with the unflattering advantage of hindsight.

A year after Lester's death they demolish the remnants of Waxy's Travel Lounge to make room for a giant high-rise. Dori goes out to see the ruins. As she wanders among the shockingly staid and unromantic rubble, there's another of those slips in the fabric of Fate, and Dori is approached by a Vision.

Thomas Hardy used to call it the Immanent Will and in China it might have been the Tao, but we late 20th-cent. postmoderns would probably call it something soothingly pseudoscientific like the 'genetic imperative.' Dori, being Dori, recognizes this glowing androgynous figure as The Child They Never Had.

'Don't worry, Mrs. Bangs,' the Child tells her, 'I might have died young of some ghastly disease, or grown up to shoot the President and break your heart, and anyhow you two woulda been no prize as parents.' Dori can see herself and Lester in this Child, there's a definite nacreous gleam in its right eye that's Lester's, and the sharp quiet left eye is hers; but behind the eyes where there should be a living breathing human being there's *nothing*, just a kind of chill galactic twinkling.

'And don't feel guilty for outliving him either,' the Child tells her, 'because you're going to have what we laughingly call a natural death, which means you're going to die in the company of strangers hooked up to tubes when you're old and helpless.'

'But did it *mean* anything?' Dori says.

'If you mean were you Immortal Artists leaving indelible grafitti in the concrete sidewalk of Time, no. You've never walked the earth as Gods, you were just people. But it's better to have a real life than no life.' The Child shrugs. 'You weren't all that happy together, but you *did* suit each other, and if you'd both married other people instead, there would have been *four* people unhappy. So here's your consolation: you helped each other.'

'So?' Dori says.

'So that's enough. Just to shelter each other, and help each other up. Everything else is gravy. Someday, no matter what, you go down forever. Art can't make you immortal. Art can't Change the World. Art can't even heal your soul. All it can do is maybe ease the pain a bit or make you feel more awake. And that's enough. It only matters as much as it matters, which is zilch to an ice-cold interstellar Cosmic Principle like yours truly. But if you try to live by my standards it will only kill you faster. By your own standards, you did pretty good, really.'

'Well okay then,' Dori says.

After this purportedly earth-shattering mystical encounter, her life simply went right on, day following day, just like always. Dori gave up computer-art; it was too hairy trying to keep up with the hotshot hightech cutting edge, and kind of undignified, when you came right down to it. Better to leave that to hungry kids. She was idle for a while, feeling quiet inside, but finally she took up watercolors. For a while Dori played the Crazy Old Lady Artist and was kind of a mainstay of the Kansas regionalist art scene. Granted, Dori was no Georgia O'Keeffe, but she was working, and living, and she touched a few people's lives.

Or, at least, Dori surely would have touched those people, if she'd been there to do it. But of course she wasn't, and didn't. Dori Seda never met Lester Bangs. Two simple real-life acts of human caring, at the proper moment might have saved them both; but when those moments came, they had no one, not even each other. And so they went down into darkness, like skaters, breaking through the hard bright shiny surface of our true-facts world.

Today I made this white paper dream to cover the holes they left.

LUCIUS SHEPARD

Lucius Shepard wrote the introduction to the second *Yearbook*, in which he described the genesis of his story 'The Off-Season'. This later 'just grew and grew' into a novel and will be one of his books published during 1990. Others include the collection *The Ends of the Earth* and the novella *Kalimantan*. He has also completed a novel based on his 'Dragon Griaule' series and two more books will be finished by the time this volume appears. By then, Shepard plans to be travelling in Borneo, Indonesia, Thailand and India.

He won the 1985 John W. Campbell Award for best new writer, the 1986 Nebula for his novella 'R&R', and the World Fantasy Award in 1988 for his collection *The Jaguar Hunter*. His story 'The Sun Spider' was published in the first *Yearbook*.

SURRENDER

by
LUCIUS SHEPARD

INTRODUCTION

'Surrender' was a response to a number of letters I received in the space of a week, all suggesting that while those who had written enjoyed my work, they could do with a bit less politics and a tad more whimsey: couldn't I write something nice and non-violent, with perhaps a few puns mixed in. I'm not sure why I got angry. Short of a march to Washington to redirect American foreign policy, this was the response I'd hoped for — to make a few people uncomfortable. The fact that the American science fiction reader could have ingested without complaint twenty zillion novels and stories about right-wing macho galactic imperialists, and that they found my few stories subject for complaint should have pleased me. But the witling tone of the letters, I suppose, triggered some frustration, and, furious, I wrote the story in a single day, a rate of production that I have not come close to emulating either before or since. I intended it to be my last story set in Central America and my last political piece, my attitude being, Okay, fine you don't want to hear it, suck on this . . . I give up. In the months following the publication of the story, however, I changed my mind about steering clear of politics — I may be ineffective as a polemicist, but I refuse to remain a silent complicitor in the tragedy of the 1990s.

Lucius Shepard

I've been down these rivers before, I've smelled this tropical stink in a dozen different wars, this mixture of heat and fever and diarrhea, I've come across the same bloated bodies floating in the green water, I've seen the tiny dark men and their delicate women hacked apart a hundred times if I've seen it once. I'm a fucking war tourist. My bags have stickers on them from Cambodia, Nicaragua, Vietnam, Laos, El Salvador, and all the other pertinent points of no return. I keep telling myself, enough of this bullshit, your turn to cover the homefront, where nobody gives a damn and you can write happy stories about girls with cute tits and no acting ability, in-depth features on spirit channeling and the latest in three-piece Republicans who do it to the public doggie-style and never lose that winning smile, but I always end up here again, whichever Here is in this year, sitting around the pool at the Holiday Inn and soaking up Absolut and exchanging cynical repartee with other halfwits of my breed, guys from UPI or AP, stringers from Reuters, and the odd superstar who'll drop by from time to time, your Fill-In-The-Name-Of-Your-Favorite-Blow-Dried TV Creep, the kind of guy who'll buy a few rounds, belch platitudes, and say crap like. Now Katanga, there was a *real* war, before going upstairs drunk to dictate three columns of tearstained human interest. I used to believe that I kept doing all this because I was committed, not a pervert or deluded, but I'm not too sure about that anymore.

A few years back I was in Guatemala City: Mordor with more sunshine and colonial architecture, diesel buses farting black smoke and a truly spectacular slum which goes by the nineties style name of Zone Five. I was just hanging out, doing yet another tragic piece on the disappeared, dodging carloads of sinister-looking hombres in unmarked Toyotas and pretending to myself that what I was going to write would Make A Difference, when this colleague of mine, Paul DeVries, AP, a skinny, earnest little guy with whom all the Guatemalan girls are in love because he's blond and sensitive and in every way the opposite of the local talent, who tend early on to develop beer guts along with a mania for sidearms and a penchant for left-hooking the weaker sex . . . De Vries says to me, 'Hey, Carl, let's haul our butts down to Sayaxché, I hear there's been some kinda fuck-up down there.'

'Sayaxché?' I say. 'What could happen in Sayaxché?'

Sayaxché's a joke between me and DeVries, one of many; we've been covering backfence wars together for four years, and we've achieved a rapport based on making light of every little thing that comes our way. We call Sayaxché 'the one-whore town,' because that's how many ladies of the evening it supports, and she's no bargain, with acne scars and a dumpling gut and a foul mouth, screaming drunk all the time. The town itself is a dump on the edge of the Petén rain forest, with a hotel, a regional bank office, whitewashed hovels, an experimental agricultural farm, a ferry that carries oil trucks across the Rió de la Pasión on their way to service the ranches farther east in the jungle, lots of dark green, lots of starving Indians, Joseph Conradland, what could happen?

'Forget it,' I tell DeVries at first.

But I'm getting fatigued with the disappeared, you know, I mean what's the point, if they'd been disappeared by magic everyone would love to hear about it, but another tragedy, more endless nattering of miserable Third World gossip . . . ho hum, and so I end up hopping a DC-3 for Flores with DeVries, then it's a bus ride on a potholed dirt road for an hour, and we are there, drinking beer and smoking on the screened verandah of the Hotel Tropical, a turquoise cube on the riverbank with three-dollar rooms and enormous cockroaches and framed photographs everywhere of Don Julio, the owner, a roan-colored man with gold chains and a paunch, posing proudly with a rifle and a variety of dead animals. We're listening to ooh-ooh-ah-ah birds and howler monkeys from the surrounding jungle, staring at the murky green eddies of the River of Passion, trying to pry some information out of Don Julio, but he has heard of no fuck-up. He's a real stand-up guy, Don Julio. Hates commies. One of those patriotic souls who will in drunken moments flourish his mighty pistola and declaim, 'Nobody takes this from me! A communist comes on my land, and he's a dead man.' And so he's doubtless lying to us in order to protect his pals, the secret police. He shrugs, offers more beer, and goes off to polish his bullets, leaving me and DeVries and a Canadian nurse named Sherril — she's on her way south to do volunteer work with the Sandinistas — to indulge in the town's chief spectator sport, which is watching the oil trucks rolling off the ferry getting stuck in this enormous pothole, which is artfully placed at the end of the dock and the beginning of a steep incline so that it's the rare truck that avoids getting stuck. In front of the bank across the street, a two-story building of pink cement block, some Indian soldiers with camo gear and SMGs are advising the driver of the current truck-in-distress on possible methods of becoming unstuck; they favor a combination of boards and sand beneath the tires, and rocking back and forth. The driver, who's been frustrated now for more than an hour, is close to tears.

'Well, this is fucking terrific,' I say to DeVries; he's ten years younger than me, and our relationship has been established so that I have the right to express stern fraternal disapproval. 'There's no end of newsworthy material to be found here.'

'Something might turn up,' he says. 'Let's hang for a while and see what surfaces.'

'What're you guys looking for?' Sherril asks. She's long, she's tall, she's looking good, she's got light brown hair and no bra, and she's waiting for this guy who promised to paddle her upriver to the Mexican border to see the Mayan ruins at Yaxchilan but hasn't showed up yet and, being two days late, probably won't show at all; she acts very engaged-disengaged, very feminine-in-control, like I want to do my thing with the rebels so I can live with myself, you know, and then raise my children to love animals and never say bad words in Calgary or somewhere, and me, I'm beginning to think that if she's stupid enough to go paddling up the River of Doom with some sleaze she met in an Antigua bar, she'll be idealistic enough to choose to sleep with a wartorn journalist such as myself. I can tell she's impressed by my repertoire of cynicisms, and there is definitely a mutual attraction.

'We heard there was some trouble here,' I say. 'Soldiers all over.'

'Oh, you must mean out at the farm,' she says.

DeVries and I exchange glances and say as one, 'What happened?'

'I don't know,' she says, 'but a lot of soldiers were out there the other day. I think they're still there. They'd have to come back through here if they left.'

The farm is, like Sayaxché, a kind of joke, though not so funny as the one-whore bit. Some years before in a canny exercise of graft, the Banco Americano Desarollo, the leading development bank in the region and thus first among many in the economic villainy that maintains the status quo of death squads and inhuman poverty throughout Central America, all in the cause of keeping the USA safe from Communism, negotiated an agreement with the then chief of corruption in Guatemala, a president by the name of Ydigoras Fuentes; this agreement traded the rights in perpetuity to oil leases in the Peten in return for what the agreement called an aggressive US policy directed toward land reform and agricultural develop-ment, a policy that — behind a veil of wonderfully vague promises — actually promised only to establish one experi-mental farm, this being the one in Sayaxché. It employs thirty Guatemalans and is considered a model of sanitation and efficiency; land reform and agricultural development are, needless to say, still a good ways off.

Wellsir, DeVries and I are hot to trot on out to the farm and see what's cooking, but Sherril tells us we'll never make it . . . not in the daytime anyway. Too many soldiers blocking the roads. She knows a way, however; if we wait until night, she'll take us. It seems that while waiting for her tardy tour guide, she ran into a right-wing nasty from Guat City who owned a ranch downriver and was dumb enough to go for a jungle walk with him. All he talked of were the discos, Cadillacs, his many girlfriends, and she thought him a fool, not recognizing that such fools are dangerous. When he tried to put a move on her, she was forced to run away and lose him in the jungle, and so discovered a nifty secret route to Ye Olde Experimental Farm, which appeared to be heavily guarded.

There are journalistic ethics involved here, we realize. Should two guys who're wise to the way of the world let this naïve Calgarette lead us into the mouth of hell at the risk of her all and everything? Probably not. But this is show biz, right, and so, rationalizing the shit out of the situation, we say, okay, honey, what an adventure we'll have! We drink beers, watching

oil trucks buck and hump in the Pothole of Death, and we wait
for nightfall. Toward dusk I take a little walk with Sherril, tell
her sad stories about the death of grunts, and am rewarded for
my vallorous past by several deep wet kisses and proof positive
of her no-bra-lessness. 'God!' she says, flushed and dewy with
delight, as we stroll arm in arm toward the hotel. 'God, I never
expected to meet somebody like you in this awful place.' There
is, I realize, vast potential here. Who says Canadians can't kiss?

At this point it all stopped being a joke. It really hadn't been
much of a joke up until then, but this is show biz, right, and I
just wanted to get you to here. I don't know what to tell you
people. I'm probably coming off in all this as wearing the moral
superiority hat, but it's only defensiveness. See, I'm just so used
to waxing passionate and having you look down your noses at
me as if to say, Interesting Specimen, or My Goodness, he's
certainly opinionated, or Yawn, boring, so the West is in
decline, so what, know where we can cop some Ecstasy, or
Jeez, I mean it's too bad and all, but I don't wanna hear it, I
work hard all the livelong while that lucky old sun just rolls
'round heaven all day, and when I get home at night, I wanna
kick back, pop a cold one and be entertained. so what do I tell
you people? I can't argue with you. You either give a shit or you
don't, and nothing I say is going to change your mind. But if
it's entertainment you want, I suggest you take a walk around,
say, the vicinity of Tolola in El Salvador, where you can see the
intriguing results of a foreign policy which has Apache heli-
copters dropping forty thousand pounds of bombs on the
countryside every month, repeating the tactic we used in Vietnam to destroy popular support for the VC (oh, yeah!), in this
case, the FMLN, and in the process causing one-fifth of an
entire nation to become refugees. It would be a most entertain-
ing walk. See the empty towns littered with skeletons! See the
curious collection of left hands rotting in a basket in front of
the bombed church! See the village of legless men! If you liked
The Killing Fields, you'll love Tolola!

Seriously, folks, it will live in your memory.

The smell alone will make it an Experience.

But I digress. Maybe the fact is that in the United States it's
become easy to achieve moral superiority, even for fuck-ups

like myself. In that case, I suppose I would do well to finish my story quickly and let you get back to your MTV.

Off we went, trudging through the jungle, following Sherril's perfect denim-clad butt through the slimy night air. It took us almost two hours of steady humping to reach the farm, vampire mosquitos, creepy scuttlings, and when we spotted lights shining through the foliage, we crept up to the margin of the jungle, went flat on our stomachs and peered through a bed of ferns. Personnel carriers with M-60s mounted on the rear, about a dozen altogether, ringed a one-story building of white stucco: the farm office. The lights proved to be spotlights and were aimed at a field of what appeared to be agave . . . though God only knew why anyone would want to cultivate agave. About fifty or sixty soldiers were visible, and none of them looked to be having big fun; they were all on alert, fanned out in front of the office, their guns trained on the field. It was very weird.

I don't know what we would have done. Nothing, probably. No way I was planning to get any closer. The chances are we would have gone back to town and done a little investigative reporting. But free will did not turn out to be an option. A few minutes after we had reached the farm I heard at my back the distinctive snick of an automatic weapon being readied for fire, and then a voice telling us in Spanish to lie with our face down and our arms spread. Moments later, we were hauled to our feet, blinded with flashlights, and, despite crying, '*Americanos, Americanos,*' we were herded roughly by a group of soldiers toward the farm and into the office building. Laid out in the dirt beside the door was one of your basic Central American vistas: a row of bullet-riddled naked bodies. The soldiers hustled us past the bodies before we could get a good look at them. Sherril started to object, but I pushed her along, whispering for her to keep quiet. Inside, we were met by another basic CA element, your sadist officer, this one a major named Pedroza who would have scored high in a General Noriega lookalike contest: the pitted skin, the vaguely oriental cast to the features. He gazed dreamily at us, visions of cattle prods and Louisville Sluggers dancing in his head; his eyes lingered upon Sherril.

It may seem that I was leaping to conclusions concerning the major, but not really. He had attained high rank in one of the most conscienceless and brutal military forces in existence, and one does not do that without having caused a world of torment; his face had the cruel sleekness of someone who has indulged in torture and enjoyed it. There is a slowness, a heaviness attaching to such men, a bulky slovenly grace like that of an overfed jungle predator, one whose kills have come too often and too easily. To anyone who has seen them in action, they are inimitable; their evil dispositions as manifest as are their beribboned and bemedaled chests.

Pedroza asked us a number of questions and was, I believe, about to begin getting physical, when a distinguished, silver-haired man in his early fifties entered the room. On seeing him, I felt greatly relieved. He was Duncan Shellgrave, a vice president with the development bank. His nephew was a friend of mine, and I'd stayed at his house in Guat City on a couple of occasions.

'What the hell's going on here, Duncan?' I said, hoping aggressiveness would establish some tenuous spiritual credential.

'Just take it easy, Carl,' he said, and told the major in Spanish that he'd take care of this.

The major, with a despondent sigh, said, 'As you will,' and Shellgrave led us into the adjoining office, a white room with a window of frosted glass and an air-conditioned chill.

'We're having a little problem,' Shellgrave said, favoring us with his best loan-denied smile, indicating that we should take chairs. 'I'm afraid you'll have to sit it out in here. Otherwise Major Pedroza will be quite annoyed.'

There were two folding chairs; I left them to Sherril and DeVries, and perched on the edge of the desk. 'What kind of problem?' I asked.

Another smile, hands spread in a show of helplessness.

I should tell you a story about Shellgrave to illustrate his character. A week after the Nicaraguan revolution, which I'd covered for a number of leftist rags, I was passing through Guat City when I ran into Shellgrave's nephew and he suggested we take dinner at his uncle's; he thought it would do his uncle a world of good to hear the straight shit concerning the state of affairs in Managua. Well, we got to the house, typical American paranoid chic with guard dogs, high walls topped with broken glass, and lots of electronic security, and when Shellgrave heard I'd just come from Managua, he said, 'My God! You're lucky to be alive. They're slaughtering people in the streets down there.'

I knew that this was absolutely not the case, but when I attempted to persuade Shellgrave of this, he put on that bland smile and said, 'You must not have seen it. They were probably steering you away from the action.'

I assured him that I'd been all over the streets; I'm no chump for the Sandinistas, but as revolutions go, Nicaragua had started out as a pretty clean one, and nothing like Shell-grave had suggested was going on. Still, I wasn't able to convince him. The fact that I'd just come from Managua seemed completely irrelevant to him; he gave his CIA informants ultimate credibility and me none. It didn't suit his basic thesis to believe anything I said, and so he didn't. He wasn't stonewalling me, he wasn't playing games. He simply didn't believe me. Men like Shellgrave, and you'll find them all over Latin America, they have a talent for belief; they *know* they're right about the important things, the big picture, and thus they understand that any information they receive to the contrary must be tainted. They thrive on the myth of *realpolitik*, they dance with who brung 'em, and their consciences are clear. They are very scary people. Perhaps not so scary as Major Pedroza and his ilk, but in my opinion it's a close call either way.

I knew there was no use in badgering him for details; I stared at the white walls, tried to cheer up Sherril with a wink and a smile.

DeVries started questioning Shellgrave, and I told him, 'Don't waste your time.'

He got angry at me for that; he pushed back the blond forelock that drove all the girls at the University of San Carlos to delirium, and said, 'Hey, you may have burned out, man, but not me. This is more than a little hinkey here, y'know. This is some bad shit. Don't you smell it?'

'The man —' I pointed at Shellgrave '— is not responsible. For him, heaven's a room with a view of Wall Street. He doesn't know from hinkey. He's eaten so many people he thinks it's normal.'

Shellgrave's smile never wavered; he may actually have been pleased by my characterization.

'See there,' I said to DeVries. 'He's fucking beatific. He knows the empire's crumbling, and that it's his sacred duty to hold onto the last crumb for as long as he can.'

But DeVries, God bless him, was a believer; he kept after Shellgrave, though without intelligent result.

The shouting began about ten minutes after we'd entered the white room. Caps popping, that's what it sounded like above the shuddery hum of the air conditioner, and then the heavier beat of the M-60s. Sherril jumped to her feet, and Shellgrave, smiling, told her not to worry, everything was all right. He believed it. He wanted us to believe it. For our own good.

'So what's that?' I asked him. 'The sound of Democracy in Action?'

He shook his head in bemusement: I was an incorrigible, and he just didn't know what to do with me.

The screaming began about three minutes after the shooting, and Shellgrave's reaction to this was not so calm. He stood, tried peering through the frosted glass, and that failing, started for the door, stopped, then went for it and locked it tight.

'Don't worry,' I told him. 'Everything's all right.'

Sherril said, 'What is it? What's happening?'

Her face was the color of cheesecloth, and her hands were twisting together; DeVries, too, looked shaky, and I wasn't feeling so hot myself.

'Yeah, what is happening?' DeVries asked Shellgrave.

Shellgrave was standing at the center of the room, his head tilted up and to the side, like a man who hears a distant call.

The screams were horrid, throat-tearing, screams of pure agony and fear; they were either drowning out most of the gunfire, or else there weren't as many people firing as there had been. Then somebody screamed right outside the window, and at that Shellgrave bolted for a filing cabinet, threw it open and began stacking papers on the desk. I picked one up, saw the word 'mutagenic' before he snatched it from my hand.

I still believed we were going to survive, but my faith was dwindling, and maybe that was why I decided to live in ignorance no longer. I shoved Shellgrave hard, knocking him to the floor, and began leafing through the papers. He tried to come at me again, and I kicked him in the stomach.

DeVries and Sherril came to stand beside me. I couldn't make much sense out of the papers, but they appeared to outline a project that had been going on for twenty years, something to do with a new kind of food and its effects on a local settlement of Indians, who — being severely malnutrited — had probably leaped at the chance to eat the shit.

'Jesus Christ!' said Sherril, staring at one of the documents.

'What is it?' I asked.

'Wait!' She began going through more of the papers.

Shellgrave groaned, said, 'Those are classified,' and this time it was DeVries who kicked him.

There was a sudden intensification of gunfire, as if the tide of battle had turned.

'God,' said Sherril weakly, and dropped into Shellgrave's chair.

'Tell us, damn it!' DeVries said.

'I think,' she said, and faltered; she drew a steadying breath. 'I don't believe this.' She looked at us hollow-eyed. 'Mutants. The food's worked terrible changes on the second generation. The brain tissue's degenerated. The children of the ones who first ate the food, they're idiots. There's some stuff here I can't understand. But there've been changes in the skin and the blood, too. And I think . . . I think they've become nocturnal. Their eyes . . .' She swallowed hard. 'They're killing them. They've stopped feeding them and they can't eat anything else but the plant they grow here.'

I kneeled beside Shellgrave. 'And now they're trying to kill your ass. That's them outside, right?'

He was having trouble breathing, but he managed a nod; he pointed to the papers. 'Burn 'em,' he wheezed.

'Uh-huh,' I said. 'Sure thing.'

It suddenly struck me as being metaphorical, us being in that cool white room, insulated from the screams and the gunfire and the monstrous dying that was happening out in the humid heat of the jungle. It was very American Contemplative, it was the classic American circumstance. All my years of filing horror stories, stories that had nothing of the bizarre technological horror of this one, yet were funded by equally demonic evil, stories that ended up in some city editor's wastebasket . . . I guess it was all this that allowed me then to editorialize my own existence. This was, you see, a particular poignant moment for me. I realized the horror that was transpiring outside was in character with all the other horrors I'd witnessed. I'm sure that reading this as fiction, which is the only way I can present it, some will say that by injecting a science fictional element, I'm trivializing the true Central American condition. But that's not the case. What was going on was no different from a thousand other events that had happened over the previous hundred and fifty years or so. This was not the exception, this was the *rule*. And it displayed by its lack of contrast to other horrors the hideous nature of that rule. The excesses of United Fruit, the hellish sadism of men such as Torrijos, Somoza, D'aubisson, and thousands of their less renowned minions, the slaughters, the invasions, the mass graves, the dumps piled high with smoldering corpses, cannibalism, rape, and torture on a national scale, all thoroughly documented and all thoroughly ignored, all orchestrated by a music of screams like that now playing . . . this was merely part of that, a minor adagio in a symphony of pain, the carrying-forward of a diseased tradition.

I understood that whoever won this battle would have little sympathy for journalists, and in this DeVries was way ahead of me. He'd dug out a pistol from the paperstorm of Shellgrave's desk, and after sticking it in his belt, he picked up a folding chair, told us to head for the trees, and then swung the chair at the window, clearing away shards of frosted glass. I clambered through, helped Sherril out, then DeVries — he had a folder of pertinent papers in one hand. After the coolness of the room, the fetid heat nearly caused me to gag. Glancing at the field beyond the office building, I spotted dozens, no, hundreds of dark and curiously twisted naked figures scampering through the agave; some were kneeling and tearing at the leaves, and there were bodies scattered everywhere, many showing bloody in the spotlights — the sort of flash Polaroid that takes about a second to develop fully in your mind and stays with you forever after, clear in all its medieval witchiness and savage detail. It was about fifty yards to the trees, and I thought we were going to make it without incident; all the screams and shooting were coming from the front of the office building. But then there was an agonized shout behind me, and I saw Shellgrave, who had struggled out the window, being dragged down by a group of the twisted figures. Blood on his face. The next moment more of those figures were all around me.

Since the spotlights were aimed toward the field, it was fairly dark where we were, and I never did get a good look at our attackers. I had the impression of something resembling hard bumpy rind covering their faces, of slit eyes and mouths, and punctures for nostrils. Even for Indians, they were tiny, dwarfish, and they couldn't have been very strong, because I'm not very strong and I knocked them aside easily. There were, however, a lot of them, and if it hadn't been for DeVries I'm sure we would have died. He started firing with Shellgrave's pistol, and, as if death posed for them a great allure, they left off clutching at me and Sherril, and they went for DeVries. I grabbed Sherril's arm and bolted for the jungle. We were about sixty or seventy feet in under the canopy when I heard DeVries scream.

I'd been friends with DeVries for — as I've said — four years, but our friendship went by the boards, replaced by panic, and with Sherril in tow, I kept running, busting down rocky defiles, scrambling up rises, stumbling, falling, yelling in fright at every hint of movement. We must have been in flight for about five or six minutes when after a spectacular fall, rolling halfway down a hill through decayed vegetation and ferns, I discovered the mouth of a cave.

The limestone foundation of the Peten is riddled with caves, and so this was no miraculous occurrence; but being out of breath and bone-tired, at the time I viewed it as such. The opening, into which my legs had wound up dangling at the end of my fall, was narrow, choked with vines, no more than a couple of feet wide, but I could sense a large empty space beyond. I cleared away the vines, caught Sherril's hand and led her inside. Cool musty smell, water dripping somewhere near. I held up my cigarette lighter for a torch, illuminating a portion of a large domed gallery, the walls white and smooth, except for the occasional volute of limestone; against one wall was a tarpaulin with the edge of a crate showing beneath it. I clicked off the lighter, felt my way toward the tarp; when I reached it, using the lighter again, I examined the crates — there were four of them, all stamped with code designations and marked US AIR FORCE. There was the distinct odor of machine oil.

'What are they?' Sherril asked.

'Smells like weapons,' I said. 'Automatic rifles, I hope.'

I began working at one of the crates, prying at the boards, but I wasn't making much headway. Then I heard a noise from outside the cave, something heavy moving in the brush. There was a large boulder beside the mouth, and in hopes that we could block the entrance with it, Sherril and I hurried back across the cave; but by the time we reached the entrance, the source of the noise was already halfway in, blocking out the faint gleam of moonlight from above. We flattened against the wall next to the opening. A shadow stepped into the cave, too big to be one of the Indians; a beam of light sprang from its hand. I made out camouflage gear, a holstered pistol, and knowing that we had no choice but to attack, I jumped the man, driving him onto his back. Sherril was right behind me, clawing at his face. The man cursed in Spanish, tried to throw me off, and he might have if Sherril hadn't been bothering him. I managed to grab his hair; I smashed his head against the stone; after the third blow he went limp. I rolled away from him, catching my breath. Sherril picked up the flashlight and shined it on the man's slack pitted face. It was Major Pedroza. That made sense to me — the major was likely stockpiling weapons for his own little coup, or else was making a neat profit selling to the contras or some other group of courageous freedom fighters.

While I hadn't had time to absorb DeVries's death, the whole affair of the experimental farm, it seemed those things were moving me now, that and everything else I'd seen over the years, all the bad history I'd reported to no avail, and it also seems that Sherril was directed by similar motives, by anger born of disillusionment. Although she hadn't seen as much as I, although I hadn't given her the respect she deserved, I realized she had the instincts I'd once had for compassion, for truth, for hope — in a single night all those instincts had been fouled.

We went about tying up Pedroza with lengths of vine that I cut from around the cave mouth, using the knife I'd taken from him. I felt stony and emotionless, as if I were wrapping a package of meat. I turned him onto his belly and tied his arms behind him; then I tied his legs and connected them to a noose that fitted tightly around his neck. If he struggled he would only succeed in strangling himself. I was sure of one thing — no matter what happened to me and Sherril, Pedroza was going to die. This may strike some as unfair. What certain knowledge, they may ask, did I have about him? He certainly had done nothing to me. But as I have detailed earlier, he was no innocent. In truth, it should have been Shellgrave whom I was preparing to kill; he was the true villain of the piece, or at least the emblem of true villainy. Pedrozas would be impossible without Shellgraves. But the major would do, he would satisfy. I tore my shirt to make a gag and stuffed it into his mouth, lashing it in place with my belt. This accomplished, Sherril and I pushed the boulder to seal off the entrance; then sat down to wait.

Neither of us said much. I was busy dealing with my desertion of DeVries; I knew I could have done nothing for him, but knowing that was little help. I saw him in my mind's eye firing Shellgrave's gun, a glimpse of blond hair, a pale strained face, then I saw him swarmed by the Indians, and then I heard him scream. I should have been used to that sort of quick exit, I'd had it happen many times before, but this one wan't going down easily. Maybe I'd been closer to DeVries than I had realized, or maybe it was the nightmare surrounding his death that made it seem insurmountable.

I'm not sure what was running through Sherril's mind, but I felt that the currents of our thoughts were somehow parallel. She began to shiver — it was dank in that cave — and I put an arm around her, let her lean against me. I asked her if she was okay, and she said, 'Yeah,' and snuggled up close. Her clean girl smell made me wistful and weak. Soon after that I kissed her. She pulled away at first, and said, 'No, don't . . . not now.'

'All right,' I said evenly; in my mind I was ready to go along with her, but I kept my hand on her breast.

'What are you doing?' she said.

'I don't know, I just needed to touch you.'

I took my hand away, but after a moment she put it back, held it against her breast. She made a despairing noise.

'I guess I need it, too,' she said. 'Isn't that something?'

'What do you mean?'

'To want this now. Isn't that —' she gave a dismayed laugh '— wrong or something.' Another laugh. 'Wrong.' She said the word as if it had gained a whole new meaning, one she was only now capable of understanding.

I had no answers for her. I kissed her again, and this time she kissed back; not long after that we spread our clothing on the stone for a mattress and made love. It was the only hope we had, the only thing we could do to save ourselves from the blind shadows and bloody shouts thronging our heads, and as a result our lovemaking was rough, more an act of anger than one of compassion. Involved in it, too, was the mutuality we'd had to begin with, the thing that might have grown to health, but now — I thought – fed by the food of that grotesque night, would bloom twisted, dark and futureless. And yet by engaging that mutuality, I had the sense that I was committing to it in a way from which it would be impossible to pull back.

It must have been while we were making love that the Indians found us, because when I surfaced from the heat and confusion that we had generated, I heard their voices: odd fluted whispers issuing not from the cave mouth but from somewhere overhead, leading me to realize there must be a second entrance. We struggled into our clothes, and I broke into the crates with Pedroza's knife; I had his pistol, but I doubted that would be sufficient firepower. The first crate contained anti-personnel rockets; I had no idea of how to use them. The second, however, contained M-16s and full clips. I inserted a clip into one and made ready to defend. I was surprised that they hadn't already attacked us, and when after several minutes they still hadn't made a move, I shined

Pedroza's flashlight toward the ceiling.

In the instant before they ducked away from the second entrance, which was halfway up the side of the dome, I saw the glowing yellow cores of their eyes; the sight was so alarming, I nearly dropped the flashlight. I handed it to Sherril and fired a short burst at the opening; it wasn't very big, a mere crack, but it might, I thought, be large enough to admit those twisted bodies. The drop was about forty feet.

'The papers,' I asked Sherril, 'did they say anything about whether they'd be able to take a long fall?'

She thought it over. 'There was some stuff about low calcium content. Their bones are probably pretty brittle.'

'They might think of lowering vines.'

'Maybe, but according to the papers they're . . . they're animals. Their IQs aren't measurable.'

I heard a strangled noise and had Sherril shine the flashlight toward Pedroza; his eyes were bugged, his face suffused with blood.

'Be careful,' I advised him in Spanish. 'You'll hurt yourself.'

His eyes looked more baleful than those of the Indians.

'I think we'll be all right,' Sherril said. 'If we can hold them off 'til morning, we'll be all right.'

'Because they're nocturnals?'

'Uh-huh. They can't take much light. They might be able to wait until mid-morning, what with the canopy, but by noon they'd be in terrible pain.' The flashlight wavered in her hand. 'They burrow.'

'What?' I said.

'They move around at night and when daylight comes, wherever they are, they dig burrows in the dirt, they cover themselves with dirt and sleep . . . like vampires. They scarcely breathe at all when they're asleep.'

'Christ,' I said, unable to absorb this, to feel any more revulsion than was already within me.

I glanced at Pedroza; he had a lot to answer for.

Sherril was looking at him, too, and from the loathing that registered in her expression, I knew that Pedroza would be in for a bad time even if I weren't there.

We sat down by the boulder, keeping our weight against it in case the Indians tried to move it; we kept the light shining on the entrance overhead, and we talked to drown out the incessant and unsettling fluting of their voices, not speech in all likelihood, mere noises, the music of a pitiless folly reverberating through the cave. I told Sherril stories, but they weren't the stories I would have told her under other circumstances. They were stories about the brave good things I'd seen, stories that still hoped, stories that gave storytelling a good name, and not my usual rotten-with-disgust tales of Businessmen From Hell and their global sleights-of-hand. Those stories were the best parts of my life passing before my eyes, and it wasn't that I was afraid of dying, because I thought we were going to make it; it was that the last of my foolish ideals were giving up the ghost, having their final say before wisping up into ectoplasmic nada. Although I'd convinced myself that I'd given up on my ideals a long time before, I believe it was then that I utterly surrendered to the evil of the world.

It was the same for Sherril. She talked about nursing, about the good feeling it gave her, she talked about her home, her old friends, but she kept lapsing. I kept having to tune her in with questions as if her station were fading from the dial. I watched her face. She was more than pretty, so damn pretty I couldn't believe that I'd had the fortune to make love to her — a stupid thing to consider, but stupid thoughts like that were occurring constantly. Her eyes were green with hazel flecks in the irises, her hair was silky, but her most attractive feature was that she knew what I knew. She was changing before my eyes, toughening, learning things that she shouldn't have had to learn all at once; she was a nice girl, and it was a shame for her to have to understand so young what a shuck niceness was. All the while as I listened, I could hear the sick music of the doomed tribe wanting to kill us. Pedroza grunting as he tried to enlist our attention. None of that mattered. In a way I was almost happy to be up against it, to know how bad it could get, and yet there I was, still able to look at a pretty woman and hope for something. I was aware that even this could be taken from me, but I was beyond being afraid. And I was learning, too. Although I didn't recognize it at the time, I was learning that you can fall in love through hate, by being with someone in a crucible of a moment when everything else is dying and the only thing left is to try to live. Or maybe it wasn't love, maybe it was just the thing that takes the place of love for those who have surrendered.

Just before dawn, some of the Indians began dropping through the crack. About twenty of them in all made the jump, but no more than a third of that number survived the landing, and they were incapable of swift movement, their bones shattered. The first one down startled me and drew a shriek from Sherril; but after that it wasn't even dramatic, merely pitiful. The wounded ones crawled toward us, their razor-slit mouths agape to reveal blood-red tongues within, their strangely unfinished faces displaying what struck me as a parody of desperation. I finished them off with bursts from the M-16. I didn't know what had caused them to try, nor did I know why they had stopped, why they didn't just keep coming like lemmings; perhaps both the jumping and the stopping had been stages along the path to their own surrender. When I was sure that no more would be coming, I dragged their bodies deeper into the cave, out of sight around a bend; I tried to avoid looking at them, but I couldn't help noticing a few details. Shriveled genitalia; a faint bluish cast to the skin as if they suffered from cyanosis; the S-curved spines, the knotted shoulderblades. They were light, those bodies, like the bodies of hollow children.

The sun rose about a quarter of six that morning, making a dim red glow in the crack overhead, a slit evil eye, but the voices kept fluting for a while after that. Pedroza's eyes pled with us; he had wet his pants, the poor soul. We watched him wriggle and grunt; we made it a game to see which of us could get him to produce the most interesting noise by doing things such as picking up the knife and walking behind him.

Eventually we let him alone and sat talking, planning what we'd do once we left the cave: avoid Sayaxché, strike out for Flores, maybe hitch a ride with an oil truck returning from the jungle.

Sherril looked at me and said, 'What are you going to do afterward?'

'I'm not staying around here. The States . . . maybe I'll go back to the States. How 'bout you? Nicaragua?'

She shook her head. 'I can't think of anywhere that sounds right. Maybe home.'

'Calgary.'

'Uh-huh.'

'What's Calgary like?'

She opened her mouth, closed it, then laughed. 'I don't know.' Then after a pause. 'The Rockies, they're close by.'

I thought about the Rockies, about their clean, cold rectitude, their piney stillness, so different from the malarial tumult I had traveled in for all those years. I said their name out loud; Sherril glanced at me inquiringly.

'Just seeing if it sounded right,' I said.

It was almost noon before we decided it was absolutely safe to leave the cave. I went over to Pedroza and unplugged his mouth. He had to lick his lips and work his jaw for a few moments in order to speak; then he said, 'Please . . . I . . . please.'

'Please what?' I asked him.

His eyes darted to Sherril, back to me.

'Don't shoot me,' he said. 'I have money, I can help you.'

'I'm not going to shoot you,' I said. 'I'm going to leave you tied up here.'

That was a test to see his reaction, to determine whether he had any allies left alive; if he flunked I intended to shoot him. His fear was no act, he was terrified. He babbled, promising everything, he swore to help us. I hated him so much, I cannot tell you how much I hated him. He was all the objects of my hate.

'I could shoot you,' I said. 'But I think I'll just leave you here. Of course you've got an option. I bet if you jerk real hard with your legs, you can probably kill yourself.'

'Listen,' he began.

I clubbed him in the jaw with the rifle butt; the blow twisted his head, and he had to fight to keep from overreacting and strangling himself. I kept talking to him, I told him if he confessed his sins I might give him a chance to live. I was very convincing in this. He was reluctant at first, but then his sins came pouring out: rape, massacre, torture, everything I'd expected. He seemed emptied afterward, drained of strength, as if the secret knowledge of his crimes had been all that sustained him.

'Say a hundred Hail Marys,' I told him, and made the sign of the cross in the air. 'Jesus forgives you.'

He started to say something, but I stuffed the gag back in.

Sherril was staring at him, her face cold, unrelenting.

I kissed her, intending to cheer her, boost her spirits, but when I looked at Pedroza, I had the idea that the kiss had wounded him. I kissed her again, touched her breasts. He squeezed his eyes shut, then opened them very wide; he wriggled a bit. Sherril knew what I was up to, and she was all for it; her antipathy for the major was as strong as mine. We spread out clothes on the stones and we made love a second time, showing Pedroza the sweetness that life can be, letting him understand the entire pain of his fate — once again it seemed the only thing we could do. He was nothing to us, he was simply everything, an abstract, a target as worthlessly neutral as a president.

By chance, we were making love beneath the crack in the limestone, and a slant of dusty sun like those you might see falling through a high cathedral window fell across Sherril, painting a strange golden mask over her eyes and nose, the sort of half-mask worn by women at carnivals and fancy balls, creating of her face a luminous mystery. And what we were doing did seem mysterious, directed, inspired. It was no performance, it was ritual, it was a kind of hateful worship. We were very quiet, even at the end we stifled our cries, and the silence intensified our pleasure. Afterward, though I could hear the glutinous noise of Pedroza's breath, it was as if we were alone with our god in that holy dome of stillness, the white cold walls like the inside of a skull, and we were its perfect thoughts. I felt incredibly tender. I caressed and kissed her. I accepted her caresses and kisses, bathed in that streak of gold, illuminated, blessed in our purpose. I suppose we were mad at that moment, but we were mad like saints.

We dressed, smiling at each other, unmindful of Pedroza, and it wasn't until we began shifting the stone back in front of the cave mouth that we looked at him. He was still pleading

LUCIUS SHEPARD

with his eyes, wriggling toward us and whining, making choked, gargling noises. I felt no sympathy for him. He deserved whatever was in store for him. He was trying to nod, aiming his eyes at the gun, begging me to shoot him.

'*Adios*,' I said — a word that means 'to God,' an ironic conceit of the language in these godless times.

We shifted the stone into place.

Before we set out for Flores we were brought up short by what we saw just beyond the mouth of the cave. The side of the adjoining hill was dotted with mounds of black dirt, each one about five feet long. There were hundreds of them, tucked in among ferns, under rotten logs, beneath bushes. Like infestations of ants I'd seen in South America. It was horrible to see, and thinking about those tiny deformed bodies lying moribund beneath the dirt, I became sick and dizzy. The ultimate attitude of surrender. I suppose I could have been merciful and shot them as they lay; the crates in the cave contained a sufficiency of death. But someone might have heard, and, too, I had gone beyond the concepts of mercy and humanitarian aid. I wasn't in the game anymore. I felt bad about that, but at least I'd tried, I had spent years trying, whereas most people surrender without even making an effort. There was nothing I could do except to leave. So we walked away from the cave, from Sayaxché, from Guatemala, from those pathetic little things with slit eyes and malfunctioning brains in their sleep of dirt and nightmares, from Major Pedroza in the final white church of his terror, from the whole damn world. And because we had nowhere we wanted to go any longer, we went there together.

Sometimes I look at Sherril, and she looks at me, and we both wonder why we stay together. We're still in love, but it doesn't seem reasonable that love should survive an act of surrender as complete as the one we made, and we keep expecting some vile mutation to occur, the product of that night in the jungle beyond Sayaxché. I suppose that's why we don't have any children. We don't think about all this very much, however. Life is sweet. We've got money, food, a future, a cabin in the Rockies not far from Calgary, work we care about — though perhaps not with the same passion we once evinced. It's good to make love, to walk, to smell the wind and watch the sun on the evergreens. We're not really happy, too much has happened for us to buy that chump; but we neither one of us ever required happiness. It's too great a chore to be happy when the world is going down the tubes, when the shitstorm is about ready to come sweeping in from the backside of creation and surprise us with a truly disastrous plague or cosmic rays from hell, and there are signs in the sky that it's time to get right with God or maybe make a few moves to change things, and all you hear is the same placid generic bullshit about shoring up the economy and possibly kicking a few bucks over to the extremists who would kind of like to have breathable air and keep the ice caps from melting and would prefer not to alienate the rest of humanity by supporting every sadistic tumor in a uniform who decides he's going to be God of Mangoland and run the cocaine franchise for the South Bronx in return for saying No to the Red Menace. Central America isn't just Central America. It's what's happening, it's coming soon to your local theater, and if you think I'm overstating the case. If you don't see the signs, if you haven't been taking notes on the inexorable transformation of the Land of the Free into just another human slum . . . well that's cool. Just kick back, and pop yourself a cold one, maybe catch that ABC special on the Starving Man and get a little misty-eyed, it'll make you feel cozier when it's time for 'Monday Night Football' or 'Miami Vice,' like you've paid your dues by almost feeling something.

And don't worry, everything's all right.

I promise I won't mention any of this again.

Adios.

Jayge Carr's first story was 'Alienation', published in *Analog* in 1976, and her subsequent magazine appearances have ranged from *Omni* to *Amazing*. She has had four novels published: *Leviathan's Deep*, *Navigator's Sindrome*, *The Treasure in the Heart of the Maze* and *Rebelaisian Reprise*. Her next book will be *Knight of a Thousand Eyes*, to be published in 1991.

Born in Houston, Texas, Carr once worked for NASA as a nuclear physicist. She now lives in Louisiana, across the lake from New Orleans.

She has written an afterword to her story for the *Yearbook*.

CHIMERA

by
JAYGE CARR

Her weakness was gambling.

Waste of good spendies, I told her. Null-program. Seemed like that kind of disparaging sermon only encouraged. Often that way, people not logical like systems. First lesson in Psych One.

I tried, though. *How* I tried.

Not that we that close. Acquaintances, casual friends, propinquity. My *friends* small, select, filtered program. She never make it past first filter.

But if living in Hive-city make it easy to be anonymous in crowds, also mean plenty casual acquaintances not prime friends. She owned — she and the spendie-union, she always said with a laugh — the small old-fashioned apt complex I living in. Real old-fashioned, genuine old, twenty, thirty years at least, not fakey-nostalgia only-*look*-old. (Them *way* too high-spendie for my budget.) Old, so cheap. And because cheap, she could select her tenants with double double precision parameters. Her 'family,' she called us.

But pay for cheap-spendie in other ways. Obvious ones like inadequate climate controls, and no interfaces to system except old-style holo-phone, only connectable to comm-type I/O. Unobvious ones like her: old, nosy, and she *loved* to talk.

No, cancel old. She not true-old, just passed over, as many professionals have been and will be, by relentless pace of technology. Obsoleted, as even I will be. But not yet. Not until complete all person program runs.

But she *was* lonely, nosy, and talkative.

Yet she not one to transfer spendie under false program, either. She was honest, blunt, on the evening that, print-out listings in one hand, I punched her code into a public comm console.

'I think of all the tenants in this building as one little family, my own family,' she said. Age didn't show in holo-image; she well-upholstered in current-then fashion, wearing the utter latest in bod-Grafts, inch-thick fur in a bold plaid. (Fashion ridiculous. This month, bulges and plaid body-fur; next month, stick-thin and diamond scales. Null-program, except for bod-designers and fashion fanatics.) 'So I do have to be sure each one fits in. If you'd like to come for a little visit, so we can meet properly . . .'

Old-fashioned, she; systems and holo relays made 'personal' meetings obsolete long time ago.

Could easily have refused, gone to next on list. Didn't even need holo-relay 'personal' interviews for work any more, just programmed résumé in systems. Interested employers ask for down-load, print-outs. If my qualifications, experience closest to what they need, and they willing to wait until I available (that on system, too — always), then I get job. If I choose. Mostly, booked up continuously, with waiting list. Often, never see physical bosses, just system they wanted me to work on. Liked that best, anyway.

Could have said no, disconnected. But room cheap, and I curious. Besides, unprogrammable intuition said, looks like smooth run. I not have secret of immortality, always one year older end of each year.

So went. Building small/old. Stood out among giant/new sprawl-up closed envirs, tower hives, like just erupted tooth-bud implant regrowing in otherwise full set of teeth.

Public levo-track with upper level jogging trail right next to building. Added points for that.

Punched temp code she'd given me into door; slight pause while door scanned self — more points. Inside security not so good; could have breached it half a dozen ways — subtracted points.

Had to add them back quickly. She greeted me with, 'This building may be old-fashioned in many ways, but the security system is complete and current. All entrances and exits are totally monitored. Residents have their privacy codes, of course, and privacy within their own quarters; if you want to give your privacy code to someone else, you're welcome to, but unless you register that person's idents with the security system, it won't accept the code without your presence.' She went on to describe security; standard, good enough, and unobtrusive. *I* could still have breached it, of course; but I had advantages. What she called privacy was so only long as no felony suspected; then seal on monitors could, would be broken. But since had no intention of committing felony, no worries. Her little warning/lecture unnecessary.

She played hostess, offered choice, alc or nics or canny or tranc or hi or whatever. Well-stocked juicer. But I had own plans for evening — with Friend — and stuck to straight fizz.

Initial impression on both sides mildly favorable, and soon all running smoothly. Too smoothly. Plans for evening did not include her as input. I warned her: 'I'm a neut.'

'How patriotic,' she cooed. Gigo. Some 30 percent of adult population opts for sterility and accompanying Basic-bonus spendies. I knew. My input helped generate some of psych analysis for the pro-sterile propaganda.

'Neut,' I repeated. '*All* the way.'

Eyes and mouth opened unbecomingly.

'No choice. Mediproblems,' I added; and watched, smiling inside, while she fought with self, not to *ask*. In the crowding of hives, privacy precious, right to keep one's own secrets — except from omnipresent systems, of course — legalized. Invasion of Privacy carried fine and jail sentence, though seldom taken so far. I grew up in society where people volunteered, but never *asked*. She hadn't, and it showed.

I took pity, eased her off hook. 'Complicated, but all over now. Details boring.'

She made null-noises. I volunteered more. 'That's why I can't take Grafts, not without too much fuss and bother.'

'You mean, that's all natural?' Which proved she had grown up before privacy laws. Question not *quite* IoP — but dangerously close.

I shrugged. 'Some of it.' Stood up and rotated slowly, let her get full effect.

She liked. 'That black hair and that white, white skin — all natural?'

I grinned, and pulled out a couple of hairs from just over my left ear. 'Test for yourself. Natural. Skin, too.' I scraped a little skin from back of left hand. 'Yours.' Offered samples to her.

'To test if you want.'

She refused. Thought she would. But offer convinced her. Why not? Was truth, and samples would have tested just as I said. Truth — but not all truth. Halftruth worse lie than statistics.

'Such a pity,' she sighed.

'Compensations.' Which was truth, too. Systemizers have mega advantages, like direct-brain inputs and access to simulation programs that *pale* natural sensations. I never lacked. Except now — could see she about to dump me, and could do nothing to stop it. Happy family! But oddly, was truth, her truth. She had, as I learned later, relationships with all tenants in building. Just not always what I would have meant by 'relationships.'

Was going to be deleted from her data files, but she too old-fashioned to simply boot out on ear. Gigo, no. Had to make polite null-noise program first. Which was how suddenly found self back in, to stay.

'That's what kind of work you do? Why, I was a programmer myself, once. You know what programmers did, don't you, Foster?'

Yeah. Knew about tallying on notched sticks, too. Equally obsolete. She hadn't managed to adapt, period. But our shared 'profession' proved master override, got me in, after all.

Programming around her took a bit of debugging, but quickly found knack. Some things never fixed, like her habit of running up all the time with 'home-cooked' goodies. 'I fixed 'way too much for myself, and I thought you might like ...' Null-program, tell her I raised on soypro and britburger, found natural foods distasteful. To her, treats. Ate under her eye when necessity, tossed when possible.

Like her curiosity. Knew enough not to ask, but would talk around and around until data 'volunteered.' But could switch her to a different loop, with ingenuity, if subject too uncomfortable.

Quickly found out maximum intervals she'd allow between 'cozes.' Once used to them, not too bad. Wanted someone to listen to her as much as wanted to ask questions. My lack of sex, oddly, an advantage. Sex partners usually not interested in talking. We talked. About anything, everything. Anything, everything general, that is. Mostly, anyway.

('Name Chim short for Chimera. Medinickname. But all fixed now — don't see any scars, do you?')

If program got too tight, could always divert her onto differences between life when she my current age and now. Not so many years ago at that; but enough. Interesting even, how the oldies lived . . .

'I was lucky, you know, to have had enough saved, when I was fired the last time, to buy this place. Course, I don't really own it —' I joined her in her favorite joke: '— me and the spendie-union own it.'

'Doubly lucky,' she went on, 'because I had settled in here before the last reevaluation, and managed to ride it out. Otherwise, my savings would have gone like that —' She snapped her fingers. 'I'd have nothing but Basic to live on. My pension will start when I'm fifty-five, but it was established before the JohnJohn currency juggle. I'll be able to buy an extra nic-stic or two with it, when it starts coming in. Without this building, it'd be the welfare ghettos for me, and you know —' a shudder '— what they're like.'

Last another of her null-noises. I not wear blinkers. Over 80 percent of pops live in ghettos.

'It isn't just living in the ghetto itself,' she went on. 'It's the — the being dependent. I was brought up to earn my own way, always.'

'So was I, but what of it. If you're obsoleted, you're —'

A sad smile. 'Women's lib is only words to you, Chim Foster, words from before you were born . . . and yet . . . my own mother . . . dead past, eh, Chim, child of your brave new age.' She shook her head. 'No sex differentiation. Even language, pronouns; you're always careful to use her with me, but with your own generation —'

I grinned, kept placing spangles on my new bod-do.

'Because sex doesn't matter to any of you, truly, except in a sexual relationship, and even then . . . and if one of you wants to reproduce —' I stiffened, ready to yell IoP; she going too far; '— I mean one person of your generation, Chim, not you personally, or one of your friends. But what with artificial insemination and exowombs, and compunurseries, and long-distance holorelays, and Great Mother knows what else — and so few people with real jobs any more — and the Basic spendies — and . . .' She laughed. 'Roles — they've blurred out of existence. We fought for things that don't even exist any more, that you youngsters never heard of, don't even miss.'

I relaxed and finished placing my spangles. 'Better this way.'

'Sometimes I wonder . . . Flip you for who does the dishes.' Does the dishes meant place them in the Reuser. But it important to her, who 'did the dishes.'

Always flip you with her. Gambling, her weakness. Flip you for this, flip you for that. She played everything. The fed-lottery. Maf numbers. Betting. Always on me, to 'program' her a 'system.' Told her, no way. Null-program. So she used her own. Stupid system, and her — once, anyway — a pro-grammer, *almost* like a systemizer.

She doubled losing bets.

Dumbest system in the universe.

Used to ask me, catch me going out to work (or out to a decent interface, often same thing) to place her bets. Wouldn't do it. Disapproved. Told her so. Didn't stop her, of course.

Couldn't stop her talking, either.

Asked her once for permission to ask *real* personal question.

She permitted. 'You hung up on this male-female input, right?'

'Right.'

'Make a suggestion, friendly suggestion, no IoP, no ego-beating take or leave, just there, friendly suggestion to think about.'

'Suggest away, friend.' She was giving me old-fashioned message — oddly pleasant — and never missed a beat. Twisted head around, watched her face.

'Make the Change.'

Almost lost an arm, because was what she had hands on. That the end of that.

Some Lib. Couldn't even stand *thought* of having male bod.

Gambling and talking, talking and gambling, her weaknesses.

Talked about family once. I have none, said so. No more

than that, my right. She thought I'd divorced them, disapproved, but couldn't say so.

No family for her, either. Parents dead, tube wreck, husband divorced long ago.

'Didn't know women's libbers went in for marriage,' said I.

'But that's what liberation was all about, to do what *you* wanted. I wanted to marry Jack. We didn't do it formally or legally, you understand. But we got a group of our friends together and exchanged vows and recited poems we'd made up ourselves in front of them.'

'Sounds different.'

Her mouth twisted. 'Different from what the conserves, olders did. No different from what half our generation was doing.' I nodded.

'Lots of things were like that, then,' she went on. 'The people yelling the loudest about how old standards were strangling them in conformity, were the strictest in ostracizing anyone else who didn't conform to *their* standards.'

I nodded again. 'Psych One.'

'Sometimes I think the worst thing that happened to humans was turning psychology into a hard, computer-analyzable science.'

Not computers, systems. But if she still wanted to call them computers, no glitch in my input.

Was a while later she mentioned her ex-husband again. She'd waylaid me coming back from long work session, yawning openly and hungry for sleep. Wound up instead in her 'kitchen,' where she fixed food. Real fixed, with microwave to heat and oldie freezerator to store unheated not-readies in. Too much trouble; I stick with auto-temp storepaks, synthetics. Separate eating area too, walls covered with antique 2-D posters, all (best guess) pre home-holo entertainments: *Star Wars VII: Revolt of the Clones*, Archery Tournament with live William Tell contest, *Lord of the Flies* operetta, Duran Duran revival, whatever.

'I divorced him for his own sake, really. He wanted children; and I couldn't have any.'

'That virtue, now.' In cup in front of me to drink: dark syrupy liquid she called coffee; real plant pods ground up by her and dissolved in boiling water. Smell almost enough to make me lose what little in stomach. (But odd: when finally tasted, like too-strong decaf.)

'But not then. I was sterile. One hundred percent. Uncorrectable. No chance, not at all.' A faraway look. 'I wanted children too, wanted them desperately. Why, once I even volunteered for — but it wasn't — it didn't . . .'

Voice lowered, mouth twisted, sneering. 'Freaks! Thank goodness none of them were *really* mine . . .' A sigh.

Louder, as though trying to forget something hardwired, burned too deep to forget. 'The medics tried all sorts of experiments on me for years, to restore even a fraction of fertility. I wanted, just once . . . but it wasn't any use. Sterile. Permanently and totally. I was caught in the fallout of one of the early nuclear accidents, before they orbited all the piles. It didn't damage me, I got the anti-R injections in plenty of time. But it left me sterile. Or maybe not. A certain percentage of people are naturally sterile, or so they claimed. I was sterile. No children. Not ever.'

Explained why she called us her 'family.'

Talk, talk, talk, she did.

Thank goodness for this place. I'd kill myself before I'd go live in a ghetto, with nothing to do but watch the cube and wait for my Basic spendies to be credited to my account every week.'

Null-words again. Nobody ever kills self over little loss of status.

Talk and gamble, gamble and talk. My disapproval only made her worse; had to prove me wrong, didn't she?

She consistently lived little over her total spendies, but gambling made up difference.

Told her what fool she was, told her luck couldn't hold out indefinitely, told her statistics is not mocked. Told her, and *told* her.

Not even null-program, negative feedback program. More told her, worse she got.

Until one day, patience ran out, *really* told her off. Gambling *idiot* program.

Only made her drag me along to place next bets.

Her favorite Olympics Shop mode/standard. Holorelays filled with events arranged in tiers around central core, catwalks to watch/bet on upper levels, several stories total. Bottom layer center eat/drink/meet. Top center, inside clear bubble, hotlight razztazz blast always going on. In between, stacks of transparent cages, live Olympics inside, house shills circling without, constantly shouting odds, times, taking bets from watchers on catwalks.

Hate Olympics Shops; don't know what's worse, Olympics themselves, or pops who gather to watch and make bets.

Always wondered what, in world where every individual is supplied with enough Basic spendies to live on, makes supposedly intelligent adults enter Olympics. Nastiest way to commit slow suicide ever invented. She thought so too; but watching easy way to gamble fast and high, and her weakness gambling.

Place crowded but not packed. People who run shop smart. No fee to watch, just 'free' opportunity to gamble, bet. Even side bets among customers allowed, long as house got percentage.

Saw a pair of likely looking Blues — shorter one iron — pumper thewed, G-string bulge aggressively flaunted, taller one runner-type, more intellectual, kilt filled but discreetly — watching a finish, drifted over. Timer above life-size holo ticked off seconds. They had odd-or-even personal bet going; other data said holo repeating in many other shops, most bets odd-or-even, others with higher odds available. Didn't like *any* of the odds, but then never did. Gambling *idiot* program.

Vital signs flashing; Olympics a mixed pair, male fading fast. Wished I had time to access system, could have programmed how much longer he'd last. Not accurate enough for odd-or-even bet, but good enough for plus/minus total. Seconds ticked away.

Male going, but going out in style; female urged him on, undrugged smirk plastered across sweat-drenched face. Her timer going, too, but she beginner. Male came again, score upped by one. Display showed record for age, weight. Nowhere near record, not likely to make now, fading fast. Vitals showed how many doses of Priap he'd had: too many.

Rotten business, but all voluntary. Feds long since quit meddling in free choice, even when free choice nasty, slow public suicide.

Male gasping, but reached up one hand, slammed panel, got another dose Priap. Mindless rutting animal now. Holo face, life-size, flushed maroon, dripping sweat, contorted in pleasure/pain/lust.

Seconds ticked off.

Body arched, drove into female again and again — convulsed — stiffened.

Timer stopped.

Body limp, vitals flat. Female shoved corpse off, looked up eagerly for next partner.

Loser paid winner, much macho joking how each could beat man's record — on other, of course, since they Blue — without doses of Priap. Blue on left Changee, knew the signs; much more macho than Blue on right.

Wandered over to join her; she watching a chain, urging on one contestant so fiercely I knew she already placed bet.

She won.

I said nothing, but loudly disapproved.

She placed another bet ostentatiously, much bigger one.

Still without speaking a word, disapproved even louder.

She kept betting, short series, doubling each bet when she lost until she won.

Kept raising her initial bets, too.

Crowed joyously with each 'win.'

Idiot program.

Never liked Olympics, anyway. Every contestant loses — sooner or later.

Told her not coming with her again, and never did. But she'd tell me how much she'd won.

Sometimes big winnings, so I knew had to bet several times to get there. Not true winnings, of course. Real winnings net, winnings minus *losses*.

But as long as she doubled, she argued, winnings always topped losses.

One day, told her, you have losing streak, bet too high once too often.

She laughed.

More I advised *Don't*, more she gambled. More I advised *Low bets*, higher she flew.

She brag, I badmouth. Over and over. Feedback. Bets higher and higher. More and more frequent visit Olympics, other places. Had to show me, prove herself, didn't she?

But statistics *exact* science. Like Psych, now.

One day she had losing streak and bet too high.

Knew it had happened when strange person stopped me in apt vestibule. Name null-program, but proved self new owner. Raising rent. I told te, new owner, paid to end of week. Showed rent receipts; had kept religiously in personal pouch. Her sig, amount of spendies credited, date, thumbprint. Kept on real plastic sheets, not printout. Not duplicated or duplicable. Te stared, finally nodded, repeated new rent rate. I laughed, packed and was out in five minutes, with receipts.

Never pays to meddle with Them.

Stopped off in Olympics Shop.

First time in long while. Don't like Olympics. But had reason.

She there, all right, life-size relay-holo, eyes desperate.

Never pays to meddle with Them, nobody welshes on bet. *Always* way to pay. Signing for Olympics voluntary — but what feds can't see, won't weep over.

She caught. Trapped animal in cage. No escape, never. Not for her. Like experimental subject. Who asks animal, experimental subject, you want to be part of this? Want to be tortured, maimed, experimented on? Hurt and hurt and *hurt* for eyes, eyes, eyes to watch and gloat over pain? No. No rights, animal. No rights, experimental subject. No rights, now, *her*. Nobody ask her, not like, want relief, ever, ever, ever.

Must have been *big* bet. They'd set her up in full S/M series, total medicated. (Not for pain, of course; for endurance.) Going to take her *long* time to pay. Suffering every second.

Interfaces with full access to systems, data-bases in the shop. Anybody smart enough to use systems for analysis, too smart to be in shop in first place. Synthesis already set up, only had to plug in specifics for her run. Got output almost immediately.

Went over, laid bets.

Shop rigged, not much, just enough to give Them extra percentage over legal. Feds knew, but got cut to keep quiet. Laid bets, some of which prepared — eager — to lose; now would take her long, *long* time to pay.

Her eyes, in holo, frantic, horrified, pleading. Like mine must have been, once, long time ago. But her fate sealed, last program in system, press enter, execute. No one going to Interrupt now, rescue. No one.

Called us freaks. Insult on top of injury. She went into that experiment eyes open. Her choice. I not have choice, then. Now, her turn, no choice.

All ended, her, her run, her program, far as I concerned. Didn't need to wait, didn't need to even watch start, probably wouldn't bother to collect winning bets.

Stopped in public refresher to make changes.

Had to ration self on hate, can only afford it at end of each special run. Stripped down, cleaned off all dyes and plastics, stared at self in full-length mirror, seeing, seeing, seeing. In mirror: improvements, results of long operations. Little left unchanged. But — underneath, mind could see though eyes no longer could, old I, true I, more real, more solid, always and forever *there*.

Chimera.

Nightmare.

Illegal now, all experiments with people making; too many pops as is. Not illegal, twenty-five, thirty years ago. Many experiments, some even viable.

Like — me.

Chimera.

Old word for nightmare. For mythical beast, mixture of many different animals, eagle, lion, scorpion, whatever.

Chimera — medical term now. Experiment. Tricking normal cells into meiotic — germ plasm, half chromosome complement — division. Artificial combination of more than two germ plasms, more than one blastula. All human — but all different. Sometimes deliberately different. In my case, *lots* more than two and one. Grossly different. Real 'test-tube baby.'

Saw illustration in old, old book once, 'Hunchback of Notre Dame.' Face, body all misshapen and distorted, arms, legs, back all warped, eyes, ears, everything all mismatched, different sizes, *wrong*. Patchwork person. Like chimera.

Only with chimera, patchwork *everywhere*. Hair colors: brown and black and auburn and dishwater blond and platinum and . . . Skin similar, big patches and little, pink next to sallow olive next to ebony black next to creamy chocolate next to . . . Same everywhere. Big collarbone on this side, small on that, joints all wrong, legs mismatched, this finger long and slender, that one short and stubby, face — like clumsy sculptor grabbed features all different sizes and shapes and mashed them crudely together any which way. Even worse while growing, because bones grew at different rates. Limped instead of walking, dropped things, had trouble seeing, constantly having glasses readjusted.

But brain fine. Maybe better if had had idiot brain to go with idiot body.

Freak, she said. She right. Freak. Her choice, I freak. Now she pay. And pay and *pay*.

Still, body designers did good job. Bones match now. Face human, no more than normally asymmetric, even mildly attractive. Only patchwork skin and hair left, easy to camouflage. Look all normal.

But underneath, still there in mind's eye, ugly, clumsy *freak*; always there, even if no one could see any more but me.

I the one who counts.

Decided skin color on right forearm pleasing combination with hair at nape of neck. Black and pale striking; but now time for unobtrusive pale olive and medium brown.

With popularity of Grafts, people drifted away from dyes. But still easy to get, available even in public convenience. Even changed color of contacts.

Someday I knew would get final series of Grafts, finish job of turning self into normal person. Someday — when no longer needed reminding.

Found public interface, accessed, and generated new identity. Being systemizer has advantages. New I would finish old I's current job; and who would know or care, long as job finished. Then . . .

Then could access again own private program — code in Chimera. Only records still in existence — and only I know, all others concerned thought long ago destroyed — of certain years-back genetic experiment

Access Chimera, and choose one more subject at random.

Long list, experimenters, executives, volunteers. Many dead now. Lucky ones before I could run their lives through private system, private program. Plenty left.

Wonder what the next parent's weakness will be?

The genesis of 'Chimera' was a cover story in the AAAS Journal Science, *about a genetic experiment. The patchwork mouse on the cover was a 'chimera,' an animal with multiple parents, produced by a forced mixing of fertilized cells. I looked at that poor little clown of a mouse, and thought, What would a human that looked like that feel like?*

Naaa, I tried to put it aside. What scientist would do that to a fellow human? But it kept nagging away in my subconscious, simmering, a piece of an idea; because someday someone might, scientists being what they are, and The Search for Truth sometimes demanding sacrifices.

Then one day I sat down and wrote it, whole, at a sitting, the words flowing as easily as if Chim were standing behind me dictating. For the sake of a lot of future folk, I hope it was merely a well-integrated piece of fiction, and not a flash of precognition.

Jayge Carr

CHARLES SHEFFIELD

Charles Sheffield was born in Hull and read mathematics at Cambridge. In the middle and late sixties he travelled back and forth to the USA, working with computers, and became an American citizen in 1971. He began writing fiction in 1976. His first published story was in *Galaxy* in April 1977. More stories appeared in the same magazine in May, June, July and August . . .

Since then, he has had another seventy stories published, four collections, and nine novels — as well as non-fiction books, articles and scientific papers. His latest novels are *Proteus Unbound* and *Summertide*; the next ones will be *Cold as Ice* and *Zardalu*.

In between, he is Chief Scientist of Earth Satellite Corporation and has also found time to serve as President of the Science Fiction Writers of America and President of the American Astronautical Society. He lives in Silver Spring, Maryland.

Of the story which follows, Sheffield remembers: 'My birthday, June 25th, 1987, was really hot. I rode my bike to a place called The Angler's Inn, about five miles from home, and ate lunch alone there. I had four beers (American, twelve ounces each and not very strong) and the idea for 'Out of Copyright'. I wrote it the next week, finished in on July 1st. My diary shows the original working title as 'Say, Don't You Remember', so I must have started with the end in mind.'

OUT OF COPYRIGHT
by
CHARLES SHEFFIELD

Troubleshooting. A splendid idea, and one that I agree with totally in principle. Bang! One bullet, and trouble bites the dust. But unfortunately, trouble doesn't know the rules. Trouble won't stay dead.

I looked around the table. My top troubleshooting team was here. I was here. Unfortunately, they were supposed to be headed for Jupiter, and I ought to be down on Earth. In less than twenty-four hours, the draft pick would begin. That wouldn't wait, and if I didn't leave in the next thirty minutes, I would never make it in time. I needed to be in two places at once. I cursed the copyright laws and the single-copy restriction, and went to work.

'You've read the new requirement,' I said. 'You know the parameters. Ideas, anyone?'

A dead silence. They were facing the problem in their own unique ways. Wolfgang Pauli looked half-asleep. Thomas Edison was drawing little doll-figures on the table's surface, Enrico Fermi seemed to be counting on his fingers, and John von Neumann was staring impatiently at the other three. I was doing none of those things. I knew very well that wherever the solution would come from, it would not be from inside my head. My job was much more straightforward: I had to see that when we had a possible answer, it *happened*. And I had to see that we got *one* answer, not four.

The silence in the room went on and on. My brains trust was saying nothing, while I watched the digits on my watch flicker by. I had to stay and find a solution; and I had to get to the draft picks. But most of all and hardest of all, I had to remain quiet, to let my team do some thinking.

It was small consolation to know that similar meetings were being held within the offices of the other three combines. Everyone must be finding it equally hard going. I knew the players, and I could imagine the scenes, even though all the troubleshooting teams were different. NETSCO had a group that was intellectually the equal of ours at Romberg AG: Niels Bohr, Theodore von Karman, Norbert Weiner, and Marie Curie. MMG, the great Euro-Mexican combine of Magrit-Marcus Gesellschaft, had focused on engineering power rather than pure scientific understanding and creativity, and, in addition to the Soviet rocket designer Sergey Korolev and the American Nikola Tesla, they had reached farther back (and with more risk) to the great nineteenth-century English engineer Isambard Kingdom Brunel. He had been one of the outstanding successes of the program; I wished he were working with me, but MMG had always refused to look at a trade. MMG's one bow to theory was a strange one, the Indian mathematician Srinivasa Ramanujan, but the unlikely quartet made one hell of a team.

And finally there was BP Megation, whom I thought of as confused. At any rate, I didn't understand their selection logic. They had used billions of dollars to acquire a strangely mixed team: Erwin Schrödinger, David Hilbert, Leo Szilard, and Henry Ford. They were all great talents, and all famous names in their fields, but I wondered how well they could work as a unit.

All the troubleshooting teams were now pondering the same emergency. Our problem was created when the Pan-National Union suddenly announced a change to the Phase B demonstration program. They wanted to modify impact conditions, as their contracts with us permitted them to do. They didn't have to tell us how to do it, either, which was just as well for them, since I was sure they didn't know. How do you take a billion tons of mass, already launched to reach a specific target at a certain point of time, and redirect it to a different end point with a different arrival time?

There was no point in asking them *why* they wanted to change rendezvous conditions. It was their option. Some of our management saw the action of PNU's part as simple bloodly-mindedness, but I couldn't agree. The four multinational combines had each been given contracts to perform the biggest space engineering exercise in human history: small asteroids (only a kilometer or so across — but massing a billion tons each) had to be picked up from their natural orbits and redirected to the Jovian system, where they were to make precise rendezvous with assigned locations of the moon Io. Each combine had to select the asteroid and the method of moving it, but deliver within a tight transfer-energy budget and a tight time schedule.

For that task the PNU would pay each group a total of $8 billion. That sounds like a fair amount of money, but I knew our accounting figures. To date, with the project still not finished (rendezvous would be in eight more days), Romberg AG had spent $14.5 billion. We were looking at a probable cost overrun by a factor of two. I was willing to bet that the other three groups were eating very similar losses.

Why?

Because this was only Phase B of a four-phase project. Phase A had been a system design study, which led to four Phase B awards for a demonstration project. The Phase B effort that the four combines were working on now was a proof-of capability run for the full European Metamorphosis. The real money came in the future, in Phases C and D. Those would be awarded by the PNU to a single combine, and the award would be based largely on Phase B performance. The next phases called for the delivery of fifty asteroids to impact points on Europa (Phase C), followed by thermal mixing operations on the moon's surface (Phase D). The contract value of C and D would be somewhere up around $800 billion. That was the fish that all the combines were after, and it was the reason we would all overspend lavishly on this phase.

By the end of the whole program, Europa would have a forty-kilometer — deep water ocean over all its surface. And then the real fun would begin. Some contractor would begin the installation of the fusion plants, and the seeding of the sea-farms with the first prokaryotic bacterial forms.

The stakes were high; and to keep everybody on their toes, PNU did the right thing. They kept throwing in these little zingers, to mimic the thousand and one things that would go wrong in the final project phases.

While I was sitting and fidgeting, my team had gradually come to life. Fermi was pacing up and down the room —

always a good sign; and Wolfgang Pauli was jabbing impatiently at the keys of a computer console. John von Neumann hadn't moved, but since he did everything in his head anyway, that didn't mean much.

I looked again at my watch. I had to go. 'Ideas?' I said again.

Von Neumann made a swift chopping gesture of his hand. 'We have to make a choice, Al. It can be done in four or five ways.'

The others were nodding. 'The problem is only one of efficiency and speed,' added Fermi. 'I can give you an order-of-magnitude estimate of the effects on the overall program within half an hour.'

'Within fifteen minutes.' Pauli raised the bidding.

'No need to compete this one.' They were going to settle down to a real four-way fight on methods — they always did — but I didn't have the time to sit here and referee. The important point was that they said it could be done. 'You don't have to rush it. Whatever you decide, it will have to wait until I get back.' I stood up. 'Tom?'

Edison shrugged. 'How long will you be gone, Al?'

'Two days, maximum. I'll head back right after the draft picks.' (That wasn't quite true; when the draft picks were over, I had some other business to attend to that did not include the troubleshooters; but two days should cover everything.)

'Have fun.' Edison waved his hand casually. 'By the time you get back, I'll have the engineering drawings for you.'

One thing about working with a team like mine — they may not always be right, but they sure are always cocky.

'Make room there. More over!' the guards were pushing ahead to create a narrow corridor through the wedged mass of people. The one in front of me was butting with his helmeted head, not even looking to see whom he was shoving aside. 'Move!' he shouted. 'Come on now, out of the way.'

We were in a hurry. Things had been frantically busy Topside before I left, so I had cut it fine on connections to begin with, then been held up half an hour at reentry. We had broken the speed limits on the atmospheric segment, and there would be PNU fines for that, but still we hadn't managed to make up all the time. Now the first draft pick was only seconds away, and I was supposed to be taking part in it.

A thin woman in a green coat clutched at my arm as we bogged down for a moment in the crush of people. Her face was gray and grim, and she had a placard hanging round her neck. 'You could wait longer for the copyright!' She had to shout to make herself heard. 'It would cost you nothing — and look at the misery you would prevent. What you're doing is immoral! TEN MORE YEARS!'

Her last words were a scream as she called out this year's slogan. TEN MORE YEARS! I shook my arm free as the guard in front of me made sudden headway, and dashed along in his wake. I had nothing to say to the woman; nothing that she would listen to. If it were immoral, what did ten more years have to do with it? Ten more years; if by some miracle they were granted ten more years on the copyrights, what then? I knew the answer. They would try to talk the Pan-National Union into fifteen more years, or perhaps twenty. When you pay somebody off, it only increases their demands. I know, only too well. They are never satisfied with what they get.

Joe Delacorte and I scurried into the main chamber and shuffled sideways to our seats at the last possible moment. All the preliminary nonsense was finished, and the real business was beginning. The tension in the room was terrific. To be honest, a lot of it was being generated by the media. They were all poised to make maximum noise as they shot the selection information all over the System. If it were not for the media, I don't think the PNU would hold live draft picks at all. We'd all hook in with video links and do our business the civilized way.

The excitement now was bogus for other reasons, too. The professionals — I and a few others — would not become interested until the ten rounds were complete. Before that, the choices were just too limited. Only when they were all made, and the video teams were gone, would the four groups get together off-camera and begin the horse trading. '*My ninth round plus my fifth for your second.*' '*Maybe, if you'll throw in $10 million and a tenth-round draft pick for next year . . .*'

Meanwhile, BP Megation had taken the microphone. 'First selection,' said their representative. 'Robert Oppenheimer.'

I looked at Joe, and he shrugged. No surprise. Oppenheimer was the perfect choice — a brilliant scientist, but also practical, and willing to work with other people. He had died in 1967, so his original copyright had expired within the past twelve months. I knew his family had appealed for a copyright extension and been refused. Now BP Megation had sole single-copy rights for another lifetime.

'Trade?' whispered Joe.

I shook my head. We would have to beggar ourselves for next year's draft picks to make BP give up Oppenheimer. Other combine reps had apparently made the same decision. There was the clicking of data entry as the people around me updated portable databases. I did the same thing with a stub of pencil and a folded sheet of yellow paper, putting a check mark alongside his name. Oppenheimer was taken care of; I could forget that one. If by some miracle one of the four teams had overlooked some other top choice, I had to be ready to make an instant revision to my own selections.

'First selection, by NETSCO,' said another voice. 'Peter Joseph William Debye.'

It was another natural choice. Debye had been a Nobel prizewinner in physics, a theoretician with an excellent grasp of applied technology. He had died in 1966. Nobel laureates in science, particularly ones with that practical streak, went fast. As soon as their copyrights expired, they would be picked up in the draft the same year.

That doesn't mean it always works out well. The most famous case, of course, was Albert Einstein. When his copyright had expired in 2030, BP Megation had had first choice in the draft pick. They had their doubts, and they must have sweated blood over their decision. The rumour mill said they spent over $70 million is simulations alone, before they decided to take him as their top choice. The same rumor mill said that the cloned form was now showing amazing ability in chess and music, but no interest at all in physics or mathematics. If that was true, BP Megation had dropped $2 billion down a black hole: $1 billion straight to the PNU for acquisition of copyright, and another $1 billion for the clone process. Theorists were always tricky; you could never tell how they would turn out.

Magrit-Marcus Gesellschaft had now made their first draft pick, and chosen another Nobel laureate, John Cockroft. He also had died in 1967. So far, every selection was completely predictable. The three combines were picking the famous scientists and engineers who had died in 1966 and 1967, and who were now, with the expiration of family retention of copyrights, available for cloning for the first time.

The combines were being logical, but it made for a very dull draft pick. Maybe it was time to change that. I stood up to announce our own first take.

'First selection, by Romberg AG,' I said. 'Charles Proteus Steinmetz.'

My announcement caused a stir in the media. They had presumably never heard of Steinmetz, which was a disgraceful statement of their own ignorance. Even if they hadn't spent most of the past year combing old files and records, as we had, they should have heard of him. He was one of the past century's most colorful and creative scientists, a man who had been physically handicapped (he was a hunchback), but mentally able to do the equivalent of a hundred one-hand push-ups without even breathing hard. Even I had heard of him, and you'd not find many of my colleagues who'd suggest I was interested in science.

The buzzing in the media told me they were consulting their own historical data files, digging farther back in time. Even when they had done all that, they would still not understand the first thing about the true process of clone selection. It's not just a question of knowing who died over seventy-five years ago, and will therefore be out of copyright. That's a trivial exercise, one that any yearbook will solve for you. You also have to evaluate other factors. Do you know where the body is — are you absolutely *sure*? Remember, you can't clone anyone without a cell or two from the original body. You also have to be certain that it's who you think it is. All bodies seventy-five years old tend to look the same. And then, if the body happens to be really old — say, more than a couple of centuries — there are other peculiar problems that are still not understood at all. When NETSCO pulled its coup a few years ago by cloning Gottfried Wilhelm Leibniz, the other three combines were envious at first, Leibniz was a real universal genius, a seventeenth-century superbrain who was good at everything. NETSCO had developed a better cell-growth technique, and they had also succeeded in locating the body of Leibniz in its undistinguished Hanover grave.

They walked tall for almost a year at NETSCO, until the clone came out of the forcing chambers for indoctrination. He looked nothing like the old portraits of Leibniz, and he could not grasp even the simplest abstract concepts. Oops! said the media. Wrong body.

But it wasn't as simple as that. The next year, MMG duplicated the NETSCO cell-growth technology and tried for Isaac Newton. In this case there was no doubt that they had the correct body, because it had lain undisturbed since 1727 beneath a prominent plaque in London's Westminster Abbey. The results were just as disappointing as they had been for Leibniz.

Now NETSCO and MMG have become very conservative; in my opinion, far too conservative. But since then, nobody has tried for a clone of anyone who died before 1850. The draft picking went on its thoughtful and generally cautious way, and was over in a couple of hours except for the delayed deals.

The same group of protesters was picketing the building when I left. I tried to walk quietly through them, but they must have seen my picture on one of the exterior screens showing the draft-pick process. I was buttonholed by a man in a red jumpsuit and the same thin woman in green, still carrying her placard.

'Could we speak with you for just one moment?' The man in red was very well-spoken and polite.

I hesitated, aware that news cameras were on us. 'Very briefly. I'm trying to run a proof-of-concept project, you know.'

'I know. Is it going well?' He was a different type from most of the demonstrators, cool and apparently intelligent. And therefore potentially more dangerous.

'I wish I could say yes,' I said. 'Actually, it's going rather badly. That's why I'm keen to get back out.'

'I understand. All I wanted to ask you was why you — and I don't mean *you*, personally; I mean the combines — why do you find it *necessary* to use clones? You could do your work without them, couldn't you?'

I hesitated. 'Let me put it this way. We could do the work without them, in just the same way as we could stumble along somehow if we were denied the use of computer power, or nuclear power. The projects would be possible, but they would be enormously more difficult. The clones augment our available brainpower, at the highest levels. So let me ask you: Why *should* we do without the clones, when they are available and useful?'

'Because of the families. You have no right to subject the families to the misery and upset of seeing loved ones cloned, without their having any rights in the matter. It's cruel, and unnecessary. Can't you see that?'

'No, I can't. Now, you listen to me for a minute.' The cameras were still on me. It was a chance to say something that could never be said often enough. 'The family holds copyright for seventy-five years after a person's death. So if you, personally, *remember* your grandparent, you have to be pushing eighty years old — and it's obvious from looking at you that you're under forty. So ask yourself. Why are all you petitioners people who are in their thirties? It's not *you* who's feeling any misery.'

'But there are relatives —,' he said.

'Oh yes, the relatives. Are you a relative of somebody who has been cloned?'

'Not yet. But if this sort of thing goes on —'

'Listen to me for one more minute. A long time ago, there were a lot of people around who thought that it was wrong to let books with sex in them be sold to the general public. They petitioned to have the books banned. It wasn't that they claimed to be buying the books themselves, and finding them disgusting; because if they said that was the case, then people would have asked them *why* they were buying what they didn't like. Nobody was forcing anybody to buy those books. No, what the petitioners wanted was for *other* people to be stopped from buying what the *petitioners* didn't like. And you copyright-extension people are just the same. You are making a case on behalf of the relatives of the ones who are being cloned. But you never seem to ask yourself this. If cloning is so bad, why aren't the *descendants* of the clones the ones doing the complaining? They're not, you know. You never see them around here.'

He shook his head. 'Cloning is immoral!'

I sighed. Why bother? Not one word of what I'd said had got through to him. It didn't much matter — I'd really been speaking for the media, anyway — but it was a shame to see bigotry masquerading as public spirited behavior. I'd seen enough of that already in my life.

I started to move off toward my waiting aircar. The lady in green clutched my arm again. 'I'm going to leave instructions in my will that I want to be cremated. You'll never get me!'

You have my word on that, lady. But I didn't say it. I headed for the car, feeling an increasing urge to get back to the clean and rational regions of space. There was one good argument against cloning, and only one. It increased the total number of people, and to me that number already felt far too large.

I had been gone only thirty hours, total; but when I arrived back at Headquarters, I learned that in my absence five new problems had occurred. I scanned the written summary that Pauli had left behind.

First, one of the thirty-two booster engines set deep in the surface of the asteroid did not respond to telemetry requests for a status report. We had to assume it was defective, and eliminate it from the final firing pattern. Second, a big solar flare was on the way. There was nothing we could do about that, but it did mean we would have to recompute the strength of the magnetic and electric fields close to Io. They would change with the strength of the Jovian magnetosphere, and that was important because the troubleshooting team in my absence had agreed on their preferred solution to the problem of adjusting impact point and arrival time. I called for strong coupling between the asteroid and the 5-million amp flux tube of current between Io and its parent planet, Jupiter, to modify the final collision trajectory.

Third, we had lost the image data stream from one of our observing satellites, in synchronous orbit with Io. Fourth, our billion-ton asteroid had been struck by a larger-than-usual micrometeorite. This one must have massed a couple of kilograms, and it had been moving fast. It had struck off-axis from the center of mass, and the whole asteroid was now showing a tendency to rotate slowly away from our preferred orientation. Fifth, and finally, a new volcano had become very active down on the surface of Io. It was spouting sulfur up for a couple of hundred kilometers, and obscuring the view of the final-impact landmark.

After I had read Pauli's terse analysis of all the problems — nobody I ever met or heard of could summarize as clearly and briefly as he did — I switched on my communications set and asked him the only question that mattered: 'Can you handle them all?'

There was a delay of almost two minutes. The trouble-shooters were heading out to join the rest of our project team for their on-the-spot analyses in the Jovian system; already the light-travel time was significant. If I didn't follow in the next day or two, radio-signal delay would make conversation impossible. At the moment, Jupiter was forty-five light-minutes from Earth.

'We can, Al,' said Pauli's image at last. 'Unless others come up in the next few hours, we can. From here until impact, we'll be working in an environment with increasing uncertainties.'

'The PNU people planned it that way. Go ahead — but send me full transcripts.' I left the system switched on, and went off to the next room to study the notes I had taken of the five problem areas. As I had done with every glitch that had come up since the Phase B demonstration project began, I placed the problem into one of two basic categories: act of nature, or failure of man-made element. For the most recent five difficulties, the volcano on Io and the solar flare belonged to the left-hand column: Category One, clearly natural and unpredictable events. The absence of booster-engine telemetry and the loss of satellite-image data were Category Two, failures of our system. They went in the right-hand column. I hesitated for a long time over the fifth event, the impact of the meteorite; finally, and with some misgivings, I assigned it also as a Category One event.

As soon as possible, I would like to follow the engineering teams out toward Jupiter for the final hours of the demonstration. However, I had two more duties to perform before I could leave. Using a coded link to Romberg AG HQ in synchronous Earth orbit, I queried the status of all the clone tanks. No anomalies were reported. By the time we returned from the final stages of Phase B, another three finished clones would be ready to move to the indoctrination facility. I needed to be there when it happened.

Next, I had to review and approve acquisition of single-use copyright for all the draft picks we had negotiated down on Earth. To give an idea of the importance of these choices, we were looking at an expenditure of $20 billion for those selections over the next twelve months. It raised the unavoidable question, Had we made the best choices?

At this stage of the game, every combine began to have second thoughts about the wisdom of their picks. All the old failures came crowding into your mind. I already mentioned NETSCO and their problem with Einstein, but we had had our full share at Romberg AG: Gregor Mendel, the originator of the genetic ideas that stood behind all the cloning efforts, had proved useless; so had Ernest Lawrence, inventor of the cyclotron, our second pick for 1958. We had (by blind luck!) traded him along with $40 million for Wolfgang Pauli. Even so, we had made a bad error of judgment, and the fact that others made the same mistake was no consolation. As for Marconi, even though he looked like the old pictures of him, and was obviously highly intelligent, the clone who emerged turned out to be so indolent and casual about everything that he ruined any project he worked on. I had placed him in a cushy and undemanding position and allowed him to fiddle about with his own interests, which were mainly sports and good-looking women. (As Pauli acidly remarked, 'And you say that *we're* the smart ones, doing all the work?')

It's not the evaluation of a person's past record that's difficult, because we are talking about famous people who have done a great deal; written masses of books, articles, and papers; and been thoroughly evaluated by their own contemporaries. Even with all that, a big question still remains: Will the things that made the original man or woman great still be there in the cloned form? In other words, *Just what is it that is inherited?*

That's a very hard question to answer. The theory of evolution was proposed 170 years ago, but we're still fighting the old Nature-versus-Nurture battle. Is a human genius decided mainly by heredity, or by the way the person was raised? One old argument against cloning for genius was based on the importance of Nurture. It goes as follows: an individual is the product of both heredity (which is all you get in the clone) and environment. Since it is impossible to reproduce someone's environment, complete with parents, grandparents, friends, and teachers, you can't raise a clone that will be exactly like the original individual.

I'll buy that logic. We can't make ourselves an intellectually exact copy of anyone.

However, the argument was also used to prove that cloning for superior intellectual performance would be impossible. But of course, it actually proves nothing of the sort. If you take two peas from the same pod, and put one of them in deep soil next to a high wall, and the other in shallow soil out in the open, they *must* do different things if both are to thrive. The one next to the wall has to make sure it gets enough sunshine, which it can do by maximizing leaf area; the one in shallow soil has to get enough moisture, which it does through putting out more roots. The *superior* strain of peas is the one who genetic composition allows it to adapt to whatever environment it is presented with.

People are not peas, but in one respect they are not very different from them: some have superior genetic composition to others. That's all you can ask for. If you clone someone from a century ago, the last thing you want is someone who is *identical* to the original. They would be stuck in a twentieth-century mind-set. What is needed is someone who can adapt to and thrive in *today's* environment — whether that is now the human equivalent of shade, or of shallow soil. The success of the original clone template tells us a very important thing, that we are dealing with a superior physical brain. What that brain thinks in the year 2040 *should* be different from what it would have thought in the year 1940 — otherwise the clone would be quite useless. And the criteria for 'useless' change with time, too.

All these facts and a hundred others were running around inside my head as I reviewed the list for this year. Finally I made a note to suggest that J.B.S. Haldane, whom we had looked at and rejected three years ago on the grounds of unmanageability, ought to be looked at again and acquired if possible. History shows that he had wild views on politics and society, but there was no question at all about the quality of his mind. I thought I had learned a lot about interfacing with difficult scientific personalities in the past few years.

When I was satisfied with my final list, I transmitted everything to Joe Delacorte, who was still down on Earth, and headed for the transition room. A personal shipment pod ought to be waiting for me there. I hoped I would get a good one. At the very least, I'd be in it for the next eight days. Last time I went out to the Jovian system, the pod internal lighting and external antenna failed after three days. Have you ever sat in the dark for seventy-two hours, a hundred million miles from the nearest human, unable to send or receive messages? I didn't know if anyone realized I was in trouble. All I could do was sit tight — and I mean tight; pods are *small* — and stare out at the stars.

This time the pod was in good working order. I was able to participate in every problem that hit the project over the next four days. There were plenty of them, all small, and all significant. One of the fuel-supply ships lost a main ion drive. The supply ship was not much more than a vast bag of volatiles and a small engine, and it had almost no brain at all in its computer, not even enough to figure out an optimal use of its drives. We had to chase after and corral it as though we were pursuing a great lumbering elephant. Then three members of the impact-monitoring team came down with food poisoning — salmonella, which was almost certainly their own fault. You can say anything you like about throwing away spoiled food but you can't get a sloppy crew to take much notice.

Then, for variety, we lost a sensor through sheer bad program design. In turning one of our imaging systems from star sensing to Io-Jupiter sensing, we tracked it right across the solar disk and burned out all the photocells. According to the engineers, that's the sort of blunder you don't make after kindergarten — but somebody did it.

Engineering errors are easy to correct. It was much trickier when one of the final-approach-coordination groups, a team of two men and one woman, chose the day before the Io rendez-vous to have a violent sexual argument. They were millions of kilometers away from anyone, so there was not much we could do except talk to them. We did that, hoped they wouldn't kill each other, and made plans to do without their inputs if we had to.

Finally, one day before impact, an unplanned and anomalous firing of a rocket on the asteroid's forward surface caused a significant change of velocity of the whole body.

I ought to explain that I did little or nothing to solve any of these problems. I was too slow, too ignorant, and not creative enough. While I was still struggling to comprehend what the problem parameters were, my troubleshooters were swarming all over it. They threw proposals and counterproposals at each other so fast that I could hardly note them, still less contribute to them. For example, in the case of the anomalous rocket firing that I mentioned, compensation for the unwanted thrust called for an elaborate balancing act of lateral and radial engines, rolling and nudging the asteroid back into its correct approach path. The team had mapped out the methods in minutes, written the necessary optimization programs in less than half an hour, and implemented their solution before I understood the geometry of what was going on.

So what did I do while all this was happening? I continued to make my two columns: act of nature, or failure of man-made element. The list was growing steadily, and I was spending a lot of time looking at it.

We were coming down to the final few hours now, and all the combines were working flat out to solve their own problems. In an engineering project of this size, many thousands of things could go wrong. We were working in extreme physical conditions, hundreds of millions of kilometers away from Earth and our standard test environments. In the intense charged-particle field near Io, cables broke at loads well below their rated capacities, hard-vacuum welds showed air-bleed effects, and lateral jets were fired and failed to produce the predicted attitude adjustments. And on top of all this, the pressure, isolation, and bizarre surroundings were too much for some of the workers. We had human failure to add to engineering failure. The test was tougher than anyone had realized — even PNU, who was supposed to make the demonstration project just this side of impossible.

I was watching the performance of the other three combines only a little less intently than I was watching our own. At five hours from contact time, NETSCO apparently suffered a communications loss with their asteroid-control system. Instead of heading for Io impact, the asteroid veered away, spiraling in toward the bulk of Jupiter itself.

BP Megation lost it at impact minus three hours, when a vast explosion of one of their asteroid forward boosters threw the kilometer-long body into a rapid tumble. Within an hour, by some miracle of improvisation, their engineering team had found a method of stabilizing the wobbling mass. But by then it was too late to return to nominal impact time and place. Their asteroid skimmed into the surface of Io an hour early, sending up a long tear-shaped mass of ejecta from the moon's turbulent surface.

That left just two of us, MMG and Romberg AG. We both had our hands full. The Jovian system is filled with electrical, magnetic, and gravitational energies bigger than anything in the Solar System except the Sun itself. The two remaining combines were trying to steer their asteroid into a pinpoint landing through a great storm of interference that made every control command and every piece of incoming telemetry suspect. In the final hour I didn't even follow the exchanges between my troubleshooters. Oh, I could *hear* them easily enough. What I couldn't do was comprehend them, enough to know what was happening.

Pauli would toss a scrap of comment at von Neumann, and, while I was trying to understand that, von Neumann would have done an assessment, keyed in for a databank status report, gabbled a couple of questions to Fermi and an instruction to Edison, and at the same time be absorbing scribbled notes and diagrams from those two. I don't know if what they were doing was *potentially* intelligible to me or not; all I know is that they were going about fifty times too fast for me to follow. And it didn't much matter what I understood — they were getting the job done. I was still trying to divide all problems into my Category One — Category Two columns, but it got harder and harder.

In the final hour I didn't look or listen to what my own team was doing. We had one band of telemetry trained on the MMG project, and more and more that's where my attention was focused. I assumed they were having the same kind of communications trouble as we were — that crackling discharge field around Io made everything difficult. But their team was handling it. They were swinging smoothly into impact.

And then, with only ten minutes to go, the final small adjustment was made. It should have been a tiny nudge from the radial jets; enough to fine-tune the impact position a few hundred meters, and no more. Instead, there was a joyous roar of a radial jet at full, uncontrolled thrust. The MMG asteroid did nothing unusual for a few seconds (a billion tons is a lot of inertia), then began to drift lazily sideways, away from its nominal trajectory.

The jet was still firing. And that should have been impossible, because the first thing that the MMG team would do was send a POWER-OFF signal to the engine.

The time for impact came when the MMG asteroid was still a clear fifty kilometers out of position, and accelerating away. I saw the final collision, and the payload scraped along the surface of Io in a long, jagged scar that looked nothing at all like the neat, punched hole that we were supposed to achieve.

And we did achieve it, a few seconds later. Our asteroid came in exactly where and when it was supposed to, driving in exactly vertical to the surface. The plume of ejecta had hardly begun to rise from Io's red-and-yellow surface before von Neumann was pulling a bottle of bourbon from underneath the communications console.

I didn't object — I only wished I were there physically to share it, instead of being stuck in my own pod, short of rendezvous with our main ship. I looked at my final list, still somewhat incomplete. Was there a pattern to it? Ten minutes of analysis didn't show one. No one had tried anything — this time. Someday, and it might be tomorrow, somebody on another combine would have a bright idea; and then it would be a whole new ball game.

While I was still pondering my list, my control console began to buzz insistently. I switched it on expecting contact with my own troubleshooting team. Instead, I saw the despondent face of Brunel, MMG's own team leader — the man above all others that I would have liked to work on my side.

He nodded at me when my picture appeared on his screen. He was smoking one of his powerful black cigars, stuck in the side of his mouth. The expression on his face was as impenetrable as ever. He never let his feelings show there. 'I assume you saw it, did you?' he said around the cigar. 'We're out of it. I just called to congratulate you — again.'

'Yeah, I saw it. Tough luck. At least you came second.'

'Which, as you know very well, is no better than coming last.' He sighed and shook his head. 'We still have no idea what happened. Looks like either a programming error, or a valve sticking open. We probably won't know for weeks. And I'm not sure I care.'

I maintained a sympathetic silence.

'I sometimes think we should just give up, Al,' He said. 'I can beat those other turkeys, but I can't compete with you. That's six in a row that you've won. It's wearing me out. You've no idea how much frustration there is in that.'

I had never known Brunel to reveal so much of his feelings before.

'I think I do understand your problems,' I said.

And I did. I knew exactly how he felt — more than he would believe. To suffer through a whole, endless sequence of minor, niggling mishaps was heartbreaking. No single trouble was ever big enough for a troubleshooting team to stop, isolate it, and be able to say, there's dirty work going on here. But their cumulative effect was another matter. One day it was a morass of shipments missing their correct flights, another time a couple of minus signs dropped into computer programs, or a key worker struck down for a few days by a random virus, permits misfiled, manifests mislaid, or licenses wrongly dated.

I knew all those mishaps personally. I should, because I invented most of them. I think of it as the death of a thousand cuts. No one can endure all that and still hope to win a Phase B study.

'How would you like to work on the Europan Metamorph?' I asked. 'I think you'd love it.'

He looked very thoughtful, and for the first time, I believe I could actually read his expression. 'Leave MMG, you mean?' he said. 'Maybe. I don't know what I want anymore. Let me think about it. I'd like to work with you, Al — you're a genius.'

Brunel was wrong about that, of course. I'm certainly no genius. All I can do is what I've always done — handle people, take care of unpleasant details (quietly!), and make sure things get done that need doing. And of course, do what I do best: make sure that some things that need doing *don't* get done.

There *are* geniuses in the world, real geniuses. Not me, though. The man who decided to clone me, secretly — *there* I'd suggest you have a genius.

'*Say, don't you remember, they called me Al . . .*'

Of course, I don't remember. That song was written in the 1930s, and I didn't die until 1947, but no clone remembers anything of the forefather life. The fact that we tend to be knowledgeable about our originals' period is an expression of interest in those individuals, not memories from them. I know the Chicago of the Depression years intimately, as well as I know today; but it is all learned knowledge. I have no actual recollection of events. I don't *remember*.

So even if you don't remember, call me Al anyway. Everyone did.

JAMES MORROW

James Morrow has written children's books and screenplays, devised computer and board games, and is the author of four sf novels: *The Wine of Violence, The Continent of Lies, This Is the Way the World Ends and Only Begotten Daughter.* In 1989 he won the Nebula for his short story 'Bible Stories for Adults, No. 17. The Deluge.'

He lives in State College, Pennsylvania, and future publications include the novella 'City of Truth'.

Of the story which follows, Morrow says: 'The American upper middle class has always elicited in me a certain morbid fascination — their country clubs, their swimming pools, their hired help. I've always suspected that, had the Civil War failed to bring about the end of slavery, the children of privilege would have embraced the institution with great relish. Not that they would have treated their slaves cruelly — we Americans are much too nice for that, much too sentimental. But if owning a particular slave ever became inconvenient, well ...'

__ ABE LINCOLN IN MCDONALD'S __
by
JAMES MORROW

He caught the last train out of 1863 and got off at the blustery December of 2009, not far from Christmas, where he walked well past the turn of the decade and, without glancing back, settled down in the fifth of July for a good look around. To be a mere tourist in this place would not suffice. No, he must get it under his skin, work it into his bones, enfold it with his soul.

In his vest pocket, pressed against his heart's grim cadence, lay the final draft of the dreadful Seward Treaty. He needed but to add his name — Jefferson Davis had already signed it on behalf of the secessionist states — and a cleft nation would become whole. A signature, that was all, a simple 'A. Lincoln.'

Adjusting his string tie, he waded into the chaos grinding and snorting down Pennsylvania Avenue and began his quest for a savings bank.

'The news isn't good,' came Norman Grant's terrible announcement, stabbing from the phone like a poisoned dagger. 'Jimmy's test was positive.'

Walter Sherman's flabby, pumpkinlike face whitened with dread. 'Are you sure?' *Positive*, what a paradoxical term, so ironic in its clinical denotations: nullity, disease, doom.

'We ran two separate blood tests, followed by a fluorescent antibody check. Sorry. Poor Jim's got Blue Nile Fever.'

Walter groaned. Thank God his daughter was over at the Sheridans'. Jimmy had been Tanya's main Christmas present of three years ago — he came with a special note from Santa — and her affection for the old slave ran deep. Second father, she called him. Walter never could figure out why Tanya had asked for a sexagenerian and not a whelp like most kids wanted, but who could know the mind of a preschooler?

If only one of their others had caught the lousy virus. Jimmy wasn't the usual chore-boy. Indeed, when it came to cultivating a garden, washing a rug, or painting a house, he didn't know his nose from a nine of spades. Ah, but his bond with Tanya! Jimmy was her guardian, playmate, confidant, and yes, her teacher; Walter never ceased marveling at the great discovery of the past century — how, if you chained a whelp to a computer at the right age (no younger than two, no older than six), he'd soak up vast tracts of knowledge and subsequently pass them on to your children. Through Jimmy and Jimmy alone, Tanya had learned a formidable amount of plane geometry, music theory, American history, and Greek before ever setting foot in kindergarten.

'Prognosis?'

The doctor sighed. 'Blue Nile Fever follows a predictable course. In a year or so, Jimmy's T-cell defenses will collapse, leaving him prey to a hundred opportunistic infections. What worries me, of course, is Marge's pregnancy.'

A dull dread crept through Walter's white flesh. 'You mean — it could hurt the baby?'

'Well, there's this policy — the Centers for Disease Control urge permanent removal of Nile-positive chattel from all households containing pregnant women.'

'Removed?' Walter echoed indignantly 'I thought it didn't cross the pigmentation barrier.'

'That's probably true.' Grant's voice descended several registers. 'But *fetuses*, Walter, know what I'm saying? *Fetuses*, with their undeveloped immune systems. We don't want to ask for trouble, not with a retrovirus.'

'God, this is depressing. You really think there's a risk?'

'I'll put it this way. If my wife were pregnant —'

'I know, I know.'

'Bring Jimmy down here next week, and we'll take care of it. Quick. Painless. Is Tuesday at 2:30 good?'

Of course it was good. Walter had gone into orthodontics for the flexible hours, the dearth of authentic emergencies. That, and never having to pay for his own kids' braces. 'See you then,' he replied, laying a hand on his shattered heart.

The President strode out of Northeast Federal Savings and Loan and continued toward the derby-hatted Capitol. Such an exquisite building — at least some of the city remained intact, all was not glass-faced offices and dull, boxy banks. 'If we were still on the gold standard, this would be a more normal trans-action,' the assistant manager, a fool named Meade, had whined when Abe presented his coins for conversion. Not on the gold standard! A Democrat's doing, no doubt.

Luckily, Aaron Green, Abe's Chief Soothsayer and Time-Travelling adviser, had prepared Abe for the wondrous monstrosities and wrenching innovations that now assailed his senses. The self-propelled railway coaches roaring along cause-ways of black stone. The sky-high mechanical condors whisking travelers across the nation at hundreds of miles per hour. The dense medley of honks, bleeps, and technological growls.

So Washington was indeed living in its proper century — but what of the nation at large?

Stripped to their waists, two slave teams were busily trans-forming Pennsylvania Avenue, the first chopping into the asphalt with pickaxes, the second filling the gorge with huge cylindrical pipes. Their sweat-speckled backs were free of gashes and scars — hardly a surprise, as the overseers carried no whips, merely queer one-chamber pistols and portable Gatling guns.

Among the clutter at the Constitution Avenue intersection — signs, trash receptacles, small landlocked lighthouses regulating the coaches' flow — a pair of green arrows commanded Abe's notice. *Capitol Building*, announced the eastward-pointing arrow. *Lincoln Memorial*, said its opposite. His own memorial! So this particular tomorrow, the one fated by the awful Seward Treaty, would be kind to him.

The President hailed a cab. Removing his stovepipe hat, he wedged his six-foot-four frame into the passenger compartment — don't ride up front, Aaron Green had briefed him — and offered a cheery, 'Good morning.'

The driver, a blowsy woman, slid back a section of the soft rubbery glass. 'Lincoln, right?' she called through the opening like Pyramus talking to Thisbe. 'You're supposed to be Abe Lincoln. Costume party?'

'Republican.'

'Where to?'

'Boston.' If any city had let itself get mired in the past, Abe figured, that city would be Boston.

'Boston, *Massachusetts?*'

'Correct.'

'Hey, that's crazy, Mac. You're talking five hours at least, and that's if we push the speed limit all the way. I'd have to charge you my return trip.'

The President lifted a sack of money from his greatcoat. Even if backed only by good intentions, twentieth-century currency was aesthetically satisfying: that noble profile on the pennies, that handsome three-quarter view on the fives. As far as he could tell, he and Washington were the only ones to score twice. 'How much altogether?'

'You serious? Probably four hundred dollars.'

Abe peeled the driver's price from his wad and passed the bills through the window. 'Take me to Boston.'

'They're so *adorable*!' Tanya exclaimed as she and Walter strolled past Sonny's Super Slaver, a Chestnut Hill Mall emporium second only in size to the sporting goods store. 'Ah, look at *that* one — those big ears!' Recently weaned babies jammed the glass cages, tumbling over themselves, clutching stuffed jackhammers and toy garden hoses. 'Could we get one, Pappy?'

As Walter fixed on his daughter's face, its glow nearly made him squint. 'Tanya, I've got some bad news. Jimmy's real sick.'

'Sick? He looks fine.'

'It's Blue Nile, honey. He could die.'

'Die?' Tanya's angelic face crinkled with the effort of fighting tears. What a brave little tomato she was. 'Soon?'

'Soon.' Walter's throat swelled like a broken ankle. 'Tell you what. Let's go pick out a whelp right now. We'll have them put it aside until . . .'

'Until Jimmy' . . . a wrenching gulp . . . 'goes away?'

'Uh-huh.'

'Poor Jimmy.'

The sweet, bracing fragrance of newborn chattel wafted into Walter's nostrils as they approached the counter, behind which a wiry Oriental man, tongue pinned against his upper lip, methodically arranged a display of Tarbaby Treats. 'Now *here's* a girl who needs a friend,' he sang out, flashing Tanya a fake smile.

'Our best slave has Blue Nile,' Walter explained, 'and we wanted to —'

'Say no more.' The clerk lifted his palms as if stopping traffic. 'We can hold one for you clear till August.'

'I'm afraid it won't be that long.'

The clerk led them to a cage containing a solitary whelp chewing on a small plastic lawn mower. *Male*, the sign said. *Ten months. $399.95.* 'This guy arrived only yesterday. You'll have him litter-trained in two weeks — this we guarantee.'

'Had his shots?'

'You bet. The polio booster's due next month.'

'Oh Daddy, I *love* him,' Tanya gushed, jumping up and down. 'I completely *love* him. Let's bring him home tonight?'

'No, tomato. Jimmy'd get jealous.' Walter gave the clerk a wink and, simultaneously, a twenty. 'See that he gets a couple of really good meals this weekend, right?'

'Sure thing.'

'Pappy?'

'Yes, tomato?'

'When Jimmy dies, will he go to slave Heaven? Will he get to see his old friends?'

'Certainly.'

'Like Buzzy?'

'He'll definitely see Buzzy.'

A smile of intense pride leaped spontaneously to Walter's face. Buzzy had died when Tanya was only four, yet she remembered, she actually remembered!

So hard-edged, the future, Abe thought, levering himself out of the taxi and unflexing his long, cramped limbs. Boston had become a thing of brick and rock, tar and glass, iron and steel. 'Wait here,' he told the driver.

He entered the public gardens. A truly lovely spot, he decided, sauntering past a slave team planting flower beds — impetuous tulips, swirling gladioli, purse-lipped daffodils. Not far beyond, a white family cruised across a duck pond in a swan-shaped boast peddled by a scowling adolescent with skin like obsidian.

Leaving the park, he started down Boylston Street. A hundred yards away a burly Irish overseer stood beneath a gargantuan structure called the John Hancock Tower and began raising the scaffold, thus sending aloft a dozen slaves equipped with window-washing fluid. Dear Lord, what a job — the facade must contain a million square yards of mirrored glass.

Hard-edged, ungiving — and yet the city brought Abe peace.

In recent months he had started to grasp the true cause of the war. The issue, he realized, was not slavery. As with all things political, the issue was power. The southerners had seceded because they despaired of ever seizing the helm of state; as long as its fate was linked to a grimy, uncouth industrialized North, Dixie could never fully flower. By endeavouring to expand slavery into the territories, those southerners who hated the institution and those who loved it were speaking with a single tongue, saying, 'The Republic's true destiny is manifest — an agrarian Utopia, now and forever.'

But here was Boston, full of slaves and steeped in progress. Clearly, the Seward Treaty would not prove to be the recipe for feudalism and inertia that Abe's advisers feared. Crude, yes; morally ambiguous, true: and yet slavery wasn't dragging the Republic into the past, wasn't retarding its bid for modernity and might.

'Sign the treaty,' an inner voice instructed Abe. 'End the war.'

Sunday was the Fourth of July, which meant the annual backyard picnic with the Burnsides, boring Ralph and boorish Helen, a tedious afternoon of horseshoe tossing, conspicuous drinking, and stupefying poolside chat, the whole ordeal relieved only by Libby's barbecued spareribs. Libby was one of those wonderful yard-sale items Marge had such a knack for finding, a healthy, well-mannered female who turned out to be a splendid cook, easily worth ten times her sticker price.

The Burnsides were an hour late — their rickshaw puller, Zippy, had broken his foot the day before, and so they were forced to use Bubbles, their unathletic gardener — a whole glorious hour of not hearing Ralph's views on the Boston sports scene. When they did finally show, the first thing out of Ralph's mouth was, 'Is it a law the Sox can't own a decent pitcher? I mean, did they actually pass a *law*?', and Walter steeled himself. Luckily, Libby used a loose hand with the bourbon, and by three o'clock Walter was so anesthetized by mint juleps he could have floated happily through an amputation — not to mention Ralph's vapid views on the Sox, Celtics, and Patriots.

With the sixth drink, his numbness segued into a kind of contented courage, and he took unflinching stock of himself. Yes, his wife had probably bedded down with a couple of teachers from the Wellesley Adult Education Center — that superfluously muscled pottery instructor, most likely, though the drama coach also seemed to have a roving dick — but it wasn't as if Walter didn't occasionally use his orthodontic chair as a motel bed, wasn't as if he didn't frolic with Katie Mulligan every Wednesday afternoon at the West Newton Hot Tubs. And look at his splendid house, with its Jacuzzi, bowling alley, tennis court, and twenty-five-meter pool. Look at his thriving practice. His portfolio. Porsche. Silver ricksaw. Graceful daughter flopping through sterile turquoise waters (damn that Happy, always using too much chlorine). And look at his sturdy, handsome Marge, back-floating, her pregnancy rising from the deep end like a volcanic island. Walter was sure the kid was his. Eighty-five percent sure.

He'd achieved something in this life.

At dusk, while Happy set off the fireworks, the talk got around to Blue Nile. 'We had Jimmy tested last week,' Walter revealed, exhaling a small tornado of despair. 'Positive.'

'God, and you let him stay in the house?' wailed Ralph, fingering the grip of his Luger Parabellum PO8. A cardboard rocket screeched into the sky and became a dozen crimson starbursts, their reflections cruising across the pool like phosphorescent fish. 'You should've told us. He might infect Bubbles.'

'It's a pretty hard virus to contract,' Walter retorted. A buzz bomb whistled overhead, annihilating itself in a glittery blue-and-red mandala. 'There has to be an exchange of saliva or blood.'

'Still, I can't believe you're keeping him, with Marge pregnant and everything.'

Ten fiery spheres popped from a roman candle and sailed into the night like clay pigeons. 'Matter of fact, I've got an appointment with Grant on Monday.'

'You know, Walter, if Jimmy were mine, I'd allow him a little dignity. I wouldn't take him to lousy clinic.'

The pièce de résistance blossomed over the yard — Abe Lincoln's portrait in sparks. 'What would you do?'

'You know perfectly well what I'd do.'

Walter grimaced. Dignity. Ralph was right, by damn. Jimmy had served the family with devotion and zest. They owed him an honorable exit.

The President chomped into a Big Mac, reveling in the soggy sauces and sultry juices as they bathed his tongue and rolled down his gullet. Were he not permanently lodged elsewhere — rail-splitter, country lawyer, the whole captivating myth — he might well have wished to settle down here in 2010. Big Macs were a quality commodity. The whole menu, in fact — the large fries, vanilla shakes, Diet Cokes, and Chicken McNuggets — seemed to Abe a major improvement over nineteenth-century cuisine. And such a soothing environment, its every surface clean and sleek, as if carved from tepid ice.

An enormous clown named Ronald was emblazoned on the picture window. Outside, across the street, an elegant sign — Old English characters on whitewashed wood — heralded the Chestnut Hill Country Club. On the grassy slopes beyond, smooth and green like a billiard table, a curious event unfolded, men and women whacking balls into the air with sticks. When not employed, the sticks resided in cylindrical bags slung over the shoulders of sturdy male slaves.

'Excuse me, madam,' Abe addressed the chubby woman in the next booth. 'What are those men doing? Is it religious?'

'That's quite a convincing Lincoln you've got on.' Hunched over a newspaper, the woman wielded a writing implement, using it to fill tiny squares with alphabet letters. 'Are you serious? They're golfing.'

'A game?'

'Uh-huh.' The woman started on her second Quarter Pounder. 'The game of golf.'

'It's like croquet, isn't it?'

'It's like golf.'

Dipping and swelling like a verdant sea, the golf field put Abe in mind of Virginia's hilly provinces. Virginia, Lee's stronghold. A soft moan left the sixteenth President. Having thrown Hooker and Sedgwick back across the Rappahannock, Lee was ideally positioned to bring the war to the Union, either by attacking Washington directly or, more likely, by forming separate corps under Longstreet, Hill, and Ewell and invading Pennsylvania. Overrunning the border towns, he could probably cut the flow of reinforcements to Vicksburg while simultaneously equipping the Army of Northern Virginia for a push on the capital.

It was all too nightmarish to contemplate.

Sighing heavily, Abe took the Seward Treaty from his vest and asked to borrow his neighbor's pen.

Monday was a holiday. Right after breakfast, Walter changed into his golfing togs, hunted down his clubs, and told Jimmy they'd be spending the day on the links. He ended up playing the entire course, partly to improve his game, partly to postpone the inevitable.

His best shot of the day — a three hundred and fifty yard blast with his one-iron — carried straight down the eighteenth fairway and ran right up on the green. Sink the putt, and he'd finish the day one under par.

Sweating in the relentless fifth of July sun, Jimmy pulled out the putter. Such a fine fellow, with his trim body and huge, eager eyes, zags of silver shooting through his steel-wool hair like the aftermath of an electrocution, his black biceps and white polo shirt meeting like adjacent squares on a chessboard. He would be sorely missed.

'No, Jimmy, we won't be needing that. Just pass the bag over here. Thanks.'

As Walter retrieved his .22 caliber army rifle from among the clubs, Jimmy's face hardened with bewilderment.

'May I ask why you require a firearm?' said the slave.

'I'm going to shoot you.'

'Huh?'

'Shoot you.'

'*What*?'

'Results came Thursday, Jimmy. You have Blue Nile. Sorry. I'd love to keep you around, but it's too dangerous, what with Marge's pregnancy and everything.'

'Blue Nile?'

'Sorry.'

Jimmy's teeth came together in a tight, dense grid. 'In the name of reason, *sell* me. Surely that's a viable option.'

'Let's be realistic. Nobody's going to take in a Nile-positive just to watch him wilt and die.'

'Very well — then turn me loose.' Sweat spouted from the slave's ebony face. 'I'll pursue my remaining years on the road. I'll . . .'

'Loose? I can't go around undermining the economy like that, Jim. I'm sure you understand.'

'There's something I've always wanted to tell you, Mr. Sherman.'

'I'm listening.'

'I believe you are the biggest asshole in the whole Commonwealth of Massachusetts.'

'No need for that kind of talk, fellow. Just sit down on the green, and I'll —'

'No.'

'Let's not make this difficult. Sit down, and you'll receive a swift shot in the head — no pain, a dignified death. Run away, and you'll get it in the back. It's your choice.'

'Of course I'm going to run, you degenerate moron.'

'Sit!'

'No.'

'Sit!'

Spinning around, Jimmy sprinted toward the rough. Walter jammed the stock against his shoulder and, like a biologist focusing his microscope on a protozoan, found the retreating chattel in his high-powered optical sight.

'Stop!'

Jimmy reached the western edge of the fairway just as Walter fired, a clean shot right through the slave's left calf. With a deep, wolfish howl, he pitched forward and, to Walter's surprise, rose almost instantly, clutching a rusty, discarded nine-iron that he evidently hoped to use as a crutch. But the slave got no farther. As he stood fully erect, his high, wrinkled forehead neatly entered the gunsight, the cross hairs branding him with an X, and Walter had but to squeeze the trigger again.

Impacting, the bullet dug out a substantial portion of cranium — a glutinous divot of skin, bone, and cerebrum shooting away from Jimmy's temple like a missile launched from a brown planet. He spun around twice and fell into the rough, landing behind a clump of rose bushes spangled with white blossoms. So: an honorable exit after all.

Tears bubbled out of Walter as if from a medicine dropper. Oh Jimmy, Jimmy . . . And the worst was yet to come, wasn't it? Of course, he wouldn't tell Tanya the facts. 'Jimmy was in pain,' he'd say. 'Unbearable agony. The doctors put him to sleep. He's in slave Heaven now.' And they'd give him a classy send-off, oh yes, with flowers and a moment of silence. Maybe Pastor McClellan would be willing to preside.

Walter staggered toward the rough. To do a funeral, you needed a body. Doubtless the morticians could patch up his head, mold a gentle smile, bend his arms across his chest in a posture suggesting serenity . . .

A tall, bearded man in an Abe Lincoln suit was on the eighteenth fairway, coming Walter's way. An eccentric, probably. Maybe a full-blown nut. Walter locked his gaze on the roses and marched straight ahead.

'I saw what you did,' said the stranger, voice edged with indignation.

'Fellow had Blue Nile,' Walter explained. The sun beat against his face like a hortator pounding a drum on a Roman galley. 'It was an act of mercy. Hey, Abe, the Fourth of July was yesterday. Why the getup?'

'Yesterday is never too late,' said the stranger cryptically, pulling a yellowed sheaf from his vest. 'Never too late,' he repeated as, swathed in the hot, buttery light, he neatly ripped the document in half.

For Walter Sherman, pummeled by the heat, grieving for his lost slave, wearied by the imperatives of mercy, the world now became a swamp, an all-enveloping mire blurring the stranger's methodical progress toward McDonald's. An odd evening was coming, Walter sensed, with odder days to follow, days in which all the earth's stable things would be wrenched from their moorings and unbolted from their bases. Here and now, standing on the crisp border between the fairway and the putting green, Walter apprehended this discomforting future.

He felt it more emphatically as, eyes swirling, heart shivering, brain drifting in a sea of insane light, he staggered towards the roses.

And he knew it with a knife-sharp certainty as, searching through the rough, he found not Jimmy's corpse, but only the warm hulk of a humanoid machine, prostrate in the dusk, afloat in the slick, oily fluid leaking from its broken brow.

ORSON SCOTT CARD

Orson Scott Card's first published story was 'Ender's Game', which appeared in *Analog* in August 1977. His first book was a collection, *Capitol*, and his first novel was *Hot Sleep*. Both of these were published in 1978, which was the year he won the John W. Campbell Award as best new writer. His novel *Ender's Game* won both the Nebula and Hugo in 1986. The following year its sequel repeated this achievement: *Speaker for the Dead* won both the Nebula and Hugo as best novel in 1987.

In 1987, he also won the World Fantasy Award for his novella 'Hatrack River'. This was the first part of the novel *Seventh Son*, which in turn is the first of an alternate world series 'The Tales of Alvin Maker'. The second novel in the sequence is *Red Prophet*, and the third volume is *Prentice Alvin*. Each of the three have been nominated for either the Nebula or Hugo. Amongst his other novels are *A Planet Called Treason*, *Hart's Hope*, *Wyrms* and *The Folk of the Fringe*.

Card lives in Greensboro, North Carolina, and is a regular reviewer for *The Magazine of Fantasy and Science Fiction*. He founded the review magazine *Short Form*, and is chairman of the judges for the Sturgeon Memorial Award for best short fiction.

The following story was a finalist for the Hugo.

DOGWALKER

by
ORSON SCOTT CARD

I was an innocent pedestrian. Only reason I got in this in the first place was I got a vertical way of thinking and Dogwalker thought I might be useful, which was true, and also he said I might enjoy myself, which was a prefabrication, since people done a lot more enjoying on me than I done on them.

When I say I think vertical, I mean to say I'm metaphysical, that is, simular, which is to say, I'm dead but my brain don't know it yet and my feet still move. I got popped at age nine just lying in my own bed when the goat next door shot at his lady and it went through the wall and into my head. Everybody went to look at them cause they made all the noise, so I was a quart low before nobody noticed I been poked.

They packed my head with supergoo and light pipe, but they didn't know which neutron was supposed to butt into the next so my alchemical brain got turned from rust to diamond. Goo Boy. The Crystal Kid.

From that bright electrical day I never grew another inch, anywhere. Bullet went nowhere near my gonadicals. Just turned off the puberty switch in my head. Saint Paul said he was a eunuch for Jesus, but who am I a eunuch for?

Worst thing about it is here I am near thirty and I still have to take barkeepers to court before they'll sell me beer. And it ain't hardly worth it even though the judge prints out in my favor and the barkeep has to pay costs, because my corpse is so little I get toxed on six ounces and pass out pissing after twelve. I'm a lousy drinking buddy. Besides, anybody hangs out with me looks like a pederast.

No, I'm not trying to make you drippy-drop for me — I'm used to it, okay? Maybe the homecoming queen never showed me True Love in a four-point spread, but I got this knack that certain people find real handy and so I always made out. I dress good and I ride the worm and I don't pay much income tax. Because I am the Password Man. Give me five minutes with anybody's curriculum vitae, which is to say their autopsychoscopy, and nine times out of ten I'll spit out their password and get you into their most nasty sticky sweet secret files. Actually its usually more like three times out of ten, but that's still a lot better odds than having a computer spend a year trying to push out fifteen characters to make just the right P-word, specially since after the third wrong try they string your phone number, freeze the target files, and call the dongs.

Oh, do I make you sick? A cute little boy like me, engaged in critical unspecified dispopulative behaviors? I may be half glass and four feet high, but I can simulate you better than your own mama, and the better I know you, the deeper my hooks. I not only know your password *now*, I can write a word on a paper, seal it up, and then you go home and *change* your password and then open up what I wrote and there it'll be, your *new* password, three times out of ten. I am *vertical*, and Dogwalker knowed it. Ten percent more supergoo and I wouldn't even be legally human, but I'm still under the line, which is more than I can say for a lot of people who are a hundred percent zoo inside their head.

Dogwalker comes to me one day at Carolina Circle, where I'm playing pinball standing on a stool. He didn't say nothing, just give me a shove, so naturally he got my elbow in his balls. I get a lot of twelve-year-olds trying to shove me around at the arcades, so I'm used to teaching them lessons. Jack the Giant Killer. Hero of the fourth graders. I usually go for the stomach, only Dogwalker wasn't a twelve-year-old, so my elbow hit low.

I knew the second I hit him that this wasn't no kid. I didn't know Dogwalker from God, but he gots the look, you know, like he been hungry before, and he don't care what he eats these days.

Only he got no ice and he got no slice, just sits there on the floor with his back up against the East Shi'ite game, holding his boodle and looking at me like I was a baby he had to diaper. 'I hope you're Goo Boy,' he says, 'cause if you ain't, I'm gonna give you back to your mama in three little tupperware bowls.' He doesn't sound like he's making a threat, though. He sounds like he's chief weeper at his own funeral.

'You want to do business, use your mouth, not your hands,'

I says. Only I say it real apoplectic, which is the same as apologetic except you are also still pissed.

'Come with me,' he says. 'I got to go buy me a truss. You pay the tax out of your allowance.'

So we went to Ivey's and stood around in children's wear while he made his pitch. 'One P-word,' he said, 'only there can't be no mistake. If there's a mistake, a guy loses his job and maybe goes to jail.'

So I told him no. Three chances in ten, that's the best I can do. No guarantees. My record speaks for itself, but nobody's perfect, and I ain't even close.

'Come on,' he says, 'you got to have ways to make sure, right? If you can do three times out of ten, what if you find out more about the guy? What if you meet him?'

'Okay, maybe fifty-fifty.'

'Look, we can't go back for seconds. So maybe you can't get it. But do you *know* when you ain't got it?'

'No,' says I. ''Cause half the time when I'm right, I don't know I'm right.'

'Shee-it.' he says. 'This is like doing business with my baby brother.'

'You can't afford me anyway,' I says. 'I pull two dimes minimum, and you barely got breakfast on your gold card.'

'I'm offering a cut.'

'I don't want a cut. I want cash.'

'Sure thing,' he said. He looks around, real careful. As if they wired the sign that said Boys Briefs Sizes 10-12. 'I got an inside man at Federal Coding,' he says.

'That's nothing,' I says. 'I got a bug up the First Lady's ass, and forty hours of tape of her breaking wind.'

I got a mouth. I know I got a mouth. I especially know it when he jams my face into a pile of shorts and says, 'Suck on this, Goo Boy.'

I hate it when people push me around. And I know ways to make them stop. This time all I had to do was cry. Real loud, like he was hurting me. Everybody looks when a kid starts crying. 'I'll be good.' I kept saying it. 'Don't hurt me no more! I'll be good.'

'Shut up,' he said. 'Everybody's looking.'

'Don't you ever shove me around again,' I says. 'I'm at least ten years older than you, and a hell of a lot more than ten years smarter. Now I'm leaving this store, and if I see you coming after me, I'll start screaming about how you zipped down and showed me the pope, and you'll get yourself a child-molesting tag so they pick you up every time some kid gets jollied within a hundred miles of Greensboro.' I've done it before, and it works, and Dogwalker was no dummy. Last thing he needed was extra reasons for the dongs to bring him in for questioning. So I figured he'd tell me to get poked and that'd be the last of it.

Instead he says, 'Goo Boy, I'm sorry, I'm too quick with my hands.'

Even the goat who shot me never said he was sorry. My first thought was, what kind of sister is he, abjectifying right out like that. Then I reckoned I'd stick around and see what kind of man it is who emulsifies himself in front of a nine-year-old-looking kid. Not that I figured him to be purely sorrowful. He still just wanted me to get the P-word for him, and he knew there wasn't nobody else to do it. But most street pugs aren't smart enough to tell the right lie under pressure. Right away I knew he wasn't your ordinary street hook or low arm, pugging cause they don't have the sense to stick with any kind of job. He had a deep face, which is to say his head was more than a hairball, by which I mean he had brains enough to put his hands in his pockets without seeking an audience with the pope. Right then was when I decided he was my kind of no-good lying son-of-a-bitch.

'What are you after at Federal Coding?' I asked him. 'A record wipe?'

'Ten clean greens,' he says. 'Coded for unlimited international travel. The whole i.d., just like a real person.'

'The President has a green card,' I says. 'The Joint Chiefs have clean greens. But that's all. The U.S. Vice-President isn't even cleared for unlimited international travel.'

'Yes he is,' he says.

'Oh, yeah, you know everything.'

'I need a P. My guy could do us reds and blues, but a clean green has to be done by a burr-oak rat two levels up. My guy knows how it's done.'

'They won't just have it with a P-Word,' I says. 'A guy who can make green cards, they're going to have his finger on it.'

'I know how to get the finger,' he says. 'It takes the finger and the password.'

'You take a guy's finger, he might report it. And even if you persuade him not to, somebody's gonna notice that it's gone.'

'Latex,' he says. 'We'll get a mold. And don't start telling me how to do my part of the job. You get P-words, I get fingers. You in?'

'Cash,' I says.

'Twenty percent,' says he.

'Twenty percent of pus.'

'The inside guy gets twenty, the girl who brings me the finger, she gets twenty, and I damn well get forty.'

'You can't just sell these things on the street, you know.'

'They're worth a meg apiece,' says he, 'to certain buyers.' By which he meant Orkish Crime, of course. Sell ten, and my twenty percent grows up to be two megs. Not enough to be rich, but enough to retire from public life and maybe even pay for some high-level medicals to sprout hair on my face. I got to admit that sounded good to me.

So we went into business. For a few hours he tried to do it without telling me the baroque rat's name, just giving me data he got from his guy at Federal Coding. But that was real stupid, giving me second-hand face like that, considering he needed me to be a hundred percent sure, and pretty soon he realized that and brought me in all the way. He hated telling me anything, because he couldn't stand to let go. Once I knew stuff on my own, what was to stop me from trying to go into business for myself? But unless he had another way to get the P-word, he had to get it from me, and for me to do it right, I had to know everything I could. Dogwalker's got a brain in his head, even if it is all biodegradable, and so he knows there's times when you got no choice but to trust somebody. When you just got to figure they'll do their best even when they're out of your sight.

He took me to his cheap condo on the old Guilford College campus, near the worm, which was real congenital for getting to Charlotte or Winston or Raleigh with no fuss. He didn't have no soft floor, just a bed, but it was a big one, so I didn't reckon he suffered. Maybe he bought it back in his old pimping days, I figured, back when he got his name, running a string of bitches with names like Spike and Bowser and Prince, real hydrant leg-lifters for the tweeze trade. I could see that he used to have money, and he didn't anymore. Lots of great clothes, tailor-tight fit, but shabby, out of sync. The really old ones, he tore all the wiring out, but you could still see where the diodes used to light up. We're talking neanderthal.

'Vanity, vanity, all is profanity,' says I, while I'm holding out the sleeve of a camisa that used to light up like an airplane coming in for a landing.

'They're too comfortable to get rid of,' he says. But there's a twist in his voice so I know he don't plan to fool nobody.

'Let this be a lesson to you,' says I. 'This is what happens when a walker don't walk.'

'Walkers do steady work,' says he. 'But me, when business was good, it felt bad, and when business was bad, it felt good. You walk cats, maybe you can take some pride in it. But you walk dogs, and you know they're getting hurt every time —'

'They got a built-in switch, they don't feel a thing. That's why the dongs don't touch you, walking dogs, cause nobody gets hurt.'

'Yeah, so tell me, which is worse, somebody getting tweezed till they scream so some old honk can pop his pimple, or somebody getting half their brain replaced so when the old honk tweezes her she can't feel a thing? I had these women's bodies around me and I knew that they used to be people.'

'You can be glass,' says I, 'and still be people.'

He saw I was taking it personally. 'Oh hey,' says he, 'you're under the line.'

'So are dogs,' says I.

'Yeah well,' says he. 'You watch a girl come back and tell about some of the things they done to her, and she's *laughing*, you draw your own line.'

I look around his shabby place. 'Your choice,' says I.

'I wanted to feel clean,' says he. 'That don't mean I got to stay poor.'

'So you're setting up this grope so you can return to the old days of peace and propensity.'

'Propensity,' says he. 'What the hell kind of word is that? Why do you keep using words like that?'

'Cause I know them,' says I.

'Well you *don't* know them,' says he, 'because half the time you get them wrong.'

I showed him my best little-boy grin. 'I know,' says I. What I don't tell him is that the fun comes from the fact that almost nobody ever *knows* I'm using them wrong. Dogwalker's no ordinary pimp. But then the ordinary pimp doesn't bench himself halfway through the game because of a sprained moral qualm, by which I mean that Dogwalker had some stray diagonals in his head, and I began to think it might be fun to see where they all hooked up.

Anyway we got down to business. The target's name was Jesse H. Hunt, and I did a real job on him. The Crystal Kid really plugged in on this one. Dogwalker had about two pages of stuff — date of birth, place of birth, sex at birth (no changes since), education, employment history. It was like getting an armload of empty boxes. I just laughed at it. 'You got a jack to the city library?' I asked him, and he shows me the wall outlet. I plugged right in, visual onto my pocket sony, with my own little crystal head for ee-i-ee-i-oh. Not every goo-head can think clear enough to do this, you know, put out clean type just by thinking the right stuff out my left ear interface port.

I showed Dogwalker a little bit about research. Took me ten minutes. I know my way right through the Greensboro Public Library. I have P-words for every single librarian and I'm so ept that they don't even guess I'm stepping upstream through their access channels. From the Public Library you can get all the way into North Carolina. Records Division in Raleigh, and from there you can jumble into federal personnel records anywhere in the country. Which meant that by nightfall on that most portentous day we had hardcopy of every document in Jesse H. Hunt's whole life, from his birth certificate and first grade report card to his medical history and security clearance reports when he first worked for the feds.

Dogwalker knew enough to be impressed. 'If you can do all that,' he says, 'you might as well pug his P-word straight out.'

'No puedo, putz,' says I as cheerful as can be. 'Think of the

fed as a castle. Personnel files are floating in the moat —
there's a few alligators but I swim real good. Hot data is deep in
the dungeon. You can get in there, but you can't get out clean.
And P-words — P-words are kept up the queen's ass.'

'No system is unbeatable,' he says.

'Where'd you learn that, from graffiti in a toilet stall? If the
P-word system was even a little bit breakable, Dogwalker, the
gentlemen you plan to sell these cards to would already be
inside looking out at us, and they wouldn't need to spend a meg
to get clean greens from a street pug.'

Trouble was that after impressing Dogwalker with all the
stuff I could find out about Jesse H., I didn't know that much
more than before. Oh, I could guess at some P-words, but that
was all it was — guessing. I couldn't even pick a P most likely to
succeed. Jesse was one ordinary dull rat. Regulation good
grades in school, regulation good evaluations on the job,
probably gave his wife regulation lube jobs on a weekly
schedule.

'You don't really think your girl's going to get his finger,'
says I with sickening scorn.

'You don't know the girl,' says he. 'If we needed his flipper
she'd get molds in five sizes.'

'You don't know this guy,' says I. 'This is the straightest
opie in Mayberry. I don't see him cheating on his wife.'

'Trust me,' says Dogwalker. 'She'll get his finger so smooth
he won't even know she took the mold.'

I didn't believe him. I got a knack for knowing things about
people, and Jesse H. wasn't faking. Unless he started faking
when he was five, which is pretty unpopulated. He wasn't going
to bounce the first pretty girl who made his zipper tight.
Besides which he was smart. His career path showed that he
was always in the right place. The right people always seemed
to know his name. Which is to say he isn't the kind whose brain
can't run if his jeans get hot. I said so.

'You're really a marching band,' says Dogwalker. 'You can't
tell me his P-word, but you're obliquely sure that he's a limp or
a wimp.'

'Neither one,' says I. 'He's hard and straight. But a girl
starts rubbing up to him, he isn't going to think it's because she

heard that his crotch is cantilevered. He's going to figure she wants something, and he'll give her string till he finds out what.'

He just grinned at me. 'I got me the best Password Man in the Triass didn't I? I got me a miracle worker name Goo-Boy, didn't I? The icebrain they call Crystal Kid. I got him, didn't I?'

'Maybe,' says I.

'I got him or I kill him' he says, showing more teeth than a primate's supposed to have.

'You got me,' says I. 'But don't go thinking you can kill me.'

He just laughs. 'I got you and you're so good, you can bet I got me a girl who's at least as good at what she does.'

'No such,' says I.

'Tell me his P-word and then I'll be impressed.'

'You want quick results? Then go ask him to give you his password himself.'

Dogwalker isn't one of those guys who can hide it when he's mad. 'I want quick results,' he says. 'And if I start thinking you can't deliver, I'll pull your tongue out of your head. Through your nose.'

'Oh, that's good,' says I. 'I always do my best thinking when I'm being physically threatened by a client. You really know how to bring out the best in me.'

'I don't want to bring out the best,' he says. 'I just want to bring out his password.'

'I got to meet him first,' says I.

He leans over me so I can smell his musk, which is to say I'm very olfactory and so I can tell you he reeked of testosterone, by which I mean ladies could fill up with babies just from sniffing his sweat. 'Meet him?' he asks me. 'Why don't we just ask him to fill out a job application?'

'I've read all his job applications,' says I.

'How's a glass-head like you going to meet Mr. Fed?' says he. 'I bet you're always getting invitations to the same parties as guys like him.'

'I don't get invited to *grown-up* parties,' says I. 'But on the other hand, grown-ups don't pay much attention to sweet little kids like me.'

He sighed. 'You really have to meet him?'

'Unless fifty-fifty on a P-word is a good enough odds for you.'

All of a sudden he goes nova. Slaps a glass off the table and it breaks against the wall, and then he kicks the table over, and all the time I'm thinking about ways to get out of there unkilled. But it's me he's doing the show for, so there's no way I'm leaving, and he leans in close to me and screams in my face. 'That's the last of your fifty-fifty and sixty-forty and three times in ten I want to hear about, Goo Boy, you hear me?'

And I'm talking real meek and sweet, cause this boy's twice my size and three times my weight and I don't exactly have no leverage. So I says to him, 'I can't help talking in odds and percentages, Dogwalker, I'm vertical, remember? I've got glass channels in here, they spit out percentages as easy as other people sweat.'

He slapped his hand against his own head. 'This ain't exactly a sausage biscuit, either, but you know and I know that when you give me all them *ex*act numbers it's all guesswork anyhow. You don't know the odds on this beakrat anymore than I do.'

'I don't know the odds on *him*, Walker, but I know the odds on *me*. I'm sorry you don't like the way I sound so precise, but my crystal memory has every P-word I ever plumbed, which is to say I can give you exact to the third decimal percentages on when I hit it right on the first try after meeting the subject, and how many times I hit it right on the first try just from his curriculum vitae, and right now if I don't meet him and I go on just what I've got here you have a 48.838 percent chance I'll be right on my P-word first time and a 66.667 chance I'll be right with one out of three.'

Well that took him down, which was fine I must say because he loosened up my sphincters with that glass-smashing table-tossing hot-breath-in-my-face routine he did. He stepped back and put his hands in his pockets and leaned against the wall. 'Well I chose the right P-man, then, didn't I,' he says, but he doesn't smile, no, he *says* the back-down words but his eyes don't back down, his eyes say don't try to flash my face because I see through you, I got most excellent inward shades all polarized to keep out your glitz and see you straight and clear. I never saw eyes like that before. Like he knew me. Nobody ever knew me, and I didn't think he *really* knew me either, but I didn't like him looking at me as if he *thought* he knew me cause the fact is *I* didn't know me all that well and it worried me to think he might know me better than I did, if you catch my drift.

'All I have to do is be a little lost boy in a store,' I says.

'What if he isn't the kind who helps little lost boys?'

'Is he the kind who lets them cry?'

'I don't know. What if he is? What then? Think you can get away with meeting him a second time?'

'So the lost boy in the store won't work. I can crash my bicycle on his front lawn. I can try to sell him cable magazines.'

But he was ahead of me already. 'For the cable magazines he slams the door in your face, if he even comes to the door at all. For the bicycle crash, you're out of your little glass brain. I got my inside girl working on him right now, very complicated, because he's not the playing around kind, so she has to make this a real emotional come-on, like she's breaking up with a boyfriend and he's the only shoulder she can cry on, and his wife is so lucky to have a man like him. This much he can believe. But then suddenly he has this little boy crashing in his yard, and because he's paranoid, he begins to wonder if some weird rain isn't falling, right? I know he's paranoid because you don't get to his level in the fed without you know how to watch behind you and kill the enemy even before *they* know they're out to get you. So he even suspects, for one instant, that somebody's setting him up for something, and what does he do?'

I knew what Dogwalker was getting at now, and he was right, and so I let him have his victory and I let the words he wanted march out all in a row. 'He changes all his passwords, all his habits, and watches over his shoulder all the time.'

'And my little project turns into compost. No clean greens.'

So I saw for the first time why this street boy, this ex-pimp, why he was the one to do this job. He wasn't vertical like me, and he didn't have the inside hook like his fed boy, and he didn't have bumps in his sweater so he couldn't do the girl part, but he had eyes in his elbows, ears in his knees, by which I mean he noticed everything there was to notice and then he thought of new things that weren't even noticeable yet and noticed them. He earned his forty percent. And he earned part of my twenty, too.

Now while we waited around for the girl to fill Jesse's empty aching arms and get a finger off him, and while we were still working on how to get me to meet him slow and easy and sure, I spent a lot of time with Dogwalker. Not that he ever asked me, but I found myself looping his bus route every morning till he picked me up, or I'd be eating at Bojangle's when he came in to throw cajun chicken down into his ulcerated organs. I watched to make sure he didn't make sure he didn't mind, cause I didn't want to piss this boy, having once beheld the majesty of his wrath, but if he wanted to shiver me he gave me no shiv.

Even after a few days, when the ghosts of the cold hard street started haunting us, he didn't shake me, and that includes when Bellbottom says to him, 'Looks like you stopped walking dogs. Now you pimping little boys, right? Little cata-mites, we call you Catwalker now, that so? Or maybe you just keep him for private use, is that it? You be Boypoker now?' Well like I always said, somebody's going to kill Bellbottom just to flay him and use his skin for a convertible roof, but Dogwalker just waved and walked on by while I made little pissy bumps at Bell. Most people shake me right off when they start getting splashed on about liking little boys, but Doggy, he didn't say we were friends or nothing, but he didn't give me no Miami howdy, neither, which is to say I didn't find myself floating in the Bermuda Triangle with my ass pulled down around my ankles, by which I mean he wasn't ashamed to be seen with me on the street, which don't sound like a six-minute orgasm to you but to me it was like a breeze in August, I didn't ask for it and I don't trust it to last but as long as it's there I'm going to like it.

How I finally got to meet Jesse H. was dervish, the best I ever thought of. Which made me wonder why I never thought of it before, except that I never before had Dogwalker like a parrot saying 'stupid idea' every time I thought of something. By the time I finally got a plan that he didn't say 'stupid idea,' I was almost drowned in the deepest lightholes of my lucidity. I mean I was going at a hundred watts by the time I satisfied him.

First we found out who did babysitting for them when Jesse H. and Mrs. Jesse went out on the town (which for Nice People in G-boro means walking around the mall wishing there was something to do and then taking a piss in the public john). They had two regular teenage girls who usually came over and ignored their children for a fee, but when these darlettes were otherwise engaged, which meant they had a contract to get squeezed and poked by some half-zipped boy in exchange for a humbuger and a vid, they called upon Mother Hubbard's Homecare Hotline. So I most carefully assinuated myself into Mother Hubbard's estimable organization by passing myself off as a lamentably prepubic fourteen-year-old, specializing in the northwest section of town and on into the county. All this took a week, but Walker was in no hurry. Take the time to do it right, he said, if we hurry somebody's going to notice the blur of motion and look our way and just by looking at us they'll undo us. A horizontal mind that boy had.

Came a most delicious night when the Hunts went out to play, and both their diddle-girls were busy being squeezed most delectably (and didn't we have a lovely time persuading two toddle-boys to do the squeezing that very night). This news came to Mr. and Mrs. Jesse at the very last minute, and they had no choice but to call Mother Hubbard's, and isn't it lovely that just a half hour before, sweet little Stevie Queen, being moi, called in and said that he was available for baby-stomping after all. Ein and ein made zwei, and there I was being dropped off by a Mother Hubbard driver at the door of the Jesse Hunt house, whereupon I not only got to look upon the beatific face of Mr. Fed himself, I also got to have my dear head patted by Mrs. Fed, and then had the privilege of preparing little snacks for fussy Fed Jr. and foul-mouthed Fedene, the five-year-old and the three-year-old, while Microfed, the one-year-old (not yet human and, if I am any judge of character, not likely to live long enough to become such) sprayed uric acid in my face while I was diapering him. A good time was had by all.

Because of my heroic efforts, the small creatures were in their truckle beds quite early, and being a most fastidious baby-tucker, I browsed the house looking for burglars and stumbling, quite by chance, upon the most useful information about the beak-rat whose secret self-chosen name I was trying to learn. For one thing, he had set a watchful hair upon each of his bureau drawers, so that if I had been inclined to steal, he would know that unlawful access of his drawers had been attempted. I learned that he and his wife had separate containers of everything in the bathroom, even when they used the same brand of toothpaste, and it was he, not she, who took care of all their prophylactic activities (and not a moment too soon, thought I, for I had come to know their children). He was not the sort to use lubricants or little pleasure-giving ribs, either. Only the regulation government-issue hard-as-concrete rubber rafts for him, which suggested to my most pernicious mind that he had almost as much fun between the sheets as me.

I learned all kinds of joyful information, all of it trivial, all of it vital. I never know which of the threads I grasp are going to make connections deep within the lumens of my brightest caves. But I never before had the chance to wander unmolested through a person's own house when searching for his P-word. I saw the notes his children brought home from school, the magazines his family received, and more and more I began to see that Jesse H. Hunt barely touched his family at any point. He stood like a waterbug on the surface of life, without ever getting his feet wet. He could die, and if nobody tripped over the corpse it would be weeks before they noticed. And yet this was not because he did not care. It was because he was so very very careful. He examined everything, but through the wrong end of the microscope, so that it all became very small and far away. I was a sad little boy by the end of that night, and I whispered to Microfed that he should practice pissing in male faces, because that's the only way he would ever sink a hook into his daddy's face.

'What if he wants to take you home?' Dogwalker asked me, and I said, 'No way he would, nobody does that,' but Dogwalker made sure I had a place to go all the same, and sure enough, it was Doggy who got voltage and me who went limp. I ended riding in a beak-rat buggy, a genuine made-in-America rattletrap station wagon, and he took me to the for-sale house where Mama Pimple was waiting crossly for me and made Mr. Hunt go away because he kept me out too late. Then when the door was closed Mama Pimple giggled her gig and chuckled her chuck, and Walker himself wandered out of the back room and said, 'That's one less favor you owe me, Mama Pimple,' and she said, 'No, my dear boyoh, that's one more favor *you* owe *me*' and then they kissed a deep passionate kiss if you can believe it. Did you imagine anybody ever kissed Mama Pimple that way? Dogwalker is a boyful of shocks.

'Did you get all you needed?' he asks me.

'I have P-words dancing upward,' says I, 'and I'll have a name for you tomorrow in my sleep.'

'Hold onto it and don't tell me,' says Dogwalker. 'I don't want to hear a name until after we have his finger.'

That magical day was only hours away, because the girl — whose name I never knew and whose face I never saw — was to cast her spell over Mr. Fed the very next day. As Dogwalker said, this was no job for lingeree. The girl did not dress pretty and pretended to be lacking in the social graces, but she was a good little clerical who was going through a most distressing period in her private life, because she had undergone a premature hysterectomy, poor lass, or so she told Mr. Fed, and here she was losing her womanhood and she had never really felt like a woman at all. But he was so kind to her, for weeks he had been so kind, and Dogwalker told me afterward how he locked the door of his office for just a few minutes, and held her and kissed her to make her feel womanly, and once his fingers had all made their little impressions on the thin electrified plastic microcoating all over her lovely naked back and breasts, she began to cry and most gratefully informed him that she did not want him to be unfaithful to his wife for her sake, that he had already given her such a much of a lovely gift by being so kind and understanding, and she felt better thinking that a man like him could bear to touch her knowing she was defemmed inside, and now she thought she had the confidence to go on. A very convincing act, and one calculated to get his hot naked handprints without giving him a crisis of conscience that might change his face and give him a whole new set of possible Ps.

The microsheet got all his fingers from several angles, and so

Walker was able to dummy out a finger mask for our inside man within a single night. Right index. I looked at it most skeptically, I fear, because I had my doubts already dancing in the little lightpoints of my inmost mind. 'Just one finger?'

'All we get is one shot,' said Dogwalker. 'One single try.'

'But if he makes a mistake, if my first password isn't right, then he could use the middle finger on the second try.'

'Tell me, my vertical pricket, whether you think Jesse H. Hunt is the sort of burr oak rat who makes mistakes?'

To which I had to answer that he was not, and yet I had my misgivings and my misgivings all had to do with needing a second finger, and yet I am vertical, not horizontal, which means that I can see the present as deep as you please but the future's not mine to see, que sera, sera.

From what Doggy told me, I tried to imagine Mr. Fed's reaction to this nubile flesh that he had pressed. If he had poked as well as peeked, I think it would have changed his P-word, but when she told him that she would not want to compromise his uncompromising virtue, it reinforced him as a most regular or even regulation fellow and his name remained pronouncedly the same, and his P-word also did not change. 'InvictusXYZrwr,' quoth I to Dogwalker, for that was his veritable password, I knew it with more certainty than I had ever had before.

'Where in hell did you come up with that?' says he.

'If we knew how I did it, Walker, I'd never miss at all,' says I. 'I don't even know if it's in the goo or in the zoo. All the facts go down, and it all gets mixed around, and up come all these dancing P-words, little pieces of P.'

'Yeah but you don't just make it up, what does it mean?'

'Invictus is an old poem in a frame stuck in his bureau drawer, which his mama gave him when he was still a little fed-to-be. XYZ is his idea of randomizing, and rwr is the first U.S. President that he admired. I don't know why he chose these words now. Six weeks ago he was using a different P-word with a lot of numbers in it, and six weeks from now he'll change again, but right now —'

'Sixty percent sure?' asked Doggy.

'I give no percents this time,' says I. 'I've never roamed

through the bathroom of my subject before. But this or give me an assectomy, I've never been more sure.'

Now that he had the P-word, the inside guy began to wear his magic finger every day, looking for a chance to be alone in Mr. Fed's office. He had already created the preliminary files, like any routine green card requests, and buried them within his work area. All he needed was to go in, sign on as Mr. Fed, and then if the system accepted his name and P-word and finger, he could call up the files, approve them, and be gone within a minute. But he had to have that minute.

And on that wonderful magical day he had it. Mr. Fed had a meeting and his secretary sprung a leak a day early, and in went Inside Man with a perfectly legitimate note to leave for Hunt. He sat before the terminal, typed name and P-word and laid down his phony finger, and the machine spread wide its lovely legs and bid him enter. He had the files processed in forty seconds, laying down his finger for each green, then signed off and went on out. No sign, no sound that anything was wrong. As sweet as summertime, as smooth as ice, and all we had to do was sit and wait for green cards to come in the mail.

'Who you going to sell them to?' says I.

'I offer them to no one till I have clean greens in my hand,' says he. Because Dogwalker is careful. What happened was not because he was not careful.

Every day we walked to the ten places where the envelopes were supposed to come. We knew they wouldn't be there for a week — the wheels of government grind exceeding slow, for good or ill. Every day we checked with Inside Man, whose name and face I have already given you, much good it will do, since both are no doubt different by now. He told us every time that all was the same, nothing was changed, and he was telling the truth, for the fed was most lugubrious and palatial and gave no leaks that anything was wrong. Even Mr. Hunt himself did not know that aught was amiss in his little kingdom.

Yet even with no sign that I could name, I was jumpy every morning and sleepless every night. 'You walk like you got to use the toilet,' says Walker to me, and it is verily so. Something is wrong, I say to myself, something is most deeply wrong, but I cannot find the name for it even though I know, and so I say nothing, or I lie to myself and try to invent a reason for my fear. 'It's my big chance,' says I. 'To be twenty percent of rich.'

'Rich,' says he, 'not just a fifth.'

'Then you'll be double rich.'

And he just grins at me, being the strong and silent type.

'But then why don't you sell nine,' says I, 'and keep the other green? Then you'll have the money to pay for it, and the green to go where you want in all the world.'

But he just laughs at me and says, 'Silly boy, my dear sweet pinheaded lightbrained little friend. If someone sees a pimp like me passing a green, he'll tell a fed, because he'll know there's been a mistake. Green don't go to boys like me.'

'But you won't be dressed like a pimp,' says I, 'and you won't stay in pimp hotels.'

'I'm a low-class pimp,' he says again, 'and so however I dress that day, that's just the way pimps dress. And whatever hotel I go to, that's a low-class pimp hotel until I leave.'

'Pimping isn't some disease,' says I. 'It isn't in your gonads and it isn't in your genes. If your daddy was a Kroc and your mama was an Iacocca, you wouldn't be a pimp.'

'The hell I wouldn't,' says he. 'I'd just be a high-class pimp, like my mama and my daddy. Who do you think gets green cards? You can't sell no virgins on the street.'

I thought that he was wrong and I still do. If anybody could go from low to high in a week, it's Dogwalker. He could be anything and do anything, and that's the truth. Or almost anything. If he could do *anything* then his story would have a different ending. But it was not his fault. Unless you blame pigs because they can't fly. I was the vertical one, wasn't I? I should have named my suspicions and we wouldn't have passed those greens.

I held them in my hands, there in his little room, all ten of them when he spilled them on the bed. To celebrate he jumped up so high he smacked his head on the ceiling again and again, which made them ceiling tiles dance and flip over and spill dust all over the room. 'I flashed just one, a single one,' says he, 'and a cool million was what he said, and then I said what if ten? And he laughs and says fill in the check yourself.'

'We should test them,' says I.

'We can't test them,' he says. 'The only way to test it is to use it, and if you use it then your print and face are in its memory forever and so we could never sell it.'

'Then sell one, and make sure it's clean.'

'A package deal,' he says. 'If I sell one, and they think I got more but I'm holding out to raise the price, then I may not live to collect for the other nine, because I might have an accident and lose these little babies. I sell all ten tonight at once, and then I'm out of the green card business for life.'

But more than ever that night I am afraid, he's out selling those greens to those sweet gentlebodies who are commonly referred to as Organic Crime, and there I am on his bed, shivering and dreaming because I know that something will go most deeply wrong but I still don't know what and I still don't know why. I keep telling myself, You're only afraid because nothing could ever go so right for you, you can't believe that anything could ever make you rich and safe. I say this stuff so much that I believe that I believe it, but I don't really, not down deep, and so I shiver again and finally I cry, because after all my body still believes I'm nine, and nine-year-olds have tear ducts very easy of access, no password required. Well he comes in late that night, and I'm asleep he thinks, and so he walks quiet instead of dancing, but I can hear the dancing in his little sounds, I know he has the money all safely in the bank, and so when he leans over to make sure if I'm asleep, I say, 'Could I borrow a hundred thou?'

So he slaps me and he laughs and dances and sings, and I try to go along, you bet I do, I know I should be happy, but then at the end he says, 'You just can't take it, can you? You just can't handle it,' and then I cry all over again, and he just puts his arm around me like a movie dad and gives me play-punches on the head and says, 'I'm gonna marry me a wife, I am, maybe even Mama Pimple herself, and we'll adopt you and have a little spielberg family in Summerfield, with a riding mower on a real grass lawn.'

'I'm older than you *or* Mama Pimple,' says I, but he just laughs. Laughs and hugs me until he thinks that I'm all right. Don't go home, he says to me that night, but home I got to go, because I know I'll cry again, from fear or something, anyway, and I don't want him to think his cure wasn't permanent. 'No thanks,' says I, but he just laughs at me. 'Stay here and cry all you want to, Goo Boy, but don't go home tonight. I don't want to be alone tonight, and sure as hell you don't either.' And so I slept between his sheets, like with a brother, him punching and tickling and pinching and telling dirty jokes about his whores, the most good and natural night I spent in all my life, with a true friend, which I know you don't believe, snickering and nickering and ickering your filthy little thoughts, there was no holes plugged that night because nobody was out to take pleasure from nobody else, just Dogwalker being happy and wanting me not to be so sad.

And after he was asleep, I wanted so bad to know who it was he sold them to, so I could call them up and say, 'Don't use those greens, cause they aren't clean. I don't know how, I don't know why, but the feds are onto this, I know they are, and if you use those cards they'll nail your fingers to your face.' But if I called would they believe me? They were careful too. Why else did it take a week? They had one of their nothing goons use a card to make sure it had no squeaks or leaks, and it came up clean. Only then did they give the cards to seven big boys, with two held in reserve. Even Organic Crime, the All-seeing Eye, passed those cards same as we did.

I think maybe Dogwalker was a little bit vertical too. I think he knew same as me that something was wrong with this. That's why he kept checking back with the inside man, cause he didn't trust how good it was. That's why he didn't spend any of his share. We'd sit there eating the same old schlock, out of his cut from some leg job or my piece from a data wipe, and every now and then he'd say, 'Rich man's food sure tastes good.' Or maybe even though he wasn't vertical he still thought maybe I was right when I thought something was wrong. Whatever he thought, though, it just kept getting worse and worse for me, until the morning when we went to see the inside man and the inside man was gone.

Gone clean. Gone like he never existed. His apartment for rent, cleaned out floor to ceiling. A phone call to the fed, and he was on vacation, which meant they had him, he wasn't just moved to another house with his newfound wealth. We stood there in his empty place, his shabby empty hovel that was ten times better than anywhere we ever lived, and Doggy says to me, real quiet, he says, 'What was it? What did I do wrong? I thought I was like Hunt, I thought I never made a single mistake in this job, in this one job.'

And that was it, right then I knew. Not a week before, not when it would do any good. Right then I finally knew it all, knew what Hunt had done. Jesse Hunt never made *mistakes*. But he was also so paranoid that he haired his bureau to see if the babysitter stole from him. So even though he would never *accidentally* enter the wrong P-word, he was just the kind who would do it *on purpose*. 'He doublefingered every time,' I says to Dog. 'He's so damn careful he does his password wrong the first time every time, and then comes in on his second finger.'

'So one time he comes in on the first try, so what?' He says this because he doesn't know computers like I do, being half-glass myself.

'The system knew the pattern, that's what. Jesse H. is so precise he never changed a bit, so when *we* came in on the first try, that set off alarms. It's my fault, Dog, I knew how crazy paranoidical he is, I knew that something was wrong, but not till this minute I didn't know what it was. I should have known it when I got his password, I should have known, I'm sorry, you never should have gotten me into this, I'm sorry, you should have listened to me when I told you something was wrong, I should have known, I'm sorry.'

What I done to Doggy that I never meant to do. What I done to him! Anytime, I could have thought of it, it was all there inside my glassy little head, but no, I didn't think of it till after it was way too late. And maybe it's because I didn't want to think of it, maybe it's because I really wanted to be wrong about the green cards, but however it flew, I did what I do, which is to say I'm not the pontiff in his fancy chair, by which I mean I can't be smarter than myself.

Right away he called the gentlebens of Ossified Crime to warn them, but I was already plugged into the library sucking news as fast as I could and so I knew it wouldn't do no good, cause they got all seven of the big boys and their nitwit taster, too, locked up good and tight for card fraud.

And what they said on the phone to Dogwalker made things real clear. 'We're dead,' says Doggy.

'Give them time to cool,' says I.

'They'll never cool,' says he. 'There's no chance, they'll never forgive this even if they know the whole truth, because look at the names they gave the cards to, like they got them for their biggest boys on the borderline, the habibs who bribe presidents of little countries and rake off cash from octopods like Shell and ITT and every now and then kill somebody and walk away clean. Now they're sitting there in jail with the whole life story of the organization in their brains, so they don't care if we meant to do it or not. They're hurting, and the only way they know to make the hurt go away is to pass it on to somebody else. And that's us. They want to make us hurt, and hurt real bad, and for a long long time.'

I never saw Dog so scared. That's the only reason we went to the feds ourselves. We didn't ever want to stool, but we needed their protection plan, it was our only hope. So we offered to testify how we did it, not even for immunity, just so they'd change our faces and put us in a safe jail somewhere to work off the sentence and come out alive, you know? That's all we wanted.

But the feds, they laughed at us. They had the inside guy, see, and he was going to get immunity for testifying. 'We don't need you,' they says to us, 'and we don't care if you go to jail or not. It was the big guys we wanted.'

'If you let us walk,' says Doggy, 'then they'll think we set them up.'

'Make us laugh,' says the feds. 'Us work with street poots like you? They know that we don't stoop so low.'

'They bought from us,' says Doggy. 'If we're big enough for them, we're big enough for the dongs.'

'Do you believe this?' says one fed to his identical junior officer. 'These jollies are begging us to take them into jail. Well listen tight, my jolly boys, maybe we don't want to add you to the taxpayers' expense account, did you think of that? Besides, all we'd give you is time, but on the street, those boys will give you time and a half, and it won't cost us a dime.'

So what could we do? Doggy just looks like somebody sucked out six pints, he's so white. On the way out of the fedhouse, he says, 'Now we're going to find out what it's like to die.'

And I says to him, 'Walker, they stuck no gun in your mouth yet, they shove no shiv in your eye. We still breathing, we got legs, so let's *walk* out of here.'

'Walk!' he says. 'You walk out of G-boro, glasshead, and you bump into trees.'

'So what?' says I. 'I can plug in and pull out all the data we want about how to live in the woods. Lots of empty land out there. Where do you think the marijuana grows?'

'I'm a city boy,' he says. 'I'm a city boy.' Now we're standing out in front, and he's looking around. 'In the city I got a chance, I know the city.'

'Maybe in New York or Dallas,' says, I, 'but G-boro's just too small, not even half a million people, you can't lose yourself deep enough here.'

'Yeah well,' he says, still looking around. 'It's none of your business now anyway, Goo Boy. They aren't blaming *you*, they're blaming *me*.'

'But it's my fault,' says I, 'and I'm staying with you to tell them so.'

'You think they're going to stop and listen?' says he.

'I'll let them shoot me up with speakeasy so they know I'm telling the truth.'

'It's nobody's fault,' says he. 'And I don't give a twelve-inch poker whose fault it is anyway. You're clean, but if you stay with me you'll get all muddy, too. I don't need you around, and you sure as hell don't need me. Job's over. Done. Get lost.'

But I couldn't do that. The same way he couldn't go on walking dogs, I couldn't just run off and leave him to eat my mistake. 'They know I was your P-word man,' says I. 'They'll be after me, too.'

'Maybe for a while, Goo Boy. But you transfer your twenty percent into Bobby Joe's Face Shop, so they aren't looking for you to get a refund, and then stay quiet for a week and they'll forget all about you.'

He's right but I don't care. 'I was in for twenty percent of rich,' says I. 'So I'm in for fifty percent of trouble.'

All of a sudden he sees what he's looking for. 'There they are, Goo Boy, the dorks they sent to hit me. In that Mercedes.' I look but all I see are electrics. Then his hand is on my back and he gives me a shove that takes me right off the portico and into the bushes, and by the time I crawl out, Doggy's nowhere in sight. For about a minute I'm pissed about getting scratched up in the plants, until I realize he was getting me out of the way, so I wouldn't get shot down or hacked up or lased out, whatever it is they planned to do to him to get even.

I was safe enough, right? I should've walked away, I should've ducked right out of the city. I didn't even have to refund the money. I had enough to go clear out of the country and live the rest of my life where even Occipital Crime couldn't find me.

And I thought about it. I stayed the night in Mama Pimple's flophouse because I knew somebody would be watching my own place. All that night I thought about places I could go. Australia. New Zealand. Or even a foreign place, I could afford a good vocabulary crystal so picking up a new language would be easy.

But in the morning I couldn't do it. Mama Pimple didn't exactly ask me but she looked so worried and all I could say was, 'He pushed me into the bushes and I don't know where he is.'

And she just nods at me and goes back to fixing breakfast. Her hands are shaking she's so upset. Because she knows that Dogwalker doesn't stand a chance against Orphan Crime.

'I'm sorry,' says I.

'What can you do?' she says. 'When they want you, they get you. If the feds don't give you a new face, you can't hide.'

'What if they didn't want him?' says I.

She laughs at me. 'The story's all over the street. The arrests were in the news, and now everybody knows the big boys are looking for Walker. They want him so bad the whole street can smell it.'

'What if they knew it wasn't his fault?' says I. 'What if they knew it was an accident? A mistake?'

Then Mama Pimple squints at me — not many people can

tell when she's squinting, but I can — and she says, 'Only one boy can tell them that so they'll believe it.'

'Sure, I know,' says I.

'And if that boy walks in and says, Let me tell you why you don't want to hurt my friend Dogwalker —'

'Nobody said life was safe,' I says. 'Besides, what could they do to me that's worse than what already happened to me when I was nine?'

She comes over and just puts her hand on my head, just lets her hand lie there for a few minutes, and I know what I've got to do.

So I did it. Went to Fat Jack's and told him I wanted to talk to Junior Mint about Dogwalker, and it wasn't thirty seconds before I was hustled on out into the alley, and driven somewhere with my face mashed into the floor of the car so I couldn't tell where it was. Idiots didn't know that somebody as vertical as me can tell the number of wheel revolutions and the exact trajectory of every curve. I could've drawn a freehand map of where they took me. But if I let them know that, I'd never come home, and since there was a good chance I'd end up dosed with speakeasy, I went ahead and erased the memory. Good thing I did — that was the first thing they asked me as soon as they had the drug in me.

Gave me a grown-up dose, they did, so I practically told them my whole life story and my opinion of them and everybody and everything else, so the whole session took hours, felt like forever, but at the end they knew, they absolutely knew that Dogwalker was straight with them, and when it was over and I was coming up so I had some control over what I said, I asked them, I begged them, Let Dogwalker live. Just let him go. He'll give back the money, and I'll give back mine, just let him go.

'Okay,' says the guy.

I didn't believe it.

'No, you can believe me, we'll let him go.'

'You got him?'

'Picked him up before you even came in. It wasn't hard.'

'And you didn't kill him?'

'Kill him? We had to get the money back first, didn't we, so we needed him alive till morning, and then you came in, and your little story changed our minds, it really did, you made us feel all sloppy and sorry for that poor old pimp.'

For a few seconds there I actually believed that it was going to be all right. But then I knew from the way they looked, from the way they acted, I knew the same way I know about passwords.

They brought in Dogwalker and handed me a book. Dogwalker was very quiet and stiff and he didn't look like he recognized me at all. I didn't even have to look at the book to know what it was. They scooped out his brain and replaced it with glass, like me only way over the line, way way over, there was nothing of Dogwalker left inside his head, just glass pipe and goo. The book was a User's Manual, with all the instructions about how to program him and control him.

I looked at him and he was Dogwalker, the same face, the same hair, everything. Then he moved or talked and he was dead, he was somebody else living in Dogwalker's body. And I says to them, 'Why? Why didn't you just kill him, if you were going to do this?'

'This one was too big,' says the guy. 'Everybody in G-boro knew what happened, everybody in the whole country, everybody in the world. Even if it was a mistake, we couldn't let it go. No hard feelings, Goo Boy. He *is* alive. And so are you. And you both stay that way, as long as you follow a few simple rules. Since he's over the line, he has to have an owner, and you're it. You can use him however you want — rent out data storage, pimp him as a jig or a jaw — but he stays with you always. Every day, he's on the street here in G-boro, so we can bring people here and show them what happens to boys who make mistakes. You can even keep your cut from the job, so you don't have to scramble at all if you don't want to. That's how much we like you, Goo Boy. But if he leaves this town or doesn't come out, even one single solitary day, you'll be very sorry for the last six hours of your life. Do you understand?'

I understood. I took him with me. I bought this place, these clothes, and that's how it's been ever since. That's why we go out on the street every day. I read the whole manual, and I figure there's maybe ten percent of Dogwalker left inside. The part that's Dogwalker can't ever get to the surface, can't ever talk or move or anything like that, can't ever remember or even consciously think. But maybe he can still wander around inside what used to be his head, maybe he can sample the data stored in all that goo. Maybe someday he'll even run across this story and he'll know what happened to him, and he'll know that I tried to save him.

In the meantime this is my last will and testament. See, I have us doing all kinds of research on Orgasmic Crime, so that someday I'll know enough to reach inside the system and unplug it. Unplug it all, and make those bastards lose everything, the way they took everything away from Dogwalker. Trouble is, some places there ain't no way to look without leaving tracks. Goo is as goo do, I always say. I'll find out I'm not as good as I think I am when somebody comes along and puts a hot steel putz in my face. Knock my brains out when it comes. But there's this, lying in a few hundred places in the system. Three days after I don't lay down my code in a certain program in a certain place, this story pops into view. The fact you're reading this means I'm dead.

Or it means I paid them back, and so I quit suppressing this cause I don't care anymore. So maybe this is my swan song, and maybe this is my victory song. You'll never know, will you, mate?

But you'll wonder. I like that. You wondering about us, whoever you are, you thinking about old Goo Boy and Dogwalker, you guessing whether the fangs who scooped Doggy's skull and turned him into self-propelled property paid for it down to the very last delicious little drop.

And in the meantime, I've got this goo machine to take care of. Only ten percent a man, he is, but then I'm only forty percent myself. All added up together we make only half a man. But that's the half that counts. That's the half that still wants things. The goo in me and the goo in him is all just light pipes and electricity. Data without desire. Lightspeed trash. But I have some desires left, just a few, and maybe so does Dogwalker, even fewer. And we'll get what we want. We'll get it all. Every speck. Every sparkle. Believe it.

RICHARD PAUL RUSSO

Richard Paul Russo's first two stories were published in 1979, in a small literary magazine called *The Reed*. A few other stories followed, but it was not until 1986 that he began to publish regularly. He has sold seventeen stories to magazines such as *Isaac Asimov's Science Fiction Magazine, Twilight Zone, The Magazine of Fantasy and Science Fiction* and *The Gate* and anthologies such as *In the Field of Fire* and *Pulphouse*. His first novel was *Inner Eclipse*, published in 1988; the second, *Subterranean Gallery*, appeared the following year — and won the Philip K. Dick Award; he is currently at work on a third.

Like several other authors in the *Yearbook* series, Russo is a graduate of the Clarion sf writers' workshop. He lives in Cannon Beach, Oregon.

He has little to say about the story which follows except that it 'is a personal favourite of mine.'

LUNAR TRIPTYCH:
EMBRACING THE NIGHT
by
RICHARD PAUL RUSSO

SIDE PANEL

You must not embrace the night, Karyn said.

Carter did not understand. In part, she was telling him to stay on Earth, to stay off the shuttles; but there was little chance of spaceflight for him, or anyone, in the near future, and they had been through all that before. So what was she trying to tell him now?

Carter stepped out onto the apartment balcony and looked up into the night sky. He left the sliding door open so Karyn could follow, but he knew she would stay inside. For seven and a half weeks now Karyn had not once left the apartment unless the sun was out, the sky clear and blue without a trace of cloud.

Far to the west, across the open plaza and just above the lowest building of the apartment complex, Carter could see the lights of the gantry blinking in the warm night air, flickering like the stars overhead. He sat in the chair nearest the railing, where he could look down at the smallest of the plaza's three pools, five stories directly below him. Although it was close to midnight, a lone figure swam steadily back and forth, in and out of the cone of light from the underwater lamp. The swimmer — a woman, he thought — did not slow or miss a beat, even when making the smooth flip-turns at each end of the pool. Perfectly at home in the water, even though not born to it.

Maybe that was the analogy he needed for his testimony at the Congressional hearings, Carter thought. That there were people, like the swimmer, always at home in the water, while others never were. The same should be true of outer space, he believed, and he could see no reason for halting manned space exploration because of those who could *not* go into space. The answer was to go on with those who could.

Carter's hand reached to his empty shirt pocket, a reflex action that remained even after four years. Right now he wished he still smoked. His hands wanted something to do.

'Are you coming to bed?' Karyn asked.

Carter turned to look through the open doorway at her. Fair-haired, fair-skinned, she was already between the white sheets, wrapped in a heavy flannel nightgown and propped against the headboard, the white spread pulled up over her bent knees. One of the two lamps on the stand beside her was lit, and she reached over to switch on the other.

Karyn would not even sleep in the dark any more. At night there was at least one light on in each room of the apartment, illuminating her noctural wanderings which were growing more frequent; she rarely slept the night through now. Two weeks earlier, when she had only a single lamp on the nightstand, the bulb had gone out at three in the morning, plunging the room into darkness. Karyn had jerked up convulsively, instantly awake and screaming. Her screams had continued until Carter managed to retrieve the living room lamp and plug it in, returning light to the bedroom. Now Karyn slept with two lamps next to her, spare bulbs in easy reach.

Carter turned back to look down at the pool. But the swimmer had emerged from the water and now sat in a lounge chair, looking up at him, wearing dark sunglasses. He felt certain it was the same woman he had seen around the complex lately, often enough so it seemed she was following him. With black hair, and always wearing the sunglasses, she only appeared at night. Maybe she thought the darkness and the sunglasses gave her some kind of protection. She never spoke to him, but when he encountered her she watched him continuously, her head turning to follow wherever he went, and he wished that just once he could see her eyes.

He watched the woman a few moments longer, her face still directed up towards him, glanced once more at the gantry lights in the distance, then stood and went inside.

'You *are* going to testify tomorrow, aren't you?' Karyn asked as he got into bed next to her.

'Yes.'

She sighed heavily, shook her head. 'It doesn't much

matter,' she said. 'Your testimony won't help anyway, it's too late now, the verdict's almost in.'

'Probably so.'

There was a long silence, and they lay beside each other without touching. Carter could not remember the last time they had made love. It had been back in their house in Massachusetts, that was all he knew. Not once since they had moved out here and into this apartment.

'The eternal night,' Karyn whispered. 'We aren't meant to join it.'

Carter rolled onto his side and looked at her. This was new, like what she had said earlier. She was beginning to sound like a newly converted mystic.

'Can't you see the pattern, Carter? All the problems, the accidents, the mechanical failures, the nervous breakdowns, and now the collapse of the Mars Expedition. They'll go on, growing worse all the time until we stop trying, until we realize we belong here, only on Earth. Until we stop trying to leave.'

Carter did not know what to say. He had heard the same ideas before; they had all heard them, more often in recent weeks. Voiced by what NASA liked to call the 'lunatic fringe.' For a while it had been a kind of in joke. Luna, lunatic. But with the Congressional hearings nearly concluded, and the effective demise of NASA practically a foregone conclusion, the joke had quickly palled.

He turned over and looked out through the glass door, unable to see much of the night with the two lamps burning brightly behind him. He tried to sleep, but his eyes remained open, and he began to wish he had sunglasses of his own to shade his eyes as he searched for sleep, for signs of the night sky.

CENTER PANEL

Two nights after the Congressional hearings had ended, there was an enormous outdoor party at the apartment complex, celebrating the end of NASA and manned exploration of space. Residents and invited guests only were permitted, but still Carter guessed there were nearly six hundred people milling around the main pool and through the lush plaza lit by a hundred burning torches, dancing on the large cement patios to the loud music of a local rock band. The music was techno-punk, complete with rainbowed lasers blazing forth from the instruments. Carter stood at the balcony railing, watching, and wondered how all these people, many of whom would soon be losing their jobs, could be so happy.

He turned and looked into the bedroom through the screen door at Karyn, who sat in a corner chair reading.

'You want to go down to the party?' he asked, knowing she wouldn't. 'This ought to be your victory celebration.'

She looked up at him, but didn't respond. Carter shrugged and opened the screen door, stepped inside. 'I'm going down,' he said. He slid the door shut and started towards the hall.

'Wait,'she said, 'Before you go . . .'

Carter stopped, turned, and leaned against the wall, watching her.

'I've lost you, Carter.'

Yes, he thought, a long time ago, though he had not really known it, or known why. 'Do you really want me?' he asked.

'Not any more. We've become too . . . different.'

No, we've always been different, we just never saw it. But he did not say anything.

'I wanted to wait until the hearings were finished,' she said. 'Until you were done. I've already talked to an attorney. I told him I didn't think there would be any problems, any fighting. That it would be an amicable divorce.'

He looked at her for a long time without speaking, then nodded once. 'All right,' he said.

'I want the house.'

He nodded again. 'It's yours.' he paused for a moment, then added, 'The kids, too.'

She turned away from him, her fingers trembling for a moment before she clasped her hands together. They had no children.

'I'm sorry,' he said, meaning it.

She breathed deeply twice. 'You can have the car.' Another pause, another deep breath. 'I'm leaving tomorrow morning. Will you drive me to the train station?'

'Of course.'

She looked back at him. 'What will you do now, Carter?

Your job won't last much longer.'

He shrugged. 'I really don't know.'

Karyn nodded, returned her attention to her book, and said no more. So simple, Carter thought. He turned away from her and walked out.

At the edge of the plaza, Carter hesitated a moment, then pushed into the crowd. He welcomed the press of people, the feel of bodies in motion and close contact, flesh touching flesh. He breathed deeply, inhaling the aroma of sweat and smoke and pot, alcohol and perfume, the gas-like smell of the torches. The babble of the crowd was almost as loud as the band, and the noise, too, he relished. He felt lost and anonymous, and was content.

Carter passed one of the open bars and squeezed up to the counter, where he ordered scotch on the rocks. Drink in hand, he pushed back into the crowd. As he neared the elevated stage, the music and singing from the band became more distinct. Surprisingly, some of the lyrics were intelligible, though shouted rapidly, almost erupting from the singer's mouth. He caught the words 'silver' and 'light' and 'sucking illusions,' and the word 'night' repeated several times, but he could never quite make any sense of what he heard.

A hand gripped his shoulder, pulled him around. Carter found himself staring into dark sunglasses reflecting torchlight directly back at him. The woman.

She smiled, hooked her arm through his, and led him through the crowd. He didn't resist, too curious. She was dressed in a short, dark jumper, her legs bare, her feet in white ballet skippers. As they passed another of the bars, Carter quickly finished his drink and set the empty glass on the counter.

The woman led the way towards the lobby of the south building. The security guard, recognizing them both, let them through without a word. When the door closed behind them, a heavy quiet filled the lobby.

They stood in front of the elevator doors, waiting. Her glasses were so dark and mirrored he could not see her eyes, only a doubled, distorted version of himself reflected back at him.

'My name is Carter,' he said.

'I know. Carter Strang. I'm Nicole.'

'How do you know me?'

The elevator opened, Nicole smiled, and they stepped inside. Nicole touched the sixth floor circle, which lit up a pale orange. She leaned back against the elevator wall, looking at him, and they began to rise.

'I know you,' she said. 'You've shot up. To the stations, to Luna.'

She made it sound like a drug trip. Maybe that was how she saw it.

'I follow all the astronauts,' she went on. 'All who leave this prison and sail up into the night.'

Carter started to protest, then said nothing. He never thought of himself as an astronaut. He was a head psychologist for NASA, so he had made seven previous trips off Earth — four tours of the stations and three trips to Luna. But people like Nicole saw them all as astronauts, and it would not matter what he said to her about it.

They stopped at the sixth floor and the elevator doors slid apart. Carter hesitated before leaving the elevator; he was beginning to realize what she was. But something, simple curiosity perhaps, continued to draw him, and he followed her along the hall.

'I watched the hearings on TV,' Nicole said. 'I watched when you talked. They didn't listen to you, but I did, and *I* understood what you were trying to tell them.'

Carter wasn't so sure he had understood himself, and almost asked her to explain it to him, but he didn't. At the fifth door on the right, Nicole stopped and inserted a key. Before she turned it she reached out with her other hand and took his arm.

'Quickly, please,' she said. She turned the key and opened the door just enough to reach inside. Carter could see that the interior of the apartment was brightly lit, but only for a moment. Nicole's hand touched a switch, the apartment went dark, and she pulled him inside, closing the door behind them.

Points of fluorescent light, thousands of them like stars in the night sky, were everywhere. Walls, ceiling, furniture, even the floor sparkled with the tiny pinpoints of silver. Although he did not recognize any constellations, Carter would not have been surprised to see one.

There was enough light from all the flourescent dots to barely make out furniture outlines, to see Nicole just a foot away. She faced him and slowly removed her sunglasses. He had expected her eyes to be something special, shining with a strange, dazzling light, but they appeared to be quite ordinary. In the darkness he could not make out their color.

'What you were saying was so right,' she said. 'About some people being at home in the water, and some being terrified of it no matter how well they swam, and how that's how it is with space, that some people can't handle it, but that some people *can*, that some people might even be more at home in space than on Earth. *I* understand. *I* believe you're right, because I think that that's where I belong, out in deep space among all the stars.'

She took his hand and gently guided him along the short hall into the bedroom. He knew he should leave, perhaps should never have come in at all but he was still too curious.

The bedroom was like the rest of the apartment, dark and filled with stars. Carter had trouble maintaining his balance, his referents hazy, almost invisible — he felt cast adrift, loose and without moorings.

In front of the sliding glass door that led out onto the balcony was a telescope. It was directed slightly downward and to the east. Carter walked unsteadily to it and looked into the eye piece.

As he expected, the telescope was trained on the balcony of his apartment. He could see the bright glow emanating from the bedroom, and wondered if Karyn was still reading, or sleeping . . . or packing to leave the next morning.

'Come here,' Nicole whispered.

Carter turned toward her, shaking his head. It was time to go.

Nicole reached for him, a dark phantom, and he backed away, jostling the telescope. He turned from her and, still disoriented, staggered out of he bedroom. His lungs seemed to tighten, cutting his breath, and he bumped into walls twice moving along the hallway.

'Carter, come back,' Nicole called, little more than a whisper.

He stumbled through the front room, crashed into a chair, then found the front door and opened it. He stepped out into the light of the hall, closed the door quickly behind him and leaned against it, breathing heavily.

The terrible thing was, he *did* want to go back to her, despite the dizziness, despite the fear. But he couldn't. Not yet.

After a minute or two his breathing was almost back to normal, his balance steady. Surprised that Nicole had not followed him, but relieved, Carter pushed away from the door and started slowly down the hall.

Emerging from the elevator and into the lobby, Carter saw a vaguely familiar man dressed in a dark suit seated in one of the chairs near the street entrance. The man stood — he was tall and large with sandy, gray-streaked hair — and casually approached. His tie was loose, top shirt button undone.

'Carter Strang? I'm William Knopfler, with the Defense Department.' He put out his hand. 'We've met once before.'

'I think twice, actually,' Carter said. They shook hands. 'And I believe I saw you at the hearings.'

'I was extremely interested in what you had to say.'

'No one else was.'

Knopfler smiled. 'Let's go for a walk. I'd like to talk to you.'

'What about?'

'A job. You're probably going to need one soon.' The smile didn't falter. Carter gave Knopfler a half smile in return, and nodded.

Knopfler led the way out through the street entrance, into warm fresh air and relative quiet. The sounds of the party were muted, distant, and street traffic was light, just an occasional car or truck driving slowly past. They began walking along the sidewalk around the complex, silent at first, but eventually Knopfler started speaking.

'What interested me was your idea about people having an ingrained affinity, established either by genetics or early life, for a specific environment. Also the converse, that people have ingrained antipathies to different environments. Of particular interest was the notion that these affinities and antipathies, especially subtle and complex variants thereof — things much more delicate and specific, for example, than simple claustrophobia — can be detected and identified through more refined, precise, and extensive procedures than currently exist.'

Knopfler paused, and Carter felt he was waiting for a response. He looked up at the sky, but though there were no clouds, the stars were dimmed by the rising glow of the city lights.

'As you say, it's just a notion.' Carter shrugged. 'I've never really had the opportunity to develop anything along those lines. And as the committee chairperson pointed out so emphatically, I do not really have any empirical evidence to support my ideas. A notion, yes. Nothing more.'

'Just a gut feeling?' Knopfler offered.

'I suppose.'

They passed a break in the buildings, where a gate led into the plaza, and for a few moments the noise increased, then gradually faded again.

'Several of my colleagues and I give your ideas much credence, however, and we would like you to work for us.'

'Why? Manned space flight will be effectively defunct, at least for the next few years. Unless you're looking at long term . . .'

Knopfler shook his head. 'We aren't interested in space flight. We're not interested in space at all, not from a human standpoint.' He paused to light a cigarette, but did not offer one to Carter. 'We have recently developed new high-tech fighting suits for our infantry. You may have heard something about them.'

'Something, yes.'

'They are completely self-enclosed, self-contained, computer-monitored, designed to be worn around the clock for days at a time, even weeks. We've done extensive testing in labs, on domestic bases and training grounds, testing of both the suits and the soldiers, and now we've begun field testing in the jungles of Guatemala.' Knopfler paused, inhaled on his cigarette. 'Frankly, we've had a few problems not unlike those encountered by the Mars Expedition. The Rigger syndrome, some have started to call it. The men we've sent into the field, none of them have claustrophobia, all of them have spent at least two continuous weeks during training inside the suits without once breaking the body or helmet seals, and all with no adverse effects, no panic reactions, nothing like that. And yet, some of them, within hours of being dropped into the jungle inside their suits, have . . . fallen apart. Panic reactions, auditory and visual hallucinations, complete breakdowns. Nothing like a majority, just a few here and there. But a significant number. I'm sure you can understand that we cannot afford that happening in actual military operations.'

Knopfler stopped, apparently finished, and they continued their circuit of the complex in silence for some time.

'And what is it you want from me?' Carter finally asked.

'We want you to develop a testing and evaluation program along the lines of what you suggested for the space program, capable of identifying those who will thrive in the fighting suits under various conditions — jungle, desert, mountains, snow, urban centers — and those who will not. We offer you a position with complete freedom, choice of staff, whatever facilities you require. There will be large financial and technical resources at your disposal. You will be allowed essentially to do whatever you want, explore any lines of research you wish, within reason.' Knopfler smiled. 'What more could you ask for?'

'Why have you come here to talk to me?' Carter asked. 'Why tonight?'

'We've tried reaching you at your office. You haven't shown there since the hearings. We are under some time pressure, to produce success. The problems in the field have, on occasion, been serious. We have had . . . a few deaths. As you are more aware than most, money is becoming difficult for everyone, and mistakes and failures are not much tolerated. We, too, are in danger of losing funding for this program, and we'd like your assistance as soon as possible. In fact, if you accept, we will want to fly you into Guatemala immediately.'

They had completed the circuit and now stopped, once again at the street entrance to the south building. Knopfler dropped his cigarette to the cement, crushed it with a brief twisting motion of his shoe.

'I'll need time to think about it,' Carter said.

'Of course. I don't expect an answer tonight. But tomorrow would be best.'

Carter nodded. The entire proposition seemed absurd to him, but he could not tell Knopfler that.

Knopfler handed him a white card with only his name and two telephone numbers. 'Any time, day or night.'

Carter nodded again, pocketed the card. They shook hands, the Knopfler turned and strode down the street without another word. Carter remained in front of the building and listened to the crisp, regular footsteps retreat into the night.

Carter walked through the hushed quiet of the lobby, then opened the door to the blast of sound from the party still going strong. He continued along a short stretch of empty cobblestone, and pushed his way back into the throng.

If anything, there were more people now than before, and Carter could hardly move of his own accord. Instead, he let the flow and surge of the crowd guide him randomly about the plaza, and he was reminded of film clips he'd seen of Carnival in Rio. The band had cranked up the amps another notch or two, but still only barely managed to overcome the shouts and laughter of the crowd.

Somehow he ended up with a drink in his hand, scotch fortunately, and he sipped at it as he was bumped and shoved along. Near the main pool, the crush eased, then broke up completely leaving a perimeter of relatively clear space around the pool's edge. People sat in pool chairs, lay on chaise longues, talking and drinking and laughing. Carter squeezed free of the crowd and wandered among the chairs until he spotted an empty one and sat on it. Next to him, two people squirmed about inside a sleeping bag, only the tips of their heads visible.

A roar welled up to his right, and when Carter turned to look, he saw a giant ball, ten or twelve feet in diameter, bouncing slowly up and down along a jungle of upraised hands. The ball was gray, with patterns and words he could not yet distinguish. It looked like the kind of giant inflated ball he had first seen as a kid at an Earth Day Festival, a hippie holdover celebration his mother had taken him to once. Then, the large, stitched leather ball filled with air had been called an Earth Ball, and had been painted with swirls and slashes of bright colors. But as this gray Earth Ball rolled and bobbed closer, Carter saw that it had been painted with craters and maria to resemble the moon. Graffiti had been added, slogans of the protesters who had marched outside the gates of the launch fields day after day for the last few months — NO MORE $$ FOR $PACE; YANKEE STAY HOME; STOP ASKING FOR THE MOON!

The people lost control of the ball, and it began rolling over them towards the pool, gradually picking up speed though hands shot into the air to try to stop it. Near the edge of the crowd a few people were knocked to the ground by the weight and momentum of the ball as it struck them and tumbled to the ground. It bounced across several chairs, jolting people and spilling drinks, then rolled into the pool with a splash. A cheer erupted as the large, gray ball floated serenely about the pool.

Carter finished his drink, set the glass under his chair, and was about to get up when a gunshot sounded from nearby. A few cries cut the air, then gradually transformed into laughter and more cheers as air hissed out of the new hole in the ball. Carter remained in the chair and watched the Moon Ball slowly deflate until it was just a limp, bulging mass floating listlessly across the surface of the water.

Carter got up from the chair and slowly worked his way towards his building, searching the faces around him for a pair of dark sunglasses. Why did he want to find her again? What was it about her that both frightened and intrigued him? Why did flashes of her apartment — the telescope, the vast array of bright dots, the star-covered bed — keep rising in his mind?

He entered his building, nodded to the security guard. Instead of going to the elevators, Carter approached the stair-well, opened the door. He stepped through, let the door slam shut behind him, and began climbing.

The stairwell was quiet, the air hollow and warm, the cement walls echoing each of his footsteps. For a moment he felt as if he was walking along the hushed, hollow corridors of one of the stations — Luther King, Lagrange, Challenger.

and her hands moved to his shirt, delicately working the buttons loose, running her cool fingers along his chest and down towards his belly. Carter felt his body respond to her touch, and he brushed his fingertips lightly across the dark reflecting lenses, her soft nose, her firm mouth. Yes, he thought, this is where I belong, here among the stars. Nicole breathed in sharply and kissed his hands, pressed her hips against his.

With the blood now rushing through him, Carter reached out to embrace her, and to embrace the night as the stars continued to spin and dance in delicate, bright patterns all around them.

SIDE PANEL

Early the next morning, Carter drove Karyn to the train station, the trip endured in silence. They had nothing to say to each other any more, and he did not stay to see her off. That part of his life was over.

On the way back to the apartment he filled the car with gas, checked water and oil, brake and transmission fluids, put air in the tires. He cleaned all the windows, bought a map of the United States. On impulse, he stopped at a bookstore and bought maps of Canada and Mexico as well.

Carter spent the day packing whatever remained in the apartment, filling boxes and bags and suitcases, sorting through it all and deciding what he would take with him, what he would leave behind.

Knopfler called twice during the day, and Carter finally promised him an answer the following morning. By then he would be gone, and Knopfler would get no answer at all.

He would go to the mountains or the desert, that much he knew. Somewhere he could really see the stars, the moon, and the clear, black skies of night. He would be ready when the space program revived, ready if not to go into space himself, then to prepare others who would.

★

Night fell, and Carter loaded the car with everything he planned to take with him. Back in the apartment, he sat one more time on the balcony, the apartment dark for the first time in months. The night air was warm, the plaza below nearly empty, quiet. Someone had pulled the deflated Moon Ball out of the pool and draped it over a chaise longue.

Carter gazed up at the night sky, but though it was free of clouds, the stars above seemed dull and lifeless. The lights of the city sent up too much glow, and there were too many stars he knew should have been visible but which he could not see. Even the moon, which was rising, remained hidden, blocked from view by the brick and cement of the apartment building. This is no place to be, he thought, this is no place to live.

He looked across the plaza to the south building. In a sixth floor window he caught a glint of light, probably from the telescope. So, she was still watching him. After tonight, though, he would be gone, and she would be watching a deserted balcony, a dark and empty room.

At midnight he locked the apartment and walked out to the parking lot. Nicole stood next to his car with a single suitcase and the telescope. The building lights reflected at him from her dark glasses. Carter breathed in deeply.

All right, he thought. For now.

They squeezed the suitcase into the trunk, then packed the telescope in the back seat. He secured the lens cover, and they wrapped the telescope carefully in thick blankets, wedged it tightly into the luggage for protection.

They left under clear skies. Mountains or desert, he would decide later. He drove north, away from the city and the rows of amber street lamps. On the freeway the moon blazed down upon them, lighting the way.

DAVID BRIN

David Brin's first published science fiction was his novel *Sundiver*, and three of his subsequent novels have been award winners: *Startide Rising* won the 1983 Nebula; *The Postman* won the 1986 John W. Campbell Memorial Award; *The Uplift War* won the 1988 Hugo. In 1988, readers of the sf news magazine *Locus* voted him 'Favorite '80s Author'.

His other books are *Heart of the Comet* (with Gregory Benford), *The Practice Effect*, and *The River of Time*. The last is a collection of short stories, including 'The Crystal Spheres' which won a Hugo in 1985. And his story 'The Giving Plague' topped the *Interzone* 1987/8 readers' poll.

Brin's latest novel is *Earth*, and the next two will be *Sooners*, which is a sequel to *The Uplift War*, and *Stratos*.

He wrote the following story as a reaction to some contemporary sf stereotypes, such as 'young punk kids who somehow get to be more technologically competent than the best engineers, and a complete aversion to depicting the place of old people in the future.'

PRIVACY
by
DAVID BRIN

'Watching, all the time watching ... goggle-eye geeks. Soon as I get out, I'm gonna Patagonia, buy it? *That's* where the youth growth is. More ripe fruit like us, cuzz. And not so many barrel-spoilers . . . rotten old apples that sit an' stink and *stare* atcha . . .'

Remi agreed with Crat's assessment of the situation. As the three of them strode side by side, Roland also expressed approval, nudging Crat's shoulder. 'That's staccato code, boy-oh.'

What brought on Crat's sudden outburst was the sight of yet another babushka, glaring at them from a park bench under one of the force-grown trees as Remi and Roland and Crat scrambled up a grassy bank from the culvert where they'd been smoking. The very moment they came into view, the old woman laid her wire-knitting aside and fixed them with the bug-eyed opaque gape of her True-Vu lenses — staring as if they were *freaks* or *aliens* out of some space-fic vid, instead of three perfectly normal guys, just hanging around, doing nobody any harm.

'My, my!' Remi whined sarcastically. 'Is it my *breath?* Maybe she smells . . . *tobacco!*'

'No joke, bloke,' Roland replied. 'Some of those new goggles've got sniffer sensors on 'em. I hear the geek lobby in Indianapolis wants to put even homegrown on the restrict list.'

'No shit? *Tobacco?* Even? Roll over, Raleigh! I just gotta move outta this state.'

'Settlers ho, Remi?'

'Settlers ho.'

The stare got worse as they approached along the gravel path. Remi couldn't see the babushka's eyes, of course. Her True-Vu's burnished lenses didn't really have to be aimed directly at them to get a good record. Still, she jutted out her chin and faced them square on, aggressively making the point that their likenesses, every move they made, were being transmitted to her home unit, blocks from here, in real time.

Why do they have to do that? To Remi, it felt like a provocation. Certainly no one could mistake that tight-lipped expression of hers as *friendly.*

Remi and his pals had promised their local Tribes Supervisor they'd keep their tempers with 'senior citizens on self-appointed neighborhood watch.' Remi tried. He really tried. *It's just another geek. Just ignore her.*

But there were so damned *many* geeks! By the running census on the Net, almost one in four Americans were over sixty-five now. And it felt even worse here in Bloomington — as if oldsters were the *majority,* staking out every shady spot with their electronic sun hats and goggle-scanners, watching from porches, watching from benches, watching from lawn chairs . . .

It was Crat whose reserve broke as they approached that baleful inspection. Suddenly he capered.

'Hey, Granny!' Crat bowed with a courtly flourish. 'Why don't you record *this!*' Roland giggled as Crat swept off his straw cowboy hat to display a garish scalp tattoo.

Merriment redoubled when she actually reacted! A sudden moué of surprise and revulsion replaced that glassy, impervious stare. She actually rocked back and turned away.

'*Astonishing!*' Roland cried, mimicking their least favorite Teen Behaviors teacher at J.D. Quayle High School. He continued in a snooty Midwestern drawl. 'It should be noted that this small urban band's totemistic innovation achieved its desired effect . . . which was? Anybody?'

'*Shock value!*' all three shouted in unison, clapping hands, celebrating a minor victory over their natural enemy.

Used to be, you could break a babushka's stare with an obscene gesture, or a show of muscular bluster — both protected forms of self-expression. But the biddies and codgers were getting harder to shake. Anytime nowadays you actually made one of them yank back that awful, silent scrutiny was a triumph worth savoring.

'Freon!' Crat cursed. 'Just *once* I'd like to catch some goggle-geek alone with fritzed sensors and no come-go record. *Then* I'd teach 'em its *not polite to stare.*'

Crat emphasized his point with a fist, smacking his palm. Today, since it was cloudy, he had forsaken his normal Stetson for a plaid baseball cap, still acceptable attire for a Settler. His sunglasses, like Remi's, were thin, wire-framed, and strictly for protection. Nothing electronic about them. They were a statement, repudiating the rudeness of geriatric America.

'Some people just got too much free time,' Roland commented as the three of them sauntered near the babushka, barely skimming outside the twenty-centimeter limit that would violate her Personal Space. Some oldsters were gearing up with sonar, even radar, to catch the most innocent infraction. They went out of their way to tempt you, creating slowmoving bottlenecks across sidewalks whenever they saw young people hurrying to get some somewhere. They hogged the centers of escalators, acting as if they *hoped* you'd bump them, giving any excuse to squeeze that police-band beeper, or raise the hue and cry, or file a long list of nuisance charges.

These days, in Indiana, juries were composed mostly of Twen Cen grads. Fellow retirement geeks who seemed to think youth itself was a crime. So naturally, a guy *had* to accept the endless dares, skirting the edge whenever challenged.

'Granny could be doin' something useful,' Crat paused to snarl, bending his head to really scrape the zone. 'She could be gardening, or collectin' litter. But no! *She's* gotta stare!'

Remi worried Crat might spit again. Even a miss would be a four-hundred-dollar fifth offense, and, despite Granny's averted gaze, those sensors were still active.

Fortunately, Crat let Remi and Roland drag him out of sight into the Formal Hedge Garden. Then he leaped, fist raised, and shouted 'Yow!' pumped by nicotine and a sweet if minor, victory.

'Patagonia, yeah!' Crat gushed. 'Would that be dammit great? Kids like us run everything there, not like here in the Land o' the Old. I hear it's better'n even Alaska, or Tasmania.'

'Better for Settlers!' Roland and Remi agreed.

'And the music? Fuego-fire's the only beat that Yakuti Bongo-Cream *can't* meet.'

Remi himself didn't care much about stuff like that. He was attracted to the idea of emigrating for other reasons.

'Naw, cuzz. Patagonia's only the first step. It's a *staging area*, see? When they open up *Antarctica*, settlers from Patagonia'll have the jump. Just a hop across the water.

He sighed. 'Antarctica. We'll have new tribes, *real* tribes. When the ice melts enough, a few years' time, we'll set it up our way. Real freedom. Real people.'

Roland looked at him sidelong. Ever since they'd qualified as a youth gang a year ago, and had to start attending Tribal Behavior Class, his friends kept on giving him looks like that, as if worrying maybe he was actually listening to what the profs said. Or even worse yet, *caring*.

'Real *privacy*, maybe,' Roland agreed. 'You just make sure *that's* in the Constitution, Rem, if they nom you to help set it up.'

Remi nodded. 'Dammed right! Privacy! I hear back in Twen Cen . . . aw, shit.'

Sure enough, bored with just talking, Crat had gone straight over the top again. With no one in view from this hedge-lined stretch of gravel path, Crat began drum-hopping up and down a line of multicolored trash bins, rattling their plastic sides with a stick, leaping up to dance on their flexing rims.

'*Sweet perspiration . . . Sweet inspiration . . .* ,' Crat chanted, skipping to the latest jingle by Phere-o-Moan.

'*Sniffin' it stiffin's it . . .* ,' Roland countertimed, catching the excitement. He clapped, keeping the beat.

Remi winced, waiting for one of the bins to collapse.

'Crat!' he called.

'Damn what, damn who?' His friend crooned from on high, dance-walking the green container, shaking its contents of grass cuttings and mulch organics.

'U-break it — U-buys it,' Remi reminded.

Crat gave a mock shiver of fear. 'look around, droggie. No civic-minded geepers, boy-chik. And cops need warrants.' He hopped across the blue bin for metals, making the cans and other junk rattle.

True, no goggle-faces were in sight. And the police were limited in ways that didn't apply to citizens . . . or else even the aphids on the nearby oleander bushes might be transmitting this misdemeanor to Crat's local Youth Officer, in real time.

'An aroma for home-a, and a reek for the street . . .'

Remi tried to relax. Anyway, what harm was Crat doing? Just having a little fun, was all.

Still, he reached his limit when Crat started kicking wrappers and cellu-mags out of the paper-recycle bin. Misdemeanor fines were almost badges of honor. But mandatory-correction *felonies* were another matter!

Remi hurried to pick up the litter. 'Get him down, Rollie,' he called over his shoulder as he chased a flapping page of newsprint.

'Aw, petrol! Lemme 'lone!' Crat bitched as Roland grabbed him around the knees and hauled him out of the last container. 'You two aren't sports. You just —'

The complaint cut short suddenly, as îf choked off. Picking up the last shred of paper, Remi heard clipped, rhythmic clapping from the path ahead. When he stood up and turned, he saw they were no longer alone.

Bleeding sores, he cursed inwardly. *All we need are Ra Boys.*

Six of them slouched by the curving hedge, not five meters away, grinning and watching this tableau — Remi clutching his flapping load of paper, and Roland holding Crat high like some really homely ballerina.

Remi groaned. *This could be really bad.*

Each Ra Boy wore from a thick pendant chain the gleaming symbol of his cult — a sun-sigil with bright metal rays as sharp as needles. Those overlaid open-mesh shirts exposing darkly tanned torsos. The youths wore no head coverings at all, of course, which would 'insult Ra by blocking the fierce love of his rays.' Their rough, patchy complexions showed where anti-onc creams had recently sloughed away precancerous lesions.

Sunglasses were their only allowance for the sleeting ultraviolet, though Remi had heard of fanatics who preferred going slowly blind to even that concession.

One thing the Ra Boys had in common with Remi and his friends. Except for wristwatches, they strode stylishly and proudly unencumbered by electronic gimcrackery . . . spurning the kilos of tech-crutches everyone over twenty-five seemed to love carrying around.

What *man* after all, had to rely on crap like that?

Alas, Remi didn't need Tribal Studies 1 to know that was as far as teen solidarity went in year 2038.

'Such a *lovely* song and dance,' the tallest Ra Boy said with a simper. 'Are we rehearsing for a new *amateur show* to put on the Net? Do please tell us so we can tune in. Where will it be playing? On *Gong* channel 4003?'

Roland dropped Crat so hurriedly he fell to the ground, breaking the Ra Boys up again. As for Remi, he was torn between a dread of felonies and the burning shame of being caught picking up litter like a Citizen. To walk just three steps and put it in the bin would cost him too much in pride so he crumpled the mass and stuffed it in his pockets as if he had *plans* for the garbage.

Another Ra Boy joined the leader, sauntering forward slowly, taunting 'Naw, what we have here, you see, are some neo-fem girlie-girls *dressed up* as Settlers. Only, we caught them being girlie when they thought no one was looking.'

'Hmmm,' the tall one nodded. 'Only problem with that *hypothesis* is, why would anyone *want* to dress up like a dammit Settler?'

Out of the corner of his eye, Remi knew Roland had seized the growling Crat, holding him back. Clearly the Ra Boys would love to have a little physical humor with them. And just as clearly, Crat didn't give a damn about the odds.

But even though no geeps were watching right now, dozens must have recorded both parties converging on this spot . . . chronicles they'd happily fax to police investigating a brawl after the fact.

Not that fighting was strictly illegal itself. Some gangs with good lawyer programs had found loopholes and tricks. Ra Boys, in particular, were clever and brutal with sarcasm . . . pushing a guy so hard he'd lose his temper and accept a night-time battle-rendezvous, or some suicidal dare, just to prove he wasn't a sissy.

The tall one swept off his sunglasses and sighed. He minced several delicate steps and simpered. 'Perhaps, they are *Gaians*, dressing up as Settlers in order to portray yet another *endangered species*. Ooh. I really must watch their show!' His comrades giggled at the foppish act. Remi worried how much longer Roland could restrain Crat.

'Funny,' he retaliated in desperation. 'I wouldn't figure you could still *see* a holo show, with eyes like those.'

The tall one sniffed. Accepting Remi's weak gambit, he replied in Posh Speech.

'And what, sweet child of Mother Dirt, do you imagine is wrong with my eyes?'

'You mean besides mutant ugliness? Well, it's obvious you're going *blind*, oh thou noonday mad dog.'

Sarcasm gave way to direct retort. 'The Sun's rays are to be *appreciated* earthworm. Mama's pet. Even at risk.'

'I wasn't talking about U.V. damage to your retinas, dear Mr. Squint. I was referring to the traditional penalty for self-abuse.'

Pay dirt! The Ra Boy flushed. Roland and Crat laughed uproariously, perhaps a little hysterically. '*Got* him, Rem!' Roland whispered. 'Go!'

From the scowls on the Ra Boys' patchy faces, Rami wondered if this was wise. Several of them were fingering their chains, with the gleaming, sharp-rayed amulets. If one or more had temperaments like *Crats* . . .

The lead Ra Boy stepped closer. 'Was that a slur on my stamina, oh physical lover of fresh mud?'

Remi shrugged; it was too late to do anything but go on autopilot 'Fresh mud, or fecund fem, they're all equally out of reach to one like you, whose only wet licks come from his own sweaty palm.'

More appreciative laughter from Roland and Crat hardly made up for the lead Ra Boy's seething wrath, turning him several shades darker. *I didn't know I'd strike such a nerve with that one*, Remi thought. Apparently this guy had a lousy sex life.

Some little victories just aren't worth the price.

'So maybe *you're* the manly man, Joe Settler?' Ra Boy sneered. 'I guess you must be Mr Testo, with a stacked stock and hormones enough for all of Indiana.'

Here it comes, Remi knew, and foresaw no way to avoid exchanging Net Access Codes with this character, which in turn would lead inevitably to a meeting in some dark place, with no

Neighborhood Watch busybodies around to interfere.

With a small part of his mind, Remi noted that the encounter had built momentum almost exactly along the positive-feedback curve described in class by Professor Jameson ... bluster and dare and counterbluff, reinforced by a need to impress one's own gang ... leading unstoppably to the inevitable showdown.

And that knowledge hadn't helped prevent a thing. Remi wished he'd never been taught any of that shit, anyway. He shrugged and accepted the Ra-worshipper's gambit.

'Well, I'm already man-ugly enough that I don't have to pray for help from a great big gas ball in the sky. Though I must say, *your* prayers sure look like they've been —'

Remi realized, mid-insult, that both groups had begun to turn, to face a new set of interlopers in the Hedge Garden. He glanced back along the path, and saw at least a dozen figures in cowled white gowns approaching, slim and graceful, down the center of the path. Their own pendants were much more delicate than the Ra Boys', and were patterned in the womb-like Orb of the Mother.

'*NorA ChuGa,*' one of the Ra Boys said in disgust. Still, Remi noticed the guys in both gangs stand up straighter, taking up masculine poses they must have thought subtle.

Feminine conversation and laughter cut off as the newcomers saw the male gathering ahead. But they scarcely slowed. The North American Church of Gaia hardly slowed for anybody.

'Good afternoon, gentlemen,' several in the front rank said, almost simultaneously. Even shaded by their cowls, Remi thought three of the leaders heartbreakingly beautiful. Two he recognized from the halls of Quayle High.

'Can we interest you in donating to the Trillion Trees Campaign?' one of them asked. In her open palm, she held out brightly colored leaflet data chips for them to take. Remi suppressed laughter. These were young, naive Gaians if they thought to hit up *Ra Boys* for reforestation money!

Settlers, on the other hand, weren't as ideologically incompatible. More important, this offered an out from an impossible situation.

'Why, yes, sisters!' he effused. 'You *can* interest us. I was just saying to my Settler friends here that the tree planting will have to be our very first priority when we get to Patagonia. Soon as it's warmed up down there. Yup, planting trees . . .'

Crat, of course, was stll exchanging glares with the craziest-looking Ra Boy. Grabbing his arm in a vicelike grip, Remi helped Roland tow him amidst the gliding tide of white-garbed girls. All the way, Remi asked enthusiastic questions about current Gaian projects, ignoring the taunts and jeers that followed them from the harsh-faced young sun worshippers.

It didn't matter. The Ra Boys could say whatever they wanted. On the scale of coups in gang Tribal Warfare, scoring with girls beat winning an insult match, hands down.

Not that actually *scoring* was likely here. Hard-core Gaian women tended to be hard to impress.

'. . . don't you see that hardwood reforestation in Amazonia is *far* more important than planting conifers down in Tierra del Fuego or Antarctica? Those are new ecologies, still delicate and poorly understood. You Settlers are *much* too impatient. Why, by the time those new areas are well understood and ready for humans to move in, the main battle, to save the *earth*, could be lost!'

Anxious to make good their getaway, Remi and Roland nodded attentively until the Ra Boys were well out of sight. 'I see your point,' Remi agreed. He continued smiling and nodding for the *next* twenty meters or so because of the speaker's heart-shaped face and beautiful complexion. Also, he liked her walk, and what he could make out of her figure under the gown. At one point he made a show of depositing the trash from his pocket in a brown recycle bin, giving the impression litter-gathering was his routine habit, and winning a brief approving pause in her lecture.

He held on even longer, accepting dozens of chip-brochures, until at last she ran low on breath as they passed under the superconducting rails of the Cross-Park rapitrans line. Then, while a gaggle of youngsters in school uniforms spilled out of a train, running amidst and distracting the other Gaians, Remi told her he'd like to see her personally, and asked for her Net Code to arrange a date.

She, in turn, met his gaze with soulful brown eyes and asked him sweetly to show her his vasectomy certificate.

'I'm sorry,' she said with sincerity, 'but I couldn't be interested in a man so egotistical as to insist, in a world of 10 billion people, that *his* genes are desperately needed for the future. If you haven't done the right thing for a certificate, can you, point instead to some great accomplishment or virtue, to justify clinging to ... ?

Her words trailed off in perlexity, addressing their backs as Remi and his friends rapidly departed.

'I'd show her something more important than *genes*.' Crat snarled.

Roland was only slightly more forgiving. 'Too damn much theory, an' not enough experience. Imagine, invading a guy's privacy like that! Tell you one thing, that's one little bird who'd be a lot happier and a *whole* lot quieter as a farm wife.'

'Right!' Crat agreed. 'Farm wife's got what life's about. There's plenty room in Patagonia for lots of kids. Overpop's just propa-crap —'

'Oh, shut up!' Remi snapped. His face still burned with shame, made worse by the fact that the girl obviously hadn't been aware what she was doing. 'You think I care what a bleeding NorA ChuGa thinks? They only teach 'em how to be — *what!*'

Roland was holding up his wristwatch, in front of Remi's face, tapping its tiny screen. Lights rippled, and the machine emitted a warning tone.

Remi blinked. They were being scanned again, and it wasn't just someone's True-Vu this time, but real eavesdropping. 'Some dork's got a dammit Big Ear on us,' Roland said irritably.

One thing after another! Remi felt like a caged tiger. Hell, even *tigers* had more privacy nowadays, in the Wildlife Survival Arks, than a young guy got here in Bloomington. *The park used to be a place where you could get away from it all, but not anymore!*

He looked around quickly, searching for the voyeur. Over to the south, Citizens of many ages were busy tending high-yield vegetables in narrow strip gardens, leased by the city to those without convenient rooftops. Bean-pole detectors watched for poachers, but those devices couldn't have set off Roland's alarm.

Nor could the children, running about in visors and sun-goggles, playing tag or beamy.

There were other teens around, too . . . though none in sight wore gang colors. The silent, boring majority, students dressed for fashion or conformity, some carrying banners for tonight's game between the Quayle High Golfers and the Letterman Hecklers.

Turning nearly all the way around, he finally saw the geek — a codger this time — leaning against one of the pillars of the monorail line, watching them. Sure enough, amid the bushy gray curls spilling under his white sun hat, Remi saw a thin wire leading from an earpiece to a vest made of some sono-magnetic fabric.

Maneuvering in step, the three boys reacted to this new provocation by striding toward the geezer. As they neared, they made out the ribbons of a Helevetian War veteran on his chest, with radiation and pathogen clusters. *Shit,* Remi thought. *Veterans are the worst.* It would be hard winning any points over this one.

Then Remi realized the coot wasn't wearing goggles! Of course he could still be transmitting, using smaller sensors, but it broke the image, especially when the gremper removed even his sunglasses as they approached, and actually smiled!

'Hello, boys,' he said amiably. 'I guess you caught me snooping. I owe you an apology.'

Out of habit, Crat accelerated all the way to the edge of the fellow's Personal Zone, and even swayed over a bit as he flashed his obscene scalp tattoo. But the geek didn't respond by flourishing his police beeper. Rather, he acted as if he neither had one nor needed one.

'Beautiful!' he laughed aloud. 'So artistic. I had a messmate . . . a Russki commando, he was — died in the drop on Liechtenstein. *He* had a tattoo like that one, only it was on his butt. Could make it dance, too.'

Remi grabbed Crat's arm when the idiot seemed on the verge of spitting. 'You know using a Big Ear's illegal without wearing a sign, tellin' everyone in range you've got one,' Remi informed the veteran. 'We could cite you, man.'

The oldster nodded. 'Fair enough. I violated your privacy, and will accept in situ judgment, if you wish.'

Remi and his friends looked at one another. This was bizarre. Geriatrics . . . especially those who had suffered in the war . . . hardly ever used the word 'privacy' except as an epithet, when accusing someone else of hiding some foul scheme. Certainly Remi had never heard of a codger willing to settle a dispute as gang members would, man to man and away from the all-intrusive eye of the Net.

'Shit, no, gremper! We *got* you —'

'Crat!' Roland snapped. He glanced at Remi, and Remi nodded back. 'All right,' Roland agreed. 'Over by that tree. You pitch; we'll swing.'

That brought another smile. 'I used that expression when *I* was your age. Haven't heard it since, though. Did you know slang phrases often come and go, in cycles?'

Still chatting amiably, he led the way toward the designated open-air courtroom, leaving Remi to try to visualize this wrinkled remnant as a youth, once filled as they now were with hormones and anger.

At least they had a war for you to fight, Remi thought bitterly. After the Helvetian Holocaust, the frightened international community finally acted to prevent any more big ones. But that didn't seem like much of a solution to Remi. The world was going straight to hell anyhow, no detours. So why not do it in a way that was at least honorable and interesting?

Do not go gently, into that good night . . . Poetry class was just about the only one Remi really liked. *Yeah. Back before Twen Cen, there were guys who had it right.*

From a grassy step near the tree, they could look out over much of downtown Bloomington, a skyline still dominated by preserved Twen Cen towers, though several of the more recent, slablike 'topias canted like ski slopes to the north. From somewhere beyond the park boundaries could be heard the ubiquitous sound of jackhammers as the city waged its unwinnable war against decay, renovating crumbling sidewalks and sewer pipes originally designed to last a hundred years . . . back more than a century ago, when a hundred years must have sounded like forever. Bloomington looked and felt seedy . . . like almost any other town, anywhere.

'I like listening to people, watching people,' the codger said as he sat cross-legged before them, displaying a surprising limberness.

'So what?' Roland shrugged. '*All* you geeks listen and watch. *All* the time.'

The old man shook his head. 'No, *they* stare and record. That's different. They try to compensate for their failing bodies by waging a war of intimidation against youth.

'Oh, it started as a way to fight street crime — retired people staking out streets with video cameras and crude beepers. And the Seniors' Posse really worked, to the point where perps couldn't steal anything or hurt anybody in public anymore without getting caught on tape.

'But after the crime rate plummeted, did that stop the paranoia?' He shook his gray head. 'Naw. You see, it's all *relative.* That's how human psych works. Nowadays Seniors — you call us geeks — imagine threats where there aren't any anymore. It's become a tradition. They're so busy warning off potential trouble, challenging threats before they materialize, they almost *dare* young men like you —'

Roland interrupted. 'Hey, gremper. We get this basic-interaction crap in tribes. What's your point?'

The old man shrugged. 'Maybe pretending there's still a need for Neighborhood Watch makes them feel useful. There's a saying I heard sometimes back: *Geeks find their own uses for technology.* It all happened naturally, day by day.'

'I wish they never invented all this tech shit,' Remi muttered.

The war veteran heard him and sighed. 'The world would be dead, dead now if it weren't for tech stuff, my young friend. You want to go back to the farm? Send 10 *billion* people back to subsistence farming? Feeding the world's a job for trained experts now, boy. You'd only fuck things worse than they are. At least in cities, you can be fed, and with less eco-impact.

'But in cities there used to be so much violence. Tech eventually solved that also, and keeps us urban prisoners from dying of boredom. Tech helps people have a million zillion low-impact hobbies . . .'

'Yeah, and helps 'em *spy* on each other, too. That's one of the biggest hobbies, isn't it? Gossip and snooping!'

The old man shrugged. 'You might not complain so much if you lived through the alternative. Anyway, *I* wasn't trying to catch you fellows in some infraction. I was just listening. I *like listening to people. I like you* guys.'

Crat and Roland laughed out loud at the absurdity of the remark. But Remi felt a queer chill. The geezer really seemed to mean it.

Of course, Professor Jameson kept saying it was wrong to overgeneralize. ' . . . *because you are gang members, that will color your view of everything. Young males do that when engaged in us-versus-them group bonding. They have to stereotype their enemies, dehumanize them. The problem's really bad here in this part of the city, where the young-old conflict has deteriorated* . . .'

Everybody hated Jameson, all the girlie gangs and dudie gangs — staying in his class only because a pass was required for any hope of earning a self-reliance card . . . as if half the kids were ever going to qualify for *that.* Shit.

'I like you because I remember the way it was for me,' the gremper went on, unperturbed. 'I remember when I felt as you do . . . as if I could bend steel, topple empires, fuck harems, burn cities . . .'

He closed his wrinkled eyelids for a moment, and when he reopened them, he seemed briefly to be looking into space and time. 'I did burn cities, y'know.'

The codger shook himself out of a memory that Remi somehow knew had to be more vivid than anything in his own paltry store of recollections. Remi felt suddenly awash in envy.

'But then, each generation's got to have a cause, right?' the oldster continued. '*Ours* was *ending secrecy.* It's why we fought the bankers, and the bureaucrats and mobsters, and all the damned socialists, to bring everything out into the open once and for all, and stop all the under-the-table dealing and mega-giga-cheating.

'Only now our solution's causing *other* problems . . . That's the way things go with revolutions, y'know.

'So when I overheard you guys dreaming aloud of privacy
. . . talking about *privacy* as if it were something holy . . . Jesus,
how it took me back. You reminded me just then of my own
dad! I remember people used to talk that way, back at the end
of Twen Cen, until my generation saw through the scam —'

'Privacy's no scam!' Roland snapped. 'It's . . . it's simple
human dignity!'

'Yeah!' Crat added. 'You got no right to follow a guy's every
move . . .'

But the old man lifted one hand placatingly. 'Hey, I agree!
At least partly. What I was trying to say is that I think *my*
generation went too far. We overcompensated against the evils
of secrecy — of numbered bank accounts and insider deals —
and now you guys are rejecting *our* excesses, replacing them
with some of your own.

'Seriously, though, what would you boys do if you had your
way? You can't just ban Tru-Vu and the other tech stuff. You
can't put the genie back into the bottle. The world had two
choices. Let *governments* control surveillance tech . . . and
therefore give a monopoly on snooping to the rich and powerful
. . . or let *everybody* have it! Let everyone snoop everyone else,
including snooping the government! I mean it, fellows. That
was the choice. There *weren't* any other options.'

'Come on,' Roland said.

'All right, you tell me. Would *you* let the rich and powerful
have a monopoly on secrecy?'

Crat glowered. 'Maybe. Why not? At least when they did,
they weren't so dammit rude! People could at least *pretend* they
were being left alone.'

Remi nodded, impressed with Crat's momentary eloquence.
'There's somethin' to that. Who was it, said life's just an
illusion, anyway?'

'Only most of the transcendental philosophers in history,'
the gremper answered dryly.

Remi lifted his shoulders. 'Oh yeah. That's right. It was on
the tip of my tongue.'

The old man burst out in delighted laughter, slapping Remi
on the knee. In an odd way, Remi felt warmed by the gesture,
as if it didn't matter that they disagreed in countless ways, or

that a gap of half a century yawned between them.

'Damn,' the gremper said. 'I wish I could take you back in time. The guys in my outfit . . . the guys would've liked you. We could've shown you some times!'

To his amazement, Remi believed him. He couldn't help but smile. After a momentary pause, he asked. 'Tell us . . . tell us about the guys.'

The three of them deliberated later, some distance from the tree, as dusk shadows stretched across the park. Naturally the old man left his Big Ear unplugged while they passed judgment. He looked up attentively when they returned to squat before him.

'We decided on a penalty for the way you invaded our privacy,' Roland said, speaking for them all.

'I'll accept your justice, sirs,' he said, inclining his head.

Even Crat smiled as Roland told him. 'You gotta come back here again next week, same time, and tell us more about the war.'

The old man nodded — in acceptance, gratitude, and obvious pleasure. 'My name is Joseph,' he said, holding out his hand. 'And I'll be here.'

Over the next few weeks, he told them tales they had never imagined, even after watching a thousand videos — about climbing the steep flanks of the Pennine Alps, and then the Bernese Oberland, slogging through gas and bugs and radioactive mud, digging out booby traps nearly every meter, and prying out the bankers' mercenaries every ten or so. He told them about his comrades, dying beside him, choking in their own sputa as they coughed their lungs out, still begging to be allowed to press on, to help bring the Last War to an end.

He told them about the fall of Bern, and the last gasp of the Gnomes, whose threat to 'take the world down with us' turned out to be backed up by three hundred cobalt-thorium bombs . . . bombs that were defused only at the last minute, when Swiss draftees finally turned their rifles on their own officers and emerged from their shattered warrens, hands over their heads, into a new day.

As spring turned to summer, Joseph asked them about themselves. He commiserated over the futility of high school, even under the New Education Plan — which forced on them lots of supposedly 'practical' models, but which never did a guy any good anyway. He held them transfixed when he spoke of the way girls *used* to be, back before they were taught all that modern crap about psychology and 'sexual choice criteria.'

'Boy-crazy, that's what they were like, lads. No girlie wanted to be caught dead without a boyfriend. It was where they got their sense of worth, you see? Their alpha to omega. Wishful thinking most of the time, of course. They'd do anything for you, believe most anything you said, just so long as you promised you loved 'em . . .'

Remi suspected Joseph was exaggerating. But that didn't matter. Even if it was bullshit, it was *great* bullshit. For the first time in his life, he contemplated the prospect of getting older — actually living beyond the ripe age of twenty-five — with anything other than a vague sense of horror. Now, when he thought about it, the idea of someday being somebody like Joseph didn't seem so bad, after all.

Roland and Crat agreed also, each in his own way. It was the profession of soldiering itself that fascinated Roland. Its camaraderie and traditions of honor. To Crat, it was liberation from the tight structures of urban life.

But Remi felt he was getting something more . . . the beginnings of a trust in *time*.

Joseph was a great source of practical advice, too — subtle verbal put-downs nobody here in Indiana had heard in years, but which would burrow like smart bombs dropped among the gang's foes, only to blow up minutes, even hours, later with devastating effect. One day they met the same group of Ra Boys in the park, and left them all scratching their heads in confusion, reluctant even to think of tackling Settlers anytime soon.

Roland began talking about joining the Guard, maybe trying out for one of the peacekeeping units.

Remi began reading turn-of-the-century history of the Net.

Even Crat seemed to grow more reflective. It was as if, every time he seemed about to lose his temper, he'd stop and think what the old man would say.

No one worried overmuch when Joseph failed to show up for one Saturday-afternoon meeting. On the second unexplained absence, though, Remi and the others grew concerned. At home, sitting at his desk-comp, Remi wrote up a quick ferret program and set it loose into the Net.

The ferret came back in under two seconds, having fetched with it Old Joseph's obituary notice.

The mulching ceremony was peaceful. A few detached-looking adult grandchildren showed up, looking as if they would rather be elsewhere. If they had been the sort to cry, Remi, Roland, and Crat would have been the only ones to shed any tears.

Still, he had been old. 'If any man's led a full life, it was me,' Joseph had said one time. And Remi believed him.

I only hope I do half as well, he thought.

So it came to Remi as a shot from the sky when he answered the message light on his home comp one evening, and found logged there a terse note from Roland.

Our names listed in Program Guide for a Net Show . . .

'Right!' Remi laughed. The law said anytime *anyone* was depicted, anywhere in the Net, it had to go into the listings. That made the weekly worldwide directory bigger in itself than all the world's libraries before 1910.

'Probably some Quayle High senior's doing a Net version of the year book . . .'

But his laughter trailed off as he read the rest.

It's on a reminiscence database for war vets. And guess who's listed as author . . .

Remi read the name and felt cold.

Now, don't jump to conclusions, he told himself. *He might've just mentioned us . . . a nice note about getting to know three young guys before he died.*

His heart raced as he dialed up the correct Net address, sifting through layer after layer, from general to specific to superspecified, until at last he arrived at the file, dated less than a month ago.

The Remembrances of Joseph Moyers:
Epilogue: My Last Weeks —
Encounters with Three Confused Young Men.

This was followed by full sight and sound, with narration, beginning on that afternoon when they had met, and held impromptu court where the elm tree shaded them from the glaring sky.

Perhaps someone neutral would have called the account compassionate, friendly. Someone neutral might even have described Joseph's commentary as warm and loving.

But Remi *wasn't* neutral. He watched, horrified, as his image, Roland's, and Crat's were depicted in turn, talking about private things, things spoken of as if to a confessor, but picked up by some hidden high-fidelity camera.

He listened, numb, to Jospeh's editorial voice, describing how he really felt about the youths who shared his final weeks.

... had I the heart to tell them! To break it to them that they were never going to Patagonia, or Antarctica? That the New Lands are nearly all reserved for refugees from flooded-out or dried-up catastrophe nations? And even then, there isn't going to be enough thawed tundra to go around. Not enough to replace what's been lost. They dream of emigrating to some promised land of opportunity, when Indiana is their destiny, now and tomorrow ...

I knew that, Remi thought bitterly. *But did you have to tell the world I was stupid enough to have a dream, Joseph? Did you really have to bare it all to everybody?*

A neutral party might have told Remi that Joseph hadn't really told very many people. It was in the nature of the Net, that vast ocean of data, that most published missives were read by only one or two others besides the author. Maybe 1 percent were accessed by a hundred or more. And fewer than one piece in ten thousand ever had enough viewers worldwide to fill even a good-size meeting hall.

Perhaps all that had gone through Joseph's mind when he made this his last testament . . . that it would be seen by only a few old men like himself and never come to his young friends' attention. Perhaps he never understood how far ferret tech had come, or that someone else might use the directories better than he ever imagined.

Remi knew it wasn't very likely Joseph's memoirs would work their way up, through good reviews and word of mouth, to best-seller status. But that hardly mattered. It *could* happen, after all. Joseph had been careless with a trust. For all the old man knew, Remi's nonchalant ramblings and dreams might be sifted and pored over by a million voyeurs, or more!

' *Why*, Joseph,' he asked aloud hoarsely. ' *Why?*'

Then another face came on screen, with delicate features framed in white. It was a voice Remi had managed to purge from memory — until now.

I'm sorry, but I just couldn't be interested in a man so egotistical as to insist, in a world of 10 billion people, that his genes are desperately needed for the future. If you haven't done the right thing for a certificate, can you point instead to some great accomplishment or virtue . . . ?

Remi picked up the unit and screamed as he threw it through the breaking glass of his bedroom window.

Strangely, Roland and Crat didn't seem to see what he was so upset about. Perhaps, for all their stylish talk, they didn't really understand privacy, not really.

They worried, though, over his listlessness, and learned not to speak of Joseph when each of them received small royalty checks in their accounts, for their parts in what was fast becoming a small-time social-documentary classic. They spent their shares on their new, diverging interests, while Remi took his own in cash and gave it to the next NorA ChuGa he met . . . for the Trillion Trees.

And so there came a day when he encountered, once again, a small band of Ra Boys in the park, this time without his friends, without anybody but his loneliness. His questions.

This time the odds mattered not at all. He tore them up, top to bottom, using sarcasm as he might a slug rifle, treating them as he might have done the Gnome mercenaries, had he been born in a time when there was honorable work for soldiers, when there was an evil that could be grappled with.

To the Ra Boys' amazement, it was *he* who demanded to exchange Net Codes. It was he who issued the challenge for a rendezvous.

They understood, however, by the time Remi actually met them later, in the darkness behind the monorail tracks. By then they'd done their own research in the Net, and understanding made sure their greeting was subdued, respectful.

Their champion bowed to him as they faced off within the makeshift arena. He even held back his best tricks, letting Remi draw honorable blood before it was time. Then, dutifully, one tribesman to another, he gave Remi what he wanted. And for weeks afterwards, the Ra Boys spoke his name in honor under the Sun.

The Sun, they said, was where at last he had settled.

The Sun was the final home of warriors.

ROBERT SILVERBERG

Robert Silverberg won a Hugo in 1956 as 'most promising new author'; his other Hugo Awards, and Nebula honours, are listed at the back of this book.

The April 1974 issue of *The Magazine of Fantasy and Science Fiction* was a special Silverberg issue. He was still under 40 at the time, and he 'retired' soon after. By then, he was already the author of some 70 sf novels and collections, 60 non-fiction books, hundreds of short stories, and he had also edited dozens of anthologies. He returned to writing with his 1980 novel *Lord Valentine's Castle* and is again amongst the most prolific of all sf writers. During 1989, he probably published more short fiction in the genre magazines and anthologies than any other author; he also had two sf stories in *Playboy*.

Silverberg was the second President of the Science Fiction Writers of America. For many years he edited his own original anthology series *New Dimensions*. He has now taken over the late Terry Carr's *Universe*, editing a new series with his wife Karen Haber.

His recent novels include *Nightfall*, which is the first of three books to be written with Isaac Asimov, *To the Land of the Living*, *At Winter's End* and its sequel *The Queen of Springtime*, and *The Mutant Season* (co-authored by Haber). Forthcoming is *The Face of the Waters*.

THE ASENION SOLUTION
by
ROBERT SILVERBERG

INTRODUCTION

I've known Isaac Asimov since somewhere about 1955, and in all that time there's been only one disharmonious moment in what has otherwise been a relationship of affection and mutual respect. It occurred when, at a science-fiction convention in New York about 1970, I made a jocular reference to the imaginary isotope Plutonium-186 during a panel discussion in which Isaac was also taking part. I knew, of course, that a heavy element like plutonium wasn't likely to have so light-weight an isotope — that was the point of my remark, in fact. Isaac seemed tickled by it. And went home and started writing a short story for an anthology I was editing, a story in which he intended to work out a plausible scientific rationale for the existence of PU-186.

And so he did; but one thing led to another and the 'story' turned into his first science-fiction novel in a decade and a half, The Gods Themselves. Well and good: I had inspired his return to the field with a remarkable work. The only trouble was that Isaac thought I was serious about Plutonium-186, and took an extremely public, although gentle and loving, way of berating me for my scientific ignorance.

I wasn't amused. I told him so. He was surprised by my irritation, and told me so. We went around and around on it for a little while, and then each of us came to understand the other one's point, and the whole squabble was dropped. And we went back to being good friends and

237

high admirers of each other's work and intelligence, and eventually, through a set of circumstances nobody could have predicted, we even wound up as collaborators. But all these years I continued to suspect that Isaac still felt guilty/defensive/touchy/uneasy/wronged by our Plutonium-186 contretemps.

So when the time came for me to write a story for a festschrift commemorating his fifty years as a professional author, I thought I'd send Isaac a signal that I carried no lingering bitterness over the misunderstanding, that in fact the whole thing now seemed to me a trifle that could be chuckled over. Thus I wrote 'The Asenion Solution,' yoking together Isaac's classic 1948 'thiotimoline' article with good old PU-186, by way of telling him that I bore no lasting resentment. It was fun to do and, I hope, for ever obliterated the one blemish on our long and pleasing friendship.

'Asenion,' by the way — as long as we're explaining all the inside jokes — is a famous typographical error for 'Asimov,' dating back close to fifty years. It was famous then, anyway. Isaac had his own sport with it in his Robot series, but I figured it was good for one more go-round here.

Robert Silverberg

Fletcher stared bleakly at the small mounds of gray metal that were visible behind the thick window of the storage chamber.

'Plutonium-186,' he muttered. 'Nonsense! Absolute nonsense!'

'Dangerous nonsense, Lew,' said Jesse Hammond, standing behind him. 'Catastrophic nonsense.'

Fletcher nodded. The very phrase, 'plutonium-186,' sounded like gibberish to him. There wasn't supposed to be any such substance. Plutonium-186 was an impossible isotope, too light by a good fifty neutrons. Or a bad fifty neutrons, considering the risks the stuff was creating as it piled up here and there around the world. But the fact that it was theoretically impossible for plutonium-186 to exist did not change the other, and uglier, fact that he was looking at three kilograms of it right this minute. Or that as the quantity of plutonium-186 in the world continued to increase, so did the chance of an uncontrollable nuclear reaction leading to an atomic holocaust.

'Look at the morning reports,' Fletcher said, waving a sheaf of faxprints at Hammond. 'Thirteen grams more turned up at the nucleonics lab of Accra University. Fifty grams in Geneva. Twenty milligrams in — well, that little doesn't matter. But Chicago, Jesse, Chicago — three hundred grams in a single chunk!'

'Christmas presents from the Devil,' Hammond muttered.

'Not the Devil, no. Just decent serious-minded scientific folk who happen to live in another universe where plutonium-186 is not only possible but also perfectly harmless. And who are so fascinated by the idea that *we're* fascinated by it that they keep on shipping the stuff to us in wholesale lots! What are we going to do with it all, Jesse? What in God's name are we going to do with it all?'

Raymond Nikolaus looked up from his desk at the far side of the room.

'Wrap it up in shiny red and green paper and ship it right back to them?' he suggested.

Fletcher laughed hollowly. 'Very funny, Raymond. Very, very funny.'

He began to pace the room. In the silence the clicking of his shoes against the flagstone floor seemed to him like the ticking of a detonating device, growing louder, louder, louder . . .

He — they, all of them — had been wrestling with the problem all year, with an increasing sense of futility. The plutonium-186 had begun mysteriously to appear in laboratories all over the world — wherever supplies of one of the two elements with equivalent atomic weights existed. Gram for gram, atom for atom, the matching elements disappeared just as mysteriously: equal quantities of tungsten-186 or osmium-186.

Where was the tungsten and osmium going? Where was the plutonium coming from? Above all, how was it possible for a plutonium isotope whose atoms had only 92 neutrons in its nucleus to exist even for a fraction of a fraction of an instant? Plutonium was one of the heavier chemical elements, with a whopping 94 protons in the nucleus of each of its atoms. The closest thing to a stable isotope of plutonium was plutonium-244, in which 150 neutrons held those 94 protons together; and even at that, plutonium-244 had an inevitable habit of breaking down in radioactive decay, with a half-life of some 76 million years. Atoms of plutonium-186, if they could exist at all, would come dramatically apart in very much less than one seventy-six millionth of a second.

But the stuff that was turning up in the chemistry labs to replace the tungsten-186 and the osmium-186 had an atomic number of 94, no question about that. And element 94 was plutonium. That couldn't be disputed either. The defining characteristic of plutonium was the presence of 94 protons in its nucleus. If that was the count, plutonium was what that element had to be.

This impossibly light isotope of plutonium, this plutonium-186, had another impossible characteristic about it: not only was it stable, it was so completely stable that it wasn't even radioactive. It just sat there, looking exceedingly unmysterious, not even deigning to emit a smidgen of energy. At least, not when first tested. But a second test revealed positron emission, which a third baffled look confirmed. The trouble was that the third measurement showed an even higher level of radioactivity than the second one. The fourth was higher than the third. And so on and so on.

Nobody had ever heard of any element, of whatever atomic number or weight, that started off stable and then began to demonstrate a steadily increasing intensity of radioactivity. No one knew what was likely to happen, either, if the process continued unchecked, but the possibilities seemed pretty explosive. The best suggestion anyone had was to turn it to powder and mix it with nonradioactive tungsten. That worked for a little while, until the tungsten turned radioactive too. After that graphite was used, with somewhat better results, to damp down the strange element's output of energy. There were no explosions. But more and more plutonium-186 kept arriving.

The only explanation that made any sense — and it did not make *very* much sense — was that it was coming from some unknown and perhaps even unknowable place, some sort of parallel universe, where the laws of nature were different and the binding forces of the atom were so much more powerful that plutonium-186 could be a stable isotope.

Why they were sending odd lumps of plutonium-186 here was something that no one could begin to guess. An even more important question was how they could be made to stop doing it. The radioactive breakdown of the plutonium-186 would eventually transform it into ordinary osmium or tungsten, but the twenty positrons that each plutonium nucleus emitted in the course of that process encountered and annihilated an equal number of electrons. Our universe could afford to lose twenty electrons here and there, no doubt. It could probably afford to go on losing electrons at a constant rate for an astonishingly long time without noticing much difference. But sooner or later the shift toward an overall positive charge that this electron loss created would create grave and perhaps incalculable problems of symmetry and energy conservation. Would the equilibrium of the universe break down? Would nuclear interactions begin to intensify? Would the stars — even the Sun — erupt into supernovas?

'This can't go on,' Fletcher said gloomily.

Hammond gave him a sour look. 'So? We've been saying that for six months now.'

'It's time to do something. They keep shipping us more and more and more, and we don't have any idea how to go about telling them to cut it out.'

'We don't even have any idea whether they really exist,' Raymond Nikolaus put in.

'Right now that doesn't matter. What matters is that the stuff is arriving constantly, and the more of it we have, the more dangerous it is. We don't have the foggiest idea of how to shut off the shipments. So we've got to find some way to get rid of it as it comes in.'

'And what do you have in mind, pray tell?' Hammond asked.

Fletcher said, glaring at his colleague in a way that conveyed the fact that he would brook no opposition, 'I'm going to talk to Asenion.'

Hammond guffawed. 'Asenion? You're crazy!'

'No. *He* is. But he's the only person who can help us.'

It was a sad case, the Asenion story, poignant and almost incomprehensible. One of the finest minds atomic physics had ever known, a man to rank with Rutherford, Bohr, Heisenberg, Fermi, Meitner. A Harvard degree at twelve, his doctorate from MIT five years later, after which he had poured forth a dazzling flow of technical papers that probed the deepest mysteries of the nuclear binding forces. As the twenty-first century entered its closing decades he had seemed poised to solve once and for all the eternal riddles of the universe. And then, at the age of twenty-eight, without having given the slightest warning, he walked away from the whole thing.

'I have lost interest,' he declared. 'Physics is no longer of any importance to me. Why should I concern myself with these issues of the way in which matter is constructed? How tiresome it all is! When one looks at the Parthenon, does one care what the columns are made of, or what sort of scaffolding was needed to put them in place? That the Parthenon exists, and is sublimely beautiful, is all that should interest us. So too with the universe. I see the universe, and it is beautiful and perfect. Why should I pry into the nature of its scaffolding? Why should anyone?

And with that he resigned his professorship, burned his papers, and retreated to the thirty-third floor of an apartment building on Manhattan's West Side, where he built an elaborate laboratory-greenhouse in which he intended to conduct experiments in advanced horticulture.

'Bromeliads,' said Asenion. 'I will create hybrid bromeliads. Bromeliads will be the essence and center of my life from now on.'

Romelmeyer, who had been Asenion's mentor at Harvard, attributed his apparent breakdown to overwork, and thought that he would snap back in six or eight months. Jantzen, who had had the rare privilege of being the first to read his astonishing dissertation at MIT, took an equally sympathetic position, arguing that Asenion must have come to some terrifying impasse in his work that had compelled him to retreat dramatically from the brink of madness. 'Perhaps he found himself looking right into an abyss of inconsistencies when he thought he was about to find the ultimate answers,' Jantzen suggested. 'What else could he do but run? But he won't run for long. It isn't in his nature.'

Burkhardt, of Cal Tech, whose own work had been carried out in the sphere that Asenion was later to make his own, agreed with Jantzen's analysis. 'He must have hit something really dark and hairy. But he'll wake up one morning with the solution in his head, and it'll be goodbye horticulture for him. He'll turn out a paper by noon that will revolutionize everything we think we know about nuclear physics, and that'll be that.'

But Jesse Hammond, who had played tennis with Asenion every morning for the last two years of his career as a physicist, took a less charitable position. 'He's gone nuts,' Hammond said. 'He's flipped out altogether, and he's never going to get himself together again.'

'You think?' said Lew Fletcher, who had been almost as close to Asenion as Hammond, but who was no tennis player.

Hammond smiled. 'No doubt of it. I began noticing a weird look in his eyes starting just about two years back. And then his playing started to turn weird too. He'd serve and not even look where he was serving. He'd double-fault without even caring. And you know what else? He didn't challenge me on a single out-of-bounds call the whole year. That was the key thing. Used to be, he'd fight me every call. Now he just didn't seem to care. He just let everything go by. He was completely indifferent. I said to myself, This guy must be flipping out.'

'Or working on some problem that seems more important to him than tennis.'

'Same thing,' said Hammond. 'No, Lew, I tell you — he's gone completely unglued. And nothing's going to glue him again.'

That conversation had taken place almost a year ago. Nothing had happened in the interim to change anyone's opinion. The astounding arrival of plutonium-186 in the world had not brought forth any comment from Asenion's Manhattan penthouse. The sudden solemn discussions of fantastic things like parallel universes by otherwise reputable physicists had apparently not aroused him either. He remained closeted with his bromeliads high above the streets of Manhattan.

Well, maybe he *is* crazy, Fletcher thought. But his mind can't have shorted out entirely. And he might just have an idea or two left in him —

Asenion said, 'Well, you don't look a whole lot older, do you?'

Fletcher felt himself reddening. 'Jesus, Ike, it's only been eighteen months since we last saw each other!'

'Is that all?' Asenion said indifferently. 'It feels like a lot more to me.'

He managed a thin, remote smile. He didn't look very interested in Fletcher or in whatever it was that had brought Fletcher to his secluded eyrie.

Asenion had always been an odd one, of course — aloof, mysterious, with a faint but unmistakable air of superiority about him that nearly everyone found instantly irritating. Of course, he *was* superior. But he had made sure that he let you know it, and never seemed to care that others found the trait less than endearing.

He appeared more remote than ever, now, stranger and more alien. Outwardly he had not changed at all: the same slender, debonair figure, surprisingly handsome, even striking. Though rumor had it that he had not left his penthouse in more than a year, there was no trace of indoor pallor about him. His skin still had its rich deep olive coloring, almost swarthy, a

Mediterranean tone. His hair, thick and dark, tumbled down rakishly over his broad forehead. But there was something different about his dark, gleaming eyes. The old Asenion, however preoccupied he might have been with some abstruse problem of advanced physics, had nearly always had a playful sparkle in his eyes, a kind of amiable devilish glint. This man, this horticultural recluse, wore a different expression altogether — ascetic, mist-shrouded, *absent*. His gaze was as bright as ever, but the brightness was a cold one that seemed to come from some far-off star.

Fletcher said, 'The reason I've come here —'

'We can go into all that later, can't we, Lew? First come into the greenhouse with me. There's something I want to show you. Nobody else has seen it yet, in fact.'

'Well, if you —'

'Insist, yes. Come. I promise you, it's extraordinary.'

He turned and led the way through the intricate pathways of the apartment. The sprawling many-roomed penthouse was furnished in the most offhand way, cheap student furniture badly cared for. Cats wandered everywhere, five, six, eight of them, sharpening their claws on the upholstery, prowling in empty closets whose doors stood ajar, peering down from the tops of bookcases containing jumbled heaps of coverless volumes. There was a rank smell of cat urine in the air.

But then suddenly Asenion turned a corridor and Fletcher, following just behind, found himself staring into what could have been an altogether different world. They had reached the entrance to the spectacular glass-walled extension that had been wrapped like an observation deck around the entire summit of the building. Beyond, dimly visible inside, Fletcher could see hundreds or perhaps thousands of strange-looking plants, some hanging from the ceiling, some mounted along the sides of wooden pillars, some rising in stepped array on benches, some growing out of beds set in the floor.

Asenion briskly tapped out the security-combination code on a diamond-shaped keyboard mounted in the wall, and the glass door slid silently back. A blast of warm humid air came forth.

'Quickly!' he said. 'Inside!'

It was like stepping straight into the Amazon jungle. In place of the harsh, dry atmosphere of a Manhattan apartment in mid-winter there was, abruptly, the dense moist sweet closeness of the tropics, enfolding them like folds of wet fabric. Fletcher almost expected to hear parrots screeching overhead.

And the plants! The bizarre plants, clinging to every surface, filling every available square inch!

Most of them followed the same general pattern, rosettes of broad shining strap-shaped leaves radiating outward from a central cup-shaped structure deep enough to hold several ounces of water. But beyond that basic area of similarity they differed wildly from one another. Some were tiny, some were colossal. Some were marked with blazing stripes of yellow and red and purple that ran the length of their thick, succulent leaves. Some were mottled with fierce blotches of shimmering, assertive, bewilderingly complicated combinations of color. Some, whose leaves were green, were a fiery scarlet or crimson, or a somber, mysterious blue, at the place where the leaves came together to form the cup. Some were armed with formidable teeth and looked ready to feed on unwary visitors. Some were topped with gaudy spikes of strangely shaped brilliant-hued flowers taller than a man, which sprang like radiant spears from their centers.

Everything glistened. Everything seemed poised for violent, explosive growth. The scene was alien and terrifying. It was like looking into a vast congregation of hungry monsters. Fletcher had to remind himself that these were merely plants, hothouse specimens that probably wouldn't last half an hour in the urban environment outside.

'These are bromeliads,' Asenion said, shaping the word sensuously in his throat as though it were the finest word any language had ever produced. 'Tropical plants, mainly. South and Central America is where most of them live. They tend to cling to trees, growing high up in the forks of branches, mainly. Some live at ground level, though. Such as the bromeliad you know best, which is the pineapple. But there are hundreds of others in this room. Thousands. And this is the humid room, where I keep the guzmanias and the vrieseas and some of the aechmeas. As we go around, I'll show you the tillandsias — they like it a lot drier — and the terrestrial ones, the hechtias and the dyckias, and then over on the far side —'

'Ike,' Fletcher said quietly.

'You know I've never liked that name.'

'I'm sorry. I forgot.' That was a lie. Asenion's given name was Ichabod. Neither Fletcher nor anyone Fletcher knew had ever been able to bring himself to call him that. 'Look, I think what you've got here is wonderful. Absolutely wonderful. But I don't want to intrude on your time, and there's a very serious problem I need to discuss with —'

'First the plants,' Asenion said. 'Indulge me.' His eyes were glowing. In the half-light of the greenhouse he looked like a jungle creature himself, exotic, weird. Without a moment's hesitation, he pranced off down the aisle toward a group of oversized bromeliads near the outer wall. Willy-nilly, Fletcher followed.

Asenion gestured grandly.

'Here it is! Do you see? *Aechmea asenionii!* Discovered in northwestern Brazil two years ago — I sponsored the expedition myself — of course, I never expected them to name it for me, but you know how these things sometimes happen —'

Fletcher stared. The plant was a giant among giants, easily two meters across from leaf-tip to leaf-tip. Its dark green leaves were banded with jagged pale scrawls that looked like the hieroglyphs of some lost race. Out of the central cup, which was the size of a man's head and deep enough to drown rabbits in, rose the strangest flower Fletcher ever hoped to see, a thick yellow stalk of immense length from which sprang something like a cluster of black thunderbolts tipped with ominous red globes like dangling moons. A pervasive odor of rotting flesh came from it.

'The only specimen in North America!' Asenion cried. 'Perhaps one of six or seven in the world. And I've succeeded in inducing it to bloom. There'll be seed, Lew, and perhaps there'll be offsets as well — I'll be able to propagate it, and cross it with others — can you imagine it crossed with *Aechmea chantinii*, Fletcher? Or perhaps an interspecific hybrid? With *Neoregelia carcharadon*, say? No. Of course you can't imagine it. What am I saying? But it would be spectacular beyond belief. Take my word for it.'

'I have no doubt.'

'It's a privilege, seeing this plant in bloom. But there are others here you must see too. The puyas — the pitcairnias — there's a clump of *Dyckia marnier-lapostollei* in the next room that you wouldn't believe —'

He bubbled with boyish enthusiasm. Fletcher forced himself to be patient. There was no help for it: he would simply have to take the complete tour.

It went on for what seemed like hours, as Asenion led him frantically from one peculiar plant to another, in room after room. Some were actually quite beautiful, Fletcher had to admit. Others seemed excessively flamboyant, or grotesque, or incomprehensibly ordinary to his untutored eye, or downright grotesque. What struck him most forcefully of all was the depth of Asenion's obsession. Nothing in the universe seemed to matter to him except this horde of exotic plants. He had given himself up totally to the strange world he had created here.

But at last even Asenion's manic energies seemed to flag. The pace had been merciless, and both he and Fletcher, drenched with sweat and gasping in the heat, paused for breath in a section of the greenhouse occupied by small gray gnarly plants that seemed to have no roots, and were held to the wall by barely visible wires.

Abruptly Asenion said, 'All right. You aren't interested anyway. Tell me what you came here to ask me, and then get on your way. I have all sorts of things to do this afternoon.'

'It's about plutonium-186,' Fletcher began.

'Don't be idiotic. That's not a legitimate isotope. It can't possibly exist.'

'I know,' Fletcher said. 'But it does.'

Quickly, almost desperately, he outlined the whole fantastic story for the young physicist-turned-botanist. The mysterious substitution of a strange element for tungsten or osmium in various laboratories, the tests indicating that its atomic number was that of plutonium but its atomic weight was far too low, the absurd but necessary theory that the stuff was a gift from some parallel universe and — finally — the fact that the new element, stable when it first arrived, rapidly began to undergo radioactive decay in a startlingly accelerative way.

Asenion's saturnine face was a study in changing emotions as Fletcher spoke. He seemed bored and irritated at first, then scornful, then, perhaps, furious; but not a word did he utter, and gradually the fury ebbed, turning to distant curiosity and then, finally, a kind of fascination. Or so Fletcher thought. He realized that he might be altogether wrong in his interpretations of what was going on in the unique, mercurial mind of the other man.

When Fletcher fell silent Asenion said, 'What are you most afraid of? Critical mass? Or cumulative electron loss?'

'We've dealt with the critical mass problem by powdering the stuff, shielding it in graphite, and scattering it in low concentrations to fifty different storage points. But it keeps on coming in — they love to send it to us, it seems. And the thought that every atom of it is giving off positrons that go around looking for electrons to annihilate —' Fletcher shrugged. 'On a small scale it's a useful energy pump, I suppose, tungsten swapped for plutonium with energy gained in each cycle. But on a large scale, as we continue to transfer electrons from our universe to theirs —'

'Yes,' Asenion said.

'So we need a way to dispose of —'

'Yes.' He looked at his watch. 'Where are you staying while you're in town, Fletcher?'

'The Faculty Club, as usual.'

'Good. I've got some crosses to make and I don't want to wait any longer, on account of possible pollen contamination. Go over to the club and keep yourself amused for a few hours. Take a shower. God knows you need one: you smell like something out of the jungle. Relax, have a drink, come back at five o'clock. We can talk about this again then.' He shook his head. 'Plutonium-186! What lunacy! It offends me just to say it out loud. It's like saying — saying — well, *Billbergia yukonensis*, or *Tillandsia bostoniae*. Do you know what I mean? No. No. Of course you don't.' He waved his hands. 'Out! Come back at five!'

It was a long afternoon for Fletcher. He phoned his wife, he phoned Jesse Hammond at the laboratory, he phoned an old friend and made a date for dinner. He showered and changed. He had a drink in the ornate lounge on the Fifth Avenue side of the Club.

But his mood was grim, and not merely because Hammond had told him that another four kilograms of Plutonium-186 had been reported from various regions that morning. Asenion's madness oppressed him.

There was nothing wrong with an interest in plants, of course. Fletcher kept a philodendron and something else, whose name he could never remember, in his own office. But to immerse yourself in one highly specialized field of botany with such intensity — it seemed sheer lunacy. No, Fletcher decided, even that was all right, difficult as it was for him to understand why anyone would want to spend his whole life cloistered with a bunch of eerie plants. What was hard for him to forgive was Asenion's renunciation of physics. A mind like that — the breadth of its vision — the insight Asenion had had into the greatest of mysteries — dammit, Fletcher thought, he had owed it to the world to stick to it! And instead, to walk away from everything, to hole himself up in a cage of glass —

Hammond's right, Fletcher told himself. Asenion really is crazy.

But it was useless to fret about it. Asenion was not the first supergenius to snap under contemplation of the Ultimate. His withdrawal from physics, Fletcher said sternly to himself, was a matter between Asenion and the universe. All that concerned Fletcher was getting Asenion's solution to the plutonium-186 problem; and then the poor man could be left with his bromeliads in peace.

About half past four Fletcher set out by cab to battle the traffic the short distance uptown to Asenion's place.

Luck was with him. He arrived at ten of five. Asenion's house-robot greeted him solemnly and invited him to wait. 'The master is in the greenhouse,' the robot declared. 'He will be with you when he has completed the pollination.'

Fletcher waited. And waited and waited.

Geniuses, he thought bitterly. Pains in the neck, all of them. Pains in the —

Just then the robot reappeared. It was half past six. All was blackness outside the window. Fletcher's dinner date was for seven. He would never make it.

'The master will see you now,' said the robot.

Asenion looked limp and weary, as though he had spent the entire afternoon smashing up boulders. But the formidable edge seemed gone from him, too. He greeted Fletcher with a pleasant enough smile, offered a word or two of almost-apology for his tardiness, and even had the robot bring Fletcher a sherry. It wasn't very good sherry, but to get anything at all to drink in a teetotaler's house was a blessing, Fletcher figured.

Asenion waited until Fletcher had had a few sips. Then he said, 'I have your answer.'

'I knew you would.'

There was a long silence.

'Thiotimoline,' said Asenion finally.

'Thiotimoline?'

'Absolutely. Endochronic disposal. It's the only way. And, as you'll see, it's a *necessary* way.'

Fletcher took a hasty gulp of the sherry. Even when he was in a relatively mellow mood, it appeared, Asenion was maddening. And mad. What was this new craziness now? Thiotimoline? How could that preposterous substance, as insane in its way as plutonium-186, have any bearing on the problem?

Asenion said, 'I take it you know the special properties of thiotimoline?'

'Of course. Its molecule is distorted into adjacent temporal dimensions. Extends into the future, and, I think, into the past. Thiotimoline powder will dissolve in water one second *before* the water is added.'

'Exactly,' Asenion said. 'And if the water isn't added, it'll go looking for it. In the future.'

'What does this have to do with —'

'Look here,' said Asenion. He drew a scrap of paper from his shirt pocket. 'You want to get rid of something. You put it in this container here. You surround the container with a shell made of polymerized thiotimoline. You surround the shell with a water tank that will deliver water to the thiotimoline on a timed basis, and you set your timer so that the water is due to arrive a few seconds from now. But at the last moment the timing device withholds the water.'

Fletcher stared at the younger man in awe.

Asenion said, 'The water is always about to arrive, but never quite does. The thiotimoline making up the plastic shell is pulled forward one second into the future to encounter the water. The water has a high probability of being there, but not quite high enough. It's actually another second away from delivery, and always will be. The thiotimoline gets dragged farther and farther into the future. The world goes forward into the future at a rate of one second per second, but the thiotimoline's velocity is essentially infinite. And of course it carries with it the inner container, too.'

'In which we have put our surplus plutonium-186.'

'Or anything else you want to dispose of,' said Asenion.

Fletcher felt dizzy. 'Which will travel on into the future at an infinite rate —'

'Yes. And because the rate is infinite, the problem of the breakdown of thiotimoline into its stable isochronic form, which has hampered most time-transport experiments, isn't an issue. Something traveling through time at an infinite velocity isn't subject to little limitations of that kind. It'll simply keep going until it can't go any farther.'

'But how does sending it into the future solve the problem?' Fletcher asked. 'The plutonium-186 still stays in our universe, even if we've bumped it away from our immediate temporal vicinity. The electron loss continues. Maybe even gets worse, under temporal acceleration. We still haven't dealt with the fundamental —'

'You never were much of a thinker, were you, Fletcher?' said Asenion quietly, almost gently. But the savage contempt in his eyes had the force of a sun going nova.

'I do my best. But I don't see —'

Asenion sighed. 'The thiotimolone will chase the water in the outer container to the end of time, carrying with it the plutonium in the inner container. To the end of time. *Literally.*'

'And?'

'What happens at the end of time, Fletcher?'

'Why — absolute entropy — the heat-death of the universe —,'

'Precisely. The Final Entropic Solution. All molecules equally distributed throughout space. There will be no further place for the water-seeking thiotimoline to go. The end of the line is the end of the line. It, and the plutonium it's hauling with it, and the water it's trying to catch up with, will all plunge together over the entropic brink into antitime.'

'Antitime,' said Fletcher in a leaden voice. 'Antitime?'

'Naturally. Into the moment before the creation of the universe. Everything is in stasis. Zero time, infinite temperature. All the universal mass contained in a single incomprehensible body. Then the thiotimoline and the plutonium and the water arrive.' Asenion's eyes were radiant. His face was flushed. He waved his scrap of paper around as though it were the scripture of some new creed. 'There will be a tremendous explosion. A Big Bang, so to speak. The beginning of all things. You — or should I say I? — will be responsible for the birth of the universe.'

Fletcher, stunned, said after a moment, 'Are you serious?'

'I am never anything but serious. You have your solution. Pack up your plutonium and send it on its way. No matter how many shipments you make, they'll all arrive at the same instant. And with the same effect. You have no choice, you know. The plutonium *must* be disposed of. And —' His eyes twinkled with some of the old Asenion playfulness. 'The universe *must* be created, or else how will any of us get to be where we are? And this is how it was done. *Will* be done. Inevitable, ineluctable, unavoidable, mandatory. Yes? You see?'

'Well, no. Yes. Maybe. That is, I think I do,' said Fletcher, as if in a daze.

'Good. Even if you don't, you will.'

'I'll need — to talk to the others —'

'Of course you will. That's how you people do things. That's why I'm here and you're there.' Asenion shrugged. 'Well, no hurry about it. Create the universe tomorrow, create it the week after next, what's the difference? It'll get done sooner or later. It has to, because it already has been done. You see?'

'Yes. Of course. Of — course. And now — if you'll excuse

me —' Fletcher murmured. 'I — ah — have a dinner appointment in a little while —'

'That can wait too, can't it?' said Asenion, smiling with sudden surprising amiability. He seemed genuinely glad to have been of assistance. 'There's something I forgot to show you this afternoon. A remarkable plant, possibly unique – a nidularium, it is, Brazilian, not even named yet, as a matter of fact — just coming into bloom. And this one — wait till you see it, Fletcher, wait till you see it —'

JOHN CROWLEY

John Crowley is the author of the novels *The Deep, Beasts, Engine Summer, Little Big* and *Aegypt. Little Big* — which Ursula Le Guin described as 'a book that all by itself calls for a redefinition of fantasy' — won the World Fantasy Award in 1982. These five novels have been published over the space of eighteen years, and his short stories are almost as rare. They have appeared in such diverse publications as the anthologies *Interfaces, Elsewhere* and *Shadows*, and the magazines *Omni, Interzone, Gallery* and *Isaac Asimov's Science Fiction Magazine*.

Crowley also writes and narrates film and television documentaries, such as 'The World of Tomorrow' which used archival film of the 1939 World's Fair. He lives in Conway, Massachusetts, and is now working on the second volume of the proposed four book sequence which began with *Aegypt*.

IN BLUE

by
JOHN CROWLEY

The route they took every morning from their dormitory to the project's buildings took them through very old parts of the city. They crossed a square where weeds grew up between enormous paving stones, a square so vast it could diminish even the long, square-columned, monolithic buildings that bordered it. The square was usually deserted and silent; not even the indigenous population of the city, descendants of those who had built this square or at least of men and women who had inhabited it when it was still a living place, ever came here much. It was too open, too lifeless: or rather it had a life too large, too intimidating; nothing could be done with it. The new populations of the city, the squatters and refugees, also rarely came here; probably most of them weren't even aware of its existence.

Hare's group passed out of the square beneath an arch the height of ten men and as thick as a room. Looking up as they passed under it, Hare could see that the honeycomb pattern of its vaulting was distorted deliberately to make the arch seem even higher, even more intimidating than it was. The hexagons high up, in the center of the arch, were actually smaller than the ones on the sides, lower down; the circles inscribed inside the hexagons were really ovals, making the center of the curve of the arch seem to retreat into a space within itself, a space that could not exist, a space into which Hare's heart seemed to be drawn.

Then he had passed under the arch and moved on with the others.

Why had they done it that way? Every morning he wondered. Why had it occurred to anyone to expend so much ingenuity on a trick like that, who had then been willing to take the trouble to execute it? Slaves. But they must have been skilled nonetheless, and proud of their skills. The effort of it, the enterprise of it, at once oppressed and lightened him, drawing his mind apart.

He looked back, as he always did, to see the whole if it, and to study the band of letters that ran across the top. Each letter must have been a meter long; between the words there were diamond-shaped stops as large as a hand. But what were the words? What was the language? He tried to memorize the first few letters, as he always did, but as always by the time he reached work he would forget their exact shapes.

He turned away. One or two of the others had also glanced back, to see what it was that Hare looked at, but they couldn't see it, and looked curiously at Hare; the woman who worked beside him at the project smiled at him, enjoying his oddness. Hare returned the smile and looked ahead.

Farther on were narrow streets, and these, too, contained fragments of the ancient city, not ruins so much as antiquities in the process of being packed up in new construction. That the old cornerstones and bits of columned fronts were being preserved in this way was an illusion; the incremental plan for new housing, for places to put the thousands who were coming in from the countryside, made it necessary to squeeze modular units wherever Applications determined they could go, leaving the old disorder to be carted away later. Hare supposed it wouldn't be long before the gray boxes, which stacked to any height, which could be piled up anyhow wherever there was room, would spill out into the square, growing with the shy persistence of ivy, higgledy-piggledy, full of children, strung with lines of laundry and hung with gaudy hectoring posters in country dialects. In these streets the uniform units had already climbed above all but the tallest of the older buildings, their zigzag stairways like ivy's clutching roots.

Through the open doors of some units, Hare's group passing by could glimpse women at stoves, or nursing children; more often, though, doors and shutters would be quietly closed as the group passed, the faces that looked out suddenly occluded by a door. These country people were shy; if they found themselves observed, they would turn away, or even cover their faces with their hands. Had they used to do so in their old home places? Where Hare had grown up, people had been friendly and talkative. He thought it must be the city, the sight of strangers, cadre in Blue who had an uncertain but real control over their lives. When Hare's group came upon children playing in the labyrinthine streets, they would stop playing and withdraw into doorways or behind pillars, silent, their dark eyes large; they wouldn't come out though Hare's group waved and called to them.

It was a problem in figure-ground mechanics, Hare thought: that the cadre in Blue knew themselves to be the servants of masters, the people; but the people thought that the servants were their masters — and of course there were instances when the servants did seem to be directing the lives of their masters. It must be hard for them, Hare thought: the uniforms of Blue meant survival, food, shelter, help, and before them even the grownups were as shy as children offered sweets or kindnesses by great strangers.

But most of Hare's group had, like Hare, also come here from the country or from small towns, and also felt themselves to be displaced — perhaps that's why they smiled and waved at the elusive children of the altered streets, and why they talked little or in low voices as they walked through this many-layered necropolis where the living trod on the dead, who when they had lived had trod on other dead. Hare, in the city, felt for the first time sharply how many more dead there are than living.

The dead had carved in stone; the living wrote on paper. The long, bannerlike posters were everywhere, explaining, exhorting, encouraging: not only explaining how not to waste water, but why it was important that water not be wasted. Some were torn off in midsentence, by hands or wind; kindly teachers whose mouths were suddenly stopped.

'Look,' Hare said to the woman who walked next to him. He read from a poster: '"If you don't know how to read, begin learning now."'

'Yes,' the woman said. 'There's a lot of illiteracy still.'

She took the hand of the woman next to her, who smiled without looking at her. Hare said nothing.

Hare's work at the project was the preparation of training manuals, introductory lessons in act-field theory and social calculus. Presently he was working on an introduction to coincidence magnitude calculations.

It was not difficult work; it was far less demanding than the work for which Hare had been trained, and for which he had shown such early promise in school, when it was thought that he might be one of those few who could alter the calculus that altered the lives of men and women. When he walked the long halls of the project building, he passed the open doors of rooms where men and women sat together, without tools beyond a terminal or a pad or without even those, men and women at work on that calculus; Hare, as he passed their doors, hearing their low voices or their laughter, could almost see the networks of their thought growing. If they caught sight of Hare, they might wave, for he had worked with some of them in these rooms and in rooms like these in other places. Then he passed on, through other rooms, meeting rooms and commissariats and the communications annex, to the cubicles where work like his was done. Beyond these cubicles lay the maintenance sheds, the shops and warehouses. Then that was the end. Hare, sitting down at his work station and turning on the dim light above it, wondered how long it would be before he was shifted that one last degree.

Not long, he thought. He wasn't sure he could even complete the manual he was working on in any form that could be submitted. And beyond the maintenance sheds, the shops and warehouses? Only the world that Hare's manuals taught about: life: the whole act-field. He would most likely go on moving, as he had moved, by degrees down from the highest realm of thought about it, to a mere place in it: or no place.

He opened the composer on his desk and retrieved the notes he had made the day before.

'Introduction. Definitions. Description of contents. Figure-ground mechanics a necessity for coincidence magnitude calculation. Probabilities and how they differ from coincidence magnitudes: example. Problems and strategies: synchronicity, self-reference paradoxes, etc. Conclude introduction: importance of coincidence magnitude calculation to the social calculus, importance of the calculus to act-field theory, importance of act-field theory to the Revolution.'

He considered these notes for a long time. Then, keyed to the line about the difference between probabilities and coincidence magnitude, he wrote this:

'Example:

'It was once believed that no two snowflakes are exactly alike. More properly we can say that the probability of any two snowflakes' being exactly alike is very low. The fall, at the same moment, of two snowflakes that are exactly alike, and the fall of those two snowflakes on this word "snowflake" that you are now reading, would be a coincidence of a probability so low as to be virtually incalculable.

'But the *magnitude* of the coincidence, if it were to be calculated by the methods you will learn here, would not be high.

'This is because coincidence magnitude is a function of *meaningfulness* as well as of probability. We know that only acts (as defined by the special and general act theories) can have meaningfulness; an act's meaningfulness is a function of its definition as an act, a definition made possible by the infinitesimal social calculus. An act bearing high meaningfulness and low probability generates a high coincidence magnitude. To calculate meaningfulness against probability, and thereby arrive at the magnitude of the coincidence, requires that coincidence magnitude calculation be operable within act-field theory as a *differential* social calculus.

'Act-field theory predicts the occurrence, within any given parameters of the field, of coincidences of a certain magnitude. It is said to *account for* these. The appearance within those parameters of coincidences greater in magnitude than the theory accounts for is a coincidence of implicitly high magnitude, generating its own parameters in another dimension, parameters calculable within the theory, which then *accounts for* the higher level of coincidence. The generation of such new parameters is called an *implicit spike*, and the process is itself *accounted for*.'

Here Hare's thought branched.

'Implicit spikes,' he wrote, and then erased it.

'Act-field theory, then,' he wrote, and erased that.

Whichever way his thought branched it seemed likely to take him to the tolstoy edge.

Once (Hare had no conception of how long ago, but long

ago) they had thought that if the position and velocity and mass of every atom in the universe could be known, at some given moment, then the next moment and thus each succeeding moment could be predicted with certainty. Of course such complete knowledge could not be assembled, no computer could be built large enough to contain all the facts, or to calculate with them; but if they could be. And then they learned that the universe was not made like that at all, that only probabilities of states and events could ever be known with certainty, and that the very act of measuring and perceiving those probabilities entailed altering them. Some people (Hare had heard) had gone mad when this was proven, out of the awful loss of certainty, the loss even of the possibility of certainty. Others rejoiced: the loss of false certainty made real knowledge possible. The calculations began again, and were fruitful. The universe of events danced inexhaustibly, and the mind could dance with it, if it would.

And there had also been a time (the same time, perhaps, the same olden days) when people had thought that history might also be calculated: that if the weather and the size of harvests and the productivity of factories and the rate of invention and every other possible variable could be known, though it could not be, and every hurt every person had suffered, every belief or thought each one had — every man's position and mass and velocity — then it could be known with certainty why every event that happened had happened, and what would happen next.

But the human universe was no more like that than the universe of stars and stones. Such calculations would fail not because they were impossibly difficult but because no such certainties as were aimed at could possibly exist. It could not even be determined what units were to be measured — human acts — and where one stopped and another began. All conceivable plans for making the measurements met a mirror paradox, a self-reference, an infinite regression: the tolstoy edge.

But only give in to that; only rejoice in it; only be not surprised to find that the points plotted on your graphs make a figure like your own face, and the calculations begin again. And are fruitful: the special theory of acts, empty now of any concrete content, defines an act, the definition including the meaningful activity of looking for such a definition; the general theory defines their entrainments, heterarchies, and transformations. Act-field theory creates a virtually infinitely dimensional simplex for operating in, and the infinitesimal social calculus separates the inseparable, one act from another, dissolving in its simplicity the self-reference paradox as completely as the infinitesimal calculus in mathematics had dissolved the paradoxes of division that had plagued it for so long. And the social calculus makes possible the Revolution: once frozen before the infinite divisions of distance to be crossed before the target is reached, the Revolution now is loosed by the archer's fingers and leaps the distance into the unfigurable, ultimately unknowable heart of man.

And how could he, Hare, sitting here now, know all that, know it so well that when he was a boy he had in one tiny way added to it (some refinements of figure-ground mechanics for which he had won a prize in school), how could he sit here now before it and be unable to describe it? How could it ever make him afraid?

And yet he could not bring himself to continue.

He leaned back in his chair, which groaned beneath his weight. He pressed a key on the composer and held it down, and letter by letter his story about the snowflakes was removed from the screen.

Hare sat at lunch with Dev, a woman of about his age. He didn't know her well, but she for some reason chose him to talk to. She ate little, and seemed to be full of a story she both wanted to tell and didn't want to tell, about a young friend of hers, and their friends, whom Hare didn't know. Hare listened, nodding, sympathetic, for the woman felt some grief, a grief that the story she told should have revealed; but the way she told it made it impossible to understand. She said 'you know' several times, and 'all that kind of thing,' and waved her hand and shook her head as at a cloud of gnatlike complications that she could see in her story but couldn't or wouldn't describe. Hare lost the thread; there were too many 'she's in the story for him to remember which was which.

'So we all *did* go swimming,' the woman said. 'That night, by the bridge where there's the embankment. Well, I said I'd go. And then she said she and her new friend, the other one from the one she came with, the one she'd just met, didn't want to — but they said, Oh, come on, everybody needs to cool off. You know.'

Hare was listening carefully now.

'So they all took their clothes off. And they're really very young.' She laughed. 'And, well. With *her* it never bothered me, but you know they can be so unkind, or no, not that, I just couldn't. I mean I'm too old really for those games they play, you know? Girls together, like in school. You get beyond that kind of thing. I laughed about it, you kids go ahead, I just like to watch, I'm an old grandma. And they just let me sit.'

Hare put down his bowl. He was smiling, too, and nodding, as though sharing with the woman this amusing part of the story, where she'd tried to act her age with offhand grace; and trying to feel the other feeling that the woman felt: exclusion from happy comradeship, and jealousy; and trying also to transmute his own sudden strong feelings, by careful attention to her, into sympathy. He shook his head, smiling at how life sometimes goes on.

'Kids,' she said. 'At that age you just don't care.'

Hare wanted to ask: What did they do together in the water? But he could not have asked this and maintained his air of casual interest; and he thought that if she told him he would not understand her answer rightly anyway, because what the young women did together in the water would be three times masked from him: by their own young feelings, by the feelings of the woman who watched them from the bank, and worst of all, by the obstruction of his own feelings, so irrelevant to the young women in the water and what they did together, and yet so fierce.

'I know what you mean,' he said, remembering a day in spring years ago, when he was at school.

The school Hare had gone to as a boy was built in the shape of a T. In one branch of the T the girls were taught by female teachers; in the other branch the boys were taught by men. Where the branches met, the corridor of Hare's part ended, crossed by the corridor of the girls' part running at right angles. Going from class to class, coming near this juncture, boys could watch the girls walking in their part: books under their arms, or held up before them, embraced in that way that girls so often held their books but boys for some reason never did; talking together in groups or walking singly. Glances and waves could be passed from one part to the other, and brief conversations held there. There was a gymnasium in the school — Hare could not remember now just how it attached to the body of the school building — where alternately through the day boys' and girls' exercise classes met; it could also be filled with folding chairs when visiting cadre came to lecture. For these events the boys used one half of the floor, and the girls the other, separated by a wide aisle.

On fine days, after they had had their lunch, older students who had permission from their teachers were allowed to walk outside for a while on a strip of pavement that ran before the wide back doors of this gymnasium, to talk and smoke cigarettes. There was a proctor to watch them, but he usually absented himself. These were good students; they were being given a taste of the sort of privileges cadre had, and that they themselves might someday have. The boys understood that, and talk was usually serious. On a burning spring day, a first summer afternoon, Hare was walking with three or four other boys, smoking and talking. They were all laughing too loud, because of the day, and the sun, and summer coming. Then — either blown open by a gust of wind because they hadn't been properly closed, or opened from within by someone on purpose to bring cool air into the hot gymnasium — the double doors of the gymnasium opened.

There was a girls' class in progress. A girl Hare knew slightly, a cheerful laughing girl, stood framed in the doorway, legs wide apart, hair lifted by the sudden inrush of air. She wore only a band across her breasts and a sort of strap around her waist and between her legs. She waved to Hare, surprised but unashamed. Beyond her, in the comparative darkness of the gymnasium, were the others in the class. There were mats laid out on the floor. Two girls on each mat were wrestling; some wore the same breast band that the girl standing in the doorway wore, some who didn't need them yet didn't. Those not wrestling stood to watch the others. Hare saw all this in a moment. The girls within shouted and laughed, the wrestlers stopped and looked, some of the girls ran to hide. Around Hare the boys were laughing. Hare only stood staring, become eyes, his heart become eyes, his hands and mouth become eyes. Then the girl pulled the doors shut with a boom.

The boys around Hare laughed together, pummeling each other and shouting in an access of energy, until the proctor came smiling to see what was up, what the joke was. Hare turned away from the closed doors, feeling an almost unbearable sense of loss and exclusion; feeling withered and desiccated within, made old, by loss.

Hare wanted to ask the woman Dev if that was what she had felt by the river, watching her friend and the other young women: that sense of loss and exclusion.

But it couldn't be. Because she had, once, herself been one of those girls on the mats, among others. She had always been in the other part. The young woman swimming with the others was her friend; they were all her friends. Hare couldn't imagine then what she felt, whether her feelings were of the same kind as his, or a different kind altogether, and whether it hurt as much, or more, or less: her loss of what he had never had.

'I know what you mean,' he said again.

Willy said to him: 'You look tired. You always look tired now. You look as though someone knew something terrible about you, and you were afraid he was going to tell all your friends, and you can't stop worrying about it. But I know everything about you, and there isn't anything terrible at all.'

Willy shared Hare's room in the dormitory building where the project staff were housed. Willy wasn't exactly cadre, he hadn't much education, he was good with his hands and worked in the project maintenance shops. But Hare, when he saw that he wouldn't be able to have a room of his own because the project staff had grown too large, had got Willy into his room. Willy didn't mind living with project cadre, he had no sense of inferiority, and everybody liked Willy, his goodness, his jokes, his sympathy with everyone. Willy got along.

Though they had often lost touch in the intervening years, Hare had known Willy since school. Willy was four years younger than he, and at summer work-camp when Hare was proctor, Willy, alone and unhappy at his first camp, had adopted Hare to be his friend and protector. He'd sneak out of his own bunk with the young children and make his way to Hare's bed, shyly but insistently climbing in with him. Hare, half asleep, didn't resist the boy's affection; he was embarrassed to find him there in the morning, as immovable as a log in his deep childish sleep, and the other proctors made fun of him, but they were jealous, too, that Hare had someone so devoted, to run errands for him; once there had been a fight with another proctor over Willy. Willy understood — he always understood the context, the human net of desires and fears, the act-field, in a concrete way that Hare never would — and after that when he crept into bed in Hare's cubicle, he would be silent; would lie with Hare almost not moving, and with his face pressed into the hollow of Hare's shoulder would masturbate him with small motions, sometimes seeming to fall asleep amid it. When Hare made noises, Willy would whisper *shhh* in his ear, and giggle.

Willy called it playing. He always did. It was more intense pleasure than eating, without that daily compulsion but no less automatic; as refreshing as football or hard calisthenics, but imbued with affection and intimacy. The continuum in Willy from simple affection and shared good times to those cryings-out, those spasms, was unbroken; it had no parts; it was the social calculus in reality, and Hare loved it in Willy and envied him for it.

Because for all he, Hare, knew the integral social calculus, in him there was such a division. There was a breaking into parts, as in the oldest and wrongest paradoxes; an infinite number of discrete distances to cross between himself and what he desired.

'It's because I want the other,' he told Willy when long ago he'd tried to say it in words. 'You want the same. So it wouldn't occur to you.'

'That's not it,' Willy said, laughing. 'Because I've been with women, too. I bet more than you have. I like people, that's the difference. You have to like people. If you like people, they'll like you back. Men or women. If you're interested in them, they like you for it. It's simple.'

Hare had laughed, too, shame-faced, uneasy with the humility he had to learn in order to take advice from the boy whom he'd protected and taught. Pride: it was a fault cadre were liable to, he knew, a fault that must be erased. Why shouldn't he take advice from Willy? While Hare had grown up in the thin atmosphere of schools, study camps, and project dormitories, Willy had been moving in the sea of the people, the endless flux of the Revolution, with all its accidents and coincidences. Never cease learning from the people: that was a maxim of the Revolution grown old and unfeelable for Hare.

But he had tried to learn. He had tried to meld himself with the common play of desire and pleasure, hope and disappointment, pleasure and work. He became, or seemed to become, wise; became someone to whom others told stories, because of his calm, sensible sympathies. The endless voices: Hare heard stories everywhere, people told him of their plans and desires, Hare nodded and said *I know what you mean.*

But he had no stories himself that he could tell.

The dormitories where the cadre that worked in Hare's project lived were modular, like the people's housing, though the units were smaller. Above the communal facilities, the refectories and common rooms and work stations, the units were bolted on seemingly at random; but in fact Applications worked and reworked the building's program to assure that every unit got as much sun and air, as many windows, as short a walk to toilets, as possible; and so optimized along many dimensions it accreted as complexly and organically as a coral reef, and with the same stochastic logic.

Toward the summer's end the man who had lived alone in the unit next to Hare and Willy was shifted to another project. The people associated with his part in the project gave him a farewell party in one of the common rooms. They gave him a few small gifts, mostly jokes relating to work, and they ate cakes and drank tea spiked with some alcohol someone had got from the dispensary. Willy, to whom things like this were important, who remembered the birthdays of many people, had spent some time decorating the corner of the room where they sat, and he gave the departing man a real gift, an antiquity he'd found somewhere in the city and made a box for in the shop. The antiquity, a small white-enameled cube of thin metal, had a little door in the front that opened to show an interior space, and four red spirals symmetrically painted on its top, and representations of dials or knobs here and there. It was passed from hand to hand, everyone marveling at how old it must be and wondering what it might have been for. Willy was pleased with the effect. The man who was leaving was very touched, even surprised, Hare thought, and embraced Willy; and then, somewhat clumsily, all the others. Then the party was over.

The next week two young women came to live together in the empty room.

They were young, in training in the project, and inseparable; shy amid new people, but making their way together. Hare talked with them now and then when he found himself opposite them at dinner. They weren't sisters, though they looked enough alike to be sisters: both dark, with luminous eyes and full, childlike yet maturely sensual faces. Their light clothes of Blue (they had come up from a project in the south) revealed them as though without their knowledge or consent. They had a funny way of finishing each other's sentences. When Hare came upon one of them alone and began a conversation with her, she talked of little but her friend, her opinions and feelings, and kept looking around to see if she had come. When at last her friend appeared, a calm joy transformed her face. Hare watched her, his polite smile stuck on his face: watched love come and settle on her features and in the repose of her body.

Because they lived next to him, because he could hear through the thin wall the indistinct murmur of their voices and the sounds of their movements, Hare thought often about the two of them. The time he spent alone in his room was punctuated by the small sounds they made: a laugh over some joke Hare couldn't hear; obscure sounds of things moved or handled. Without willing it, he found himself growing alert to these sounds, his attention pricking up at them like a dog's ears. When Willy was also in the room, Hare paid no attention to the next room; his and Willy's noises drowned them out. But alone he listened; even held still to listen, found himself making the silent movements of a spy with his glass or his book, so as not to miss — What? he asked himself; and went on listening.

There was a night when loud scrapings, sounds of effort, laughter, business, went on some time next door; something bumped against Hare's wall. He could make nothing of all this until, after general lights-out, he climbed into bed and heard, close by him and more distinctly than before, the sound of their voices, the jounce and squeak of their bed.

They had shifted the few furnishings of their room, and moved the bed they shared from the far side of the room up against the wall that divided their room from Hare's, the same wall against which his own bed was placed. It was as though the three of them were now in the same bed, with the thin wall between them dividing it in two.

Hare lay still. There were long silences; a word from one of the two of them, a brief answer; the noise of the bed when one of them moved. He heard one of them get up, the pat of her naked feet on the floor; she returned, the bed spoke. With slow care he rolled over in his bed so that he lay next to the wall. Still he could hear no intelligible voices, only the sounds of their speech. But now, with the lights out, alone next to them close enough to touch them but for the wall, he knew he must hear, hear it all.

His mouth was dry, and there was a kind of intense constriction in him. Where had he once heard that you could eavesdrop on an adjoining room by putting a glass against the wall, and listening as though to a megaphone? He only thought about this for a time, lying still; then he slid from the bed, lit his nightlight, and took his glass from the sink. His knees were watery-weak. The feelings he felt didn't seem to him to be sexual, weren't like the feelings caused by sexual fantasies, they were more dangerous somehow than that; and yet he knew now what he wanted to hear. He got silently back into bed; he placed the glass against the wall, and his ear against the glass, his heart beating slow and hard.

There was a sort of roar, like the sound of the sea in a shell, the sound of his own blood rushing; then one of the two women spoke. She said: 'When the first boy has passed the last marker.'

'All right,' said the other. 'I don't know.'

Silence.

What were they talking about? They were together, in bed. Lights were out. They might still have a night-light on: that he couldn't tell. He waited.

'Last boy passes the first marker . . .,' said the second who spoke.

'No,' said the first, laughing. '*First* boy passes the *last* marker. You got the last boy.'

More silence. Their voices were distinct, and not far away, but still remote, as though they spoke from the bottom of a clear pool. Hare knew he could listen all night long, but at the same time he grew horribly impatient. He wanted a sign.

'I don't like that one. Let's do another.'

'You're just lazy. Listen again.'

'Oh, let's stop.'

Hare understood then. They were solving a puzzle, the kind printed in the back pages of mathematical journals. Aimlessly, without paying it much attention, they were working out a relay-race problem. Hare did them himself sometimes, when he had nothing better to do.

How could that be? They had one another, they were alone in a room, in a bed, they loved each other, they were free, free together in circumstances so enviable that desire only to be a witness of it, only to know a little of it, had driven Hare to this shameful contrivance, the glass against the wall, the wanting ear against the glass: and they were working out — or not even really bothering to work out — a puzzle in a magazine. But why would they? How could they?

He lowered the glass from the wall. Desire must not be what he thought it was: if its satisfaction was always present, it must grow blunted, it must not even be often thought of. That must be so. If you lived with the one you loved you did puzzles, had arguments, sometimes made love, slept. Couldn't he have supposed that to be so? It was obvious. Desire was a wholer, though not a larger, thing than the thing that was within himself. Of course it must be: and that cut him more deeply than anything he had expected to overhear.

There was further talk from the next room. He picked up the glass and listened again, willing them to show each other love, for his sake. But the talk was unintelligible to him now, private, or perhaps directed at something visible to them alone: anyway, meaningless. Then speech grew infrequent. Still he listened. Then, when silence had gone on so long that it might as well have been an empty room he listened to, he gave up, exhausted by the effort of attention; no doubt they slept.

Hare didn't sleep. He lay awake, feeling irremediably cheated, cheated of their desire. He wouldn't have minded the hurt he would have suffered that their desire faced away from him, so long as he could have witnessed it; yet even that they had withheld from him — not even on purpose, not conscious of him at all, having no intention toward him whatever.

On other nights he listened again. He sometimes heard things he could interpret as lovemaking if he chose to, but nothing clear enough to gain him what he wanted — entrance, commonality, whatever it was. When he slept with Willy, he made a joke of it, telling Willy in a whisper that the two could be heard; Willy smiled, intrigued for a minute, then bored when nothing immediately amusing could be heard; then he slept. Desire kept Hare awake beside him. Desire lay heavily in him: his own, the two women's desire that faced away from him. Desire seemed lodged hard in his throat and gut, distorting his nature and his natural goodness, something foreign, not a part of him, which yet cut every part of him, like a knife he had swallowed.

That month when Willy was moved to the night shift and Hare saw him only at dinner and for a few moments when Hare was preparing to leave for the project and Willy had just returned, Hare felt a certain relief. He couldn't have stopped, now, listening to the undersea sounds that came through his drinking glass, and of course he couldn't do it when Willy was present — but it was more than that. He couldn't have put Willy out of his room, that would have been like cutting a lifeline, but he couldn't now have him nearby either. His presence was like a reproach, a sign that what had become of Hare need not have happened.

★

History no longer existed. Hare had had to reinvent it. On his free days he would find excuses to avoid the communal activities of the dormitory, the classes and criticism sessions and open committee meetings, and with a tablet and pencil he would wander in old parts of the city, working and dreaming — working by dreaming — over this invention of his, history.

On a bench in a crowded park he sat opposite a great and now unused building, fronted with fluted pillars and crowned in the middle of its roofline with complex statuary, a group of men and women victorious or defeated, winged infants, and horses, which seemed to be bursting out of the unknowable old interior into the air of the present.

The building was a favorite of his, partly because it was still whole, partly because the present had not been able to think of a use for it, but mostly because as he sat before it — closing one eye, then the other, measuring with his thumb and with lengths of the pencil held up before him — he saw most clearly the one sure fact he had learned about the past. The past thought in geometry: in circles, sections of circles, right triangles, squares, sections of squares. The building before him was nothing but an agglomerate of regular geometrical figures, cut in stone and overlaid with these striving figures continually trying, but never succeeding, in bursting them apart. He imagined that the whole structure — even the fluting of the pillars, the relation of different bits of molding to one another — could be expressed in a few angles, in small whole numbers and regular fractions. Even the statues, with their wild gestures and swirling draperies, were arranged in a simple rhythm, a graspable hierarchy.

He thought it was odd that it should be so; and he thought it was odd that he should derive so much pleasure from it.

Why had the past thought that the world, life, should be pressed into the most abstract and unliving of shapes — the regular geometrical solids that were foreign to all human experience? Except for a few crystals, Hare thought there were no such things in the world. The mind contained no such shapes; the shapes the mind contained, if they were to be projected into the world, would look like — they *did* look like —

the clusters of people's housing that crept up to the edges of this park. They would look like the stacked, irregular dormitories Hare had lived in for years, restless accumulations always seeking optima, the result of a constant search amid shifting variables. Those were the mind's shapes, because the computers that designed the dormitories and the people's housing contained and used the logic of the mind: contained it so completely that the shapes that lay within the human mind, truly there in the resulting structures, were no more immediately apparent there than the shapes of the mind are in a casual conversation, with all its strategies, accommodations, distributions, and feedback loops.

But this building was part of the past. The past wasn't like the present. The past hadn't understood the shapes the mind naturally contained, it had no way of ascertaining them — no mirror as the present had in its big, linked computers; the past had longed for absolutes, for regularities foreign to the mind's nature, and (if the stories Hare had heard were true) had enforced them brutally on a heterarchical world. What peace, then, when all those hierarchies, when the very striving for hierarchy itself, had been dissolved in the Revolution! Peace; Perpetual Peace. The false and hurtful geometries had bent and melted and yielded to the unpredictable, immense stochastic flow of the act-field, leaving only a few memorials like this building, obdurate things caught in the throat of time.

Afternoon sunlight fell slantwise across the broad face, coloring its gray stone pink. There was a band of tall letters, Hare saw, running across the whole length of it, obscured by dirt: the light had cleansed them for a moment, and Hare, with many glances from his tablet to the building, copied them:

*IAM * REDIT * ET * VIRGO * REDEUNT * SATURNIA * REGNA *

He closed his tablet, and rose.

In the broad avenue that led away from the park and the building, people went by, an endless stream of them, bicycles and trucks, cadre in Blue, children and workers and country people. Two young women, one in shorts pedaling a bicycle, the other half-running beside her, holding with one hand the teetering bicycle that tried to match her slower pace. Both young, and smiling; they smiled at Hare when they saw that he watched them — happy, it seemed to him, and proud of their young health and beauty on a summer day. He smiled for them, paying them the compliment of being proud of it, too.

The people were a corrosive against all hierarchies.

Still smiling, Hare followed the avenue to where the cathedral stood on a square of its own. Its high doors stood open on this day; in winter they were closed, and only a small wicket let people in and out. And for whom had these immense doors been built, then, what beings needed such a space to go in and out by? As he passed through, he looked up at the ranked carvings of figures, human but attenuated and massed like a flight of birds, that swooped up the sides of the archway, ascending toward those seated at the top like a committee. Who were they all? The dead, he thought.

The interior of the church had been cleared of its benches. The great floor was being used (though vast spaces rose unused and useless overhead) as a clearing house for newcomers to the city. Groups of people stood before long tables waiting for housing and ration allocations. The sound of their footsteps, of the answers they gave to questions asked of them, even the taps of a pencil or the click of a terminal, rose into the upper volume of air and came to Hare's ears magnified and dislocated from their sources. Behind the tables low walls of board had been set up all along the stone walls of the church, whether to protect the walls, the windows and statuary, or simply for a place to pin up directions and information, Hare didn't know. He walked, head bent back, trying to follow the lines of the arches into the upper dimness. This, he thought, more than the other building across the park, mirrored the mind: the continual exfoliation of faces, birds, flowers, vines; the intersecting curves of vaulting, like the multiplane ellipsoids of a whole-program simplex; the virtually infinite reaching-away of it all into unseeable darkness. The colored, pictured glass, like the bright but immaterial reflections of the world in the thinking brain.

It wasn't so, though, really. His eyes, growing accustomed to the dimness, began to follow the lines of arches into the circles out of which they had been taken. He measured the regular spaces between pillars, and counted the repeated occurrences of squares, rectangles, triangulations, symmetries.

It was breathtaking how they had bent and tortured those simple ratios and figures into something that could approximate the mind. He felt a fierce joy in the attempt they had made, without understanding why they had made it. He thought this church must have been built later than the less complex but also somehow more joyful building beyond the park. He wondered if there was a way of finding out.

The low wall of flimsy board closed off some deep recesses even more full of figuration and glittering metalwork than the body of the church: like hollows of memory, if this were a mind, memory at once bright and dark. Peering into one such recess, Hare could see the statue of a woman atop a sort of table heaped up with what looked like gilt bushes. She wore robes of blue and a crown, a crown circled with pearls; some of the pearls had come out, leaving dark holes like caries. She stood beneath a little vaulted dome; a band of mosaic around the dome made letters, letters like those across the top of the arch he passed under every day, or the facade of the building down the avenue. He opened his tablet to a clean page and carefully copied the letters:

** A * V * E * E * V * A **

Ave Eva. 'Ave Eva,' he said aloud.

The woman's face — modest, with lowered eyes, despite her crown — did not look to Hare like the Eva he knew, his Eva. And yet he thought she did look, in her self-contained remoteness, a little like the Eva he sometimes dreamed of: dreams from which he would awake in a sweat of loneliness and cold loss.

He went out of the church.

No: now the building down the avenue, washed in sun, looked far the younger of the two, cheerful and new. Older or younger? He thought about it, blinking in the sunlight.

It seemed there ought to be enough of the past to make an act-field in itself; it rose vastly enough in Hare's mind, teasing him with limitless complexity. But it wasn't so. Even if everything that could be known about the past were known, it would still be far too thin to make an act-field. Even now, in order to construct a human act-field, the Revolution's computers ingested so much random matter that it was hard to find room in them for ordinary computations, food production, housing allocation: and even so, what the computers possessed was only a virtuality — a range of acts that was virtually but not truly infinite; enough for the Revolution's work, but still only a shadow cast by the immensity of the real act-field in which the people lived.

And history — out of which all old theories about society had been made — was a shadow of a shadow, so thin as to be for the program's purposes nonexistent. The whole of the past was less nutritious to the browsing search programs than the most meager meal of daily motions, truck accidents, school schedules, dew point, paper consumption, hospital discharges, decibel levels. The kinds of postulates that could be derived from history would not be recognized within act-field theory as postulates; out of the paucity of history, closed systems only could be constructed, those hurtful tautologies that ended in *ism*, once thrust onto the world like bars — systems less interesting than common arithmetic.

Hare knew all that. It didn't matter that the past was made of stone, and the present of thin walls of board bolted and stapled over it: history was a dream. History was Hare's dream. He didn't expect to learn from it; he knew better than that; he meant only to escape to it for a while.

Amid the crowds of the people; mounting up old stone steps, cut beside narrow cobbled streets; moving with the traffic along the broad avenues bordered with shuttered buildings; in the center of the great square, measuring its size by the diminution of a lone bicycle progressing toward the mouth of a far arch, Hare was in history, and his heart was calm for a while.

Hare wondered if the magnitude of the coincidence that had brought him together with Eva could be calculated, and if it were, what the magnitude would be. To daydream in that way meant to suspend his own knowledge of how such calculations worked — they could never work backward, they were abstracting and predictive; they could never calculate the magnitude of coincidences that had actually occurred. And Eva herself would have hated it that he should try to calculate her, predict her, account for her in any way.

Outlaw in a world without law, how had she come to be the way she was? Remembering the distances within her eyes, or waking from a dream of her regard turning away from him, he would think: she was trying to go far off. Loving Hare had not been a stopping or a staying but had been part of that going; and when he had explained to her that no, she couldn't go far off, didn't need to, and couldn't really even if she wanted to, then she went farther off by not loving him any longer — walking away, wearing her pregnancy like defiance, not hearing him call to her.

Hare sat at his desk at the project, looking at the notes for his manual on coincidence magnitude calculation, but thinking of Eva and the years since, years in which an automatic grasp he had once had of the Revolution's principles had weakened, a gap had opened between himself and his work, and the project that had been so eager to get him had begun to have difficulty finding something he could do. Eva had thought she could walk away from the world; Hare, standing still, had felt the world move away from him, grow less distinct, smaller.

No, that wasn't possible either. And any work he could do had its real importance to the Revolution, the same real importance as any other work; work for the Revolution had all the same formal properties and was all included; what it consisted of hour to hour didn't matter, it was all accounted for.

Importance of coincidence magnitude calculation to the social calculus. Importance of the calculus to act-field theory. Importance of act-field theory to the Revolution.

When Hare had been in school, that had been part of every lecture, on no matter what topic: its importance to the Revolution, its place in Revolutionary thought. Even in those days the boys hadn't listened closely; the Revolution was too old; it was either self-evident or meaningless to say that a thing was important to the Revolution, because there wasn't anything that was not the Revolution. *Dedicate yourself daily to the work of the Revolution,* said the tall letters that ran above the blackboards in his classroom. But that was like saying, Dedicate yourself to the activity of being alive: how could you do otherwise? If act-field theory, which lay at the heart of the Revolution and all its work, meant anything, then no act — no defiance of the Revolution, no grappling to oneself the principles of it, no ignoring or rejecting of it — could be not part of it. If any act could be not part of the Revolution, if any act could be conceived of as being not governed by act-field theory, then the field would dissolve; the Revolution would founder on the prediction paradox. But act-field theory was precisely the refutation of that paradox.

It was what he could not make Eva see. She was haunted by the thought that all her acts were somewhere, somehow, known in advance of her making them, as though the Revolution hunted her continually.

Importance of act-field theory to the Revolution. Hare twisted in his chair, linked his hands, changed the way his legs were crossed. The morning sped away.

There was a woman he had known in cadre training, at summer camp, in those days of night-long earnest conversations in screened wooden common-rooms, conversations that absorbed all the sudden feelings of young men and women for the first time thrust into daily contact. She had believed, or had told Hare she believed, that there was no such thing as act-field theory. She was sure, and argued it well, that for the Revolution to succeed, for the people to live within it happily and take up their burdens and do their work, it was only necessary for the people to believe that the theory *did* work. Once-upon-a-time, she said, social theories made predictions about behavior, and thus could be disproved or weakened or shown to be self-contradictory when behavior was not as the theory predicted, or when unwanted results arose when the theory was applied. But act-field theory simply said: whatever you do, whatever comes about in the whole act-field, is *by definition* what act-field theory predicts.

Every shocking or astonishing turn of events; every failed harvest, street riot, cadre shake-up; every accident or reversal in every life, are all as act-field theory says they must be. They are all accounted for, every spike, every rising curve, every collapse. And when the Revolution has swept away those failed and hurtful systems that attempt to predict and direct the future, there is nothing left to rebel against, nothing to complain of. There is Perpetual Peace. Street riots slacken in force, go unnoticed, are aberrations that have been accounted for even before they occur; the people go to work, harvests are steady, cadre do their jobs, there are no longer shake-ups and purges, none at least beyond those that have been accounted for. The Revolution is permanent. In the midst of its eternal mutability and changefulness, society no longer needs to change, or to hope for an end to change either. Life goes on; only the hierarchies are gone.

She said she didn't object to any of that. She felt herself to be in training precisely to do that work, to maintain the illusion that act-field theory governs human life in the same way that axioms govern a mathematical system. She felt (Hare remembered her uplifted face, almost aglow in the dark common-room, long after lights-out) that there could be no higher a task than to dedicate oneself to that work, which was cadre's work within the Revolution. Act-field theory dissolved social truisms like an acid, but it itself could never be dissolved; its works were its truth, the happiness of the world was its truth, the Revolution was its truth.

Hare listened, warmed by her certainty, by the strength of her thought; and he smiled, because he knew what she did not know. He had been where she couldn't go. She was no mathematician; she had not, as he had, just completed a multiplane ellipsoidal simplex and entered it onto the central virtual act-field and seen — he *saw* it, saw it like a landscape full of unceasing activity — the interior of the Revolution's data base, virtually as limitless as the actual act-field it reflected: and then saw it, at the bidding of his program, turn and look at itself.

How could he communicate that mystery? Ever since, as a schoolboy, he had learned that there are problems — in topology, in chaos description, in the projection of fractals — problems with true and verifiable solutions that only computers can construct, and only other computers verify, Hare had known how it was that computers could truly contain a virtual act-field, an image of the world larger than he could access within himself. He could put real questions about the world to the computers and receive real answers, answers not he nor any human mind could predict, answers only the computers themselves could prove true.

There *was* an act-field, and a theory by which it could be constructed. Just as Hare knew there was an interior in the young woman who sat beside him, which he could apprehend through her words and through the strength of her thought touching him as he listened and looked, an interior bounded by the planes of her pale temples and the warm body real beneath her clothes of Blue, so he knew truth to be contained within the interiors of the Revolution's computers: truth both unbounded and boundless, endless by definition and somehow kind.

He remembered that feeling. He remembered it, but he no longer felt it. He could not ever, knowing what he knew, think as that woman had, that act-field theory was a lie or a kind of trick. He imagined, guiltily, what a relief it might be to think so, but he could not. But act-field theory no longer seemed to him kind, as it once had. It seemed to be hurting him, and on purpose.

But if act-field theory underlay the Revolution, and the Revolution could not hurt him or anyone, then act-field theory could not hurt him.

He sat back, his hands in his lap, unwilling to touch the keys of the composer, reasoning with himself — tempted to reason with himself, as a man with a wound is tempted to probe it, pull at the scab, pick at the hurt flesh.

He *did not need to feel* these things, he told himself. He did not need to write an introduction to his manual. It needed none. Of course any part of act-field theory could be introduced by an explanation of all of it, but no part *needed* such an introduction. The project knew that. Certainly the project knew that. In fact the project had given him this job precisely because it would not require him to think about the whole of act-field theory, but only about the simple mechanics of its application. And yet the fact that he could no longer think clearly about the whole (which was why he was here now before this antiquated composer) meant that when he was confronted with this simple introduction, he felt like a man confronted with a small symptom, not in itself terrible, not even worth considering, of a fatal systemic disease.

Perhaps, though, the project *had* thought of all that; perhaps it had put him here, in this cubicle, and presented him with the concrete, the explicit and fearful consequences of act-field theory, to punish him for no longer being able to think about the theory itself: for betraying, through no fault of his own, the Revolution. No fault of his own: and yet he felt it to be his fault.

No, that was insane. If the Revolution was not always kind, it was never vindictive, never; for a heterarchy to be vindictive was a contradiction in terms: the Revolution could not be if it could be vindictive.

Unless there was a flaw in the theory that underlay the Revolution, act-field theory, which made heterarchy in the world conceivable, which made the integral social calculus possible and therefore all the daily acts and motions of the human world, including his sitting here before his unwritable manual.

But there could be no flaw in act-field theory. Hare knew that as well as he knew that he was alive. Act-field theory proved that all possible disproofs of act-field theory were themselves provable parts of act-field theory, just as were all other acts. It was not even possible for Hare to consider act-field theory without the act of his considering having been accounted for by the theory.

All possible strategies for avoiding paradox within act-field theory were also parts of the theory; they were acts the theory defined. Just as his sitting here pursued by paradox was defined and accounted for.

Hare had entered into an infinite-regression fugue; the taste of infinity was in his mouth like metal. That which had freed the world held Hare like a vise, like a cell in which a madman runs eternally, beating his head first on one wall, then the other.

Hare got permission to go and visit Eva and his son in the country. It was never hard to get such permission, but it was often hard to find transportation for such a purely personal trip. Hare's cadre status was no help; in fact it was considered not quite right for cadre to be seen traveling for private reasons. It didn't look serious; it could seem like unearned privilege and might be offensive to the people. Hare learned of a convoy of trucks that was taking young people out of the city to help with the harvest, and he was promised a ride on one of these.

When Willy returned from his night shift, he shook Hare awake, and as Hare, yawning and blinking, dressed, Willy undressed and climbed into the warmth Hare had left in the hollow of the bed. Hare went out into the empty, frosted streets, still tasting the dream from which Willy had awakened him.

Hare wondered if there were different names for different kinds of dream. This dream had been the kind where you seem to be telling a story to someone, and at the same time experiencing the story you are telling. Hare had been telling a story to Willy, a shameful and terrible secret that he had always kept from him, but which he had to confess to him now because Willy wanted to play. He had to confess how when he was a boy — and here he seemed not only to remember the episode but to experience it as well — when he was a boy, he had cut off his penis. He had done it deliberately, for what seemed like sufficient and even sensible reasons; he had kept the cut-off penis in a box. He saw himself opening the box in which he had kept it, and looking at it: it was erect but dead-looking, white, the veins in it pale. As he looked at it, the dream rising away from him, he realized how stupid he had been — how horribly stupid to have done this irrevocable thing that could never, ever be repaired, why, why had he done it — and as he contemplated the horror, Willy's hand awoke him. Relief of the purest kind washed over him, the dreadful burden fell away: it was all a dream, he hadn't done it at all. He grasped Willy's hand and laughed. Willy laughed, too. 'Just a dream,' Hare said.

Hare walked through the streets to the truck depot, shivering, feeling alternatively the horror of the dream and the relief of waking. He had been distant with Willy lately: he ought to stop that, there was no reason for it.

Young men and women, students and younger cadre, filled the open trucks, mostly in Blue, mostly laughing and pleased at the prospect of a day in the country. Hare found the driver who had promised him a ride, and he was helped into the truck by several hands. The convoy started its engines, and as dawn threw long bars of sun between the buildings, they drove out of the city. The young people in Hare's truck began to sing, their strong high young voices clear, and the truck's engine a bass accompaniment to their song. It was stirring.

More somber, across the bridge, were the wide tracts of old city suburbs, long straight streets crossed by dirt roads where pools of water colored with oil stood in the truck ruts. Children, who perhaps belonged to the flowerets of modular housing growing over the dumps and shacks and abandoned factories, looked up to watch them pass. The young people stopped singing and began to find places within the truck's bed where they could sit comfortably through the long ride. Some opened books or journals they had brought. Some of the women lit cigarettes, though none of the men did.

Almost all the boys Hare had known who smoked cigarettes gave them up at a certain age, once out of school, but many women didn't. Women who smoked were of a certain kind, Hare thought; or at least they all seemed to roll and smoke their cigarettes in the same way, with the same set of gestures. Like that one, sitting with another out of the wind in the shelter of the cab: tall, lean, her hair cut short and carelessly, she used her cigarette in a curt, easy way, dangling it in her long hand that rested over her knee, flicking it now and then with her thumbnail. She rolled it within her fingers to lift it to her lips, drew deeply though it had grown almost too short to hold, and gracefully, forcefully, two-fingered it away over the truck's side, at the same time dismissing the smoke from herself through mouth and nostrils. The hard way she smoked seemed like the mark of a sisterhood; her friend beside her smoked in much the same way, though not tempered by the grace, the young eyes, or the kind smile that this one paid to Hare when she caught him studying her. Hare returned the smile, and the woman, still smiling, looked away, running her hand through her hair.

Hare laughed, enjoying the way what she did to mask herself, the smoking, revealed her to him. Young: when she was older, and more practiced, it wouldn't reveal her, but just now, in this morning, it did. Perched on the truck's scuppers, among youth — among the unmarked who desired so much to be marked, and in their desire, showing their tender just-born selfhoods the more cleanly, the more tartly to his senses — Hare for a moment felt how well after all the world is put together, and how well the people in it fit into it; a seamless act-field into which, no matter what fears he felt, Hare too fitted; into which even his fears of not fitting also fitted in the end.

He thought of Eva.

The truck left him off at a bare crossroads, where it turned toward the broad garden lands. He walked the two or three miles to the cadre crèche where Eva lived and worked, and where their son was growing up: three years old now. Hare had with him some books for Eva — she always complained there weren't enough, or the ones she could get weren't interesting — and a gift for his son, which Willy had made: a nesting set of the five regular geometric solids, all inside a sphere. They could be taken apart, and with some trouble, put back together again.

It had never been the case that anyone, any bureau or person or committee, ever forbade a marriage or some permanent arrangement between Eva and Hare. There was no committee or person who could have done that. Eva believed from the beginning, though, that such a barrier existed; it made her at once fearful and angry. Hare couldn't convince her that, whatever stories she may have heard, whatever rumors circulated, cadre weren't forbidden to regularize affairs like theirs. 'They don't want it,' Eva would say. 'They don't care about anyone's happiness, so long as the work gets done. They never think about anything but the work.' And Hare could not make her believe that, in the very nature of the Revolution, there was no 'they,' there could not be a 'they' of the kind she feared and hated.

Certainly there was a tedious set of procedures that had to be gone through, but none of them were restrictive, Hare insisted, they were only informational. Many different people, yes, had to be informed; Hare and Eva's plans had to be passed outward into wider and wider circles of diffusion, first to the proctors and flow people at the project, then to the committee representatives at the dormitory, then the neighborhood and city committees; eventually the whole Applications system would have to be informed — would in the course of things become informed even if they only made their intentions known to the first levels of this diffusion. And it was true that in some ways they, Hare and Eva, would stick out: the two of them would make a spike within the regularities of cadre life, which was almost entirely unmarried, assumed to be celibate out of dedication and the pressure of work, and communal in ways that made strong pacts between individuals unusual; which meant that strong pacts between individuals upset people who were upset by unusual things. But why, Hare asked Eva, shouldn't the two of them be an oddity? Didn't she know that such oddities, such spikes, were implicit in the forms of communal life if that life isn't imposed by a hierarchy, is not tyrannical, is chosen, is the Revolution itself? They are assumed; they are already accounted for.

She did know that. But when Hare said — carefully, mildly, without insistence, a plan only for her to consider — that they could make their plans known at the first levels, within the first circles, and see if they were prevented even in the most subtle ways, and at the first signs of such resistance (though he knew there could be no such resistance) draw back if she liked: then she looked away and bit her nails (they were small, and bitten so short that the flesh of her fingertips folded over them; it hurt Hare to look at them) and said nothing.

She wanted something to defy, and there was nothing. She didn't want to hear his explanations of heterarchy, and when he made them, he felt as though he were betraying her.

He knew so much. He knew nothing.

He remembered her face, the day when she told him she was pregnant: her eyes questioning him even as her mouth said she didn't care what he did, this act was hers, she alone had decided on it. She expected some declaration from him, he knew: a denunciation of her for having done this, or a sudden pact offered that he would join her in it, as though joining a conspiracy. It didn't even seem to matter which he did — join her or denounce her. In fact he did neither, not being able to imagine either, not knowing why she should set such terms for him, yet knowing also that it was not really he who was being challenged; and obscurely certain he was failing her by not being able to feel as she did — that her act was a crossroads, a crux, a turning point where a fatal choice had to be made.

He thought: *What if I had pretended to understand?* If she thought she was surrounded by watching authorities, who wanted her not to do what she wanted, if the child had been a defiance of those authorities, then what if he had somehow pretended to join her in her defiance? Would she have believed him? Would she not have gone away? He thought it was possible, and it hollowed his chest to think so.

The cadre crèche was a cluster of low buildings, dormitories, a barn, yards, infirmary, school; beyond were the gardens and fields that the commune worked. In and out the doors, through the halls bright with autumn sunlight, boys and girls came and went, and women tending groups of children. Hare thought this must be a good place for children; it was crowded with the things children like — tools, growing things, farm animals, other children.

He wandered from room to room with his gift and books, asking for Eva. All the men and women who lived and worked in the crèche were parents of children being raised here, but many other children of cadre were here whose parents had chosen not to stay with them. Hare thought of them, the parents, separated also from each other perhaps, attached to faraway long-term projects, or working with the people in distant cities.

It's just hard for cadre, that's all, he thought, very hard. The people acted as they acted, their actions describable by theory but otherwise unbound; for cadre it was different. There were no *theoretical* barriers to their acting just as they would; theoretically, they did exactly that. In practice it was different, or seemed to be different; there seemed to be a gap there, a gap that only kindness and a little good humor could cross. He and Eva were bound by that now, if by nothing else; bound by what separated them, by the whole front of the Revolution sweeping forward at once, which could not be otherwise. With kindness and humor they could cross the gap. It was enough; no one had anything better. It was hard but fair.

In the summer refectory the long tables were now heaped with gourds and vegetables to be put by for the winter; men and women were stringing onions and peppers, hanging up bunches of corn to dry, packing potatoes for storage. Hare stood at the threshold of the broad, screened room filled with harvest, sensing Eva among them before he saw her.

'Hello, Eva.'

She turned to find him behind her, and a smile broke on her face that lifted his heart as on a wave. 'Hello,' she said. 'How did you get here?'

'I found a ride. How are you?'

She only regarded him, still smiling; her cheeks were blushed with summer sun, like fruit. 'Where's Boy?' Hare asked.

She had called their son only 'the boy' or 'boy' from the start, refusing to give him any other name; eventually 'Boy' had become simply his name, a name like any other.

'He's here,' Eva said. She leaned to look under the table at which she sat and called: 'Boy! Come see.'

He came out from beneath the table, dark curls first, and lifted his enormous eyes (they seemed enormous to Hare) first to his mother, and then to Hare. 'Hello,' said Hare. 'I've brought this for you.'

He held out the sphere to Boy, without revealing its secret, and Boy took it from him cautiously; the length of his eyelashes, when his eyes were cast down to study the gift, seemed also extraordinary to Hare. He opened the sphere; inside it was the pyramidal tetrahedron.

'I sent a message,' he said. 'Didn't you get it?'

'No,' she said. 'I never go to the terminals. You haven't come to stay, have you?'

'No,' he said. 'No, of course not.'

'You still have work, at the project?'

'Yes.' If he had said no, would her face have darkened, or brightened? 'It's not the same work.'

'Oh.'

She had done nothing since he had known her but pose questions he could not answer, problems without solutions; why then did he hunger for her as though for answers, the answers that might unburden him? All at once his throat constricted, and he thought he might sob; he looked quickly around himself, away from Eva. 'And you?' he said. 'What will you do now?'

Eva was coming near the end of her time at the crèche; she would soon have to decide what she would do next. She couldn't return to work on any of the major projects whose people were housed in the agglomerate dormitories such as Hare and Willy lived in. There were cadre who lived outside such places, among the people, but for the most part they did work for which Eva wasn't trained.

She could also ask to be released from cadre: put off her clothes of Blue and join the people, and live however she could, as they did. She and Boy.

'What will you do?' Hare said again, because she hadn't answered; perhaps she hadn't heard him. Eva only looked down at Boy absorbed in opening the tetrahedron. For a moment it seemed to Hare she resembled the statue of the crowned woman in the cathedral. Ave Eva.

'It might be,' he said, 'that they would have work for you here, if you asked for it. For another year or more. So that you could stay on here. Isn't that so?'

Boy had turned and stood between his mother's legs, lifting the tetrahedron to her, patient to be helped. Eva only laughed, and picked him up.

'Would you want to do that?' he asked. And just then Boy, in Eva's arms, reached out for him, gleefully, and clambered from his mother to Hare.

The first thing Hare perceived was the boy's weight, much greater than he had expected from the compact miniature body; yet heavy as he was he seemed to fit neatly within Hare's lap and the compass of his arms, as though they were made to go together — which they were, in a way, Hare thought. The second thing he perceived was Boy's odor, a subtle but penetrating odor that widened Hare's nostrils, an odor of skin in part and a sweetness Hare couldn't name. He could almost not resist thrusting his face into the crook of Boy's neck to drink it in.

Eva had begun to talk of her life at the crèche. It was

tedious, she said, and every day was much like every other, but
she had come to prefer it to the city. All summer, she said, she
had worked in the gardens, learning the work with a man who
had been a long time in the country, working with the people.
He was someone who couldn't be predicted, she said, just as she
was herself such a person; someone outside the predictions that
were made for everyone, for every person. She had liked
talking with him, hearing about other ways of life in other
places, other possibilities; after work they had often gone
walking with Boy, in the evenings that had seemed to her so
huge and vacant here, quiet, as though waiting to be filled.

'As though you could step into them and keep walking away
forever,' she said.

'Yes.'

'That's what he said.'

'Yes.' But Hare had not been listening; he had been hearing
Boy, and feeling him, the solidity of him in his lap. He had
begun to imagine what it would be like to live here, as Eva and
Boy did. He thought of the passage of days, the work that there
would be to do — work which Hare had never done but which
he could just now imagine doing. *Have you come to stay?* Eva
had asked him, as though it were possible he might. He was
Boy's father, after all; he had a place here with him, too.
Perhaps, if he did, if he came to stay with Eva and Boy, he
might in the course of a year recover the balance he had lost,
shake off the lethargy that bound him.

'Would you want to do that?' he asked again.

'Do what?'

'Stay here. If you could.'

She looked at Hare as though he had said something not
quite intelligible. 'I'm not going to stay here,' she said.

'Where are you going?' Hare asked.

'I'm going,' Eva said. 'They can't have me any longer.'

'But where?' Hare insisted. 'What city? What town? Are you
going to look for another project? Are you going to give up
Blue?'

She had begun to shake her head, easily but certainly rejecting each of these possibilities. It would not be, her face seemed
to say, anything that could be predicted.

'Eva,' Hare said. 'You know you can't just . . . just fall out of the universe.' He had begun to experience an awful swooning vertigo. 'You can't, you can't. You'll be alone, you . . .'

'I won't be alone.'

'What? What do you mean?'

'I told you,' Eva said. 'I told you about him. I was telling you all about him. Weren't you listening?'

'Oh,' Hare said. 'I see.'

'You tell me there's no place to go. But there has to be.'

'I didn't mean that. I meant —'

'There has to be,' Eva said, looking away.

Hare sat still and said nothing further, but it seemed at that moment that the color began to be drained from everything that he looked at: the fruits and orange gourds on the tables, the people in Blue, the colored tiles of the floor. The boy he held, who a moment ago seemed as large as himself, no, larger, seemed to grow small, distant within his arms, a foreign thing, something not connected to him at all, like a stone. He looked up. Had the sun gone behind clouds? No, it still shone. Where did this awful chill come from? 'It's not what I meant,' he said again, but did not hear himself speak it; he could only marvel at what had happened, what had happened and would not cease happening. Boy fell silent, and slipped out of his arms to the floor.

'I don't feel well,' he said, and stood abruptly. 'I'd better go.'

Both Boy and Eva were looking at him, curious and not unkind, not kind either; not anything. Their faces were stones or closed doors, the faces of those at accidents or public quarrels. Hare thought he would see such faces if he were to die in the street.

'Do you want to go to the infirmary?' Eva asked.

'No. I'll go.'

'Are you sure?'

'I'll go,' Hare said. 'I'll go. I'll go. I'll go.'

He had thought it was just a story he was being told, about working in the gardens, about summer evenings, empty and vast. He hadn't listened carefully; he hadn't known that there would come this sickening reversal of figure and ground, showing him a story he had not suspected, that he was all unready for. Nothing had been as he thought it was; he had walked into what was the case as into a truck's path.

Hare stood at the crossroads awaiting the trucks returning from the farmlands to the city. The strange gray blindness that had afflicted him at the cadre crèche had not passed, nor had the dreadful stonelike weight in his chest. He patted his chest as he stood waiting, trying to press it down. He thought perhaps he would go to the infirmary when he returned.

It was true what he told her, though, what he knew about heterarchy and she did not, that it was limitless, that it could not be got outside of, that to think about it as though it had an inside and an outside was a kind of pain, the pain of error that is fruitless, unnecessary, because self-inflicted: this conviction that by choice or by some dreadful mistake it is possible to fall out of the universe. Hare knew (it was all that he had ever tried to make her see) that it was not possible to fall out of the universe.

He thought of her and Boy and the man they were going away with. His thought followed them into a featureless stony landscape, without weather or air, under a vault of dun sky. Forever and ever would they be there.

He tried to draw breath deeply, but the painful bolus beneath his sternum seemed to prevent it; he could not get the air he needed.

Perhaps he would die. He wasn't old, but he seemed to be suffering some irreversible debility that quickened almost daily. He could not clearly remember, but he thought he had not really been well since the time when he was a boy and had cut off his penis.

No, that was a dream. Wasn't it? Yes, of course it was. With horror Hare realized that for some hours he had actually been assuming it to be so: that he had done such a thing and was now living with the consequences.

No. He wasn't truly ill. It was only this weather oppressing him, airless and chill, this close vault of dirty sky. He was grievously thirsty. Perhaps he would die.

The trucks surprised Hare, appearing suddenly past sundown; apparently he had been standing and waiting for hours without noticing time pass. He waved. The truck that stopped to pick him up was not the one that had brought him out; the young people who helped him in were not the same, were not the cheerful boys and girls who had sung children's songs and talked and laughed. These looked at Hare in silence, their faces in the twilight pale and reserved.

Hare thought he should explain himself to them. Perhaps he could ask them for help. He opened his mouth, but his throat was so dry and constricted that no words came out; he gaped foolishly, he supposed, but no one smiled. He forced his throat to open, and a gout of language came out that Hare did not intend or even understand.

He had better not talk more, he thought. He sought for a place to sit down; the silent young people drew away from him as he crept toward the shelter of the cab. He supposed that after all no one had heard the nonsense he had spoken, not over the noise of the truck's engine: an awful imploding roar that grew steadily worse, sucking the air from Hare's mouth and the thoughts from his head. He leaned against the cab, his hand hanging loosely over his knee; with his thumbnail he flicked the fragment of cigarette he held between his fingers. He was certain now that he would die of his old wound, or, far worse, that he would live forever. Forever and ever. 'Ave Eva,' he said, and a woman laughed. Hare laughed, too. The words seemed the only thing that could relieve his thirst. *Ave Eva*, he said again, or thought he said, unable any longer to hear himself under the withering roar. *Ave Eva. Ave Eva. Ave Eva. Ave Eva.*

The committee had high seats behind a long desk. This was not so that they sat above those who came before them to be examined — Hare's guard explained this to Hare — but so that everyone in the room could see them clearly. The committee leader had a seat on one side, and before her she had some dossiers and some things taken from Hare's room, including the sketches of old buildings and the attempts Hare had made to decipher their inscriptions. Hare found it hard to recognize these things; when the committee leader held up a sketch and asked Hare if he had made it, he couldn't answer. He tried to answer; he opened his mouth to answer, but could not make an answer come out.

The committee was patient. They listened to testimony about Hare, what he had done, how he had been found. They rested their cheeks in their hands, or they leaned back in their chairs with their hands folded in their laps; they asked gentle, unsurprised questions of the people who came before them, trying to get a clear story. When there seemed to be a contradiction, they would ask Hare what had happened. Hare opened his mouth to answer; he thought he could answer, possible answers occurred to him, then other possibilities, opening and branching like coincidence-magnitude calculations, switching figure and ground. Still he thought he could answer, if he could only say everything at once, describe or state the whole situation, the whole act-field, at once; but he could not, so he only struggled for a while with open mouth while the committee waited, watching him. Then they returned to questioning the others.

The two women who lived in the dormitory room next to Hare described how he had got into their room late at night: how he had forced his way in, though talking all the time very strangely and gently, about how he meant them no harm, wanted only to explain. They told (interrupting each other, finishing each other's sentences, until the committee head had to speak sharply to them) of their fear and confusion, of how they had tried to get out of the room, how Hare had prevented them. A torn nightdress was shown to the committee. The committee talked among themselves about attempted rape, asking questions that embarrassed the two women, but asking them so gently that answers were got at last.

Some others from the dormitory described how they had come to the women's room, and their struggle with Hare. They were eager to explain how or why it was that they had let Hare go, had not apprehended him and taken him then and there to security or to the committee representative. The committee head, not interested in hearing this, kept guiding the witnesses back to the facts of Hare's struggle: what weapons he had had, how he had behaved, what he had said.

Willy came in. He wanted to go and stand next to Hare, but

the committee asked him to stand where the other witnesses had stood; and all through his story he kept looking at Hare, as though pleading with him to say something, to behave in some way that Willy understood. Hare saw that Willy's hands shook, and he wanted to take his hand, to say something to calm him, but he couldn't move. His guard sat behind him with his hands in his lap and probably wouldn't have prevented his going to Willy or speaking to him, Hare thought; but he couldn't do it, any more than he could answer the committee's questions.

Much of Willy's story was taken up with how tired and upset Hare had been before this incident, the bad dreams he had had, the troubles at the project. Hare couldn't remember any of the things Willy told about — any more than he could remember going into the women's room, or fighting with the people in the dormitory — but it seemed to him that the more that Willy, with every kind intention, tried to explain away Hare's behavior, the worse it looked to the committee. It sounded as if Willy knew something really terrible about Hare, and out of love was covering it up.

But Willy had once said to Hare that he knew all about him, and there wasn't anything terrible.

Hare wanted to say that, more in Willy's defense somehow than his own, but he could not.

Then, as Willy told about going out after Hare, and searching the city for him, Hare began to remember something of the events that were being told to the committee. In the same way that a dream that is forgotten on waking can be brought into the mind, disconnected but vivid, by some event of the day, some word or sight, Hare caught sight of bits of the story he had been in. When Willy told of finding him at last, huddled on the wide steps of the building whose inscription he had copied out, he remembered. Not how he had come to be there, or what had happened to him before, but that alone: Willy's hand on his shoulder, Willy's face before him, speaking to him. And he knew also, with a deep horror that deafened him to the committee's further proceedings, that that had not happened yesterday, or the day before, but weeks ago; and he remembered nothing at all of what had happened between then and now.

The committee leader was speaking, summing up the

committee's findings. The case was really out of their provenance, she thought, and should probably not have been brought before the committee. She asked Hare if he had anything further to say.

The guard behind Hare leaned forward and tapped Hare's shoulder. Hare stood.

'Do you have anything you want to say?' the committee leader said again, patiently and without insistence.

'It's hard,' Hare said. This came out of his mouth as though it were a stone he had dislodged from his throat, not like something he had decided to say. 'It's very hard!'

He looked at the faces in the room, the committee, his neighbors, Willy. He knew, suddenly, that they would understand: they must, for they were all engaged with Hare in this hard thing together. 'We all know how hard it is,' he said. 'The work of the Revolution. To grasp its principles isn't easy. To *live* them isn't easy. I've tried hard. We all have.' They would understand how he had stumbled, they must; they would help him to rise. Together, in the face of the awful difficulties of the Revolution, they would go on. If he could lean on them, then as soon as he regained his feet, he could try again to be someone on whom others leaned. He smiled, and waited for their smile in return. 'It's hard, always grappling with these difficulties. Act-field theory: that's hard to think about.' He shook his head in self-deprecation. 'Oh, I know. And the duties of cadre. The duty to *understand*. The committee knows how hard it is; everyone knows. I only want to say that I've tried. I want the committee to understand that. The committee understands. You understand.'

He stopped talking. The circle of faces around him had not changed. It watched him with what seemed to him a terrible reserve, and something like pity. He knew he had not been recognized. He said, to the calm, closed face of the committee head: 'Don't you think it's hard?'

'No,' she said. 'Frankly, I don't.'

Frankly. Hare could not stand up any longer; his knees were unable to support him. Frankly. She had spoken with that remote, unmoved concern, the remote concern with which an adult will speak to a child in moral difficulties, difficulties the adult doesn't feel; without anger, with some impatience, without collusion: collusion would be inappropriate. Hare knew himself to be absolutely alone.

He had stopped speaking. After a moment the committee head gave the committee's resolution. Hare was to be remanded to a hospital. The committee head said she was sure that with rest and attention, Hare would return to normal. When he was better, they might have another meeting, and consider what amends Hare might be able to make for his behavior, if any were thought to be necessary then. Her last words to Hare were the usual formula spoken at the end of committee deliberations, when disposition of someone's case was made. She said: 'Did you hear that?'

In the spring, discharged from the hospital, Hare was given a paper with an address on it, an address in an older part of the city where he had used to go often, to look at buildings.

It was strange to be once again alone on the street. Not often in the last months had he been alone at all, and never on the street. Except that a thin rain was falling, cold and hastening, he might have wandered for a while through the squares and alleys of the quarter; they seemed at once new and familiar to him, and the sensation of walking there was both vivifying and sad: the mixture of emotions made him feel painfully alive, and he wondered how long it would persist. But he turned up his collar and went on to the building to which he had been sent.

It was an old one, and one he remembered. He had stood before it more than once, feeling with his sight and his sense of proportion the curves of its stonework and its iron window-grilles. He had used to look in through the barred glass doors, down a long marble-floored hall bordered by columns, but he had never dared to go in. He went in now. There was an aged doorkeeper who took Hare's paper, made a remark about the rain and shuddered as though it were he who was wet and not Hare, and entered something on the terminal before him. He waited for a reply in the display, and when he had it, he left the little cage or box that was his station and led Hare down the long hall, past the columns pinkish and blue-veined like the legs of old people, to a tall open door. He waited for Hare to enter, then closed the door behind him.

The big room was empty. There was only a work station — a desk and two chairs, a terminal, a pile of printouts and other papers — which stood in the center of the floor, or not quite in the center, as though whoever had placed them there hadn't known that the room had a center. It did, though: it was clearly marked by the radiating diamonds of the parquet floor; it was plumb with the central diamond-shaped pendant of the chandelier, a multitiered forest of swagged lights and what seemed to be strings of jewels, that hung from the center of the ceiling above. Hare looked up at it as he crossed the floor to the desk; it swung around its axis, or rather seemed to swing, as he moved. He sat down in the chair beside the desk, crossed his hands in his lap, and waited. He didn't know who it was he waited for, or what disposition would be made of him now; he only supposed, with a sort of automatic humility he hardly even recognized in himself any longer, that whomever he waited for would be wiser than himself, would be able to see him clearly and know what was best.

That was one thing he had come to learn, over the last months — not how wise others were, but how unwise he was himself. He had learned to trust those who trusted in the world in a way that he could not: that way he hoped he might once again come to trust in the world himself. And even if he could not — even if there remained in him always some fatal mistrust — still there was no better thing that he could do: nothing else at all that he could do.

It hadn't been easy, learning that.

In the first weeks of his stay in the hospital, he had mostly been aware of the difference between himself and others, both those in difficulties like himself, and those attempting to help them. It seemed to him important, desperately important, to make those differences clear: to explain what it was in him that made him unlike others and unable to be as they were. It frightened him to be among so many who were bewildered, hurt, angry, or sad, not because he was not all these things himself, but because he felt himself to be unimaginable to them; and it frightened him more to be with the staff, because he could not define for them, in any way that he felt they could truly grasp, the perplexities within himself that made him unlike them: made him unwise, unwhole, divided and in pain, as they were not.

They were not even cadre for the most part, the staff, not anyway in the wing to which Hare was moved after a series of tests had determined there were no metabolic disorders at the root of his condition. (He had briefly hoped that some such disorder would be discovered, to relieve him of the awful burden of finding the explanation elsewhere. But there was none.) In his wing were those whose troubles were unanalyzable, and the staff there were only kind, only experienced and sympathetic, only set to watch the disorders take their course, and give what common help they could. And how could Hare explain to them — heavy women who nodded and patted his hand, male nurses who spoke in banalities — about act-field theory, its unchallengeable truth, its danger to him?

He knew so much. In his long, long silences his own explanations were his only occupation, and seemed to him all that sustained him over an abyss. He knew, with great precision, what stood between him and happiness; he knew quite well that he did not need to feel as he did, that just beyond his feelings, just past his really quite simple and explainable error, lay the real world, which he could reach if he could only stop making this error, or even stop explaining the error to himself: but when he tried to say these things aloud, to explain this predicament to the nurses and the staff or the other patients, the explanations hurt him; and the real world, as he talked, grew more fearsomely remote.

The explanations broke, in the end, like a fever. Then there were tears, and shameful incontinence of grief, and helplessness; no help at all but kindness and attention, the help of those who knew how little help they could be.

He had not believed it was possible to fall out of the universe: yet he had experienced exactly that. He had fallen out of the universe into explanations of why he could not fall out of the universe. And he had to reach for the hands of those who could not even envisage such a thing and be drawn back in. In the common-rooms, with their old furniture worn and stained as though by the sorrows of those who used it; in the kitchens, where he clumsily helped with meals; in the winter yards and the crossing paths of the grounds, he would be swept by waves of healing integration, unwilled, as though some severed part of him were drawing back within him: waves of feeling that left him weak and still afraid of the strange things he contained. When those diminished, too, like the terrible explanations, then he was empty. He looked around himself at the world and knew that though he did not know it, it knew him. He ate its nourishing breakfasts, blinked in its watery winter sunlight, joined its talk tentatively, washed its dishes with humility. He could not fall out of it.

Willy, who had visited him weekly, bringing good food and (what Hare hungered more for) stories of the people Willy knew, came on a spring day to take him away. In his dossier, encoded now with thousands of others in the hospital's records, the course of his illness and its resolution were charted, he knew; and when the magnitude of his difference from others was accounted for, his absolute otherness factored in, they were exactly as act-field theory predicted. It was all right.

All right. He sat, hands folded in his lap, waiting beneath the chandelier.

When a dark woman in Blue of about his own age came through the far double doors, Hare stood. The woman waved to him apologetically across the vast room, picking up a folder from a cart of them by the door; smiling, she crossed the geometrical floor to where Hare stood.

Among cadre there was no rank, and therefore no marks of rank beyond the simple clothes of Blue they all wore. But subtle distinguishing marks had nevertheless arisen; Hare knew that the cluster of pens in this woman's pocket meant heavy responsibilities. There was more, though. In the last months the faces of those he met were often charged for him with intense but imaginary familiarity; and yet about this woman he was sure.

'I know you,' he said.

She raised her eyebrows. She didn't know him.

'Yes,' Hare said. 'Years ago.' He named the study camp where in the summer of Hare's seventeenth year they had known one another, studied together, hiked together. As he spoke, he remembered the summer darkness of the common-room where late at night they had talked.

'Oh, yes,' she said. 'Yes, yes, I remember now. A long time ago.' She smiled, remembering. 'A long time.'

She had opened Hare's dossier, and now drew out the drawings of buildings and the calculations of their geometries that Hare had made. The last time Hare had seen them was when he stood before the committee: so long ago.

'Do you know why you do this?' she asked. 'Copy these things?'

'No. I like them, I like to look at such places, old places, and wonder how they came to be; what the people thought and felt who built them.'

'History,' she suggested, 'The past.'

'Yes.'

'That interests us, too,' she said. 'My project, I mean.'

'Oh,' said Hare, not knowing what else to say. 'Is yours . . . is it an Applications project?'

She smiled. 'No,' she said.

'Oh.'

She rested her cheek again in the palm of her hand. 'I think,' she said, 'that long ago there was another time like this one, when people lived in places whose history they didn't know, whose history they had forgotten. They had lost history because they knew so little. They called that ignorance "darkness," and when they began to relearn history, they called that knowledge "light." But we're in darkness, too. Not because we know so little, but because we know so much. It's not different.'

'Knowing everything is not different from knowing nothing,' Hare said. 'Is that what you mean?'

She quoted an old principle of act theorists, one that had become an adage of Revolutionary cadre: 'We seek no solution — only knowledge of the problem.'

She turned to the drawing of the building opposite the cathedral, whose lettering Hare had copied out. Her finger touched the words.

'Do you know what they mean?' Hare asked her.

'No,' she said. She folded her hands before her. 'When you went out to do these things . . .'

'It was always on my own time,' Hare said. 'On free days.'

'Did you tell anyone where you were going, what you were doing?'

'Not usually. Not all of it.' Hare stared down at the hat he held in his hands. He felt, like an old secret wound, his taste for history, like a peasant child's taste for eating dirt.

'It must have seemed,' she said, 'that you were leading a double life. Did you feel that way? That you were leading a double life?'

At her words hot tears rose to Hare's eyes with awful quickness, and he felt for a moment that he would sob, as he had sobbed so often at just such small remarks that winter. A double life: a life inside, and another outside, between which Hare was pulled apart.

'Will you go on doing this, now?' the woman asked gently, her eyes watching Hare's evident distress.

'I don't know,' he said. He looked up. 'I want to help,' he said. 'I want to do useful work. I know that I haven't been much help for a long time, but I'm stronger now. I want to be of use.'

She turned over the picture, and pushed the pile toward Hare. For a moment he didn't understand that she was giving them back to him. 'I think your project made a mistake when they removed you from the work you'd been doing,' she said.

'You do?'

'I think the better thing would have been to release you from cadre altogether.' She rested her cheek again in the palm of her hand. 'What do you think?'

A storm of shame arose within Hare, a storm that made the dreadful imploding roar he had first heard in the truck returning from the country. It broke so quickly over him that he had to suppose he had all along been expecting precisely these words to be said to him. Through its great noise he could not hear his own answer: 'I'll do as you think best,' he said. 'Whatever you think.'

'Go to the people,' the woman said.

Hare covered his eyes. 'I'm not good for much,' he said. 'There's not much I know how to do.'

'What I suggest is this,' the woman said. 'You'll get a ration card and find a place in the city. Then — go on with what you did. I mean the drawings and the investigations you liked. History.'

Hare listened.

'If you would,' she said, 'I would like you to come back here, now and then, and talk to me — to my project — about what you are doing.'

'That would be all right?' Hare said. 'I could do that?'

'You can do as you like,' she said. 'You can go back to your project, too.'

'No,' Hare said, feeling a strange warmth at his breastbone. 'No. I'll do as you say.'

'I don't know what we can learn, but I think . . . well.' Her humorous eyes regarded him steadily. 'Anyway there's probably nothing better for you to do. You are an oddity, aren't you?'

'Yes,' Hare said.

'Did you think the Revolution was not large enough to contain you?'

'No,' Hare said, 'I didn't think so.' But he had: he understood at that moment that he had thought exactly that.

She took a card from his dossier and handed it to him. 'Take this to Applications, in the old cathedral,' she said. 'They'll tell you what to do. Come back here when you like. I'll be glad to see you.'

She stood; Hare's interview was evidently at an end. He twisted the hat he held in his hands.

'I was remembering,' he said, 'something you told me. That summer, when we met at study camp.' He felt his heart fill with a familiar apprehension. 'You said . . . We were talking about act-field theory, which I was working on then, and you told me you believed that there was no such thing really as act-field theory at all; but that so long as everybody believed there was such a theory, and cadre believed that it worked, then it *did* work.'

'Yes?'

'Yes.' Dreadful as the danger Hare felt himself to be in, narrow as the ledge he stood on, he had to ask: 'Do you still think that?'

'No,' she said. Her smile hadn't passed, but it had changed, as though she not only shared a memory with Hare, but a joke as well; or a secret. 'No, I don't.'

Hare walked through the old quarter of the city, not feeling the thin rain soaking through his shoes. He seemed to himself to be naked but warm, to be already not in Blue, and walking in the world for the first time, as though his feet created it step by step: the world he had fallen out of, the world into which Eva and Boy had gone. He laughed, in fear and hunger for it.

His desire was not what he had thought it to be: his desire for history, for Eva, for Boy, none of it was what he thought it was. He knew nothing, nothing of the world he walked in; but he might learn.

What a strange, what a foolish error for him to have made, Hare thought. If he were called again before the local committee to make restitution for the trouble he had caused, he could tell them: he had come, without knowing it, to see the world in hierarchies. He, with his years of training, his excellent education, had built hierarchies in his heart. He had not known it until he had been asked to resign from cadre and had been overcome with shame: as though to be in Blue were better than to be not in Blue, to be cadre better than to be among the people.

He had believed act-field theory governed the act-field, and not the reverse. But the act-field governed. In the computers of the Revolution, as in the corridors and hollows of Hare's heart and mind, there was only a virtuality, after all; a virtual real-world, and not a whole one. He was inside the act-field and not it inside him; so was the Revolution, and all its work.

'Oh, I see,' he said aloud. He had stopped walking. At the end of the street the great square opened, crossed by a single person on foot, a single bicycle. The obscure huge buildings that bordered it were soft in the misty rain. Hare, for the first time, yet not as though for the first time, but as though coming to remember some commonplace thing of enormous, of vital, importance, saw the act-field. Still; calm; with no face, not kind, not cruel, not anything. He reached out with his mind to touch it, but everywhere he touched it, it parted, showing him spaces, interstices, emptinesses formed by the edge of himself facing the sparkling edge of the world.

Hare cried out, as though stung. He felt the sensation of an answer, a sensation like a physical shock. The answer was an answer to a figure-ground problem, the simplest figure-ground problem, a problem solved long ago. The answer was an emptiness, formed by the edges of two questions: but the sensation of the answer was like a bit of light, a point of light lit, flaring fiercely and burning out: a physical sensation, a brief coincidence, an act.

Then it was gone. Hare set out across the square.

1989:
THE YEAR IN
SCIENCE FICTION

__ WHY DIDN'T THE CROWD BOO? __
by
BRIAN W. ALDISS

The ocean poured itself into a great bay, the Bay of Dissonance. The waves that reached the shore had travelled halfway round the world, unimpeded by land, unencumbered by ship. As if the journey had robbed them of momentum, they broke upon the strand with scarcely a sound beyond a recurrent hiss.

Marking the final northern point of the bay was a rocky headland. In all the land- and sea-scape, this headland was the sole feature aspiring to something other than the horizontal. From a distance of some miles, it resembled a castle. But no being had ever piled stone on stone, or sought to defend any such eminence.

A figure was progressing towards this eminence, following the curve of the beach, with mechanical step.

The figure was metallic and of ancient construction. Externally, its body formed a simple construct of octagonal design. It had no head. The body, bulbous at the bottom, rose almost to a point before flattening to support a small looped aerial. To this geometrical body, two sturdy legs and an arm had been added.

The sturdy legs moved tirelessly at a good pace. The creature had been walking along the coastline for some while, leaving behind it a trail of deeply indented footprints which the ocean eroded.

This creature had been named by its long-defunct inventors Turth. Knowing not the pronoun for the first person singular — a proof, inevitably, that it had no soul — it referred to itself, on the rare occasions when such reference became necessary, simply as Turth.

As Turth progressed, undaunted by weather, undeterred by day or night, it kubered at irregular intervals. A kuber sometimes caused it to alter its course, to proceed farther from the shallows, or even to enter them. Some kubers caused it to accelerate or slow its pace, some to make an about turn.

The single arm would snake out and pluck diskettes from

the creature's sides, sometimes from the left side, sometimes from the right. The diskettes were stored in slots which opened at the touch of the creature's two fingers. After selecting a diskette, the arm transferred it to a slot in the 'head' of the creature. Turth then kubered according to the instructions of the diskette.

An observer would have been puzzled to decide whether the movement of the arm was under the creature's control or worked autonomously. Turth gave every appearance of paying no attention to the arm's movements.

The next diskette slotted into the blunt head was labelled COASTLINE. As had been the previous diskette. When the diskette was played out, the arm removed it, slotting it back into the creature's right side. Turth kubered on its way.

The next diskette was also labelled COASTLINE. By this means the perceptions of the creature functioned.

Following more COASTLINE diskettes was one labelled NIGHT. The creature switched on a headlight and proceeded on its way, kubering through disc-induced darkness.

After a long intermission, up came the arm. The previous diskette was replaced by one labelled DAY. The creature switched off its headlight. Always it advanced steadily.

The arm took from the left slots a diskette labelled SARABANDE. Turth danced gravely on the sand to its own music.

When it received the diskette SHIP, it turned, scanned the empty waters, and kubered a ship. Distant though the ship was, its great metallic sails, driven by wind and sunlight, could clearly be seen by the creature. It stood looking until a different diskette was inserted in its head. Then Turth proceeded again towards the distant headland.

My empathy with this creature was intense last Saturday. Someone — I knew not who — had inserted an EXISTENCE diskette in my head, and I was kubering according to its demand. For this reason, I left my story about Turth incomplete.

If I ever complete my story, I know the time will come when that arm, whether deliberately or by accident, inserts a diskette entitled NON-EXISTENCE in the creature's head, and it will instantly cease to be. I feel for my creature, and hence delay the hour.

Once the diskette SATURDAY had been inserted in my head, I wandered about at home until the diskette BLACK-WELL'S was inserted.

Blackwell's bookshop is one of the glories of Oxford. There I kubered, as so often in my leisure hours, without any clear idea of what I wanted to buy. Serendipity is a large part of the pleasure of bookshops. On this occasion, a diskette popped into my head labelled BREAKTHROUGHS, and almost at once, on the lower ground floor, in the immense Norrington Room, housing two million or more books, I encountered a book by Claire L. Parkinson entitled *Breakthroughs.*

Breakthroughs contains a list of achievements of science and mathematics, cross-referenced, and arranged in chronological order. '1720. J.G.H. Karmer (Austrian) notes that fresh vegetables have a curative effect on soldiers stricken with scurvy. 1753. James Lind (Scottish) publishes 'A Treatise on the Scurvy', asserting the value of fresh fruits and vegetables for preventing and treating the disease. Oranges and lemons specifically mentioned. 1912. Casimir Funk (Polish-American) identifies scurvy as a 'vitamine' deficiency disease. The term 'vitamine' is later changed to vitamin.'

Thus one can follow any scientific development through Parkinson's pages. It was at once apparent that this book was indispensable, although I had not previously known of its existence.

In fact, I had been wondering whether to buy Stephen King's novel, *The Dark Half.* A review in *Interzone* discouraged me. The reviewer mentioned that one of King's characters refers to a novelist as someone who is paid to tell lies.

I have always fought this particular smart-arsed saying. Although it has been put about by a number of well-known sf writers, Robert Heinlein and John Brunner among them, it represents what should be the reverse of the true situation. Without going into the question of whether novelists are 'paid', within the ordinary meaning of the term, rather than just happening to earn money if their fictions are liked, I defend the principle that fiction is in some way designed to promulgate truth, not lies. Yes, even science fiction. Truth, the vitamin of mind.

The great Russian writers would have scorned to think of themselves as being 'paid'. They believed they had a readership to educate — to educate into religion, the way of the world, injustices, civilities, the sorrows of others, and perhaps several other conflicting matters. Of course, this sort of voluntary education, unlike the kind conducted everywhere in schools, had to be spiced with interest, the illicit love of Anna Karenina, the murder by Rashkolnikov, and so on. In *Tom Jones*, Henry Fielding speaks of interest as 'indeed a most excellent medicine', which 'flies at once to the particular part of the body on which you desire to operate, whether it is the tongue, the hand, or any other member, where it scarce ever fails of immediately producing the desired effect'.

The afflicted part on which we desire to operate in sf is the head. To revert to our poor unsouled creature, Turth, still patrolling the unknown seashore, what will it experience if that autonomous arm inserts into its headless head the diskette FICTION? Truth or falsehood?

The answer, I suppose — and I know the answer no better than my average reader, beyond adding, in Fieldingesque style, that at least the attempt to toy with the question is mine rather than yours, dear reader — and to consider it an important question, with immediate bearing on what you read in this excellent anthology — is that the diskette FICTION would contain both truth and falsehood.

The invaluable OED utters, as its first two definitions of Fiction, conflicting descriptions of the word. 1, 'the action of fashioning or imitating', and, 2, 'arbitrary invention'. This implies that a fiction writer can choose merely to imitate or merely to invent arbitrarily; either is okay. You may judge Turth, trudging along his coastline, a mere arbitrary invention. But don't you notice that he nevertheless imitates some forms of behaviour, and not only electronic ones?

You, reader, can see Turth quite clearly in your mind. I have inserted, as it were, a diskette labelled TURTH into your head. This enlarges your world-view. We need to extend our vocabulary all the time. Our repertoire has to increase as culture grows more complex, spawns more departments, coins more seductive delusions.

Once, grubbing under stones on savannahs, huddling in caves, mankind possessed only the frozen vocabulary of instinct. Now we are freer. Now we need to imagine impossible things to keep alive. The unlikely is our new truth. There is a ghostly language of dreams which we downgrade as falsehood at our peril.

This last year has witnessed the extraordinary events in Eastern Europe where, just before Christmas 1989, the totalitarian regimes in Poland, East Germany, and elsewhere began to crumble. Swift was the fall thereof. The firmly entrenched 'Conductor' of Romania, Nicolae Caeucescu, proved not to be firmly entrenched at all. The crowd booed him on his balcony. He tried to flee the country. He was captured, tried, and shot on Christmas Day.

Why didn't the crowd boo previously?

If it was all so easy, why didn't it happen before?

Like climatic change, systems of belief do not alter gradually. We walk out one day and find it is spring. So, it seems, we may walk out one day and find we are free. It is not that the emperor has no clothes, not that he never had clothes — Caeucescu was clothed in the most elaborate security system the world has ever seen, employing one in three of the population — but that the same diskette went into everyone's slot at approximately the same time. BOO, it said.

Such is the power of language.

In January, an old hero died — a hero and wise man, in many ways the opposite of the Conductor who had just preceded him into the spacious world of the grave, not least in his reverence for the amenities of cities which Ceausescu was busy destroying. Lewis Mumford died at the age of 94, full of honour. His writings were diverse and always humane. Among his most celebrated books were *The Story of Utopias, Technics and Civilization, The Culture of Cities,* and *The City in History.* These works give evidence of vast erudition; their scope would be vacuous were it not for Mumford's brilliant eye for detail, Shakespearean in its command. No doubt other sf writers gladly acknowledge themselves in Mumford's debt. He's the Stapledon of city-planning.

It was in his old age, in 1966, that he produced a volume called *The Myth of the Machine*. This work postulates something Mumford calls a 'megamachine'. A megamachine is a societal energy-system which relies not on tools alone but on the bodies and beliefs of men. Belief, the willingness of individuals to become less than individual in pursuit of a god or an idea, is the true power of the megamachine.

To each age its particular form of megamachine. Once the over-riding belief has died, succeeding generations, trapped into a new belief-set, can hardly comprehend the one before. What on earth were the ancient Egyptians thinking of when they built the pyramids? We can hardly imagine. What will succeeding centuries think of the belief-set of our generation's stockpiling of obscene weapons of destruction which can destroy ourselves and our planet many times over? They will hardly imagine. Or so we hope.

Made of metal-plastic alloy, rather than language, Turth is a metaphor reduced to reality. He clanks, therefore he is. Also, I forgot to mention, he is two kilometres high, and Russian kilometres at that. The shore shakes under Turth's tread. And he can receive only one idea at a time.

Turth has to be powerful. The world he walks on has sixty times the mass of our planet. And, as Mumford says, it is only the powerful who gain from the megamachine; the rest of us tend to get ground down, trampled into the sand. Mumford puts it better:

'Only the minority . . . closely attached to the mega-machine could fully share this power; while those who resisted it courted death — as well might they resist the stars in their courses. Despite repeated setbacks and failures, these cosmic fantasies have remained intact to this day: indeed, they have come back again in the guise of "absolute weapons" and "absolute sovereignty" — the far from innocent hallucinations of the "Nuclear Age".'

We have seen in Britain during this year how reluctant the supervisors of this country's little megamachine are to remove from their crania the diskette labelled ABSOLUTE WEAPONS. That's the tune they kuber to. We pay our taxes to keep the diskette in place.

Meanwhile, at the other end of Europe, a diskette labelled DEMOCRACY has been inserted. The old order which was booed into nothingness has disappeared. Nobody understands how it prevailed for so long. Past kumbers soon become past comprehension.

As for Turth, he lumbers on along the margin which divides land from sea and belongs to neither. Does he grow tired in his long march? But then up comes that single arm again and inserts a different diskette into his headless head. REST, it is labelled.

And Turth believes he sleeps. He walks, and believes he sleeps.

WAKE says another diskette, and he believes he wakes.

Now perhaps we can understand why there are two definitions of fiction. 'Arbitrary invention' (if indeed there is such a thing) is a lie. But 'imitation (realistic fiction)' can also be a lie, since what is imitated is presumably activities taking place within the current distorted belief-set of the ruling megamachine. How can writers, therefore, avoid lying?

Well, there's accidental lying and deliberate lying. The late Robert Heinlein, mentioned earlier, was a declared supporter of the presiding megamachine (or rather, of the megamachine now rusting and becoming obsolescent); his truths fall within that illusory belief-set. Nevertheless, it seems to me that a writer of sf on the whole starts with a great advantage when it comes to attempting to tell the truth. For he can throw out all the old received beliefs, or the ones he holds to be false beliefs, and start clean with a new universe, which may well conflict with reality as widely perceived.

Sf stories are *anagrams of truth*, like Turth itself.

Readers of sf also have a special role to play, a rather different role from that of readers of other kinds of fiction. They have to decide whether the invention which follows from the new clean slate is arbitrary or — VISIONARY.

Friends, it does mean discarding a lot of old diskettes. This year in particular. Since it was powered by courage, the booing has changed things.

But now Turth's independent arm is active again. As if unaware, Turth continues to pace towards the headland, which from a distance so greatly resembles a splendid castle. The arm selects another diskette. This diskette is labelled LAST YEAR.

It clicks into place in Turth's headless head.

The massive planet vanishes from under him.

Turth goes on walking remorselessly, remorselessly through the universe. It's hard to stop a megamachine.

March 1990.

SCIENCE FICTION NOVELS
OF THE YEAR
by
JOHN CLUTE

As I walk'd through the Wilderness of this World, I lighted on a
certain place, where was a Denn: And I laid me down in that place
to sleep: And as I slept I dreamed a Dream. I dreamed, and behold
*I saw four Horsemen, cloathed in Armor, and their Names were Isaac
and Iris and Poul and Greg: And the Lines of Thought upon each Face
were of Gilt paint: And the Eye Balls were of Gilt also.* So I awoke,
and behold I saw four Horsemen, and they seemed to be making
pretty good headway, so I thought I'd better hurry on after them,
though the sky was dark, and the road was exceedingly narrow,
indeed a Tight Rope. And so I came to the last Rider, and saw that
he sat backwards within his Cage of shining armor, and bore upon
the crown of his head a gilt face which stared forward, but himself
stared back upon my countenance as I drew abreast, and waved
his tiny arms, and in his hands was a map of the path we had
already taken. And the name of that map was *Nemesis.* And I
thought, I know that face. And so I passed further on ahead, and
saw that all the Riders sat bandy-legged within their Struts and
stared thus backwards at what had been, with great longing. And
each bore a map. And the name of the maps were *Message to the
Planet,* and *Boat of a Million Years,* and *Tides of Light.* And I passed
yet further, and for a bright Instant thought to see the road ahead
in all Truth and the Chasm, but dared not give a second glance, for
the sake of my Health. And I turned back, and was passing to the
rear, and imprints of the four just maps fell into my hands (for a
sum), and I examined them. And I thought: That's all right, but
what have you done for me lately?

Lately, what has begun to happen is history. The Cold War,
after clutching Time deep-frozen to its winter heart for longer
than we dare remember, has finally cracked open, and a million
clocks have begun to turn (for Time lives again). We may have
wintered the War (or not), spring may come (or otherwise); but
suddenly there is a Present, and it burns. Suddenly (for Time

has given us air to breathe) the great globe and all that it inherit seems within our grasp to save (or spoil utterly). The deranged Punch-and-Judys who 'govern' us no longer (until they regroup) have the final say, and in March 1990 it seems that we the people may ourselves be able to call the tune as we enter Planetary Cusp and decide whether or not, as a race, we wish to live or die. Very soon now (most of us should still be alive) the verdict will be in, and we'll know whether or not we're going to survive on (or off) this planet we have asset-stripped nearly to death. So the Tight Rope lies before us, the narrow road to the egress. So what have you done — science fiction writers of the year — to chart the course ahead? Is there anything you'd like to say on our behalf? If you twist around in your saddle-cages as you ride, can you glimpse anything of the way ahead, through the pinholes in your masks?

Are there pinholes in the masks you bear?

Of course there are not quite as many bright riders around to help nowadays (are there as many of us still hoping to learn)? It looks as though, when the final figures have been checked, 1989 will have seen a slight slackening in the number of titles published in at least two of the three categories (horror, fantasy, science fiction) now commonly in use. As a percentage of a ludicrously high previous total, the largest drop should (by all that's holy) be in horror titles, but won't be, even though it's terribly hard for a non-aficionado to avoid a sense that this subgenre suffers from an intractable vacuity of premise, with only its very finest writers only very occasionally coming up with anything verging on the new. Katherine Dunn's *Geek Love* (Knopf) lets sift a tracery of horror images over a tale whose inner premises may (or may not) have an intended science-fiction base, but whose house is the house of James Purdy (or Ross Macdonald), the pore-house of family. Ramsey Campbell continues, in *Ancient Images* (Century/Legend), to explore the interstices of his water-retentive Liverpool psyche; and in *Down River* (NEL), also drenched by the undead-urban heart of Middle Britain, Stephen Gallagher once again beats to death (and beyond) an idea too dumb to remember, in prose much much too fine to waste. And Stephen King flirts once again, like a child picking at the poison ivy in the mirror, with the autobiography of a writer bound to a wheel of fire of unmerited success, but *The Dark Half* (Hodder) no more bites the bullet than *Misery* (1987) did. But Dan Simmons's *Carrion Comfort* (Dark Harvest) came close to filling its huge boots (650 huge pages) with a tale of feeding which (like the experience of reading the book itself) battened on the orchestra of what it ate.

As with the great reptiles so many millions of years ago, there may be a dragon die-off in 1989, with fantasy titles levelling out (and maybe even beginning to sink), though most of those remaining are told in Barbara Cartland Celtic. (The name Melanie Rawn appears nowhere in this essay.) The only titles worth reading all year were those that scraped at the bars of the form like birds (Storm Constantine) or beasts (Jonathan Carroll) or pushmi-pullyus (Terry Pratchett). Storm Constantine (a British writer I always find myself thinking of as 'Storm Constantinople'!) finished off her *Wraeththu* sequence with a walkabout occupying more of *The Fulfilments of Fate and Desire* (Drunken Dragon Press) than was perhaps wise, if wrapping up the loose vipers of the plot were her goal (but clearly it ·vas not); and *The Monstrous Regiment* (Orbit) was a menarche weepie pretending really to be about the political destiny of an entire cheap-servant planet, which it wasn't. Steve Erickson's novels are fantasy if Kafka (or America) is; like strobe shots of a disaster, *Tours of the Black Clock* (Poseidon) and *Leap Year* (Poseidon) afforded no full views of the land of dreams, only gasped recollections of nightmare. This Apocalypse Pointillism also marked books whose narratives were seemingly conventional enough, like Lisa Goldstein's *Tourists* (Simon and Schuster), or Jonathan Carrol's *A Child Across the Sky* (Century/Legend); in both novels, whole and rounded characters come close to choking in the bricolage of failing worlds, until they seem motley: but in both cases the protagonists survive (at what cost). In *The Stress of her Regard* (Charnel House), Tim Powers returned to the clement cartoon tapestry of the early nineteenth century England featured in *The Anubis Gates* (1983), digging deeper this time, though maybe with a dab less joy. In *The Father*

319

of Stones (Washington Science Fiction Association), Lucius Shepard lacquered the stone hide of the Dragon Griaule with yet more daubs of allegory, but the beast seems to thrive on its fleas. Howard Waldrop retold the legend of Hercules in a slow drawl, while never letting *A Dozen Tough Jobs* (Ziesing) slacken into anecdote; always, beneath the jokes, an antique thrill seemed to lurk. And *Pyramids (The Book of Going Forth)* (Gollancz), along with *Guards! Guards!* (Gollancz), continued Terry Pratchett's crystalline *Discworld* comedies, shapely and hilarious and benign; perhaps because they owe their originating premises as much to Larry Niven as to the fantasy moguls they sweetly and piercingly jape, a hard articulacy underpins the sequence (eight strong so far), so that finally its riffs and cocoricos seem *strophic.*

There will probably have been somewhere between 250 and 300 science fiction novels published during the year; the total depends in part on definition — most of the books already cited might well be called science fiction by someone, perhaps by me — and part on the Technical Concerns (or *fingers*) that the boffins at *Locus* (and other journals) refer to or count on whenever $2 + 2$ adds up to 5 shared worlds in a sharecropper tree. But the final total, however it is calculated, will almost certainly suggest that there's still a great deal of fat yet to be pruned; a sense that too many instant-martyr books still end their tiny careers bound to the Browser-Scald shelves of Dalton-Walden, where they scream their hype for a moment or two, in a quite extraordinarily cruel parody of Andy Warhol's fifteen minutes of fame, before their covers are ripped like scalps and the dead skins returned to sender.

Write on, brave riders.

Dinosaurs (as we've used the term in previous years to describe authors whose careers took off in the Golden Age) continue to paw the stained turf-labyrinth of the 1990s (Exxon marks the spot), just as though 1940 were forever, and the one future we all faced could be met by one Project we could all agree upon. None died this year. The talking heads in grey prose of Isaac Asimov's *Nemesis* (Foundation/Doubleday) confab once again to save the savourless bacon of the Good Doctor's stone prosthesis dream of Earth. (One Horseman down.) Arthur C. Clarke took once again the Chamber-of-Commerce conscience of the otiose Gentry Lee under his wing and together they betray *Rendezvous with Rama* (1973) to its sequel, *Rama II* (Gollancz), which swallows its pa down with hardly a burp and bores on through the vacancy of space insatiate: further sequels are projected, sequels to the sequel, frequent-traveller Ramas, Ramada Ramas. And Frederik Pohl continued to feel-good in *Homegoing* (Ballantine Del Rey), like a wise old horny owl caught (as we hinted last year) drinking champagne out of his Norn-mask. No other dinosaur spoke or pawed.

Like a Raft of the Medusa in a sea of drowning singletons, the books of genre band together for solace and for sales; and tales of genre interest which swim alone — through amour propre or market savvy — continue to miss our boat. Almost always we are the losers. Peter Ackroyd, whose black *Hawksmoor* (1985) spun a True Map of London out of Iain Sinclair's *Lud Heat* (1975), took on part of the Matter of Britain in *First Light* (Hamish Hamilton), but occluded it. In Martin Amis's *London Fields* (Cape) suicide and the millennium come together in a dovetail of horror, told in a scraped scathed scatological prose quite remarkably painful to read. Paul Auster might seem more soothing, for *Moon Palace* (Viking) seems to celebrate a traditional marriage of internal and external geographies, in which a quest for self mirrors the search to conquer the Moon in all her phases; what shocks in the end is that the marriage is no metaphor, and one's eyes are pinned open to naked ceremony. Nor does the element of spoof in Julian Barnes's *A History of the World in 10 1/2 Chapters* (Cape) do much to attenuate the fervent darkness of its burden. For several years now Thomas Berger, whose *Little Big Man* (1964) wrenched the West into post-modern fable-land, has been using science fiction tools for a similar prying loose of modern urban life in America; *Nowhere* (1985) is a dystopian jaunt to a Lewis Carroll Ruritania; the device that shapes *Being Invisible* (1987) is pretty obvious, and *Changing the Past* (Little, Brown) is about changing the past, but the simplicity of these tales is like the edge of a knife, the clarity is all the better to eat you with, like any true anthropology.

In *The History of Luminous Motion* (Bloomsbury), Scott Bradfield lays out California as a map of the family romance, rolls the map up with the readers still inside. Anthony Burgess wobbles his lexicon lips more chastely than sometimes in *Any Old Iron* (Hutchinson), but the survival of the eponymous Excalibur fails to lance a single boil of our secular quotidian; no Arthur lives again to save British Rail. In *Skeleton-in-Waiting* (Bodley Head), Peter Dickinson (who is never still) returns to the alternate world of *King and Joker* (1976), where a different monarch reigns over Britain, but to no avail: it is still our hedged and bounden world, for which (all the same) he conveys a wiry love. Nor do we entirely escape our servitude to the real in the exuberant thaumaturgies of *Foucault's Pendulum* (Secker) by Umberto Eco, but the tricks and turns of the book work like a rhetoric of the human urge to pry something loose from things, and we do, for a moment, feel, therefore, freed. Geraldine McLaughrean's *The Maypole* (Secker) also homes on the Middle Ages, but cannot leave, caught in a weave of tapestry and song; the tale should interest genre-readers for the washed potency of its sense that the world is new, like somewhere else. There is of course no message to the planet in *the Message to the Planet* (Chatto) by Iris Murdoch, though the dying Wittgensteinesque guru at its heart does raise the dead, and thinks hard, and squats upon a menhir on a ley line, and so forth; but then he dies mute, the throat of his spirit torn out. (If you peek through the pinhole in the mask, says the next Horseman, you will go blind.) There are deep ghosts and incest mirrors galore in *Soul/Mate* (Dutton), but none as frightening as the thought of Rosamond Smith (tasty pseudonym) meeting Joyce Carol Oates (ravenous). *The Scapeweed Goat* (Hamish Hamilton), by Frank Schaefer, limns a nineteenth century American West spot-stained with religious utopias, but in the end his art seems insufficiently obdurate to grasp the muddied God he hopes to discredit. In *Two Women of London: The Strange Case of Ms Jekyll and Mrs Hyde* (Faber), Emma Tennant rough-cuts the Robert Louis Stevenson tale for Ladbroke Grove (Jerry Cornelius's old home), where the old dichotomy between self and sharer marshalls new traumas, points the belatedness of the heroines as the world dwindles into factory farm. William Wharton, in *Franky Furbo* (Holt), shape-changes his beloved family (which, variously disguised, appears in all his work) into radiant undying foxes (literally), and snuggles down with them to an eternal Christmas, safe from us, from the rusty traps of time, and heat-death. And Marianne Wiggins, in *John Dollar* (Secker), reduces the world of men and women and children to its apodictic nub in a fable rightly much likened to William Golding's *Lord of the Flies* (1954). One must eat to live. Civilization is guts writ large.

Growls become audible. Alpha males of the first order — massive bewhiskered paterfamiliases who came into the field after World War Two and held their ground until 1975 or so — muscle into view; if either Ursula K. Le Guin or Joanna Russ had published in 1989, we might be speaking of alpha persons: but they did not. Hush now. I think I see the first of them, like Bambi full-grown, suddenly manifest. Do nothing aggressive. At all costs avoid eye contact. You'll be all right.

It's Poul Anderson himself, raising his selkie head from long immersion in the breeding tanks of fantasy, bringing us *The Boat of a Million Years* (Tor) between his jaws, grrrring softly. The book itself is complicated and epical and crabby, and its wisdom-scarred immortal protagonists end up turning their backs on the planet we have served so ill, the tightrope we walk. (Mortals to the back of the bus, the third Horseman tells us. His Weltzschmerz stings our pocked cheeks. Twilight becomes him. But his quirt sizzles.) Next, slipping demurely into the spotlight, comes sleek disgruntled Piers Anthony, fresh from the greasepaint orgy of *Bio of an Ogre* (1988) (an auto-biography) and a million puns of low degree, eager to tell us a bit more about the traps that line the path of a great hunter, as the utterly peculiar apologia-cum-scholarly-apparatus sur-rounding *But What of Earth?* (Tor) must be intended to demonstrate. The novel was originally published in 1976, as part of the loathsome Laser Book series of doctored novels, and was duly copy-edited to fit its easy-digestion, offend-thee-no-crank-Christian remit. In the long and laboured revenge he takes upon the butchers of his silly pale little tale, Anthony demonstrates mainly (and we mention the book solely to illustrate) how dangerous it is for alpha males to hunt alone too long. Gordon R. Dickson (next) plugs along with *The Earth Lords* (Ace), without cracking much of a smile, always a bridesmaid. In *Eden* (Harcourt Brace), an early novel (from 1959) now translated, Stanislaw (let's hear it for the Polish Porcupine) Lem sidles into view with another elegant diagram of the void between Us and Other (as in *Solaris* from two years later); the bureaucratic reality-games which apparently govern those native to the planet Eden might as well portray the nomenklatura of his own country, before History began again.

In *The Fugitive Worlds* (Gollancz), Bob Shaw reduced the glowing gemutlich cosmogonic game-show of *The Ragged Astronauts* (1986) to Tinker Toy operatics (matter transmitters and AIs and galactic Bangs and wooden spaceships and wicked princesses and big-domed aliens, stargates and wandering planets and lovesick commandos and other scrapings of the barrel all thresh it out in the jacuzzi); but a certain daft adroitness kept it all in play. Robert Silverberg continued, in *The Queen of Springtime* (Gollancz), to show us all how easy it was to organize a hunt, to guide the hounds, to bag a robot fox. He writes without a hitch, without a catch in the throat, without a view. He writes like a Motorway to Canterbury. In *Bugs* (Macmillan), John Sladek, who is the kind of hunter who stakes *himself* out for bait, juggles autobiography and the blackest of fabulations in a tale of exile's return to America, and of the rending teeth within the belly of the beast; Minneapolis is stripped to its fundamental Mall, Nevada is a bum rap; there are lots of laughs. In *Megalomania* (DAW), Ian Wallace brings back the world of Croyd, sounding like three Cordwainer Smiths having a squabble on their way to a dance. In *Soldier of Arete* (Tor), set in ancient Greece, Gene Wolfe continues the tale of Latro, who cannot remember events earlier than the previous day; but now a goddess brings him to a Theatre of Memory, and the book begins to sing in strophes deeper than the wine-dark sea. I think it is a song of love to Latro. And in *Land of Shadows* (Morrow), Roger Zelazny, who may have a better ear than anyone in the field, sticks his headphones on again and bikes amiably at great speed through the land of Amber for the ninth time; it may take all his very considerable skill to navigate the turns of a tale told at such a high pitch, but so what, who can follow what it is impossible to heed?

Aficionados of the Sort will find that, as we approach the present tense, categories become less stable. Some writers whose genre careers have just begun are really quite grizzled (like Jack Butler); others (like Neal Barrett Jr., or George Alec Effinger) have been working for a couple of decades, but have only recently begun to surmount (like dolphins) the medium. Some members of this cohort love the tickle of attention. Others do not take well to handling. We will put them cheek by jowl.

The Archivist (Unwin), which is a first novel, by Gill Alderman, who was born in 1941, dives with a painterly lubricity into the cities and cultures of a matriarchy dominant over part of an extremely distant planet. The urgency of her need to see and weigh and taste this pomegranate demesne does sometimes drive her plot into an outer room (where it babbles unheard); but a sense of something lived swells through the chaos and the oops-sorry jump-cuts of an almost untold tale. Like an inside-outside of the Alderman, A.A. Attanasio's *The Last Legends of Earth* (Doubleday Foundation) applies its painterly lubricity to a palette of plot-knots and icons too devious and daunting to describe, though enticing to *imbibe*; but because the worlds whirl like tops, it's impossible to sit down anywhere in the book. Iain (M.) Banks, in *The State of the Art* (Ziesing), uses his deft interstellar post-scarcity Culture to knee our own wee shambles; super folk come from far stars to the Earth of 1977 and gag. Shock egress ensues. In *Dawn's Uncertain Light* (Signet), Neal Barrett Jr. further darkens the monitory quest scenario of *Through Darkest America* (1987), sweeps dizzyingly downwards East and West through blacker and blacker outcomes of the Dream, until we find what eats what to keep the America Ball lit. And gruffish Gregory Benford, galactic insight veteran, also travels further in *Tides of Light* (Bantam), bound upon a course towards the heart of things, melancholy and bristling, brimful of the thought of it all. But the plot itself, like an old friend the author has outgrown, keeps saying the wrong thing in mixed company, staining the carpet of the stars with its pulpy feet (it is a sequel to *Great Sky River* from 1987), gassing on.

(Hello I must be going, says the fourth Horseman. I must gafiate to Ganymede. I am twinned with Far Arcturus. I have no time for Moaning Minnies. I have a huge advance. I'm off.)

In *Deus Ex Machina* (Bantam), J.V. Brummels takes on space opera, a dystopian acid bath vision of America down the line, cyberpunk, prostitution sort of stuff, and cosmogonic comeuppances all around; and it might almost be said he wins. In prose of alert muscle and good skin-tone, Jack Butler transforms the moderately dumb premise of *Nightshade* (Atlantic Monthly) — to wit, that vampires are a cul-de-sac of evolution, when in fact they are a sac out of whole cloth — into a tour-de-force of cat's-cradle plotting, set on Mars with AIs and the kitchen sink and all. Orson Scott Card skirted *The Abyss* (Pocket) by claiming that it was not a novelization of the movie but in fact a novel novelizing the movie (move over Aquinas): edged out another Alvin the Maker text with *Prentice Alvin* (Tor), bringing us only marginally closer to the true abyss of adulthood and the Land to salve for real; and couched an apologia for his Mormon culture in terms so enticingly strange (and seemingly humble) that readers might well have taken *The Folk of the Fringe* (Phantasia) for an apostasy, which it is not. After the pounding amplitude of *Cyteen* (1988), C.J. Cherryh finely compressed her bustling intelligence into the chamber-opera of *Rimrunners* (Warners), set almost entirely inside a ship, below decks, where small dramas of life and death took on countenances we all know from the moral streets that bind us all. Building on the scummy hieroglyphs of *When Gravity Fails* (1987), George Alec Effinger's *A Fire in the Sun* (Foundation/ Doubleday) seemed to begin to alphabetize his cyberpunk/ Middle East soup; further volumes may learn to spell in this new tongue. Ben Elton (mentioned last year in passing) told us all in *Stark* (Michael Joseph) that he wasn't just another pretty face, that he meant exactly what he said about the end of life on Earth and no Tight Rope; jokes and all, this highly nervous first novel (a typical Raven Book, every stanza ending in Nevermore) read like a cattle prod. It was not easy to ignore.

This year's Conrad Stargard novels from Leo A.

Frankowski, *The High-Tech Knight, The Radiant Warrior* and *The Flying Warlord* (all Ballantine Del Rey), whose time-traveller hero continues to jump-start Medieval Eastern Europe into the starring role in an alternate Renaisance, once again cast a simple spell of Anachronism, a totally untoughminded dream of infantile omniopotence whose locus classicus (for me, because I love the book) has always been Poul Anderson's *The High Crusade* (1960). And Richard Grant, in *Views from the Oldest House* (Foundation/Doubleday), drifted slowly into a coy murk of allusion, SOSing vainly to King Arthur and to M. John Harrison as he sank, having forgotten (perhaps) that King Arthur was a ringleader (not a freelance) and Viriconium was the kind of place Thomas Covenant would *believe* in.

Good-tempered but really very tired (why does one think of Henry Cooper), Joe Haldeman made more sense with *Buying Time* (Morrow) than he has for a while, but this tale of the costs (and benefits) of immortality had a much too high apparatus-to-message ratio, and bestowed all too many privileges on its high earner protagonists (I stared at the book with mute inglorious dumb resentment for quite a few minutes before managing to Think Rich for an hour). James Patrick Kelly's *Look into the Sun* (Tor), an unacknowledged sequel to *Planet of Whispers* (1984), continues to count the perils and perks of exogamy on an alien planet, in a style as slow and crafted as Gardner Dozois' of *Strangers* (1978) long ago. *Good News from Outer Space* (Tor) by John Kessel — like so much science fiction now of interest — churned tropes galore into goulash, kept its afflatus dry, hit its targets stunningly well (for those who could see them); and by refusing to unpack its alien visitor into common view indulged in an archetypal late-genre play on the absence of the Sign. (A late-genre work might well be described as any text made up of material remembered but not present.) Garry Kilworth, who should have been mentioned last year for the concise map of decline contained in *Abandonati* (1988), published this year *In the Hollow of the Deep-Sea Wave* (Bodley Head) and *Hunter's Moon* (Unwin), the one a collection of linked mellow-astringent tales edging at the numinous, the other a Fox Consciousness epic (and not our brief). The linked stories in Eric McCormack's *The Paradise Motel* (Viking) also edged, but grotesquely, like musings of Dr. Lao, into the Other-world of genre. Bruce McAllister, whose *Humanity Prime* (1971) may now gain the readership it merits, presents in *Dream Baby* (Tor) a nightmarish vision of the maelstrom of complicity of Vietnam, told in clear, so that it is hardly to be read. Pat Murphy's *The City, Not Long After* (Foundation/Doubleday) did not make one wish to nuke San Francisco (though she did coat the tale in a dire complacency of smarm about the place), because the City, in the end, is our highest craft, and carries the burden of the race, and she said so. And in America it is brave to so depose.

In *The Night Mayor* (Simon and Schuster UK), Kim Newman played with film noir, Philip K. Dick, medical ethics and pocket universes and shamus stuff, juggling the melange with weird clemency; and in *Drachenfels* (GW Books) as Jack Yeovil, he came like an agent provocateur (or Henry Fonda in *The Grapes of Wrath*) into sharecropper country, and told a tale whose licketysplit contempt for its egregious premises must have shored up the heart of any serf who cared to look. It was, in other words, pure Hollywood. Paul Park continued, in *Sugar Rain* (Morrow), to create a world vaster than empires and more slow, and a story to match. There is little dash to the book, but within its dream-retarded periods a mature love story, that sounds like life, unfolds its human limbs within the pageant, the cleansing downpour of the title. There is also a tropical redolence to the mise en scene of Geoff Ryman's first full-length novel, *The Child Garden* (Unwin), which is set in a tangled and transfigured London, though the true heat of the book lies in the close breath of its telling, the pinned proximity of its characters, the moral curvatures one must trace to catch the story as it shifts and grows. It is a science fiction tale (with learning viruses and a metaphysic of cancer in a world governed by a collective Will) and a novel of mimesis, and a bildungsroman, and an act of devotion to Dante. All these. In Richard Paul Russo's *Subterranean Gallery* (Tor), a hard negen-tropic flame of Art (in the form of SF illustrations) continued against the odds to burn against the night in police-state San Francisco; Allen Steele's *Orbital Decay* (Ace) was bonny and hard and loud; Sheri S. Tepper's *Grass* (Foundation/Doubleday) was ornate, gracile, steely, extremely savvy. We spoke of *Carrion Comfort* long pages earlier; we speak of *Hyperion* (Foundation/ Doubleday) now, Dan Simmons's second (or third) novel of 1989, a science fiction text of daunt and glint based on the Canterbury Tales (with additives). Like blind men describing the elephant which is Hyperion, the seven Pilgrims of the book tell each other of their earlier experiences upon the planet; only as the book closes (the second volume of the novel is now due) do they finally land, and begin the true pilgrimage. There is, in other words, rather more plot that Chaucer needed, whose folk found in the God-illumined world itself provender sufficient. But Chaucer wrote when the world was young (or English was), and Simmons writes in a belated genre (science fiction) very late in the day. (The Pinholes leak upon us shards of Light, visions of the Future we must plot and plot and plot to gain if we may, or baulk if need be, upon the Rope.) There are late-century additives of every hue in *Hyperion*, a surplusage of deaths, and burnings, and infinite recursives of spying, and star fleets, and the Shrike, and the Time Tombs, and the Boojum. *Hyperion* when whole may bring us home to what we can say in 1990 in the words of science fiction; or it may default to norm. Who can tell? Write on, brave rider. Say the sayable. Say us onwards.

So I awoke, and behold it was a Dream.

HEROES AND VILLAINS
by
DAVID GARNETT

Wenceslas Square and Tiananmen Square . . .
 Rushdie and Khomeini . . .
 Berlin and Panama City . . .
 Science fiction and fantasy . . .
 1989. The end of the eighties. Into the final decade of the millennium. Or is it 11 years until the new century, the most famous sf date of all: 2001. (1984 now belonging to history.)

THE PRIZE GUYS

1989 was the year that the Nebula became the Nebula™. Or maybe the Nebula®. The Science Fiction Writers of America trademarked their annual award. Like the other major sf honours, the year's Nebula winners are listed at the end of the book.

The other main awards of the year are the Hugos, which were awarded in Boston in September 1989. As well as the fiction prizes, the other awards went to:

Best Non-fiction:	*The Motion of Light in Water* by Samuel R. Delany
Best Dramatic Presentation:	*Who Framed Roger Rabbit*
Best Semi-prozine:	*Locus*
Best Professional Editor:	Gardner Dozois
Best Professional Artist:	Michael Whelan
Best Fanzine:	*File 770*
Best Fan Writer:	Dave Langford
Best Fan Artist:	Brad W. Foster
	Diana Gallagher Wu (tie)

This was Dave Langford's fourth Hugo. Having collected three for fan writing, and one for editing his literary journal *Ansible*, he has now beaten Arthur C. Clarke's record and won more Hugos than any other British writer. (Clarke, however, has won four Nebulas — Nebulae? — including a Grand Master Award.)

The World Fantasy Awards were given out in Seattle in October 1989. Some of these went to:

Best Novel:	*Koko* by Peter Straub
Best Novella:	'The Skin Trade' by George R.R. Martin
Best Short Fiction:	'Winter Solstice, Camelot Station' by John M. Ford
Best Short Story Collection:	*Storeys from the Old Hotel* by Gene Wolfe
	Angry Candy by Harlan Ellison

The 'best novel' award went to a book without any fantasy or supernatural element. The 'short story' award became 'short fiction' because the winner was a poem.

Some of the British Fantasy Awards, given by the British Fantasy Society, went to Ramsey Campbell for his novel *The Influence* and to Brian Lumley for his short story *Fruiting Bodies*.

The British Science Fiction Awards are listed at the end of this volume; but as well as the two fiction prizes, since 1980 there have also been awards for best artist and best 'media presentation'. Jim Burns has won the former five times, deservedly so. In 1989 the winner was Alan Lee for the cover of *Lavondyss*. And no doubt Steven Spielberg was absolutely delighted that *Roger Rabbit* won the media award.

The 1989 awards were not given out at the Easter Convention as usual, partly because it was held in the off-shore tax haven of Jersey. It cost as much to reach the Channel Isles as the whole previous Easter convention, held in Liverpool. But because no convention is complete without an awards ceremony, they invented some new ones. The fireworks display at the 1987 Brighton World Convention won one of these prizes, which must be a first of some kind. It was also a worthy winner, as anyone who saw the spectacular post-Hugo pyrotechnics will confirm.

The Theodore Sturgeon Memorial Award for best short fiction of 1988, which is chosen by jury and administered by the University of Kansas's Center for the Study of Science

Fiction was awarded to George Alec Effinger for 'Schrödinger's Kitten' — already a Nebula and Hugo winner.

And that, for this year, is enough on awards — until after
the afterword.

THE GOOD GUYS

In the introduction to his collection *A Romance of the Equator*,
subtitled *Best Fantasy Stories*, published in 1989, Brian Aldiss
writes that he tries 'to keep the nutty element within bounds' —
there are no dragons or elves or vampires in his fantasy.

I've attempted to make the *Yearbook* an anthology of science
fiction, but often the best sf is on the verge of something else,
the kind of material that expands the borders of the genre. Sf
has to grow and develop. Yet many of the stories that are being
published within the science fiction magazines have very little
to do with speculative fiction. Sentimental fantasies are very
much in vogue these days, nostalgic whimsy for an age that
never was. So are 'horror' stories.

This volume, however, includes fiction that a few years ago
probably would not have been considered sf. These stories
coexist with more traditional science fiction — although not *too*
traditional — all of which make up my own choice for the
dozen best stories of 1989.

Seven of this year's selection are taken from the pages of the
science fiction magazines, although only two titles are re-
presented. This partly reflects the decline of the magazines,
which always seem to be on the verge of dying, only to have
new life breathed into them by a new owner or by the foundation of new titles.

The oldest surviving magazine is *Amazing*, which was also
the first title devoted solely to science fiction. This began in
1926, started by the great Hugo Gernsback, but it seems that
the November 1990 issue may be the last. *Amazing* was taken
over a few years ago by TSR, the company which gave the
world Dungeons and Dragons, but little effort appears to have
been spent on reviving its fortunes. Its circulation has now been
exceeded by *Aboriginal*, the newest of the magazines.

There must be a reason why so many sf magazine titles

begin with an 'A'. In the case of *Aboriginal*, one explanation is probably so that it could be first in any alphabetical listing. This is subtitled 'Tales of the Human Kind' — the aboriginals of the title are meant to be the human race — and the publisher is listed as 'a crazy alien'. Earlier issues used to contain pages and pages and pages of letters from readers, all saying how great the magazine was. Combined with gushing reviews and superficial movie gossip, this all served to give the publication a very amateurish feel. Published bi-monthly in large format, *Aboriginal* previously boasted that it had the best art in the field. Whether that was true or not is debatable, but the fiction certainly wasn't the best.

All of the stories here are very short, and there aren't very many of them — which does not seem the best policy for a science fiction magazine. The editor of *Aboriginal* is Charles C. Ryan, who previously edited the magazine *Galileo* (1976–1980). Let's hope that *Aboriginal* survives long enough to maintain it slow improvement.

If *Amazing* does finally expire, the oldest sf magazine will be *Analog*. This began as *Astounding*, and in January 1990 it reached its sixtieth year. *Analog* can be relied on to avoid 'horror' stories, yet it does publish a few stories which could be categorised as 'fantasy'. On the whole, the magazine prints the safest and most traditional sf — although there are the occasional pleasant surprises. *Analog* is edited by Stanley Schmidt and published thirteen times a year.

The same company also publishes *Isaac Asimov's Science Fiction Magazine* thirteen times a year. This was started in 1977 and is now edited by Gardner Dozois, Asimov himself serving only as a figurehead. The Hugo Award used to be given to the 'best professional magazine' each year. This demonstrated the importance of magazines in the past, when there were so many of them and so few sf books. In 1973, the award was changed to 'best professional editor'. This has almost always been won by a magazine editor, however, and in 1988 and 1989 the winner was Gardner Dozois — a reflection of the significance of *Asimov's*. (Dozois also edits a 'best of the year' science fiction anthology, although he includes fantasy — even some 'nutty stuff'.)

Four stories in this *Yearbook* were first published in *Asimov's*: 'Dori Bangs' by Bruce Sterling, 'Surrender' by Lucius Shepard, 'Dogwalker' by Orson Scott Card and 'Lunar Triptych: Embracing the Night' by Richard Paul Russo.

The Magazine of Fantasy and Science Fiction also celebrated an anniversary in 1989; the October issue marked its fortieth year of publication. *F&SF*, as it is known, has been edited by Edward L. Ferman since 1966. With *Asimov's*, this is the most important source of new short fiction and of new authors in American sf.

Three stories in this *Yearbook* were first published in *F&SF*: 'Out of Copyright' by Charles Sheffield, 'Abe Lincoln in McDonald's' by James Morrow and 'Privacy' by David Brin. ('Abe Lincoln' also appears in the second volume of *What Might Have Been*, an alternate history anthology edited by Gregory Benford and Martin H. Greenberg, of whom more below.

Omni, the glossy American pop-science magazine, is often listed amongst the sf magazines. This is because it publishes a disproportionate amount of excellent stories amongst its articles on technology, UFOs, ecology, dreaming, 'new age' subjects and adverts for cars and computers, 'Girl Watching Classes' — *Omni* comes from the publishers of *Penthouse* — and flicknives: 'The Sicilian . . . a reputation from the hills of Corsica to the asphalt jungles of New York.' The fiction editor of *Omni* is Ellen Datlow, who is also the co-editor of yet another 'best of the year' anthology — fantasy and horror in this case.

'The Gates of Babel' by J.R. Dunn was first published in *Omni*. 'At the Rialto' by Connie Willis was also published here, although it first appeared in *The Microverse*, an anthology edited by Byron Preiss.

Byron Preiss is a packager, and it was he who devised such 'franchised' books as *Arthur C. Clarke's Venus Prime* and *Isaac Asimov's Robot City*. These were discussed at length in last year's *Yearbook* by both John Clute and myself. What happens is a famous author 'leases' his name to a series of books based on his own work, which are then written by other authors. 1989 saw more of these, of course, the latest being Harry Harrison's *Bill the Galactic Hero* — which was unique in that

Harrison wrote one of the new books himself.

But, credit where it's due, *The Microverse* is a very interesting volume. It consists of scientific essays and science fiction stories, photographs and paintings, all on the subject of 'the invisible world' — from particle physics to microbiology.

As well as magazines, sf stories are also published in original anthologies, of which there are too few. One such collection is George Zebrowski's *Synergy*, which seems a very slim and overpriced paperback — but you get what you pay for, and the series does contain the occasional gem such as Jayge Carr's 'Chimera' from the fourth volume.

Single author collections are usually made up of stories that have been published previously, but that was not the case with the John Crowley volume *Novelty*. The title story had appeared in *Interzone*, but the other three were all originals — including 'In Blue'.

1989 was the fiftieth anniversary of Isaac Asimov's first published story. ('Marooned off Vesta' in *Amazing*, March 1939.) The event was marked by the publication of *Foundation's Friends*, an anthology in which seventeen authors contributed stories based on Asimov's writings. Okay, so this is 'franchising' and a 'shared-world' (or universe) — but it did include Robert Silverberg's 'The Asenion Solution'. The collection was edited by Martin H. Greenberg.

THE WISE GUYS

Greenberg compiled an anthology 'to celebrate the fiftieth anniversary of his creation.' This wasn't Asimov's creation, but that of the caped crusader. *The Further Adventures of Batman*, however, featured many of the same authors as *Foundation's Friends*: George Alec Effinger, William F. Nolan, Robert Sheckley, Edward D. Hoch, Mike Resnick, Robert Silverberg (with Karen Haber) and also Isaac Asimov.

Asimov features prominently in Greenberg's amazing number of anthologies — and vice-versa.

Early in 1990, Asimov quoted his figure of published books at 424. These included 110 anthologies, almost all of which had been compiled with Greenberg. 1989 produced several of these:

Isaac Asimov Presents the Great Sf Stories # *19*, *Isaac Asimov's Wonderful Worlds of Science Fiction* # *9*, *Isaac Asimov's Magical Worlds of Fantasy* # *11*, *Visions of Fantasy, Tales of the Occult* and *The New Hugo Winners*. Some of these also list Charles G. Waugh as a third editor, or maybe the second, with Greenberg taking up the third place. *The Twelve Frights of Christmas* also listed Carolyn Rossel as editor, along with Waugh and Greenberg and Asimov. Greenberg seems to have put together *Fifty Years of Asimov* — not to be confused with *Foundation's Friends* — all by himself, however.

Asimov may have edited almost all his anthologies with Greenberg, but the converse is not the case. Greenberg began editing in 1974, and almost always seems to have had a collaborator. The first of these were Patricia Warrick, Harvey Katz, John Milstead and Jospeh Olander — or combinations thereof. Starting with six collections published that year, this has grown to a total of over three hundred, mainly reprints of already published stories. Many of these also have Charles Waugh's name on the cover. (And some have neither of their names on the cover, but only inside the book.)

In 1989 Greenberg also produced *What Might Have Been* # *1* with Gregory Benford, *Catfantastic* with Andre Norton, *Things That Go Bump in the Night* with Jane Yolen, *The Horror Hall of Fame* with Robert Silverberg, *The Best Japanese Science Fiction Stories* with John L. Apostolou, *Stalkers* with Ed Gorman, *The Legacy of Olaf Stapledon* with Patrick A. McCarthy and Charles Elkins, *Phantoms* and *Fourteen Vicious Valentines* both with Waugh and Rosalind Greenberg. There were probably more. That's without counting anthologies of mysteries, westerns, and doctor and nurse stories.

During the year, Greenberg and Waugh also collaborated with David Drake to produce *Space Gladiators* and *Space Infantry*. Drake is himself a prolific anthologist, author, and producer of outlines for other writers to fill in. Almost all of his books are on military themes. His previous anthologies include the classics — or at least the titles are classics — *Men Hunting Things* and *Things Hunting Men*, both reprint collections. Instead of having 'edited by' on the cover these were 'created by David Drake'. Maybe this is what I should do with the *Yearbook*...

1989 saw more of Drake's creativity when, with Sandra Miesel, the collections *Heads to the Storm* and *A Separate Star* both appeared. Each of these was 'a tribute to Rudyard Kipling', who is apparently a great hero to the writers of jockstrap sf. Drake is also a fan of the Roman Empire, and January 1990 saw the first of his books of the year. This was *Eternal City*, which from the cover appears to be a novel. Nowhere does it say 'edited by' or 'created by'. Only by the contents list inside is it revealed as a collection, and only from the copyright line is it discovered that Greenberg and Waugh are also the editors. Or creators.

There is also a series of novels called *Crisis of Empire* — a good old galactic empire this time — which was 'conceived by' Drake, although the books have been written by Thomas T. Thomas (what does the initial stand for?), Bill Dietz and Roger MacBride Allen. All this creating and conceiving doesn't leave time for much writing — although Drake does turn up in various anthologies, edited/devised by others.

He has a story in the Fall 1989 issue of *New Destinies*, for example, which is 'the Paperback Magazine of Science Fiction and Speculative Fact'. This is edited by Jim Baen, who publishes Baen Books. Baen Books is the publisher of most of Drake's creations.

The same issue of *New Destinies* includes stories by Dean Ing and S.M. Stirling, and also one by Anne McCaffrey which is taken from a book which promises to be *the* collection of 1990: *Carmen Miranda's Ghost is Haunting Space Station Three*. Although this will also be published by Baen, the editor this time is Don Sakers.

Baen Books has a reputation for publishing military sf, but the most famous sf series of this type comes from a different American publisher, Tor. This is Jerry Pournelle's *There Will Be War*, which has reached volume 8, *Armageddon!* Previous volumes include *Blood and Iron, Guns of Darkness, Call to Battle!* and *Day of the Tyrant*.

The success of this series has inspired imitators, but more significantly it has finally provoked a reaction against such mindless power fantasies.

Two new collections will soon be published on the opposite

theme: that violence is no solution. One of these is *There Won't Be War*, edited by Harry Harrison and Bruce McAllister, which will also be published by Tor; and the other is *When the Music's Over*, edited by Lewis Shiner. It is unlikely that these will have been 'created by' their editors.

Drake is also 'the man who brought you *Hammer's Slammers*, as we are reminded on the cover of *The Fleet* # *3 — Break Through*, edited by Drake and Bill Fawcett, which starts with a story written by Drake and Larry Niven. Let us not forget that Larry Niven is the creator of the *Man-Kzin Wars*, the second volume of which contains two stories, one by Dean Ing, the other by Pournelle and S.M. Stirling. The authors in these series are interchangeable. And somehow Rudyard Kipling has been included within such lists of contents.

Imperial Stars is yet another series, mostly of reprint stories, 'created by' Pournelle, which reached number 3 during 1989 — *The Crash of Empire.* There was probably even another volume of Pournelle's newest creation *War World*, although I didn't try too hard to trace it.

All this kind of stuff is what outsiders generally consider to be the mainstream of sf. Operation Just Cause with cosmic mercenaries; galactic empires and space-frigates. Rambo against the alien slime. Almost the kind of thing that won *Star Wars* a Hugo — and a Nebula . . .

But even *Analog* doesn't believe in this type of sf any more. (Or hardly.)

All of these blood and blaster books are published in the USA, and although the majority of sf which appears in Britain has an American origin, at least none of this is being reprinted by British publishers. Or not much . . .

THE NICE GUYS

None of the stories in this *Yearbook* are by British authors — Charles Sheffield having become American two decades ago — and none are from British sources, which is not always the same thing.

In a way, when making my selection for this volume, I am biased against stories which have first been published in

Britain. Whenever I buy a collection, I don't like finding material that I have previously read elsewhere. This is a British book, from a British publisher, by a British editor, and most of the sales will be made in Britain. Anyone who is interested enough can already have traced all the short sf published in Britain during the year, but the American stories are more difficult to locate.

Had I found fiction from Britain which was too good not to miss, which I judged to be better than the American alternatives, then it would have been included here — as has happened in previous years. This time, however, British material of an equally high standard missed out ...

I keep saying 'British' and 'American' because when it comes to sf, that's all there is. 'Foreign' science fiction is very rarely translated into English, unless it is a thirty year old book by Stanislaw Lem.

If you don't keep up with contemporary British short sf, this is what you missed (but which you can still probably find):

Interzone is still Britain's only sf magazine. Edited by David Pringle, this is the place where much of the best new science fiction can be found — anywhere. Packed with fiction, articles, reviews, news, interviews, *Interzone* is essential reading. Now monthly and distributed nationally, it can be ordered from any newsagent. A sample copy can be obtained for £2.30 from 124 Osborne Road, Brighton BN1 6LU.

The Gate: The first issue of this new magazine did appear. The kindest thing to say is that it can only improve. The magazine is due for a 'relaunch' for its second issue. We'll see.

Other Edens 3, edited by Christopher Evans and Robert Holdstock, is an original volume of fantasy, horror and science fiction. Some fine stories, as usual, but not enough emphasis on sf.

Arrows of Eros, edited by Alex Stewart, an original anthology of 'sex 'n' sf', is — alas — the kind of book you can judge by the cover. Some good material, however, although not much.

Starfield also deserves a mention. This is a hardback anthology of Scottish science fiction, mostly reprint, edited by Duncan Lunan. (There was once a Scottish sf magazine, called *Nebula*, which was where Robert Silverberg sold his first story.

There never seems to have been a magazine entitled *Hugo*, however.)

And finally there was the first volume of *Zenith*, which was edited by me. This was a collection of twelve original stories by British authors, and as a matter of policy I decided against using any of these in the *Yearbook*. (Although it was suggested that I simply reprint all of *Zenith* in the *Yearbook*, on the theory that they must be the best because I originally selected and first published them . . .) Go and buy the anthology, read it all. Half the contents were selected by American editors for their 'best' collections, or were finalists for the British Science Fiction Award* — or both.

By now, the second *Zenith* is also available. From this editor, from this publisher, from the shop where you bought this book.

The 'golden age' of science fiction is usually how the 'good old days' are regarded by veteran readers. Its exact date depends on when they began reading sf.

In *The Observer* last year, a number of writers were asked to choose the 'experts' expert' — the authors' author. Arthur C. Clarke declined to single out any individual writers for praise, because there is so much excellent science fiction now being written. He said: 'This is the golden age of sf.'

And in spite of the opposition, he's right.

*The winner was Lisa Tuttle's 'In Translation' — from *Zenith* . . .

APPENDIX

The Awards

One of the first science fiction books I ever read was *The Hugo Winners* edited by Isaac Asimov. This was in the days when Asimov was a solo anthologist, and the collection was the first of his hundred plus anthologies. The paperback was published in Britain by Penguin in 1964, when Brian Aldiss served as the consultant editor and was responsible for the company issuing many of the best books of the era. (These days, despite their reputation in some other areas, Penguin has the most abysmal sf list in British publishing.)

The Hugo Winners lived up to its title by collecting all the early short fiction winners up until 1961; and as an appendix to the book, there was a list of every winner to 1963. This included each of the novels, all of which I finally tracked down and read.

Most of these were well worth it. The first ever Hugo winner was *The Demolished Man*, one of the great science fiction novels. The second winner was *They'd Rather Be Right*, about which the less said the better. . .

This list of award-winning books and stories led me to so much good material that I have decided to include complete details of each of the current major honours in the hope that it may do the same for readers of the *Yearbook*. Last year, I listed all the International Fantasy Awards, which were the first real awards for the genre. If you want to find out these, go buy the second *Yearbook*. . .

There is no listing for the World Fantasy Awards here, partly because these fall outside the limits of this volume — even though most of the winners have been the kind of material that gives fantasy a good name — and partly because there are so many of them, because there are so many categories.

Awards have come and gone, forgotten by everyone except

the winners and those who keep records of the winners. What, for example, was the Balrog Award? An American publisher recently advertised that one of its authors had won 'Britain's coveted Balrog Award'. Coveted it may have been, but it certainly wasn't British.

The Hugo Award consists of a model spaceship — these days made in Birmingham — while the Arthur C. Clarke Award includes a cheque for £1000. In other cases, the 'award' may be nothing more than a piece of paper, perhaps a 'scroll' or a simple notification. There may not even be that, and it has happened that some prize winners were not even informed of their good fortune.

Many of the following novels are still available, while much of the shorter fiction can be found in various books such as the Hugo and Nebula anthologies — and other 'best' collections like this one and earlier volumes in the series. (Recently there was even a *Best of the Nebulas* anthology.)

Awards in themselves may not mean much, except perhaps to the people who win them, yet they serve as landmarks to demonstrate the development of the genre: the highs, and even the lows. This is where science fiction came from, it is our heritage. How else is 1959 remembered except by the Hugo winners? (Who remembers the novel *That Sweet Little Old Lady* by Mark Philips or the story 'Cat and Mouse' by Ralph Williams — both finalists that year?)

Often award winners are decided as the result of laziness and inefficiency, corruption and favouritism, lethargy and indifference. But so what? That is the way almost everything else in our society operates. Why should awards be any different?

Over the years there have been many more worthy winners than not — if it had been otherwise, the honours system would long ago have disintegrated — and this is the true significance and the importance of such awards.

Hugo Awards

The Science Fiction Achievement Awards are voted upon by the members of each year's World Science Fiction Convention.

The name 'Hugo' comes from Hugo Gernsback, who founded *Amazing Stories* in 1926. As already mentioned, this was the 'first' sf magazine. It took twenty years until the four fiction awards became fully established on the ballot.

1953
Novel: *The Demolished Man* by Alfred Bester

1954
                No Awards

1955
Novel: *They'd Rather Be Right* by Mark Clifton and Frank Riley
Novelette: 'The Darfsteller' by Walter M. Miller, Jr
Short Story: 'Allamagoosa' by Eric Frank Russell

1956
Novel: *Double Star* by Robert A. Heinlein
Novelette: 'Exploration Team' by Murray Leinster
Short Story: 'The Star' by Arthur C. Clarke

1957
                No Fiction Awards

1958
Novel: *The Big Time* by Fritz Leiber
Short Story: 'Or All the Seas with Oysters' by Avram Davidson

1959
Novel: *A Case of Conscience* by James Blish
Novelette: 'The Big Front Yard' by Clifford D. Simak
Short Story: 'That Hell-Bound Train' by Robert Bloch

1960
Novel: *Starship Troopers* by Robert A. Heinlein
Short Fiction: 'Flowers for Algernon' by Daniel Keyes

1961
Novel: *A Canticle for Leibowitz* by Walter M. Miller, Jr
Short Story: 'The Longest Voyage' by Poul Anderson

1962

Novel: *Stranger in a Strange Land* by Robert A. Heinlein

Short Fiction: The 'Hothouse' series by Brian Aldiss

1963

Novel: *The Man in the High Castle* by Philip K. Dick

Novelette: 'The Dragon Masters' by Jack Vance

1964

Novel: *Way Station* by Clifford D. Simak

Short Fiction: 'No Truce With Kings' by Poul Anderson

1965

Novel: *The Wanderer* by Fritz Leiber

Short Story: 'Soldier, Ask Not' by Gordon R. Dickson

1966

Novel: *... And Call Me Conrad* by Roger Zelazny
Dune by Frank Herbert (tie)

Short Fiction: ' "Repent, Harlequin!" Said the Ticktockman' by Harlan Ellison

1967

Novel: *The Moon is a Harsh Mistress* by Robert A. Heinlein

Novelette: 'The Last Castle' by Jack Vance

Short Story: 'Neutron Star' by Larry Niven

1968

Novel: *Lord of Light* by Roger Zelazny

Novella: 'Weyr Search' by Anne McCaffrey
'Riders of the Purple Wage' by Philip Jose Farmer (tie)

Novelette: 'Gonna Roll the Bones' by Fritz Leiber

Short Story: 'I Have No Mouth, and I Must Scream' by Harlan Ellison

1969

Novel: *Stand on Zanzibar* by John Brunner

Novella: 'Nightwings' by Robert Silverberg

Novelette: 'The Sharing of the Flesh' by Poul Anderson

Short Story: 'The Beast That Shouted Love at the Heart of the World' by Harlan Ellison

1970
Novel: *The Left Hand of Darkness* by Ursula K. Le Guin
Novella: 'Ship of Shadows' by Fritz Leiber
Short Story: 'Time Considered as a Helix of Semi-Precious Stones' by Samuel R. Delany

1971
Novel: *Ringworld* by Larry Niven
Novella: 'Ill Met in Lankhmar' by Fritz Leiber
Short Story: 'Slow Sculpture' by Theodore Sturgeon

1972
Novel: *To Your Scattered Bodies Go* by Philip Jose Farmer
Novella: 'The Queen of Air and Darkness' by Poul Anderson
Short Story: 'Inconstant Moon' by Larry Niven

1973
Novel: *The Gods Themselves* by Isaac Asimov
Novella: 'The Word for World is Forest' by Ursula K. Le Guin
Novelette: 'Goat Song' by Poul Anderson
Short Story: 'Eurema's Dam' by R.A. Lafferty
'The Meeting' by Frederik Pohl and C.M. Kornbluth (tie)

1974
Novel: *Rendezvous with Rama* by Arthur C. Clarke
Novella: 'The Girl Who Was Plugged In' by James Tiptree, Jr
Novelette: 'The Deathbird' by Harlan Ellison
Short Story: 'The Ones Who Walk Away from Omelas' by Ursula K. LeGuin

1975
Novel: *The Dispossessed* by Ursula K. Le Guin
Novella: 'A Song for Lya' by George R.R. Martin

Novelette: 'Adrift Just off the Islets of Langerhans: Latitude 38' 54' N, Longitude 77' 10'13'W' by Harlan Ellison

Short Story: 'The Hole Man' by Larry Niven

1976

Novel: *The Forever War* by Joe Haldeman
Novella: 'Home is the Hangman' by Roger Zelazny
Novelette: 'The Borderland of Sol' by Larry Niven
Short Story: 'Catch that Zeppelin!' by Fritz Leiber

1977

Novel: *Where Late the Sweet Birds Sang* by Kate Wilhelm
Novella: 'By Any Other Name' by Spider Robinson
'Houston, Houston, Do You Read?' by James Tiptree, Jr (tie)
Novelette: 'The Bicentennial Man' by Isaac Asimov
Short Story: 'Tricentennial' by Joe Haldeman

1978

Novel: *Gateway* by Frederik Pohl
Novella: 'Stardance' by Spider and Jeanne Robinson
Novelette: 'Eyes of Amber' by Joan D. Vinge
Short Story: 'Jeffty is Five' by Harlan Ellison

1979

Novel: *Dreamsnake* by Vonda McIntyre
Novella: 'The Persistence of Vision' by John Varley
Novelette: 'Hunter's Moon' by Poul Anderson
Short Story: 'Cassandra' by C.J. Cherryh

1980

Novel: *The Fountains of Paradise* by Arthur C. Clarke
Novella: 'Enemy Mine' by Barry B. Longyear
Novelette: 'Sandkings' by George R.R. Martin
Short Story: 'The Way of Cross and Dragon' by George R.R. Martin

1981

Novel: *The Snow Queen* by Joan Vinge
Novella: 'Lost Dorsai' by Gordon R. Dickson

Novelette:	'The Cloak and the Staff' by Gordon R. Dickson
Short Story:	'Grotto of the Dancing Deer' by Clifford D. Simak

1982

Novel:	*Downbelow Station* by C.J. Cherryh
Novella:	'The Saturn Game' by Poul Anderson
Novelette:	'Unicorn Variation' by Roger Zelazny
Short Story:	'The Pusher' by John Varley

1983

Novel:	*Foundation's Edge* by Isaac Asimov
Novella:	'Souls' by Joanna Russ
Novelette:	'Fire Watch' by Connie Willis
Short Story:	'Melancholy Elephants' by Spider Robinson

1984

Novel:	*Startide Rising* by David Brin
Novella:	'Cascade Point' by Timothy Zahn
Novelette:	'Blood Music' by Greg Bear
Short Story:	'Speech Sounds' by Octavia Butler

1985

Novel:	*Neuromancer* by William Gibson
Novella:	'Press Enter ' by John Varley
Novelette:	'Bloodchild' by Octavia E. Butler
Short Story:	'The Crystal Spheres' by David Brin

1986

Novel:	*Ender's Game* by Orson Scott Card
Novella:	'24 Views of Mt. Fuji, by Hokusai' by Roger Zelazny
Novelette:	'Paladin of the Lost Hour' by Harlan Ellison
Short Story:	'Fermi and Frost' by Frederik Pohl

1987

Novel:	*Speaker for the Dead* by Orson Scott Card
Novella:	'Gilgamesh in the Outback' by Robert Silverberg
Novelette:	'Permafrost' by Roger Zelazny
Short Story:	'Tangents' by Greg Bear

1988
Novel: *The Uplift War* by David Brin
Novella: 'Eye For Eye' by Orson Scott Card
Novelette: 'Buffalo Gals, Won't You Come Out Tonight'
                by Ursula K. Le Guin
Short Story: 'Why I Left Harry's All-Night Hamburgers' by
                Lawrence Watt-Evans

1989
Novel: *Cyteen* by C.J. Cherryh
Novella: 'The Last of the Winnebagos' by Connie Willis
Novelette: 'Shrödinger's Kitten' by George Alec Effinger
Short Story: 'Kirinyaga' by Mike Resnick

Nebula Awards

These are voted on each year by members of the Science
Fiction Writers of America (SFWA). The four fiction categories
have remained consistent despite endless changes in eligibility
rulings. The 'Grand Master' Award is voted by the SFWA
officers and cannot be given more than six times in any ten year
period. For a while, the SFWA also gave out a 'dramatic
presentation award'. This was voted out by the membership, a
vote repeated several times since. As soon as the idea is
defeated, someone always suggests it again. For the sake of
completeness, the 'dramatic presentation' Nebulas are also
listed below — as is the only 'special award' ever given. . .

Unlike all the other sf prizes, which are dated by the year in
which they are awarded, the Nebulas are dated by year of
publication.* The 1988 Nebulas were awarded in 1989, for
example.

1965
Novel: *Dune* by Frank Herbert

*Usually. The 1987 winning novel (prize awarded in 1988) was
published in 1986. See the second *Yearbook*.)

Novella:	'The Saliva Tree' by Brian W. Aldiss
	'He Who Shapes' by Roger Zelazny (tie)
Novelette:	'The Doors of His Face, the Lamps of His Mouth' by Roger Zelazny
Short Story:	"Repent, Harlequin!" Said the Ticktockman' by Harlan Ellison

1966
Novel:	*Flowers for Algernon* by Daniel Keyes
	Babel-17 by Samuel R. Delany (tie)
Novella:	'The Last Castle' by Jack Vance
Novelette:	'Call Him Lord' by Gordon R. Dickson
Short Story:	'The Secret Place' by Richard McKenna

1967
Novel:	*The Einstein Intersection* by Samuel R. Delany
Novella:	'Behold the Man' by Michael Moorcock
Novelette:	'Gonna Roll the Bones' by Fritz Leiber
Short Story:	'Aye, and Gomorrah' by Samuel R. Delany

1968
Novel:	*Rite of Passage* by Alexei Panshin
Novella:	'Dragonrider' by Anne McCaffrey
Novelette:	'Mother to the World' by Richard Wilson
Short Story:	'The Planners' by Kate Wilhelm

1969
Novel:	*The Left Hand of Darkness* by Ursula K. Le Guin
Novella:	'A Boy and His Dog' by Harlan Ellison
Novelette:	'Time Considered as a Helix of Semi-Precious Stones' by Samuel R. Delany
Short Story:	'Passengers' by Robert Silverberg

1970
Novel:	*Ringworld* by Larry Niven
Novella:	'Ill Met in Lankhmar' by Fritz Leiber
Novelette:	'Slow Sculpture' by Theodore Sturgeon
Short Story:	No Award

1971
Novel:	*A Time of Changes* by Robert Silverberg
Novella:	'The Missing Man' by Katherine MacLean

Novelette:	'The Queen of Air and Darkness' by Poul Anderson
Short Story:	'Good News from the Vatican' by Robert Silverberg

1972

Novel:	*The Gods Themselves* by Isaac Asimov
Novella:	'A Meeting with Medusa' by Arthur C. Clarke
Novelette:	'Goat Song' by Poul Anderson
Short Story:	'When It Changed' by Joanna Russ

1973

Novel:	*Rendezvous with Rama* by Arthur C. Clarke
Novella:	'The Death of Doctor Island' by Gene Wolfe
Novelette:	'Of Mist, and Grass and Sand' by Vonda N. McIntyre
Short Story:	'Love Is the Plan, the Plan is Death' by James Tiptree, Jr.
Dramatic Presentation:	*Soylent Green*

1974

Novel:	*The Dispossessed* by Ursula K. Le Guin
Novella:	'Born with the Dead' by Robert Silverberg
Novelette:	'If the Stars Are Gods' by Gordon Eklund and Gregory Benford
Short Story:	'The Day Before the Revolution' by Ursula K. Le Guin
Dramatic Presentation:	*Sleeper*
Grand Master:	Robert A. Heinlein

1975

Novel:	*The Forever War* by Joe Haldeman
Novella:	'Home Is the Hangman' by Roger Zelazny
Novelette:	'San Diego Lightfoot Sue' by Tom Reamy
Short Story:	'Catch That Zeppelin!' by Fritz Leiber
Dramatic Presentation:	*Young Frankenstein*
Grand Master:	Jack Williamson

1976
Novel: *Man Plus* by Frederik Pohl
Novella: 'Houston, Houston, Do You Read?' by James
                 Tiptree, Jr.
Novelette: 'The Bicentennial Man' by Isaac Asimov
Short Story: 'A Crowd of Shadows' by Charles L. Grant
Grand Master: Clifford D. Simak

1977
Novel: *Gateway* by Frederik Pohl
Novella: 'Stardance' by Spider and Jeanne Robinson
Novelette: 'The Screwfly Solution' by Raccoona Sheldon
Short Story: 'Jeffty Is Five' by Harlan Ellison
Special Award: *Star Wars*

1978
Novel: *Dreamsnake* by Vonda N. McIntyre
Novella: 'The Persistence of Vision' by John Varley
Novelette: 'A Glow of Candles, a Unicorn's Eye' by
                 Charles L. Grant
Short Story: 'Stone' by Edward Bryant
Grand Master: L. Sprague de Camp

1979
Novel: *The Fountains of Paradise* by Arthur C. Clarke
Novella: 'Enemy Mine' by Barry Longyear
Novelette: 'Sandkings' by George R.R. Martin
Short Story: 'giANTS' by Edward Bryant

1980
Novel: *Timescape* by Gregory Benford
Novella: 'The Unicorn Tapestry' by Suzy McKee
                 Charnas
Novelette: 'The Ugly Chickens' by Howard Waldrop
Short Story: 'Grotto of the Dancing Deer' by Clifford D.
                 Simak

1981
Novel: *The Claw of the Conciliator* by Gene Wolf
Novella: 'The Saturn Game' by Poul Anderson
Novelette: 'The Quickening' by Michael Bishop

Short Story: 'The Bone Flute' by Lisa Tuttle*
Grand Master: Fritz Leiber

1982
Novel: *No Enemy But Time* by Michael Bishop
Novella: 'Another Orphan' by John Kessel
Novelette: 'Fire Watch' by Connie Willis
Short Story: 'A Letter from the Clearys' by Connie Willis

1983
Novel: *Startide Rising* by David Brin
Novella: 'Hardfought' by Greg Bear
Novelette: 'Blood Music' by Greg Bear
Short Story: 'The Peacemaker' by Gardner Dozois
Grand Master: Andre Norton

1984
Novel: *Neuromancer* by William Gibson
Novella: 'Press Enter ' by John Varley
Novelette: 'Bloodchild' by Octavia E. Butler
Short Story: 'Morning Child' by Gardner Dozois

1985
Novel: *Ender's Game* by Orson Scott Card
Novella: 'Sailing to Byzantium' by Robert Silverberg
Novelette: 'Portraits of His Children' by George R.R.
                Martin
Short Story: 'Out of All Them Bright Stars' by Nancy Kress
Grand Master: Arthur C. Clarke

1986
Novel: *Speaker for the Dead* by Orson Scott Card
Novella: 'R & R' by Lucius Shepard
Novelette: 'The Girl Who Fell into the Sky' by Kate
                Wilhelm
Short Story: 'Tangents' by Greg Bear
Grand Master: Isaac Asimov

1987
Novel: *The Falling Woman* by Pat Murphy

*Award declined by the author.

Novella: 'The Blind Geometer' by Kim Stanley
               Robinson
Novelette: 'Rachel in Love' by Pat Murphy
Short Story: 'Forever Yours, Anna' by Kate Wilhelm
Grand Master: Alfred Bester

1988
Novel: *Falling Free* by Lois McMaster Bujold
Novella: 'The Last of the Winnebagos' by Connie Willis
Novelette: 'Schrödinger's Kitten' by George Alec Effinger
Short Story: 'Bible Stories for Adults, No. 17: The Deluge'
               by James Morrow
Grand Master: Ray Bradbury

John W. Campbell Memorial Award

John W. Campbell edited *Astounding,* which became *Analog,*
from 1937 until his death in 1971. He was the most influential
sf magazine editor of his era — which, for most of the time,
meant the most influential editor in the whole genre.

The Memorial Award was initiated by Harry Harrison and
Brian Aldiss, and is awarded by an international panel of judges
to the 'best novel' of the (previous) year. It is now administered
from the University of Kansas.

1973   *Beyond Apollo* by Barry N. Malzberg
1974   *Rendezvous with Rama* by Arthur C. Clarke
       Malevil by Robert Merle (tie)
1975   *Flow my Tears, the Policeman Said* by Philip K. Dick
1976   *The Year of the Quiet Sun* by Wilson Tucker*
1977   *The Alteration* by Kingsley Amis
1978   *Gateway* by Frederik Pohl
1979   *Gloriana* by Michael Moorcock
1980   *On Wings of Song* by Thomas M. Disch
1981   *Timescape* by Gregory Benford
1982   *Ridley Walker* by Russell Hoban
1983   *Helliconia Spring* by Brian Aldiss

*Awarded retrospectively: first published in 1970

1984   *Citadel of the Autarch* by Gene Wolfe
1985   *The Years of the City* by Fredrick Pohl
1986   *The Postman* David Brin
1987   *A Door into Ocean* by Joan Slonczewski
1988   *Lincoln's Dreams* by Connie Willis
1989   *Islands in the Net* by Bruce Sterling

And just to confuse things, but not to be confused with the John W. Campbell Memorial Award, is the John W. Campbell Award for 'best new writer'. This is on the Hugo ballot, voted for by members of each year's World SF Convention.

1973   Jerry Pournelle
1974   Spider Robinson and Lisa Tuttle (tie)
1975   P.J. Plauger
1976   Tom Reamy
1977   C.J. Cherryh
1978   Orson Scott Card
1979   Stephen R. Donaldson
1980   Barry B. Longyear
1981   Somtow Sucharitkul
1982   Alexis Gilliland
1983   Paul O. Williams
1984   R.A. MacAvoy
1985   Lucius Shepard
1986   Melissa Scott
1987   Karen Joy Fowler
1988   Judith Moffett
1989   Michaela Roessner

Philip K. Dick Memorial Award

Philip K. Dick died in 1982. He won a Hugo for his novel *The Man in the High Castle*, but was never given the success and recognition due to him in the USA, although in Britain and Europe he was widely recognised as a major author. In 1989, readers of *Interzone* voted him the 'all-time best sf author'. More of his books are in print now than during his lifetime, including a number of non-sf works that he could not sell while he was alive.

The film *Blade Runner* was based on his novel *Do Androids Dream of Electric Sheep?*, and the new Arnold Schwarzenegger film *Total Recall* is based on his story 'We Can Remember It for You Wholesale' — which has been novelized by Piers Anthony.

Chosen by jury, the Memorial Award was originally suggested by Thomas M. Disch. Because most of Dick's novels were originally published in paperback, the award is given to a book which first appeared in (American) paperback.

1983   *Software* by Rudy Rucker
1984   *The Anubis Gates* by Tim Powers
1985   *Neuromancer* by William Gibson
1986   *Dinner at Deviant's Palace* by Tim Powers
1987   *Homunculus* by James P. Blaylock
1988   *Strange Toys* by Patricia Geary
1989   *Wetware* by Rudy Rucker
        Four Hundred Billion Stars by Paul McAuley (tie)
1990   *Subterranean Gallery* by Richard Paul Russo

The runner-up each year is also given a 'special award' — which means they can claim to have won the 'Philip K. Dick Special Award'. As with John W. Campbell, it appears there are now two Philip K. Dick Awards . . .

The British Science Fiction Award

This is administered by the British Science Fiction Association and voted on by BSFA members and members of the annual Easter Convention, which is the main British sf convention. (Although in 1989 the award was made at Mexicon, several weeks later.) Originally, in 1966 and 1967, this was known as the British Fantasy Award. (Not to be confused with the current British Fantasy Award, of course.)

The voting for this has apparently been less organised than most. Some years, it seems, no one remembered to give any awards. Michael Moorcock is still awaiting his 1967 trophy. It was taken away to be engraved and he never saw it again.

The BSFA has to be the best bargain in science fiction. There are six mailings of the magazines *Vector*, *Paperback Inferno* and *Matrix* to members each year, for a £10 subscription. Details from: BSFA, 33 Thornville Road, Hartlepool, Cleveland TS26 8EW.

1966	John Brunner
1967	*The Three Stigmata of Palmer Eldrich* by Philip K. Dick
Special Award:	Michael Moorcock
1968	No Award
1969	No Award
1970	*Stand on Zanzibar* by John Brunner
1971	*The Jagged Orbit* by John Brunner
1972	*The Moment of Eclipse* by Brian Aldiss
1973	No Award
1974	*Rendezvous with Rama* by Arthur C. Clarke
Special Award:	*Billion Year Spree* by Brian Aldiss
1975	*Inverted World* by Christopher Priest
1976	*Orbitsville* by Bob Shaw
1977	*Brontomek!* by Michael Coney
Special Award:	*A Pictorial History of Sf* by David Kyle
1978	*The Jonah Kit* by Ian Watson*
1979	No Award
1980	
Novel:	*The Unlimited Dream Company* by J.G. Ballard
Short Fiction:	'Palely Loitering' by Christopher Priest
1981	
Novel:	*Timescape* by Gregory Benford
Short Fiction:	'The Brave Little Toaster' by Thomas M. Disch
1982	
Novel:	*The Shadow of the Torturer* by Gene Wolfe

*First published in 1975, but this award was for the paperback ...

Short Fiction:	'Mythago Wood' by Robert Holdstock

1983
Novel: *Helliconia Spring* by Brian Aldiss
Short Fiction: 'Kitemaster' by Keith Roberts

1984
Novel: *Tik-Tok* by John Sladek
Short Fiction: 'After Images' by Malcolm Edwards

1985
Novel: *Mythago Wood* by Robert Holdstock
Short Fiction: 'The Unconquered Country' by Geoff Ryman

1986
Novel: *Helliconia Winter* by Brian Aldiss
Short Fiction: 'Cube Root' by David Langford

1987
Novel: *The Ragged Astronauts* by Bob Shaw
Short fiction: 'Kaeti and the Hangman' by Keith Roberts

1988
Novel: *Grainne* by Keith Roberts
Short Fiction: 'Love Sickness' by Geoff Ryman

1989
Novel: *Lavondyss* by Robert Holdstock
Short Fiction: 'Dark Night in Toyland' by Bob Shaw

1990
Novel: *Pyramids* by Terry Pratchett
Short Fiction: 'In Translation' by Lisa Tuttle

The Arthur C. Clarke Award

This is the most recent of awards and is given by a jury to the 'best science fiction novel' published in Britain. Arthur C. Clarke is the most famous and successful British sf writer. For a third of a century he has been one of the 'big three' in world sf, the others being Isaac Asimov and Robert Heinlein.

(Heinlein died early in 1988.) The author of many of science fiction's classic novels and stories, Clarke co-wrote the film *2001* with Stanley Kubrick. He has lived in Sri Lanka for over thirty years, and in 1989 he was awarded the CBE for services to Sri Lankan culture.

1987 *The Handmaid's Tale* by Margaret Atwood
1988 *The Sea and the Summer* by George Turner
1989 *Unquenchable Fire* by Rachel Pollack
1990 *The Child Garden* by Geoff Ryman

IAIN M. BANKS is the pseudonym of sherry drinker Iain Banks, who is the author of such novels as *The Wasp Factory*, *The Bridge* and *Canal Dreams*. His sf books are *Consider Phlebas* — described by Arthur C. Clarke as 'one of the most amazing novels I've ever come across' — *The Player of Games* and *The Use of Weapons*. He lives in Edinburgh.

BRIAN W. ALDISS is also Brian Aldiss, and in 1989 he was named 'the science fiction writers' science fiction writer' in *The Observer*. His novel *Frankenstein Unbound* has become *Roger Corman's Frankenstein Unbound*. The film starring John Hurt, Raul Julia and Bridget Fonda was premiered at Cannes in May 1990. His most recent book is *Bury my Heart at W.H. Smith's*. He lives in Oxford.

JOHN CLUTE has not disclosed his middle initial. He was born in Canada, but after twenty years in Britain has recently become a British citizen. With Peter Nicholls as co-editor, he is now compiling a new edition of the indispensable *Encyclopedia of Science Fiction*. He lives in London.

DAVID S. GARNETT is David Garnett, but not the one born in 1892, although his local tax office remains unconvinced. As well as editing the *Yearbook* and *Zenith*, he also writes short stories and novels. He does not live in Edinburgh, Oxford or London.

A HIDDEN PLACE

Robert Charles Wilson
Author of GYPSIES and MEMORY WIRE

'Reminiscent of vintage Theodore Sturgeon . . .'
Michael Bishop

Into a small American town during the Depression comes
Anna Blaise, a strange, other-worldly woman. Travelling
boxcars comes Bone, a quiet, deadly man. In the small
mid-West town live Travis Fisher and Nancy Wilcox,
young and in love. They will all be drawn together by
fate and strange, unknowable forces.

A HIDDEN PLACE is both science fiction and fantasy,
love-story and thriller. It confirms Robert Charles Wilson
as an outstanding talent, transcending the genre.

'. . . a talent to watch' Lisa Goldstein

'An impressive first novel' *San Francisco Chronicle*

AN ORBIT BOOK
SCIENCE FICTION
0 7088 8341 9

MEMORY WIRE

Robert Charles Wilson
Author of GYPSIES and A HIDDEN PLACE

Seeking an escape from his past, Keller volunteers to
become an Eye – an all-seeing, unfeeling human video-
recorder. Looking where it matters, not where he wants,
being a camera. This detachment works for Keller for a
time. A *long* time. He avoids past, future *and* present.

Until he meets Teresa, a beautiful and haunted young
artist. She's addicted to oneiroliths, the extraterrestrial
dreaming jewels discovered in South America which
affect their users in a way unthinkable to Keller . . . they
make you remember.

In this dazzling tour-de-force by one of science fiction's
brightest young talents, Keller must fight his fears, his
training and above all his wiring, as he and Teresa
become swept up in murder, smuggling and far worse.

'Stay with him. He'll make it worth your while.'
Roger Zelazny

'. . . Wilson achieves the perfect balance of tension and
invention.' *Booklist*

'Profound and beautiful . . . a tense thriller.'
Orson Scott Card

AN ORBIT BOOK
SCIENCE FICTION
0 7088 8340 0

ENDANGERED SPECIES

Gene Wolfe

A brilliant new collection from the best-selling author of
THE BOOK OF THE NEW SUN

'Tonight you and I, with billions of others, are sitting
around the fire we call "the sun", telling stories; and from
time to time it has been my turn to entertain.'
Gene Wolfe

In these stories, Gene Wolfe more than fulfils his wish to
entertain. He will make you think, laugh and feel sad;
but above all, he will give you enjoyment, the most
important task for a writer to perform. The stories range
widely, through science fiction, fantasy and horror – two
are set in the universe of Wolfe's best-selling *Book of the
New Sun* novels. Once again, Gene Wolfe proves himself
a master of fiction.

'. . . a collection worthy of major attention' *Locus*

Don't miss:
THE URTH OF THE NEW SUN
SOLDIER OF THE MIST
both from Orbit

FUTURA PUBLICATIONS
AN ORBIT BOOK
SCIENCE FICTION
0 7088 8325 7

The final volume in The Pandora Trilogy

THE ASCENSION FACTOR

Frank Herbert
and Bill Ransom

By the author of the best-selling DUNE series

PANDORA – where water is the ecological equivalent of DUNE's desert . . .

Pandora's human inhabitants have been recovering land from the planet's raging seas at an increasing rate since the events of *The Lazarus Effect*. Using the massive stands of sentient kelp to buffer themselves from the wild ocean currents, they are creating new settlements; but in the shadow of those settlements, children starve.

The planet is ruled by an ambitious clone known as The Director, whose repressive regime leads to uprisings which are punished by starvation. The resistance fighters' main hope is Crista Galli, a woman believed by some to be the child of God. Pooling her talents with those of others, Crista fights to overthrow The Director and his followers.

The Ascension Factor was Frank Herbert's last book – he died soon after completing his share of the collaboration. Concluding The Pandora Trilogy, it contains all the inventiveness, complexity and exuberance readers have come to expect.

Don't miss:

THE JESUS INCIDENT   MAN OF TWO WORLDS
THE LAZARUS EFFECT   THE PRIESTS OF PSI
THE DOSADI EXPERIMENT

FUTURA PUBLICATIONS
AN ORBIT BOOK
SCIENCE FICTION
0 7088 4440 5